The Sisters

The Sisters

A Novel

Jonas Hassen Khemiri

Farrar, Straus and Giroux · New York

Farrar, Straus and Giroux
120 Broadway, New York 10271

EU Representative: Macmillan Publishers Ireland Ltd, 1st Floor,
The Liffey Trust Centre, 117–126 Sheriff Street Upper, Dublin 1, DO1 YC43

A version of this book was originally published in Swedish in 2023
by Albert Bonniers Förlag, Sweden, as *Systrarna*.

Library of Congress Cataloging-in-Publication Data
Names: Khemiri, Jonas Hassen, 1978– author.
Title: The sisters : a novel / Jonas Hassen Khemiri.
Other titles: Systrarna. English
Description: First edition. | New York : Farrar, Straus and Giroux, 2025. |
Identifiers: LCCN 2024053351 | ISBN 9780374618896 (hardcover)
Subjects: LCGFT: Novels.
Classification: LCC PT9877.21.H46 S9713 2025 | DDC 839.73/8—
    dc23/eng/20241115
LC record available at https://lccn.loc.gov/2024053351

Designed by Gretchen Achilles

Our books may be purchased in bulk for promotional,
educational, or business use. Please contact your local bookseller or the
Macmillan Corporate and Premium Sales Department at 1-800-221-7945,
extension 5442, or by email at MacmillanSpecialMarkets@macmillan.com.

www.fsgbooks.com
Follow us on social media at @fsgbooks

1   3   5   7   9   10   8   6   4   2

If you surrendered to the air, you could ride it.
—TONI MORRISON, *SONG OF SOLOMON*

I'm like a clock that always keeps time,
as long as it's left alone.
—SELMA LAGERLÖF

BOOK 1

2000 (One Year)

Part I

Chapter One

And so it was told that the story of the Mikkola sisters started on the last day of December, on the last day of the millennium, when they were standing in the elevator, heading up to the fourth floor to celebrate New Year's Eve at Mossutställningar, a temporary freelance-office-slash-art-space run by Hella d'Ailly, who once had been an artist herself, but now was more of a curator-slash-party-arranger. It was Hella who had managed to convince some bureaucrat at Statsholmen that it was a good idea to rent this empty, magnificent space of 1,000-plus square meters, with ornamented wooden floors and a ceiling height of three meters (including two non-working but really impressive fireplaces), to a bunch of artists, freelance journalists, web designers and textile printers. The contract was temporary, but the initial six months were extended to a year, and then another year and now, to celebrate their third or fourth extension, they were having a huge party, open to everyone who worked there, and their friends, and their friends' friends' friends.

There were two angry doormen downstairs and the Mikkola sisters had to skip a long line to get in, Anastasia did the talking, she claimed that she was about to start her "DJ set in less than twenty minutes" and that her sisters were joining her as back-up dancers, the doorman checked the list and let them in, despite Evelyn's suppressed laughter and Ina's red face. Now they were in the elevator heading upwards, breathing the strong smell of perfume from other guests, three sisters, one incredibly happy to be here, one already longing for the next party, one pushing the button for the fourth floor again and again, antsy to get to a dance floor and let loose some of the energy that she had been saving up during the cab ride.

Whatever happens, we stay together, Ina said as the elevator slowed to a halt. Right?

Evelyn pushed open the door, the sound of the deep bass from the sound system echoed in the staircase.

Of course, she answered and smiled.

Don't worry, we got you, Anastasia said, and followed Evelyn into the party. Twenty seconds later they were gone. Or not gone, Ina kept seeing them in different rooms as she tried to understand the layout of the huge space. There was Evelyn, in a corner, constantly surrounded by three to five people, everyone hypnotized by whatever story she was telling. And there was Anastasia, first on one dance floor and then on another, and then on top of a bar, then up on a windowsill, arms in the air, hands transformed into parentheses, palms facing forward as if she was pushing an invisible wall in front of her.

Ina did her best to try to approach them, but there was a sweaty sea of people in the way, and it was dark and the floor was covered in drifts of confetti and spilled drinks clung to the bottom of her flat shoes and she was blinded by the strobe and lost sight of her sisters. The music colliding from the two dance floors made it impossible to talk to anyone and still everyone seemed to have someone to talk to, everyone except Ina, and whenever she saw someone else who didn't have anyone to talk to, she felt pity for them, because they looked so lost and lonely and at least Ina had her backup, she knew that her sisters were here somewhere.

She kept walking from room to room, there was Evelyn again, in the third room to the right, waving from the other side, her hands up in the air, signaling that unfortunately she was stuck here, pointing towards the bar, molding her hand to an invisible glass, in a gesture that Ina interpreted as: If you go to the bar and get us some drinks I will wait for you right here. Ina was not too keen on becoming her younger sister's waitress, but she knew that it was almost eleven and if she lost sight of Evelyn now, there was a risk that she would need to celebrate midnight by herself, raising a glass to propose a toast to a random stranger, so she swallowed her pride, fought her way towards the overcrowded bar, spent fifteen minutes being ignored by the bartender, then finally got two drinks, took a quick sip from both plastic cups to make her journey back to Evelyn easier, and when she got there, Evelyn was gone.

Walking around a huge party with nobody to talk to was painful enough, but walking around the same party with two full cups was even worse. Especially for Ina, who was so tall that drunk men saw her and pretended to get scared. Of course she had alternatives, she could down one drink and head for the dance floor and try to dance in that special way that she had developed, with her knees constantly bent, to make herself look somewhat less tall than she actually was. Or she could leave both drinks on one of the marble windowsills facing the interior courtyard, and simply go home and fall asleep before midnight. Another, crazier alternative would be to approach someone, offer them a drink, and simply start talking, it wouldn't be that hard, she had prepared some suitable subjects in the cab ride over here, she could ask what they thought of the rumors that all computers would go crazy when the date flicked over from December 31, 1999, to January 1, 2000, she could talk about the Victorian tradition where they opened a random page of a novel on New Year's Eve to let the first sentence on the page predict what kind of year it would be, but no, those were the wrong kinds of subjects, they wouldn't work here, instead she should tell them a funny story about something that happened to her "on the way here" because that was what Evelyn always did, she had tons of stories that happened "earlier today" or "yesterday" or "recently," and even though Ina would stand right there knowing that this particular thing happened two and a half years ago, and hadn't even happened to Evelyn, but to a friend of hers, she would keep quiet because she saw that Evelyn brought so much life with her, and if there was something Ina needed right now, it was more life.

But Ina wasn't Evelyn. And she wasn't Anastasia. So instead of talking to someone or attacking the dance floor, she just stood there, with the two drinks, not knowing what to do with herself or the slowly passing time. She sipped on one of her drinks, she tried really hard to look like a person who was holding a drink for someone who had left to go to the bathroom, she even started looking towards the bathrooms and then checking the time, to show anyone who was watching her that she wasn't as alone as she looked, she had sisters, she had friends, they were just not here right now.

With thirty minutes to go to midnight, Ina took one of the cups and started circling the party again, using the same strategy she used when she was a teenager to disguise her loneliness, she entered each room and every corridor with intense focus, trying really hard to look like she was looking for someone, and in a way she was, she was looking for her sisters, but rather than actually looking for them, she focused on trying to look like a person who was looking for someone and she saw herself from the outside looking like a person trying to look like a person who was looking and not fooling anyone. She passed a room with a ping-pong table, she passed an office where people smoked joints and made out on a gray couch, she passed a kitchen where there was a separate party with crappy speakers, maybe because they didn't like the music being played on the main dance floors, and then, in a corridor, she saw him, his beard, his face, his freckles, as if a cluster bomb of freckles had exploded on his nose. He was standing next to the wall, and even though his size made it difficult for people to squeeze by, he didn't seem to be uncomfortable being in the way. He looked at her, he looked away, she approached him and asked if he knew where Anastasia's room was.

Who?

Anastasia, Ina said. She rents a studio here.

Is she about this tall, with red hair?

No.

Good, because that person is in there right now puking her lungs out, he said, nodding towards what looked like a conference room.

There was something about his voice, everything he said sounded like a compliment. This place is huge, Ina said, just to say something.

Yes, it took me an hour to realize that it actually covers the whole . . . what's it called. Våningsplan.

Floor, she said.

So wait, you speak Swedish? he said in Swedish. Then why are we speaking English?

I came here with my sisters, she said, which really didn't explain anything, but she didn't feel like telling him the whole story, at least not right now, maybe later, maybe tomorrow when they would wake up together, maybe in a couple of years when they had kids, a bunch of black-haired freckly kids who would have his smile and his height and her nose. They were quiet for a moment, people kept squeezing past them in the corridor.

This place is really huge, Ina said, only to realize that she had just said the same thing twice. He looked at her and smiled.

You need help finding Anastasia's room? he said.

I don't even know if she's there, she said. Both my sisters have disappeared.

I will help you look for them, he said.

Don't you have to stay here? she said and hated herself for saying it.

Well, I'm not sure if this wall will hold if I let go of it, but let's see, he said, and he slowly let go of the wall, turned to her, grabbed her hand and started plowing his way through the crowded party. She followed him, thinking to herself that he must have played sports all his life, possibly handball, more likely American football because he kept finding openings, he took her through a packed corridor, he crossed the crowded main dance floor, she saw numerous people trying to cross it who gave up and turned back, it was just too crowded, too dark, the bass was too thumping, the wall of dancing human flesh too compact, but he kept going, he kept looking for her sisters, even though he had no clue what they looked like. He pointed to a guy with his pants so low that half his butt cheeks were shining white in the fluorescent light.

Is that them?

Ina shook her head. He picked up a crushed plastic cup from

the floor, signaling to Ina that there was lipstick on it, which meant that they must have been there. Ina smiled. He walked up to people at random and asked if they had seen "Anastasia recently" and they just looked at him like he was crazy, and Ina looked at him and thought the same thing, but it was a craziness that she was growing attached to, even though she had only been close to it for the last five minutes.

Midnight was approaching when Ina realized that she didn't want to find her sisters, not now, because she knew what would happen when they did. Hector would see Anastasia and understand that there was another version of Ina, not as freakishly tall, not as afraid of life, not as prone to going to New Year's parties having memorized the timetable of the night bus to be able to leave without saying goodbye, and Hector would fall in love with Anastasia, the fun sister, the crazy sister, the "I have something in my sock, let's sneak into the bathroom and snort it" sister—and he would agree and then he would be gone for ten minutes and come out a changed man, while Ina would wait outside. And then, all teary-eyed with white powder on his upper lip, he would catch sight of Evelyn and then he would quickly let go of Anastasia's hand and become transfixed by Evelyn's eyes, her dimples, her ability to tell the same story for the fourth time that evening, and still give the impression that she was searching for words, trying to show whoever was listening that it was a special honor to hear her tell this particular story at this particular time and it would be Evelyn who took him home, and Ina who went home alone on the night bus, and Evelyn who decided that he wasn't her type after a few weeks, and that would be okay for Ina, she was used to this, she had been through it so many times, when they were kids, when they were teenagers, now she was twenty-four and Evelyn twenty-one, and Anastasia nineteen, and still Ina wouldn't blame Hector, because she knew that if she were to choose between herself and her sisters she would also choose them, but for now she just wanted time to slow down, so that she could have a few more minutes with him.

Ten minutes before midnight they found Anastasia and Evelyn in the big room with one of the non-functioning marble fireplaces.

There you are, Evelyn yelled and waved her over.

We have been looking all over for you, Anastasia said and handed her a plastic cup.

Ina reluctantly introduced Hector to her sisters.

This is Evelyn.

Evelyn took his hand, smiled and winked her green eyes at him.

And this is Anastasia.

Anastasia nodded to him but didn't shake his hand, she was too busy trying to get the stubborn cork out of the prosecco bottle. Evelyn leaned towards them and started telling Hector a story about the bottle, they had dropped it in the cab, they had smuggled it in, it had been shaken nonstop and now it would probably explode and knock someone senseless and Ina felt herself retreating, she knew it was all over, for a few seconds another world had been possible, but now Hector was hypnotized by Evelyn, still Ina was grateful for the time she had spent with Hector, it had been a marvelous fifteen minutes, she might as well leave now, nobody would notice, but the more Evelyn spoke to Hector, the more restless he looked and finally he interrupted her.

Sorry, he said. But I was just involved in this really interesting conversation with Ina and I can't stop thinking about it, so I hope it's okay if we continue this another time?

He came over to Ina and Evelyn looked like a surprised fish and with one minute until midnight Anastasia finally managed to open the bottle and the cork came shooting out and hit a guy in the eye, but luckily he was wearing glasses and Anastasia filled their cups with bubbles and gave her own cup to the guy who was nearly blinded and took the bottle for herself and then everyone started counting down from ten nine eight seven, and when everyone yelled Happy New Year, the guy who Ina had met in a corridor, who had a big beard and shoulders so wide that he had to walk sideways through doors, who sounded like he was singing even though he was speaking, he reached for her and touched the palm of her hand, they didn't kiss, that would have been too much, besides, Ina was not the kind of person who meets someone at a party and starts kissing them fifteen minutes later, that was not her style, but they looked at each other and she could feel his finger in her palm and it wasn't until afterwards, when everyone had hugged and kissed and wished each other Happy New Year, that someone double-checked the time and realized that they had been at least one minute early, actually midnight is now, when? In ten seconds! And then they did the whole thing over again, ten nine eight seven, and this time he leaned forward and kissed her.

Chapter Two

The first time I heard about the Mikkola sisters I was five or six years old, sitting on the living room floor of our old apartment, the one on Drakenbergsgatan 8, five stairs up, a two-bedroom apartment. My brothers weren't born yet, so my parents still slept in the corner bedroom, and when their bed wasn't located in the living room, the area between the couch and the windows was perfect for playing. I was remodeling the yellow Lego castle that I had received from my older half sister, she had been here on a short visit, she was four years older than I was and I felt strangely attracted to her, physically we looked rather similar. I was often mistaken for a girl, my father kept saying that I should cut my hair, but I didn't care, or maybe I did, but I wanted to keep the hair, despite it I felt very much like a boy, especially when I saw my sister, during her visit I started having strange sexual dreams about her, they would come back to haunt me in my twenties, when I desperately tried to find someone to fall in love with, that image of my older sister, who by then had fallen into serious drug abuse and had lost contact with the family, became my ideal girlfriend, not because of how she looked at the time (apparently she looked hideous, according to my dad, who had gone down to the south of Sweden to try to save her, but it was too late, she had developed a heroin addiction and later we would learn that she was HIV positive), no, my ideal girlfriend looked like my sister had looked when she visited us when I was five or six years old, and there was a lot of guilt in that, because on some level I knew that she looked a lot like me, and if that's not a serious case of narcissism, I don't know what is, a person in his twenties, desperately searching for a girlfriend who actually looks like himself when he was young, but this will all come later, now I'm five or six years old, sitting on the living room floor, sun patterns on the parquet, the smell of Dad's special briks frying on the stove, with capers for adults, without capers for me, I'm building a special gray fence that will fall down on unwanted intruders and crush their brains if they manage to get across the moat, and I hear my mother and father talking in the kitchen. They speak French, as they always did back then, or actually they went back and forth between French and Swedish, but they always spoke French if it was serious enough for them to raise their voices, and they normally only raised their voices when they spoke about money matters. But this time they didn't seem to be speaking about money, because they didn't use words like *dix milles* or *c'est trop cher* and *je ne peux plus*, instead they talked about a family that was moving to our area, Mom seemed upset about it and my dad seemed maybe not happy about it, but he had more of a what-can-you-do attitude, which was how he approached most things that seemed complicated, if you can't do anything about it, why focus on it, and it was one of the things my mom had loved most about him when they first met, when he was working as a bartender and living in an apartment without wallpaper, heating, toilet or stove, and it was one of the things that seemed to drive her insane now, when they had been married for six years and he still wasn't able to get his act together. He still hadn't finished that book he was talking about when they met, he still hadn't quit his job as a subway driver, he still hadn't applied to medical school, even though he kept saying that he was meant to study medicine, it was his destiny, since his dad had been a pharmacist and in his country, in the countryside, a pharmacist was basically the same thing as a doctor. My dad claimed he could magically sense if someone had a fever just by applying his hands to their forehead, and once he had known a girl in his village who was famous for being sort of a witch, but Dad never applied to medical school, he was just drifting along, letting life push him here and there, and now it had happened again, he had "run into" (how?) an old friend who was running away ("from what?") and told her ("her!?") about this area, that it was great for kids, that the queue for getting an apartment wasn't that long, because most people didn't want to live in brown eight-story high-rises this close to the heavily trafficked Hornsgatan. And for some reason, his "friend" thanked him for the advice and said that she would consider it, and for some reason, Mom wasn't having it. I couldn't understand why. I didn't even know Dad had friends. We were always spending time with Mom's friends, and Mom's friends' husbands, and I wondered why Mom didn't seem happy that Dad had found a friend, especially a friend that seemed to come from the same country as he did. The word *Mikkola* kept coming back, and I remember wondering what it meant, *Mikkola*, it didn't sound French and it sure didn't sound Swedish or Arabic, I stopped playing and snuck towards the kitchen when my dad said that the Mikkola family had moved numerous times, "trying to get away" (not specifying from what), and now they were just *considering* moving here, but it probably wouldn't happen, and even if it *did* happen, it wouldn't mean that he would spend time with his "amie," that chapter was closed many years ago. Then he was silent and Mom was silent, and then I heard her hissing that this was so typical of him, she called him weak, she said that he was a coward and called him another word in French that I hadn't heard before. My father left the kitchen and went to the bathroom, and then he came out and put on his shoes and left the apartment, and my mother had to take his briks out of the oven and they came out perfectly crispy. We waited for Dad to come home, and when he didn't, we ate the briks ourselves, and my mother put his briks on a plate covered with metal foil and when I went to sleep he still hadn't come home. The Mikkola sisters didn't move to our area.

Not until seven years later.

Chapter Three

The new millennium was a few weeks old when Anastasia finally decided to answer Hella d'Ailly's call. Anastasia kind of knew what to expect, she had been warned before, and now things had apparently gone too far, Hella explained that Anastasia had to give up her studio straightaway, she reminded Anastasia that this was an artist-run collective, very tolerant of complex creative processes, maybe they had even been *too* tolerant, but now the back of the camel had been broken, everyone had to feel safe here, they had had such patience and warned Anastasia before, multiple times actually, but she kept breaking the rules, she was always late with rent, she kept using the studio as an apartment even though the contract made it clear that this was a workspace, she kept scaring people when she cut bread in the kitchen with her butterfly knife, she kept annoying her office neighbors by smoking indoors, she had been caught with drugs "time after time after time" (it had only happened twice, but Anastasia knew that it was useless to contradict Hella), and she kept inviting that "lunatic" to their parties (Anastasia noticed that she smiled when Hella called Mathias a "lunatic" but she wasn't really sure why).

The chaos he created at the New Year's party will cost a fortune to fix, Hella said. Chaos? Anastasia wasn't sure what Mathias had done, she only had a few random flashes of memory from New Year's Eve.

First, they had been in the apartment that Evelyn rented on Kungsholmen, overlooking a dark park, high ceiling, turn-of-thecentury details, the three sisters had drunk prosecco and really tried not to end up in the same old fights, Ina didn't comment on the smell when Anastasia and Evelyn came back from the balcony after a smoke, Evelyn didn't get angry when Ina started rearranging her spice rack in alphabetical order, Anastasia didn't tell her sisters that she had invited Mathias to the party, it would just cause problems, Anastasia's sisters didn't understand that he was a misunderstood genius, yes, he could be kind of limitless and yes, he had a tendency to end up in fights, especially when he had been drinking, but he had a kind heart and great contacts.

All three sisters were committed to stopping this night from ending the same way as the last time they celebrated New Year's together, when Ina found weed in Anastasia's jacket pocket and started screaming that her baby sister was a drug dealer, while Anastasia calmly asked Ina what right she had to go through her pockets. That night ended at a strange after-party at Bofill's Båge, Evelyn made out with some guy in the kitchen, and during the silent cab ride home, Ina mumbled that she had had a crush on that particular guy in high school and Evelyn laughed and said that Ina had a crush on every guy in high school, and every girl and every teacher and every pet, and Ina who was always sitting up front because of her legs mumbled: Whore, and Evelyn said: Rather a whore than a coward, and the cab driver had to pull over because the two sisters had started throwing punches that risked the lives of everyone in the car.

But this year things would be different, it was the new millennium, they would say goodbye to the old and hello to the new, the doors to the party opened at nine and Ina suggested that they preorder a cab for eight thirty, and Anastasia laughed and then stopped laughing when she understood that her eldest sister was serious.

Let's wait and see, Evelyn said and poured herself another drink.

If the doors open at nine, everyone will be there at ten, and we can arrive at eleven, Anastasia said.

Eleven thirty, Evelyn said.

When they arrived the queue was longer than expected but Anastasia knew the doorman and thirty seconds after Ina had paid the cab driver (and asked for a receipt) they were in the elevator, heading up to what everyone seemed to think of as the party of the year.

Let's stay together, Ina said. If we lose sight of each other we can meet up here. Unless there's a fire, then we meet up outside on the curb. Okay?

Ina and Evelyn nodded and entered the party. It was just like any other party that Hella and her crew had organized the last couple of years, an abundance of quasi-creative boring middle-class people, the dance floors were packed with art directors from Örnsköldsvik who kept talking about the last time they were in Berlin, the DJs were playing hits, at one point Anastasia actually saw a group of blond girls approaching the DJ requesting a song, and the DJ didn't inform them that this was not a fucking school dance, no, she smiled and seemed to say that unfortunately she couldn't play "Sommartider hej hej" or whatever they were requesting.

Since Mathias hadn't arrived yet, Anastasia decided to get really drunk in order to survive, she stole a bottle from one of the bars and then the flashes of memory became vague and fragmentary, midnight, an exploding bottle, Mathias arrived, he had shaved his head, it was uneven in the back, he was bleeding behind one of his ears, a toilet, powder, metallic kisses, more focus, finally the world became what it should have been all along, the music became better, the air was easier to breathe, the people more beautiful, the bodies more harmonious, they attacked the dance floor, Mathias disconnected a few cords so that the lights went out, Mathias jumped up and held on to one of the lighting rigs, the rig fell, Mathias bled from both his ear and his nose, someone tried to start a fight with him, someone tried to kick him out, Evelyn pulled Anastasia's arm, she tried to say something, it was important, it was about Ina, Ina had gone home with someone.

Anastasia nodded, she had seen him, Ina had followed him around all evening like a puppy, at midnight she had forced her tongue into his mouth, poor him, fun for Ina, but Evelyn couldn't let it go.

She didn't say goodbye, she said, again and again. We came together and then we leave together, right?

Anastasia wanted to say that Evelyn never said goodbye when she went home with someone, she just disappeared without a trace, but her mouth didn't obey and her body just wanted to return to the dance floor. Evelyn caught sight of Mathias.

Don't tell me you're back together again, Evelyn said.

Anastasia smiled.

After what he did to you, you're inviting him back into your life?

Anastasia pulled free.

You're fucking unbelievable, Evelyn said.

And Anastasia agreed, she was unbelievable, she was amazing, she was the most perfect person that had ever graced this earth with her magnetic presence, she danced and drank and visited the toilets again and again, and then Mathias found a bag of fireworks, or maybe he had brought them in his backpack, the stairs down to the courtyard, Mathias lit one two three rockets and watched them soar towards the sky, it started raining, it wasn't until the bouncers came running and pushed them against a wall that Anastasia remembered that the courtyard had a roof, and that's why the rockets kept coming back down and exploding on the ground and that's what had set off the sprinkler system. Mathias was thrown out, the bouncers said he could come back and get his jacket another day, more fighting, Mathias was bleeding from an ear, his nose, his upper lip, Anastasia snuck back up to the party, the dance floors were half-empty, her sisters were gone, she had to make a few circuits before she finally found her office, she unlocked it on her fourth try, when she finally realized that the door hadn't been locked in the first place, then she sank down on the burgundy couch and checked her phone, she had a few missed calls and texts from Evelyn, but not from Ina, and she told herself that she should answer, just send Evelyn a few words to let her know that she was okay, she was better than okay, she was happier than she had been for years, she was finally free, she hadn't worried about their mother for at least five hours, and she held up her phone, tried to squint to find the right buttons, but then she gave up, dropped the phone to the floor and fell into a dreamless sleep.

Are you there? Hella said.

Yes, Anastasia said.

This wasn't an easy decision, Hella said.

Anastasia told Hella that she was sorry and that she would empty her room straightaway, she even thanked Hella for her call, and when they hung up, she wondered why she felt this strange sense of relief. Then she looked out of the window and saw Hella on the other side of the interior courtyard, their eyes met, Hella waved and smiled, and Anastasia waved back.

Anastasia found some folded moving boxes in the ping-pong room. She went through her things and sorted them into two piles, keep vs. throw away. The throwaway pile grew bigger and bigger. She put all of her sketches and preparatory work for the upcoming application to Konstfack in a black garbage bag and emptied it into the container in the basement. She convinced the Web designers on the other side of the hall to adopt her couch and the clothing designers by the entrance happily agreed to use her desk and her desk chair until she needed them again. Because she would be needing them again, right? She didn't want to sell them the desk?

Anastasia took a few seconds to think about it, she was seriously strapped for cash, still, she decided to keep her furniture, she would need it when she found her own studio, when she had been accepted at Konstfack, when Index and Nordenhake fought over the right to exhibit her work.

Good luck, one of the clothing designers said, and it sounded like she really meant it, even though everyone knew how incredibly tricky (see: impossible) it was to find a cheap workspace in Stockholm, especially a workspace where nobody would notice if you spent the night.

When she had emptied her room, Anastasia left her keys on the windowsill. Now she was ready for the next chapter in life, now she would show herself and the world that she could make it on her own. But first, she needed a place to stay, and their dad was dead and their mom was not an option, so the only person left was Ina.

Of course, her older sister said when Anastasia called and asked if she could stay with her for a couple of weeks. When are you coming over? There's meat sauce in the fridge. Do you need money for a cab? Ina's voice was full of that special happiness that older siblings feel when they are able to give their younger siblings what their parents were never able to give them.

The cab driver didn't need to fold any seats to transport all of Anastasia's belongings to Ina's place, located south of the city, on the red line. On the way over, Anastasia kept wondering why she wasn't sad. Was it the relief of not needing to find excuses for why she couldn't pay next month's rent? Was it the relief of realizing that because she didn't have a studio she couldn't work on her application to Konstfack, and therefore she had no choice but to fail? Was it the realization that now she had no choice but to change? She had changed already, she hadn't taken any drugs since New Year's, and she hadn't returned any of Mathias's calls or texts, and sitting there in the cab, surrounded by borrowed moving boxes with labels not describing her own belongings ("Empty binders," "Accounting 1996–1998"), slowly rolling south, passing an industrial area, the convention center, the gas stations, she decided that now she had to let go of Mathias, sure he needed help, but she was not the right person to help him, not now, not later, not ever.

Chapter Four

The second time I heard about the Mikkola sisters my father and I were heading into town, this was in May 1990, both my younger brothers had been born and now Dad and I were the men of the family, I was eleven and my dad was about to turn forty. On weekends we cleaned a restaurant called Tre Backar, I vacuumed the floor with an industrial-looking round vacuum cleaner, first the ground floor, then the basement, while he did the toilets. When we had finished, I was paid in cash and cashew nuts, then I said goodbye so that Dad could start his night shift as a bartender in the basement.

But on this day we weren't heading to work, we were heading into town, and we didn't ride the subway like normal people, hell no, we weren't normal, we had our own set of rules, and our own set of keys. Since my dad worked as a subway driver at the time he had a magic key chain, whenever some punk pushed the emergency stop of an escalator my dad pulled out the key chain, opened the metal box on the side and set the escalator in motion again, smiling to the grateful ladies who avoided the elevators due to the pee smell. And whenever we were going into town, my father pulled out the keys and let us into one of the empty driver compartments located between each car. Was he allowed to sit there with his eleven-year-old son? Well, allowed and not allowed, there are rules that have to be respected and then there are rules that are bendable, come to think of it, most rules are bendable, was my father's credo, most rules but not all rules.

There is one rule we should respect and that's this one, he said when the subway accelerated. Boys have short hair and girls have long hair.

But Mom has short hair, I said.

That's an exception, Dad said.

Didn't you have long hair when you were young?

That was a long time ago.

But I like my long hair, I said.

You look like a girl, Dad said.

I don't care, I said.

You will care, Dad said. Soon you will start to care, and then you will be angry with me for not telling you that you looked like a girl.

I want to keep it, I said.

Sure you do, Dad said.

We got off at T Centralen and took the escalator up to Sergels Square, Dad nodded to someone and hugged someone else and when I asked who it was, Dad said they were "flummare från förr" ("hippies-slash-drug-addicts from the past"). We continued past Mega, and up towards Sergelgatan, and my dad said that he wanted me to cut it short and I repeated that I had only agreed to come on the strict promise that he would tell the hairdresser to keep it long and my father said: You don't want to end up like the Mikkola sisters, and I asked him who the Mikkola sisters were, and he said they were the daughters of an old friend.

What friend? I said.

He didn't answer, instead he said that the Mikkola sisters all looked like boys, especially the youngest one, Anastasia, and that had gotten her into "all kinds of trouble."

Like what trouble? I said.

You're stubborn, he said.

I have gotten it from you, I said, and we were smiling when we opened the door to the salon, located on the right side of the blue concert hall. It was crowded, it was always crowded, dads and kids and the owner's dog and three hairdressers that were talking more than cutting. Everyone was speaking Arabic, but not the normal kind of Arabic that I almost understood, this was another kind of Arabic, different tone, different word choices.

It's because they are Egyptian, my dad said. And Palestinian. And that guy is from Jordan, and my dad nodded and gave high fives and despite the queue Dad managed to convince Mansour that I was next. The queue protested but my father claimed that he had been here this morning, reserving a time for now, and everyone laughed at the obvious lie and Mansour promised that it was going to be a quickie. I told Mansour that I wanted to keep it long, and my father said something in Arabic, and my father looked at me and said "Fehemt?" which means "Do you understand?" in Tunisian Arabic, and I nodded, because that particular word I understood.

Then my father had to step out to do some business, there was always some business to be done, someone needed to borrow money, someone else needed to pay back a loan, Mansour put away his scissors and got out his new electric razor and with a zeal that I hadn't seen before or after, he shaved my head, three millimeters all over.

When my father came back he smiled and said that I finally looked like a real boy. He asked Mansour how much he owed him and Mansour said a sum and my father laughed and gave him half, and Mansour didn't laugh and said that he wanted at least fifty more, and my father laughed and said that he would get it, of course he would get it, next time my father came by, he would get fifty and then some, and the next guy was already sitting in Mansour's chair, pulling on his sleeve, asking him to start cutting because he had a date tonight.

Mansour looked at my father and said something about the fact that he was Tunisian, and it sounded like an insult, but my father answered it like it was a compliment. As we exited the salon the cold wind touched areas of my skull that I had never been aware of before and my dad said:

Don't tell Mom.

I vowed to never speak to my dad again, not ever, and I would never ever cut my hair at a hair salon, and I would definitely tell Mom, I would tell her and I would try not to cry, but first we had to get back home without tears because I knew that if my father saw me crying he would just look at me and walk away, because nothing made him more disgusted than seeing his own son crying in public, crying like a little bitch, crying over a haircut, please, his son was eleven years old and didn't know anything about life and he was certain that in a few years his son would thank him for this insight, he would come up to him and say: Thank you, Dad, thank you for making sure that nobody thought I was a girl, thank you for overriding my explicit wish so that I didn't have to endure three years of high school while taunted for being gay, thank you for teaching me the power of language from such an early age, who knows, maybe his son would go on to do that thing that he himself had dreamed of all his life, what if he became a writer, and the name Khemiri would exist in libraries, his son could write long books about his amazing father, how he taught him important life lessons, from the early age of eleven.

We headed back home, this time we sat in the normal seats, and not the driver seat, and I remember that I wondered if he wanted to sit in the driver compartment on the way there only because he was ashamed of having a son who looked like a daughter. When we took the escalator up towards Varvsgatan I still hadn't said a word, but I had a long speech memorized that I would give to my mother as soon as we got home because I knew that the only way to hurt him was through my mom.

Ten meters from ground level we heard screams, a woman, she cried out: But help me, someone please help me, and my father started running up the already moving stairs. A drunk had taken a bunch of newspapers and now he was heading towards the exit with the newspapers with a nasty grin, the woman who worked in the kiosk screamed for help, and there was a queue of five people, two men, three women, and nobody did anything. My father just walked up to the drunk man, grabbed the newspapers and gave them back to the lady.

Thank you, she said. Thank you. And then she immediately returned to the kiosk, to avoid more trouble. The drunk looked at my dad and started spewing out racist insults.

You filthy fucking svartskalle, he said. Fucking sand monkey, fucking . . .

My dad looked at him with a face that I had never seen before, eyes big as eggs, mouth grinning like a hyena, teeth grinding, he slowly put his hand in his inner pocket.

So what, you have a gun, the drunk said. You have a knife? Dad kept his hand in his inner pocket.

I'm not scared of you, the drunk said, walking backward, almost falling over when he collided with a trash can.

My dad didn't pull out whatever he had in his inner pocket, he just looked at the drunk and said:

Three . . . Two . . .

The man turned around and ran, out towards Varvsgatan, up the stairs towards the church. The lady from the kiosk thanked him again, and my father smiled and waved to her and the people who hadn't moved from their positions in the queue.

When we got home I checked the many pockets of Dad's leather jacket and they were empty, except for a couple of toothpicks, a paper napkin and a filled-out horse betting slip. When Mom got home and when I got back to school on Monday morning, it wasn't the story of the haircut that I was telling, it was the other story, the story of how my father saved a screaming lady from being robbed of all her newspapers, and I enjoyed turning my father into a story, somehow it gave me power over him, it seemed like the only power I had.

Chapter Five

n February 2000, Evelyn's bosses (yes, there were two, Henrik and Fredrik, they were a couple) decided that no employees were allowed to check their cell phones when they could be seen by customers. So whenever Evelyn got a text, she told Kattis and Anders that she had to get something from the back, smuggled her Nokia phone from under the counter into her pocket, opened the door to the stockroom and read the message. This was back in a time when it cost money to send texts, and all phones came with a calculator showing how many letters had been used, and Evelyn knew that if the text was from her younger sister, Anastasia, it was often a never-ending rant about the crappiness of some contemporary artist who had recently been acquired by Moderna Museet (she especially hated the well-respected painter-slash-multimedia-artist Ernst Billgren), and if the text was from her older sister, Ina, it was always the exact number of letters that could be contained in one text, not that Ina was cheap, she was just practical, she planned things ahead of time, and even if the text would have fit in one message, she made up abbreviations of her own to optimize her time, or to show her younger sisters that she had more important things to do than text them, "Hi my dear sister, thanks for having me over, I hope all is well, could you please be so kind to call Mom tomorrow to remind her to pick up her medicines?" became in Ina's version: "hi, clal mom tmrw, remind medicines!!!")

And Evelyn knew that even if Ina reminded her to call their mom,

Ina would also call their mom, because she didn't trust Evelyn to do it, so therefore Evelyn could ignore the reminder.

Evelyn hadn't spoken to their mom since New Year's Eve, when her mom called seven times in an hour. First she dialed Anastasia's number, then Evelyn's cell phone started vibrating. Ina was the only one who picked up. Evelyn heard how Ina tried to calm their mom. Ina explained that everyone was doing well, nobody had been kidnapped, nobody was stabbed, nobody had been hit by a car, they were all three of them chilling in Evelyn's kitchen and soon they would go to a party at Anastasia's office.

Can I come? their mom said.

No, it's not possible, Ina said and tried to end the call.

After everything I've done for you? Selima said. Everything that I've sacrificed?

Ina sighed.

Is Evelyn there? their mom said.

Evelyn shook her head frantically.

Let me talk to Anastasia, their mom said.

Anastasia put one hand around her neck and ejected her tongue, when she removed the hand there was a red mark on her neck.

Why aren't they picking up?

I'll call you tomorrow, Ina said. Happy New Year Mo—

Selima had hung up.

At midnight on New Year's Eve, Evelyn had promised herself to quit her job, but now it was February and she was still here. She told herself that this job was just a way to make time pass, she had taken a year off after graduation, she would never be one of those people who started working and never went back to university, but then she got this job, and she got used to the salary and the VIP invitations to club openings and now she had worked here for one, two, shit, three fucking years, and the job had become so mind-numbingly boring that she had developed a number of strategies to survive each workday. One was to take really long toilet breaks. Another was to hide in one of the dressing rooms, pretending to be polishing the mirrors. A third was to pour out the milk in the sink and tell her colleagues that they were out of milk, the nearest store was only four minutes away, up the block on the next corner, but in order to buy milk Evelyn had to take money from the cash register (one minute), get her coat (one minute), exit the front door (twenty seconds), pass the tailor to ask if he had anything that was ready to be collected (two minutes), and once she was there she might as well ask the tailor about his years in the military and ask him to tell that story about how he worked for an oil company and drove a jeep without a license and got lost in the desert (five minutes) and what happened when the war broke out, was he drafted or did he go to the front voluntarily and who of his brothers had died and who had ended up in a wheelchair and who had made it here and who died on the way and how was his daughter doing, oh she had her second daughter, any photos, wow so cute, what are they calling her, Rakel is a beautiful name, I have a friend who's called Rakel, it's a lovely name, yes, it's both Muslim and Western, that's why it's so great, all my friends with Muslim parents are called Sara and Mona, there were tons of small Adams and Isaks and Jonases running around in the area where we grew up, our mom, yes, she was different, she chose another strategy, here the tailor smiled and looked down at his sewing machine, putting needles into his mouth to signal that he really needed to get back to work but Evelyn didn't give in, she asked about his second daughter, who works for UNICEF, how is she doing in Cambodia, and how is your wife and your dog and your garden (on a good day this could take almost half an hour).

When the tailor finally told her he needed to get back to work, Evelyn thanked him, she picked up the finished clothes, hanging on spidery metal hangers, and continued up the street to the corner store, she bought milk, saved the receipt and the change, to put it back in the cash register, she exited the store and then she just stood there for a few seconds, at the top of the stairs, on one of the most expensive pedestrian streets in Stockholm, always comfortably free from ice and snow, due to a special hidden heating system, she looked at the sky, thinking to herself that maybe one day she would be one of these people who was walking down this street with the swagger of someone who felt at home here, maybe one day she would be able to enter the store where she worked and buy clothing at full price, without worrying about an upcoming sale, not thinking twice before shelling out her food budget on a merino sweater or her monthly rent on a coat, and sometimes, when she descended the hill, passing people in furs, women with well-groomed dogs, men with glittering watches and polished shoes, she wondered if some of them saw her and her clothes (bought at a great discount simply because her bosses wanted all employees to wear the brands carried by the store) and thought to themselves that she was one of them, maybe she had married rich, or she came from a family of Egyptian ambassadors, or she was related to the emirs in Dubai, in her fantasy she had a two-bedroom on one of these streets that would make the person who asked where she lived pause and then blurt out an impressed "oh," maybe she lived on Strandvägen, and she had just forgotten to buy some milk and now she was on her way back home to her wooden floors and unobstructed sea view.

When she came back to the store Kattis wondered if she had milked the cows herself, and Anders checked the time and said that she had been gone for forty-five fucking minutes, and Evelyn just smiled at them and told them a story about something fascinating that had happened to Nadia in Cambodia, and Anders said: Who's Nadia? And Kattis said: It's Farid's daughter, and Anders said: Farid the tailor? and Kattis nodded and Evelyn said: Who wants coffee? and everyone raised their hands.

After lunch Evelyn received a text and since she had just been on two rather unmotivated toilet breaks, she slipped the phone into her pocket and said that she would go downstairs to get some more hangers.

Be back before closing time, Anders said with a smile.

I'll try, she said, opened the door to the back and checked her phone.

It was from Ina. But it was not a text asking her to do something for their mom, or an impromptu text informing her about some "new and cheap global index fund" (just because Evelyn once happened to mention to Ina that despite her years working at a place she hated, she still didn't have any savings). Instead Ina wrote: *Hi my dear sister. Are you at work? Can we come by?*

Evelyn looked at her phone as if it had just burped.

"We"? Who was "we"? The only "we" that existed was Ina, Evelyn and Anastasia. Since when did Ina start referring to herself in first-person plural? Evelyn answered straightaway: *Sure. I'm here, come on by.* Thirty minutes later they arrived. Ina and a bearded guy in a loose flannel shirt and polished Doc Martens. Ina smiled and said:

You remember Hector, right? From New Year's?

Yes, of course, Evelyn said and leaned in for a hug. Over his shoulder she signaled to Ina that she had no recollection of this guy whatsoever, they had celebrated New Year's at Anastasia's office, where Evelyn had met some friends, or not friends, but people who she kind of knew, and who became close friends for the night, with the same logic that you are much friendlier to a neighbor if you run into them abroad than if you meet them in your elevator, so Evelyn had continued partying with them, and here was this guy, holding her older sister's hand, looking at her like he couldn't believe his luck.

So . . . are you like . . .

Evelyn felt slightly nauseous, not really knowing why. She cleared her throat and changed subjects.

Are you looking for anything special today?

It was one of those work phrases that she said at least eighty times per day, so she should be able to say it without sounding phony, but this time, she couldn't.

Yes, Hector needs a new shirt, Ina said. And some pants.

Hector nodded and Evelyn took them over to the men's section, showing them the items that were on sale, and getting some other things from the back that weren't on sale yet, but that he could have for a reduced price if he wanted. As they strolled through the store, Ina said that Hector's dad had worked as a marine biologist for more than twenty years at an aquarium on Djurgården. To celebrate his recent decision to resign they were meeting up at a restaurant in Östermalm.

Are you going? Evelyn said.

Ina shook her head. Me? Of course not.

Well, you could if you wanted to, Hector said.

Ina's face turned red. It's way too soon, she said.

Evelyn nodded in agreement, without knowing why she agreed.

They would love to meet you, Hector said. He touched Ina's face and Evelyn had to look away.

I will take a look around, he said, and headed straight for the section of the store where there was no sale. He picked out a blue shirt and some pants in a weird dark-green-slash-brown color.

Do you have this in XL? And these in 54?

Evelyn nodded and pulled out invisible drawers from underneath the merino table, to give him his sizes. Before he headed to the dressing room he gave Ina a quick kiss on the cheek.

Evelyn looked at Ina in disbelief. She smiled.

What? she whispered.

Who *is* this?

It's Hector, Ina said, as if it was the most normal thing in the world. As if she was used to meeting guys at New Year's Eve parties and then deciding to form a union with them, and start referring to herself in the plural. Not even Hector seemed to understand how weird this was, he was just humming away in his dressing booth. It was as if he didn't understand that Ina didn't have boyfriends. She never went home with guys. Evelyn used to think that Ina had a nearsighted relationship with love, she fell in love with people at a distance, but as soon as they got close, she saw them too well and realized that she didn't like the details, she couldn't date someone who hadn't read Tolstoy's complete works in chronological order, she stopped returning a guy's phone calls just because he happened to say that he liked a popular French movie that Ina despised. But here Ina was, strolling around the store, looking for items for her . . . boyfriend? With a smile that Evelyn had never seen before, touching the fabric of random sweaters, as if she loved the sweaters as much as she loved him.

Have you heard about Anastasia? Evelyn said.

No, what?

She's back together with Mathias, Evelyn said, knowing very well that Ina would throw a fit when she heard the news. Instead Ina just shrugged her shoulders.

Well, it's her life, Ina said. I've done everything I can for her.

Evelyn noticed that her mouth was open and closed it.

Ina? Hector said. You have to see this.

Ina opened the door to the dressing room. Their laughter was so loud that two other customers started smiling as well. Evelyn wasn't sure why it felt like she was breathing through polyester.

How did it go? Evelyn said, not being able to shake the artificiality of her voice, every time she said one of those sentences that she normally only said to customers.

Well, what do you think? Hector exited the dressing room. A bit too tight, or? If the shirt had a voice, it would scream in pain.

You don't carry XXL? Ina said.

No, sorry, Evelyn said. And what about the pants? She looked down and realized that he was wearing them, but he hadn't managed to get them above his thighs.

Don't worry, he said. I'm used to this.

Hector changed outfits and came back out with the clothes he had tried on, he had tried to fold the shirt, with limited success.

We are heading for coffee, he said. If you want to join?

Sorry, I'm closing today, Evelyn said. And I have already taken all my breaks. And we have a couple of important orders coming in so . . .

I hope we will get the opportunity to speak more another time, Hector said.

Absolutely, Evelyn said and waved goodbye, went to the counter, took out some cleaning material and started cleaning the mirrors with a dedication and frenzy she hadn't had since she started working here.

Are you okay? Anders asked.

Yes, I'm fine, Evelyn said, and wondered why it felt like a lie.

Her elder sister had finally found someone. Anastasia was back with Mathias. Their mom was doing not fine, but at least she was in a stable phase. Evelyn should be happy for her family's sake. But instead she headed to the bathroom and just stood there for a while to gather her thoughts and avoid letting out a scream that would make the customers run to the street in panic. She promised herself that she would change, she would not work another day in this store, she would never have another one-night stand, she would leave this bathroom, grab her coat, go straight out to Anders and Kattis and tell them that she was through, she had already let this store steal way too much of her life.

Now it was time. Now she was doing it. She unlocked the door, returned to the counter and worked diligently until closing time.

Chapter Six

The first time I saw the Mikkola sisters was in May 1991. They came parading down to the park, three sisters looking like brothers, ready to start a fight if someone said something about their outgrown bowl cuts, dirty Lion sneakers or sweatpants with stretched-out pockets. I couldn't take my eyes off them.

Who are they? Nico said and nodded towards Ina, Anastasia and Evelyn, climbing towards the top of the jungle gym in the center of the park, a fifty-meter-long steel dragon with a water-spraying head and a slide as a tail.

Tourists, Ellet said, when he heard that the sisters spoke English. From the hostel.

No, I think they live here, I said, and it was not only because I saw that Ina had a set of keys around her neck. It was also because I sensed that we belonged together, even though I didn't know why.

Definitely tourists, Nico said, but I heard in his voice that he wasn't sure, because even though the sisters were speaking English with one another, Swedish words kept appearing in their sentences. When Anastasia had reached the head of the dragon, Ina said: Wait here, hold on and I will push the "vattenknapp."

And Evelyn answered: This is boring, who wants to go to the "pingisrum"?

That's the Mikkola sisters, I said.

Do you know them? Nico said.

Mikkola, Ellet said. It sounds Finnish. Why do they speak English with each other?

Next time we saw them in the park, Ellet approached them and tried his arsenal of Finnish curse words (jumalauta, kusi, kyrpä). Evelyn ignored him, Ina looked at him as if he was a barking dog. It wasn't until he said "perkele huora" that they understood he was rattling off insults.

Get that fucking douchebag out of my sight, Ina said, and Evelyn turned around and pushed him, and Ellet tripped over a sandbox and fell and swore to never ever try to talk with those "crazy sisters" again.

Two weeks after their move to Drakenberg, everyone knew that the Mikkola sisters lived in house 19 on the third floor, we knew that they always chewed gum, we knew that the eldest sister was taller than most adults (Ina couldn't have been more than fifteen), we knew that the youngest sister had her arm in a cast and still she was able to play outdoor ping-pong fairly well (the official story was that Anastasia had hurt her arm "jumping into an outdoor pool" a few weeks prior to the move, but none of us believed it, we knew that something else must have happened, her dad had broken her arm as a punishment for something, or she had broken her arm doing bungee jumps or being arrested for something, because how many times have you heard of someone breaking their arm jumping into a pool?).

We knew that the middle sister had the most beautiful smile the world had ever seen, and the blackest hair and the greenest eyes matching the crystal around her neck, and whenever she was in the park, the older guys who were playing basketball three-on-three stopped playing for fun and started playing for blood, they called fouls, they fought for rebounds, it didn't matter that Evelyn was way too young for them, she was already surrounded by a strange power field, grown men saw her and started jogging with new energy, fat dog-owning middle-aged women in sweatpants looked at her with hateful eyes, but Evelyn seemed totally unaware of all this, or maybe she had learned early on to conceal her awareness of the effect she had on the world.

Another thing that was special about the sisters was that they were always out in the park, rain or sunshine, and they were always out by themselves. None of us had seen their parents, we were also out without our parents from time to time, of course we were, we weren't like Isak, who never went to the park without his mom, even though he was one year older than us. We met up in the park and spent hours transforming the swings into a ninja challenge (give all swings a push and try to run through without getting hit), we dug for gold in the sandboxes, we kicked our soccer ball up the apple trees to get apples, and then we kicked more soccer balls to knock down the first ball that was stuck in the tree, and our parents weren't there the whole time, but they came by from time to time to check on us, my mom would pass the park on her way to Vivo to make sure that I kept an eye on my brothers or to remind me to be home by six, my dad would come down to the park on his way to a night shift in the subway with some fruit for me and my friends. But the Mikkola sisters were always out alone, always, and when I casually mentioned this to my mom, she said:

Well, that's a surprise, but it was obvious that she meant that it wasn't a surprise, and my dad said that their mom was a good person, she did her best to take care of her kids, just like we do.

Really? Mom said.

Just let it go, Dad said.

Really? Mom said again, and my dad looked at me with those eyes that seemed to say: Do you see what I put up with for you guys?

Soon rumors started circulating about the sisters. The rumors whispered that their dad was dead, but nobody really knew how he had been killed, if it was an overdose or car accident or drowning, or a combination of the three. The rumors said that their mom worked late and on weekends and wore a lot of perfume and black leather boots and always had her designer handbag full of cash.

The rumors whispered that the youngest sister, Anastasia, had been standing in the courtyard between houses 4 and 12, poking a dead bird with a stick, and when she touched the bird and said something the bird sprang to life and took flight. The rumors said that the middle sister had convinced one of the older guys to kiss her French-style in exchange for a chestnut and that the eldest sister was actually a boy, because it didn't seem believable that a fifteen-year-old girl could be that tall and be that good at basketball.

I never started those rumors, but sometimes I embellished them, added some details, doubled a number, and knowing very well that my mom had a hard time with the Mikkola family, for reasons that I didn't understand, I brought home everything that was said about them to our dinner table, and my mom nodded and looked at my dad with her "what-did-I-tell-you" face.

Don't believe everything you hear, he said.

Their mom was never in the park, never at any teacher-parent conference, rarely in the grocery store, but we heard her when she came home, late on Friday afternoons, first the roar of her car, a shiny red Toyota Celica with pop-up headlights, sometimes parked just outside their door, even though it was a handicap spot, then the sound of her high heels as she left the car and walked towards their door, the sound echoing between the tall buildings, click clack, like a metronome, but inhumanly fast, either she had the shortest legs in world history or she was running home to her kids (it turned out that both were true).

Look at her, my mom said, peering down from beneath the kitchen drapes. Just look at her.

I looked, but I never really understood what Mom wanted me to see. Sure they were different, their mom wore high heels, my mom wore Birkenstocks, their mom wore makeup, my mom wore makeup so rarely that my brothers became scared of her when she came home made-up after a party, their mom seemed to be traveling nonstop for work, my mom had worked for years at the same place, ten minutes from our home, a treatment center for alcoholics. Their mom gave her daughters money for takeout, my mom would never dream of ordering takeout, it would be a sign that she had failed in her mission as a parent, instead she prepared real food, and when their mom spent her Saturday evenings at the local pizzeria Rimini, our mom was at home watching *Dallas* and making lists, and when their mom came home humming a song so loudly that it drowned the sound of her high heels, my mom stood behind the kitchen drapes, shaking her head, reminding me that I could do whatever I wanted in life, except become like the Mikkola sisters.

Because you will see what happens to children who roam around freely like that, she whispered. No structure, no rules. They will not make it, not in this world.

Chapter Seven

On a Sunday in March 2000, Evelyn came home from work and, as she took a big step over the pile of unopened mail in the hallway, she realized that she longed for a phone call from Ina. It had never happened before, and normally Evelyn would let Ina's phone calls go straight to voicemail, and even if Evelyn answered, she would do it with a stressed voice so that Ina wouldn't think for a second that Evelyn had as much time to talk as Ina. But now, after a few weeks of silence, Evelyn wondered why Ina didn't call, she always used to call on Sunday evenings, there was always some important information that she needed to share with Evelyn, she had read some new comparison of home insurance policies, she had tried a new shampoo that was both very good and extremely cheap, and now she wanted Evelyn to try it. And when Evelyn didn't tell Ina anything about her life, Ina used to take advantage of the situation to give her an update about their mother, where she lived now, how she was doing, what kind of medications she was on, what the doctor had said last time they spoke, and when Evelyn still just answered with humming sounds, Ina gave up and said that she would call Anastasia now, and they hung up.

Last fall Evelyn couldn't imagine that she would miss these calls, but now she did, and when she had picked up the mail from the floor and kicked off her heels, she headed to the living room and called Ina, who answered after two rings and sounded just as happy as Evelyn had feared, fuck, this was a mistake, but now it was too late to go back, Ina refused to hang up, she told her about all the incredible things that she and Hector had been doing lately, one weekend they had taken a walk around Skeppsholmen and ended up eating lunch at the East Asian museum! Another weekend they had gone to Casablanca and rented EVERY Woody Allen movie they could find.

ALL OF THEM, Ina said, as if she could barely believe how crazy this was.

How many did they have? Evelyn said.

Four, Ina said. And do you know what we did afterwards?

Evelyn shook her head, and even though Ina couldn't hear this through the phone, she kept telling her: They had gone past the main library because Hector was picking up a book, and then they had MADE OUT in the staircase leading up to the rotunda.

Wow, Evelyn said and tried to mask how incredibly uninterested she was in all of this.

With tongue, Ina said. A couple of tourists saw us, and then we stopped, but when they left, we kept going.

Fun for you, Evelyn said, as she started to leaf through her mail. Electricity bill. Party invitation. Advertising. Advertising. Advertising. And then an envelope, addressed to Evelyn, without a stamp.

How's Anastasia? Evelyn said, just to have something to say.

She's good, Ina said. But I have barely seen her, since I have spent so much time at Hector's place.

But she's here now, a hoarse voice yelled in the background.

Evelyn smiled when she heard Anastasia. Is she okay? Evelyn said.

It's just temporary! Anastasia screamed.

What did she say?

That it's just temporary, Ina said. And it is. She's only staying here until she finds something else. And she has promised to help out with Mom because I have three exams coming up.

Evelyn nodded and didn't say what she thought, which was: It will never work, Anastasia will soon be twenty years old and is incapable of taking care of herself, how could she help their mom, they are way too similar.

How are you? Ina said.

Evelyn was turning twenty-two and had never been dependent on anyone, never, not Ina, not her mom, especially no damn boyfriend. But that didn't mean that she was lonely, absolutely not, she had offers, just this last month she had gone home with three different guys, first that older guy who worked in finance but was an avid poetry reader, then that young guy who worked as a mailman, he had terrible posture but incredible lips, and then, last weekend, that trombone player whose apartment was full of music equipment and books about Zen Buddhism. Needless to say, they all fell in love with her, of course they did, how could they not, she was so good at putting on a show for them that it was impossible not to, she knew exactly how to pause and ask those intimate questions, she knew precisely how she would look and listen with that small fascinated smile, as if she was totally blown away and lost in thought, captivated by this particular dude's rambling about the genius of Szymborska, or the challenges of getting up at 4 a.m. or the importance of a daily meditation practice, and there should be books written about her ability to give blow jobs, always starting out a bit unsure, as if this was the first time she did this, always with the humming sound so that the guy thought that this particular dick was something special, harder, bigger and more tasty than every penis out there, and then the finale, her fake orgasm, she could give courses at the university about how to time them perfectly with the guy, even if he came too soon, even if his dick was the size of a cheese doodle, nails into his back, the breathing, the eye rolling, and afterwards, leaning forward, sighing, mumbling something that made them feel special, chosen, something that made sure that they would never forget her. When they woke up she was gone, she had gathered her effects, left them her fake number and stolen something on her way out, not money, never money, or rarely money, but rather something small that they wouldn't miss, an incense candle, a cologne they didn't use, a coffee cup, just something to remember them by, and then she was out the door, never to be seen again, and they would keep calling the same fake number for months, sometimes years, trying to see if the four that she had written could have been a nine and maybe the three was an eight, and they kept ending up at the wrong person, who became angrier and angrier, please stop calling this fucking number, I don't know anyone called Evelyn, she's not here, okay, you've been played, just accept it and move on!

Are you still there? Ina said.

Yes, Evelyn said. Sorry. I just remembered I have to do . . .

But before she had the chance to hang up, Ina needed to tell her more about Hector and his family history, his Argentine marine biologist dad, his Swedish lawyer mom, his dad had been a professor, or close to being a professor, then he had left the university to "start his own thing" (and Evelyn wondered: How is it even possible for a marine biologist to "start his own thing"?) and he had dived and chased fish and imported fish to Sweden, both in legal and semi-legal ways, and it was thanks to him that the aquarium on Djurgården housed so many rare species. Evelyn listened to her sister and tried to mimic her happiness. Then she found a reason to end the call and hung up with tired cheek muscles.

Evelyn looked down at the envelope without stamps. She opened it. It was a dated letter from the person whose apartment she was subletting. He informed her that unfortunately he had broken up with his girlfriend (he actually specified in the letter that he was the one who had broken up) and that he therefore needed his flat back as soon as possible. However, seeing that this was an "unfortunate situation" (his words) for both of them, he would "be open to discussing the possibility of sharing the flat with you, if you would be interested in this." He wrote that he could sleep in the living room and that they could split the rent, simply because he knew how impossible it was to find a new flat, with short notice, in this crazy city.

Evelyn couldn't help but smile. On some level she knew this would happen, she had made the mistake of being too charming last time he was here to collect his mail. She had worn that black polo sweater and her purple tights. She had told him some stories from her past and done that thing with the spoon and even asked him if he wanted some tea, and of course he had declined, not because it would be wrong for him to have tea with the woman who was renting his flat, but rather because he knew that if he had had that cup of tea, he would never be able to leave, he would come home late to his boring ugly veterinarian girlfriend and start to wonder why she didn't look more like Evelyn, why couldn't she be full of all these fascinating stories, how could he settle down with a person who had such a boring normal background, no crazy gun-toting uncles, no paranoid mother, no nine moves in eleven years just to get away from that curse that their mom feared more than death itself, no, instead he was condemned to a life of mediocrity, with this soulless person, and he tried to keep it up, for a couple of months, he even became kinder to the person he was living with, buying flowers, seeking couples therapy, in a serious attempt to conceal his infatuation for Evelyn, but ultimately he couldn't do it, the poor thing, he ended things with her and walked over to the flat to drop off the letter that he had prepared in his mind for weeks. And even though Evelyn knew it wasn't a good idea, she decided that she would say yes, she would do anything to avoid moving in with Ina, it would be like going back in time, Ina, Anastasia and Evelyn, in the same flat, for the first time since they left home? That wouldn't end well.

She picked up her phone and called her landlord. He answered the phone with a voice that she barely recognized. It took him a few seconds to understand who was calling. She said that she would be happy to share the flat with him. She expected him to become happy, now his fantasy was coming true, he would have the chance to live in close proximity with the one and only Evelyn, for at least a few months, until she found a new place to stay, and sure, this didn't mean that they would become a couple, but just the chance to be close to her energy, her beauty, her intelligence, would make all men jealous.

I would be happy to share the flat with you, she said. He was silent for a few seconds.

Actually, he said, I have given this some thought, and I think it's better if you just move out. I'm really sorry, but this isn't going to work.

Evelyn looked at her phone as if to make sure that she had heard him correctly. Okay, she said. I will move out, no problem.

Thank you, he said and hung up before she did.

Chapter Eight

The Mikkola sisters had lived in our area for a couple of months when Nico pulled me aside one day in the park and informed me that the three of them were half Tunisian.

No way, I said.

Yes way, he said.

He had heard it from Leffe K, who had a brother who was in Ina's class at school. Their mom was from Tunisia and their dad was Swedish, even though the family name sounded Finnish. I had lived in Sweden my whole life and never met anyone else who was half Swedish, half Tunisian. In first grade there was me, an adopted kid from Chile (was his name Micke?) and then a girl who was half French (her dad had been a pilot but was dead, her name was Elise, I haven't thought about her for thirty years, but as I look her up now I see that she has her birthday in September, lives in Spånga and seems to be working as a licensed animal caretaker at the Barkaby Animal ER, specializing in anesthesia and pain relief), but that was about it, everyone else was Swedish. Ellet's dad was from Estonia, but that didn't count. A new guy in another class was half Italian, I decided that we would become best friends, his name was Daniel, but he wanted to be called Rocky, because, well, you know, he said. I didn't get it.

The movie, he said. *Rocky*.

I nodded but still didn't get it.

He's Italian, Daniel aka Rocky said, and I nodded and understood, I wanted him to call me another name, a more suitable name than

Jonas, I suggested Younes, it was the name my Tunisian relatives called me, I suggested Achraf like my oldest cousin, but Rocky thought it sounded weird.

Tell me the names of some famous Arab boxers or actors, he told me, and I couldn't name anyone.

What about scientists? he said. I shook my head.

Singers?

My head was empty of names, the only singer I could think of was Oum Kalthoum and I was not about to let Rocky call me Oum for the rest of the school year, so we decided to stick with Jonas. Rocky and I were best friends, until we entered a store and I saw him stealing at least three pieces of Chock licorice chewing gum, and he looked at me and put his finger to his mouth, and I smiled and went straight home and told Mom what had happened because I told her everything, she was my everything, and she forbid me to hang out with Rocky, and I felt a strange sense of relief when I went back to hanging out with Nico and Ellet in the park, where I knew who I was, and nobody could take my place.

Next time we saw the Mikkola sisters, close to the swings made of large black car tires, I approached them with Nico as a sidekick and asked them if it was true that they came from Tunisia.

Evelyn nodded, Ina just looked at me, Anastasia was too young to care what I was saying, she just returned to gathering sticks that she for some reason put in the dark empty space where the tire swings once had had an inner tube.

I started to bombard them with questions, questions that I hated being asked, but it felt more okay to ask them these questions because they understood that I didn't ask them with the same intention as other people (or did they?).

I asked them if they were born here or there. Here, they said, which made me feel more okay.

I asked them if they were "hel eller halv" (whole or half). Half, they said, which made me feel even more okay.

I asked them how often they "åkte ned" ("went down"), which was my attempt at casually asking how often they visited Tunisia, as if it was a half-hour car trip away, and not a flight of seven to ten hours, depending on if you stopped over in Paris with Tunisair or went via Frankfurt with Lufthansa.

We have only been there once, Ina said, and now I felt really confident, there was no way that they could know more about Tunisia than I did, because we went down every summer, or at least every other summer, and therefore they wouldn't be able to take my spot as the area's best half Tunisian. I told them that I loved the casse-crouts in Tabarka, and that the tea and the water pipes in Sidi Bou Said have become way too touristy and in Sousse there are great beaches and an amazing hamburger place, just opposite a small circus.

We have only been to Djerba, Evelyn said.

Our mom has friends there, Ina said. Don't you know Djerba?

Of course, I said. Djerba is quite close to the coast, right?

Djerba is an island, Evelyn said.

That's right, I said. I'm more familiar with Jendouba, where my dad is from. And Aïn Draham, where there's a spring with holy water, and Tabarka, which is like Sousse, but better, because there are no tourists there and . . .

That's where they met, Ina said.

Where who met? I said.

Your dad and our mom.

Evelyn looked at me with a smile.

He doesn't know, she said.

Of course he does, Ina said.

Know what, I said.

Our mom and your dad used to date, Evelyn said.

But it was a looooong time ago, Ina said.

She broke his heart, Evelyn said.

Not true, I said, even though I wasn't sure why it felt important to me to disagree with this particular fact.

Sure did, he was crazy about our mom, but she was in love with someone else, and they stayed in touch and the rest is history, Ina said.

If they know each other so well, why haven't they spoken since you moved here?

Ask your mother about that, Evelyn said, and I did, I went straight home and asked if it was true that dad had had a crush on the Mikkola sisters' mother and my mom looked at me and said that sometimes there are things in the adult world that are hard to understand and I asked her if she had forbidden our dad to see their mom, and my mom said:

Who is there to see, she's never home, she travels all over the country, leaving her kids alone. Do yourself a favor and stay away from those sisters.

But for the first time in my life, I didn't obey her wishes. Instead I dedicated every waking moment to becoming best friends with them. When Ina played basketball, I volunteered to stand under the basket to take rebounds and pass the ball back to her, so she could work on her jump shot. When Anastasia lost her necklace in the bushes next to the soccer field, I spent half an hour trying to help her find it (we found it dangling on a branch, as if someone had found it and hung it there so we wouldn't miss it, a red crystal, a metallic Fatima's hand and a blue glass pearl with a white symbol that kind of looked like an eye).

But mostly I hung out with Evelyn, we were closest in age, we went down to the yellow kiosk and dug for dropped coins under the patio, we stole plums from the garden plots on Tanto Mountain, sometimes she came over to our place to watch afternoon TV, I always checked before so that Mom wouldn't be home, I didn't want her to get angry that I wasn't following her rules.

Once Mom came home early from work, she saw Evelyn's worn-out sneakers in the hallway, she came bursting into my room, I expected her to throw a fit, to start yelling, to tell Evelyn that she was not welcome in our home, but when she saw us on the bed, with one comic each, with a safe distance between our bodies, she smiled and asked if we wanted a snack, she even came in with a tray to my room, which had never happened before, at least not when I wasn't sick.

When she put the tray down she asked if Evelyn wanted to stay for dinner. Evelyn said that she had to check with her mom.

Of course you do, Mom said. You can call her.

Evelyn got up and used the landline in our kitchen, she dialed a number, and I remember thinking that her number had too few digits.

Yes, I can stay for dinner, Evelyn said.

That was quick, Mom said.

When Dad came home from work, he found us in the kitchen, his kids, his wife and Evelyn.

What's she doing here, Dad said in French.

Someone has to feed her, Mom said in French.

I turned to Evelyn and asked her if she spoke French, she shook her head.

Mom always spoke English with us when we were kids, she said. She figured we would learn Swedish anyway, and English is a much bigger language.

What about French? Dad said. Or Arabic?

English is way bigger, Evelyn said.

Bigger is not always better, Mom mumbled.

But your mom's English is . . . Dad said.

What?

Nothing. I have heard her speak English and it doesn't really sound like English. Her pronunciation is . . .

She wanted us to be able to leave this country when we wanted to, Evelyn said, staring at Dad.

Why would you want to leave this country? Mom said. This is the best country in the world.

Everyone was silent for a few seconds.

We also have a lot of relatives who don't speak Swedish, Evelyn said. My great-grandfather emigrated to New York, he was one of the steelworkers who built Rockefeller Center.

Nobody said anything.

It's a famous high-rise, Evelyn said. In Manhattan.

But the Empire State Building is higher, right? Mom said.

Yes, it's definitely higher, Dad said, even though none of them had been in New York.

Evelyn turned to me.

You know that famous black-and-white photo with a bunch of guys who are eating their lunch on a steel beam really high up in the air?

I nodded, of course I knew the photo, everyone knew that photo, I must have seen it at least twenty times, it was sold as a stock photo at IKEA, buy a frame and get the poster for free, they had it on the wall of our local youth center, in the ping-pong room, my uncle had it framed in the corridor above his vinyl collection.

One of those guys on the beam is my dad's dad's dad, Evelyn said.

That's incredible, Mom said, but she didn't sound impressed, instead she sounded like she was comforting a kid who had just dropped an ice cream.

When Evelyn had left, Dad cleared the table, and Mom reminded me that she didn't want me to play with the Mikkola sisters.

They're not to be trusted, she said. And did you see her nails? They were like claws.

Nobody said anything, I hadn't thought about her nails, but next time I saw Evelyn I thought about her nails, and maybe they were a bit longer and dirtier than other kids' nails.

But it's not her fault, Mom added. What can you expect, after such a turbulent childhood.

After that Evelyn and I mostly met up outside. And whenever we hung out, time passed quicker than normal and everything felt meaningful and the loneliness that I had felt all my life hurt less.

One evening we sat high up on Tanto Mountain, the sun was setting. The flat rock under us was still warm from the afternoon sun.

I don't get why they store sand piles here, Evelyn said.

I looked straight ahead so she wouldn't get the idea that I had any ideas.

Maybe it's because . . . I said.

I couldn't come up with a good answer. It was a bit strange, big trucks needed to go to the top of the mountain to collect brown sand that was used to reduce the slipperiness of sidewalks and streets during the winter. And during the summers one of the city's most scenic places was occupied by gigantic brown sand piles.

Evelyn squinted against the sunset. I looked back, I saw our shadows, they were tall as . . . I searched for a good metaphor, I wanted to tell her, look at our shadows, they are tall as, tall as basketball players (come on), tall as trees (stop it), long as swimming pools (just quit), tall as your sister (she may be offended), tall as really tall, really long shadows (hmm).

What else could they do here? I said.

How about an outdoor restaurant? Evelyn said. A hotel? A cable railway? Just anything except a freaking sand dump?

I looked down at the square-shaped brown buildings that constituted our home, the long metallic shape that was the Dragon, the glistening water of Årstaviken, the dark metal of the Liljeholm Bridge.

This is so typically Swedish, Evelyn said, and I nodded, even though I wondered if this was something that she thought, or if all of this was something her mom had said to her that she was just repeating.

Can I ask you something? she said.

I nodded.

What do your parents do? Don't lie.

But she said it more like this:

What do your parents do—don't lie!

And in normal cases, I may have lied because that's what I did back then (and in some sense that's what I do still), but for some reason, I told Evelyn the truth. I said that my mom is a physiotherapist for alcoholics at Mariakliniken and my dad is a subway conductor and on the weekends we clean a bar together, and then he is a bartender there in the evenings, to make some extra cash. Evelyn was quiet for a moment. Then she asked me if I had heard any rumors about her family, and since I had already started being honest, I didn't see any point in stopping, so I nodded my head and said:

Yes, there are some rumors about your family.

Our family is a bit different, she said, and I nodded my head.

Ours too, I said.

How so?

Well, you know, having parents from two different countries, being both Arab and Swedish at the same time.

You're a bit obsessed with that aren't you? she said. No, I mean that we are special in other ways.

Because your dad is dead and your mom is a prostitute? I said.

She looked at me like my face had turned into pus.

Excuse me?

Sorry.

What did you say?

Sorry, I said again.

Our mom is a traveling salesman, she screamed. She she she sells the best handwoven carpets on the market. Who has said that?

Everyone says it, I mumbled, not really knowing how to hide my face.

Well, you can tell everyone, Evelyn said, while getting up on her feet and switching to English, that we are special because we have an ultra-strong curse placed on us, saying that everything we love will get taken from us, and despite that curse, we are still here!

She started walking down Tanto Mountain, her steps so angry that they made puffs of smoke in the gravel. I followed her, I didn't run up to her, I didn't say sorry, I just walked there, behind her, just close enough to see the words that she had written with a permanent marker on her denim jacket, thinking to myself that I somehow had managed to destroy the most valuable thing I had, simply by trying to be honest.

Chapter Nine

Evelyn was supposed to leave her flat at the end of March, but since everything had happened so fast, and since Evelyn was Evelyn, she managed to convince her landlord that she could move out a couple of weeks later, and even though her landlord was staying on a friend's couch, he accepted this and even asked her if she needed help with the move. She declined his offer, she didn't need help, or rather, she had enough friends and sisters to get through this move by herself.

Since Ina was the only sister who had her driver's license, she was responsible for renting a moving truck, and since Ina was Ina, she didn't rent the truck from the closest rental place in Vasastan. No, Ina had managed to find a place south of the city, in Midsommarkransen, where you could get a twelve-square-meter truck for only 750, plus tax, for three hours, which was almost 250 kronor cheaper than Quickrent in Vasastan.

But you're not even paying for it, Evelyn said with a sigh. I'm paying for it, and my friends will be here at noon and I just want to get this done as quickly as possible.

If you don't care about money, you could have hired a moving company, Ina said. Hector and I had plans today.

What kind of plans? Evelyn said. Do your color-coordinated calendars tell you that you have to spend the weekend watching romantic comedies in matching pajamas and then falling asleep in your sleep masks? No, of course she didn't say that, because she knew that if she said that, Ina wouldn't get the moving truck and then she wouldn't be able to move, so instead she smiled and swallowed and said:

Thanks for helping me, sis.

The three sisters had met up at Slussen and traveled south on the subway, it wasn't a long trip, but all trips are long when you don't know exactly where you are going and one third was out dancing until 4 a.m., and another third is convinced of the meaninglessness of the trip, and the last third longs to be back in Hector's warm bed.

When they reached the address for the rental place, it was nowhere to be found. Instead they found a small tobacco shop at the address that the guy had given to Ina.

I knew it, Evelyn said. Why couldn't you just have rented a normal moving van, at a normal gas station?

Sorry for trying to help, Ina said.

Tired of their fighting and hungover from the night before, Anastasia entered the tobacco shop to ask if the woman behind the counter knew of a car rental place somewhere around here. The smell of the store evoked memories, this is what their grandmother's kitchen smelled like in Tunisia, this was the courtyard in their mother's home country, this was the basement mosque on Ringvägen that they had visited once or twice when their mother had her monthlong religious phase. The woman behind the counter seemed hypnotized by the small and not particularly thin TV.

Good episode? Anastasia said to get her attention.

The woman didn't answer. Anastasia looked at the screen. A woman in a red dress drank a smoking blue potion from a wineglass, another woman stood hidden behind a plant, but she wasn't hidden, because it was obvious to everyone that she was grinning and wringing her hands.

They are enemies, the woman behind the counter said.

They don't look like enemies, Anastasia said in an attempt to be funny.

They should be enemies, the woman said, and without removing her eyes from the TV screen, she gave a short convincing summary of why the woman in red should hate the lady behind the plant.

What's the name of this show? Anastasia said.

The woman said the name.

Are they speaking Turkish? Anastasia said.

The woman looked at Anastasia as if trying to understand if she was joking or not. Not Turkish?

Arabic, the woman said. Don't you hear the difference between Arabic and Turkish? Anastasia tried to listen to the voices of the actors, yes, maybe she heard some difference, but mostly she heard her sisters' voices from the street and she remembered why she was here.

Do you know a rental car place around here?

Name? the woman said.

My name or the name of the rental place? Anastasia said.

Name of the person who booked the car.

Ina, Anastasia said. Ina Mikkola. And the lady reluctantly turned away from the TV screen (first her face, then her eyes) long enough to look at a paper in a green binder in front of her. She disappeared behind the counter and came back up with a key.

Here you go.

You don't want to see my ID?

Just be sure to bring it back before four. Anything else?

Yes, well, where is the truck?

Up the hill, the lady said, as if this was the most obvious thing she had ever uttered. Anastasia exited the tobacco store with the car keys held high, like a trophy.

You're kidding me, Ina said. Did they give the keys to *you*?

Yes, so I guess that means *I'm* driving, Anastasia said, and led them up the hill towards the truck.

Please, dear Lord, don't let it be that one, Evelyn said.

What's wrong with this one? Ina said and tried to look confident.

The moving truck had once been yellow, now the color was hard to detect behind all the dirt.

This must be an old postal truck, Anastasia said.

As long as it's rolling, I'm happy, Ina said and looked rather unhappy.

The doors were rusty, the window on the passenger side was

cracked, one of the fenders had been duct-taped in order to not fall off.

This is the last time I let you rent a moving truck, Evelyn said.

Don't worry, this is the last time I will help you move, Ina said, as they climbed up into the front seat and tried to open the windows to air out the cigarette smell.

Chapter Ten

During our last summer together I understood that my mom was wrong. The Mikkola sisters had rules, lots of rules. But their rules weren't like our rules, they didn't have rules telling them to be home at a certain time, or to only eat candy on Saturdays. Their mom had three rules, number one, and most important: They should never ever tell anyone anything about themselves, not in school, not to the cops, they should fly under the radar, they should invent fake answers to avoid attracting other people's jealousy (Even when you're talking to friends? I said. It depends on which friend, Evelyn said). Number two: Always wear your necklaces. (Even when you're doing sports? I said. Especially when we are doing sports, Evelyn said). Number three: They must touch their earlobe, knock wood three times, kiss their knuckle and touch the earlobe again, every time someone gave them a compliment, or wished for something good to happen to them, or said good luck (That's a lot of knocking, I said. I know, Evelyn said).

And the Mikkola sisters, who didn't seem to be afraid of anyone or anything, actually seemed to be following their mom's rules.

Then there were other rules that Ina had invented, and they always seemed to be about Evelyn. Ina forbid Evelyn to climb trees. She wasn't allowed to be alone with boys. She had to ask for permission if she wanted to cross the heavily trafficked Hornsgatan. She was not, *under any circumstances*, allowed to bike down to Långholmen by herself. She could get hit by a car or kidnapped by Södermannen, a local flasher who showed his dick to schoolkids.

You're not my mom, Evelyn said.

I'm just trying to keep you safe, Ina said. To avoid another Blackeberg. What happened in Blackeberg? I said.

Nothing happened in Blackeberg, both Evelyn and Ina said with one voice.

Evelyn followed her mom's rules and seemed to try her best to break Ina's rules. Sometimes I wondered if that's why she chose to restart our friendship after the fight on Tanto Mountain. Because we did spend time by ourselves, we biked down to Årstaviken to swim, we crossed Hornsgatan to buy ice cream at the Glacette store, sometimes she showed me that she had her great-grandfather's genes by climbing really high up, without any sign of vertigo.

Check this out, she said and climbed to the top of the roof of the bike shed. And this, she said and climbed from the bike shed to a nearby chestnut tree.

Even I, who was still on the ground, had a slight sense of vertigo, just imagining the view from up there. I had my head so far back that I opened my mouth and I felt the tickling of the leaves, the wind through the branches, the consequence of one small mistake, and just as I felt it, when I was up there with her, even though I was still on the ground, she let go and fell, no, she didn't fall, she jumped, she jumped from one branch to another, the tree swayed, leaves fell to the ground as if they thought she fell and wanted to stay close to her the whole way down.

Chapter Eleven

na turned the key and the motor started with a jolt. They drove back into town, in silence. Three sisters next to one another. Anastasia in the middle to avoid more fighting. Evelyn at the window to avoid sitting next to Ina. Ina at the steering wheel, because neither of her childish sisters had been responsible enough to apply for a license. How hard was it, to save some money, book a couple of lessons, take the ice test, ace the theory, schedule a driving test? Was it that hard to imagine that they would need a driving license in the future? Was it impossible for them to plan ahead? But no, her sisters didn't plan for the future, they just sat back and enjoyed the ride she offered them.

Anastasia leaned forward and tried the radio (it didn't work). She asked Evelyn about her job (it was okay, but she hated it and would quit soon). She asked Ina about her exams (she probably passed them). Then more silence. Anastasia knew she could reduce the tension in the truck by asking more questions, but she was tired of being the peacemaker. Now when they would live together all three (temporarily!) for the first time in years, she wanted her older sisters to take responsibility for resolving their own conflicts, how hard can it be, but when nobody had said anything for another five minutes, Anastasia did what she had promised herself not to do.

Do you remember Mom's red Toyota? she said.

And that was all that was needed, now they found a path back to one another, of course they remembered Mom's red Toyota Celica, the pop-up lights, the Fatima hand dangling from the rearview mirror, the chant she always mumbled when she was going on a long trip, the beaded seat cushion that helped her crooked back survive her long work trips, the chestnuts in the compartment made for sunglasses, and that time when a hare-lipped cop outside Eskilstuna pulled her over for speeding, and it ended with her a) not needing to pay the fine, and b) getting a police escort to Södertälje, because she claimed that her daughter had an inflamed appendix (and right as the cop hunched down to look in the back seat, all three sisters started moaning). The sisters smiled.

Sometimes I miss her, Evelyn said.

She would be glad if you came to visit, Ina said.

Evelyn looked out through the cracked window, they were so high up, the truck that looked like a shack from the outside was something else from the inside, now they were sailing, this reminded her of something, but she couldn't think of what, another life, high up in a pirate mast, Anastasia kept talking memories, the two-room apartment in Drakenberg, the apartment with two kitchens in Rågsved, the camping trip when it rained so much that their plastic table was washed away, Ina answered, Evelyn answered, and it was a dance, they had been practicing it for years, everyone knew exactly what to say when, and soon they were friends again, or at least less unfriendly with one another, but Evelyn couldn't escape the feeling that everything was fake, that the only reason they tried so hard was that they would soon live together again, and sometimes she looked down on her fingers and saw how they touched the car door, as if the fingers tried to remind her that there was a way out, she could open the door now, and just tumble out in freedom, whenever she wanted, now, at the next red light, or the next one.

The truck creaked and the dashboard vibrated when Ina floored the gas pedal and drove out on the Väster Bridge. They passed the treetops of Långholmen, just woken and still bare in the spring sun, then the glittering water of Riddarfjärden, the facades of Kungsholmen like a wall, the vertigo of seeing the whole city from above. The bridge's fence was full of padlocks, some people called them "love locks," but Evelyn was convinced that they had been put there by mourners, to remember everyone who had climbed over the fence and jumped, and as the car struggled towards the top, Evelyn wondered if the people who had jumped had died from drowning or from the impact, if everyone regretted it halfway down, if there was someone who had jumped and survived.

Chapter Twelve

n August 1993, the last Sunday of the Water Festival, Evelyn suggested that we should bike over to Rålambshovsparken to see the air show. I didn't need convincing, I had seen *Top Gun* so many times that I knew half of the lines by heart.

The sky was too blue to be true and our bike ride was taking longer than expected because Långholmsgatan was full of people, the police had stopped the traffic and people were pouring out of buses. Evelyn and I had to get off our bikes and walk. I checked the time, it was twelve thirty and we weren't moving fast enough. A couple of guys climbed up on lamp posts to get some kind of idea of what was happening in front, it felt like a demonstration without the banners, a carnival without the confetti. Even the balconies with a limited view of the sky were filled with people with binoculars and big black VCR cameras on their shoulders, the red recording light already beaming, preparing for what surely would be something to show the grandkids.

Evelyn and I fought our way through the crowd, dads folded strollers to save space, toddlers were put on shoulders to avoid being trampled, our bike pedals scratched strangers' ankles, a confused Spanish-speaking family was desperately trying to go in the opposite direction, but had to give up and follow the flow of the people, towards the Väster Bridge.

We won't make it to the other side in time, I said.

But Evelyn just kept going, using her green BMX bike as a battering ram, squeezing past red-faced tourists from Lidköping, ignoring angry comments from people who had been patiently waiting their turn in the heat of the sun, and I followed her, sweat running down me, breathing through my mouth to avoid the collision of smells of moose langos and licorice candy belts from street sellers.

Evelyn! I said. Let's go to Långholmen instead.

She just kept going and I followed, gliding through the brief opening in the sea of people that she and her bike created as if she was an icebreaker, and I was a seal.

It starts in fifteen minutes, I said, but she kept moving until she stopped. We had reached the beginning of the bridge, and even Evelyn understood that there was no way we would make it over there in time.

Okay, she said. Let's go to Långholmen. But don't tell Ina.

I nodded, without really understanding why this particular thing was important to hide from Ina. We wrangled ourselves out from the crowd, jumped on our bikes and raced down the hill towards the footbridge to Långholmen, an island small enough that our gym teacher could tell us to run around it in less than an hour. We passed a few drunkards on a bench who looked really puzzled by the number of people who were running and biking in the same direction. They didn't know that this was the day of our revenge, our military had been working on the Jas 39 Gripen for twenty-plus years, and there were some people, some naysayers, some haters who had claimed that we didn't need our own fighter jet, we could just buy French airplanes, or American, or heaven forbid Russian instead. Why would we, a small country in the north with eight million inhabitants, need to make our own fighter jets? Wasn't it enough that we had the audacity to have not one, but two car manufacturers? But those people didn't get it. They hadn't seen *Top Gun* forty times. They didn't know why Evelyn and I (mostly I) biked around the park shouting, "Goose, I'm hit I'm hit I'm hit," they didn't understand why we (or I)—many years later—commented on a really bad one-night stand with the words "I got caught in her tailwind," they didn't have dads who kept repeating "Life is like *Top Gun*, no points for second place, you have to be the best of the best" (even though our dads seemed pretty far from being the best at anything).

But on this special day in 1993, we, the believers, the people who never doubted, the people who knew that on the other side of clouds was eternal sunshine, we would be vindicated. We didn't even think about that incident that happened the last time the airplane was shown, when the proud generals had invited journalists to witness the miracle airplane's first prototype flight, and things didn't go exactly as planned, there were some small problems, yes, the steering system didn't really work back then and when the shiny new airplane went in for a landing in front of the rolling cameras, the plane started wobbling and then crashed sideways into a blazing wreck. Somehow the pilot made it out alive. But that was four long years ago, and since then the steering system had been updated and tried and tested and now it was put forth as one of the airplane's best features, the electronic super-advanced computer system that would stop the Russians from threatening our borders.

We biked over the footbridge and took a right, zigzagging to avoid hitting someone, the green crystal on Evelyn's necklace constantly moving in the opposite direction of her panting upper body, we were way too cool to have bicycle bells, so instead we used our voices, alerting the people that we were coming, constantly scanning the sky for airplanes because the air show should start any minute now. I had never seen the island of Långholmen this crowded, the field was full of picnickers who didn't give a damn about fighter jets, but still, they were here, and therefore they stood with their eyes towards the sky waiting for the show to start, even the boats in the harbor were full of people. As we biked into the looming shadow of the Väster Bridge, into the sudden cold and the echoing sounds of footsteps and voices, Evelyn said:

Remember, if Ina asks, we were in the park the whole time.

We leaned our bikes against a tree and found a cliff near the water with an unobstructed view of the sky. And then it started, airplane after airplane zooming through the sky, first two Drakens, then four

Viggens in formation, looping and rolling, plowing the blue color with white chemtrails, and sure it was impressive to see them soar through the sky and outrun their own sound. But we were all here for the grand finale. First we heard the sound, then we saw it, coming in fast from the east, a thin rocket of an airplane, glistening gray in the sun, spiky nose, two small wings in the front and two large wings in the back, creating that particular canard shape that was used for Viggen as well, and that people had been criticizing for years, saying that it reduced the stability of the airplane. What did they know about authentic Swedish engineering, nothing, absolutely nothing, this was proof that we still had it.

I heard Evelyn mumbling: You see it? You see it?

And of course I saw it, everyone saw it, even the hippie couple standing next to us had their mouths open and were beaming with reluctant pride.

After a turn over the city center, the pilot returned and approached us, he turned left, he turned right, and then it looked like the wings couldn't decide what was up or down, the airplane looked like the hand of my uncle when he was asked about the recent Dire Straits concert, and he was too much of a fan to be honest, and too honest to lie, so he stretched out his hand in front of him and kind of wobbled it sideways.

No no no no, Evelyn said, and in that second the airplane hit an invisible wall, the pilot hit the air brakes, the front turned upwards like a prancing horse, and I remember thinking that this has to be a trick, a part of the show, only the Jas 39 Gripen can stop in midair and then start tumbling towards the ground, the cockpit exploded and the motors started smoking and people started screaming, and Evelyn kept saying no no no, as the airplane fell like a leaf, silently and aimless it fell and fell towards Långholmen, towards us, the hippie couple turned around and ran, but Evelyn and I just stood there, our feet planted to the ground and our eyes hypnotized by the falling airplane, the steel body, this magnificent creation worth hundreds of millions of kronor, that landed somewhere between us and the bridge.

I want to remember a bang, I want to remember the sound of shattered glass, broken branches, mushed metal. But all I remember is silence. A compact silence. A silence of shame. A silence of: How could we think that we were better than we were? A silence of: Let's not try again ever. A big black cloud of smoke filled the sky.

The pilot's parachute slowly descended out over the water, and someone called my name.

It was Evelyn, she was already on her bike, she clenched her teeth and gestured to me.

Let's go, she said in English.

Roger that, I answered in English and we biked like only fourteen-year-olds can bike, we left the coastline and biked towards the impact site, we biked past people who looked weirdly stunned, everyone just walked, where? Just away from here, we biked towards the black smoke, towards the sirens, we saw burning trees, the firemen were already there, they wore black clothes with yellow reflectors, it was unfathomable how they could be so quick, had they known that this would happen? They covered the flames with white foam, there was a strong smell of gasoline and a weird sugary smell that I couldn't place, was it cotton candy? burned honey? The first cop on the scene covered his mouth with a red handkerchief, he told us to keep it moving, there was nothing to see here, please keep walking, and when nobody moved, he started screaming that there was a risk of explosion. People started backing away, some ran, but most of us just stood there, hypnotized by this glittering steel-gray fighter jet that had turned into a black foam-covered carcass in just a few seconds. More police came running, they were out of police tape so instead they spread out and started pushing people, they yelled that this was a military area, they stretched out their arms as if they wanted to spare our eyes the sight of this high-tech plane turned into a pile of metallic rubble, covered by white, snot-like foam.

Finally there were so many screaming police that we left, we walked down the hill, leading our bikes as if seeing the cadaver of the airplane made us doubt all the technological advances of the last ten thousand years, sure they look like wheels and they may turn like wheels, but who knows if they will behave like wheels. And everywhere this eerie silence. Thousands of people, walking in silence, like pale robots, not even panicking when the black cloud spread over the city. A small girl, eating an Igloo ice cream on her dad's shoulders, happily unaware that her dad kept his sunglasses on and kept wiping his cheeks so that nobody would notice his tears.

I wanted to say something, but Evelyn was quiet, so we were quiet. We crossed the small bridge and followed the coastline back to our park. Everyone we met talked about how many must have died, sure it had landed in one of the few places that day that hadn't been jam-packed with people, but still, people kept saying, there must be casualties, yes, of course, there were three hundred thousand people watching the air show.

When we reached the swings in Draken, I noticed that Evelyn was crying. Not knowing how to deal with my friend's tears I said nothing, just sat down in one of the swings pretending like I didn't see that she was upset.

It was my fault, she said.

What do you mean?

It was my energy that caused the crash, she said.

Of course not, I said.

Yes, she said. Mum warned us. She told us to spread out, otherwise something bad would happen.

Is this linked to the curse? I said.

Evelyn didn't answer.

What if it was the other way around? I said. What if it was thanks to you that it didn't get worse? What if the plane had crashed into the bridge or landed in the city?

Evelyn looked at me and smiled.

Thanks for trying, she said. But Ina will kill me.

Why?

Because she told me to watch it from Rålambshovsparken.

Okay, I said and tried to look as if I understood. I wanted to ask her about the curse, who had put it on them and wasn't there a way to break it? But I said nothing. Evelyn sighed. I looked up. Ina and Anastasia were biking towards us, Ina on her big green military bike that looked like it weighed a ton, and Anastasia on that small orange bike with robot stickers that she had gotten from Evelyn.

If she asks, we were here the whole time, Evelyn said, with her hand covering her mouth.

Got it, I said without moving my lips.

You could have died, Ina screamed before even reaching us.

I expected Evelyn to say something, she always had something to say, I had seen her stand up to teachers, drunks and random racists, but this time she just lowered her head and sat still in her swing.

We were here all the time, I said.

Shut up, liar.

I'm not lying. We biked around here and then we went down there and sat on a green bench, we were nowhere near the plane crash.

He's lying, Anastasia said. He's always lying.

Anastasia couldn't have been more than twelve at the time, but she was right. I lied about everything. The first person I kissed was the Danish supermodel Helena Christensen. My dad might come to the park dressed as a subway driver, but that was just a cover, in reality he worked as an armed agent for the Tunisian secret service and was featured in the African version of the *Guinness Book of Records* for having the world's biggest biceps. My younger brothers looked normal, but at night they turned into gremlins. But I wasn't alone, everyone lied back then, Ellet claimed to have gotten the phone number of Tupac Shakur through a friend of a friend, and Nico's older brother was the world heavyweight champion of judo, kung-fu, boxing and pool, Evelyn still claimed that her great-grandfather sat on that steel beam high up in the air and was part of the team that built Rockefeller Center, even though it was obvious to everyone that it was a lie. But the lie I was telling this day was different, I didn't even see it as a lie, I saw it as a friend helping out a friend.

I'm serious, I said. We sat on a *dark green* bench . . . really emphasizing the words *dark green*, as if that in some magical way made the bench specific (when in reality all benches in Stockholm are dark green).

No, you didn't, Ina said, not even taking her eyes from Evelyn. Because we saw you on Långholmen.

She finally looked at me.

Say goodbye to my sister.

We mumbled goodbye and Evelyn got up and left.

Chapter Thirteen

Evelyn leaned over and started honking, Ina told her to stop, but Evelyn didn't hear it, because she had already opened the door and slid down to the street. Even if they were late, she was welcomed by her friends as if she had won the Olympics, hugs and cheek kisses, and while Ina spent five minutes parking the truck as close to the front door as possible, she saw in the side mirrors that Anastasia also hugged people left and right. Ina turned off the motor and took a deep breath, reminding herself that she also had friends (at least two, Saskia in Malmö and Laura, who she'd only met when Saskia was visiting, but would they really be there for Ina if she needed to move?).

Ina climbed down from the front seat and extended her right hand, introducing herself to Sofia and Neves and Marcus and Alexandra and Anders F and Anders L and Lisa and Jenny and Max and Lugo and a bunch of other people whose names Ina instantly forgot. She kept introducing herself as "Ina, I'm the eldest," while she kept thinking: When did Evelyn meet these people, and when did Anastasia meet them, and does this mean that they hang out at parties I'm not invited to? Do they go to the cinema and go bowling, the whole crew, but choose not to invite me, just because . . . I am as I am? Of course they do, sometimes they even talk about it, Anastasia to Evelyn: "Should I call . . ." Evelyn: "No, please don't, not this time, let's for once just hang out you and me," and of course everything is lighter and more fun when she isn't around, they are more spontaneous, after the bowling they go to a bar on the corner, without

Ina pulling out a list of good bars in the area that she has prepared the night before, then they pass the window of an apartment where there's a party, and Anastasia starts throwing rocks at the window until someone opens it and the people see Evelyn and Anastasia and all their friends and immediately throw down the key, or yell the code to the front door, and the party is amazing, it's the party of a lifetime, there are multiple floors, bubble baths, orgies in masks, house-trained tigers, and they keep looking at each other whispering that NONE of this would have happened if we had brought Ina with us tonight.

Hello? Anastasia said and snapped her fingers. Can you open the back of the truck, please? Ina walked to the back of the truck and unlocked the door.

Who are all these people? she whispered to Anastasia, as they swung the doors open and jumped up into the echoing empty square space to get moving blankets.

I have no idea, Anastasia said.

Do you go bowling together?

What are you talking about? Anastasia said. Can you imagine me, bowling?

So how do you know them?

I've never met them before!

But you hugged them? Ina said.

I hug everyone, Anastasia said. And if they are Evelyn's friends they are my friends because without them we would be here until 2010.

When Ina got up to the apartment, she understood what Anastasia meant. Normal people spend a week before a move preparing, putting things in carefully labeled boxes, putting lamps in sheets, wrapping plates in newspaper, taping the corners of fragile furniture. When Ina and Evelyn's friends walked into the apartment, there were barely any signs that Evelyn had to leave the apartment the day after. Sure there were a few moving boxes in the hallway, but most of them were empty. And there were a bunch of folded boxes lined up in the kitchen. But the apartment looked more or less like it had the last time Ina was here, which was on New Year's Eve.

Evelyn cleared her throat:

Okay, she said. I know that you're thinking that this will take forever. And yes, this may be a bit harder than the last time you helped a friend to move. But I can *guarantee* you that it will be more fun. I will be supplying you with caffeine, cookies and pizza slices, the music will be extremely well chosen and very upbeat, I know it looks dark right now, but we will start seeing the light in just a few hours, let's go, people, we got this, I believe in you, Erik and Sandro, you start packing plates, cutlery and glasses, Sofia and Neves, you do the bathroom, Anders F and Anders L: couch, bed and electronics, the rest of you: clothes, we have one motto, people: if you see it, you pack it, don't worry about labeling things, just throw things in either a box or a black garbage bag and we will get this done in super time, you hear me, we can do this, we got this, who's with me?!

It was the least-prepared move Ina had ever witnessed, and she was expecting half of the crew of friends to bail, but instead they roared with motivation after Evelyn's speech and after a few sarcastic comments about "wow, she prepared this so well" and "we will be done by lunch" the music started playing and everyone got to work, Evelyn supported them with freshly brewed coffee, freshly baked banana bread, she yelled compliments, she pushed the elevator button, she stayed in touch with the cleaning firm that would arrive as soon as they were done. After only a few hours the whole apartment had been packed in boxes and Marcus, a tall guy who seemed a bit too invested in this move (he had brought his own gloves and had already explained twice to Ina that they needed to start with the bed and the big objects and then secure them with the boxes) was organizing a system for fitting as much as possible in the truck.

As the day progressed, more and more people arrived, Cecilia came, and Hector, who carried down bookshelves without asking for help. After a while they were so many that it became hard to find something to do, the boxes were swooshing down the stairs, the bathroom, bedroom and living room were already empty. When Ina and Anastasia took a break out on the sidewalk, Ina said:

I don't understand—where does she meet all these people?

It's Evelyn, Anastasia said. Next time she moves there will be even more friends of hers, but none of these friends will be invited. She changes friends like we change underwear.

Like the pope changes candles, Ina said and Anastasia laughed.

Like the bonobo changes mates, Anastasia said.

Like the wind changes direction, Ina said.

Like the flasher changes trench coat, Anastasia said.

Like Mom changed apartments, Ina said.

Anastasia smiled.

And the rest of the move, when Anastasia and Ina saw each other in the stairwell, or in the gradually fuller moving truck, they leaned in and whispered, "like the baby changes teeth" or "like the fountain changes water" or "like the politician changes views" and even though it was silly, it made both sisters feel more okay about the fact that Evelyn had managed to invite more friends to this move than both of them would be able to muster up for their wedding.

At 5 p.m., the truck was finally full, the apartment was empty and Evelyn took a last stroll through the empty echoing rooms, saying goodbye to the things she loved about this place. Goodbye, courtyard view with occasional cats, bye, immaculate wardrobe space, bye, original nineteenth-century wood floor, bye, newly installed brand-name induction stove. She had lived here for almost three years, and during that time the prices for apartments in this area had doubled, if she had listened to her gut she would have just invested in her own place while she had a comfortable monthly salary, but at the time she was convinced that her job was temporary and she chose to listen to her doomsday older sister who was convinced that they were in a housing bubble and suggested that she hold off on buying a flat, at least for a few years, just to wait and see. Now the flats in this area were way too expensive for her to buy and as she turned off the lights and locked the door for the last time, and dropped the keys in the letter box, she promised herself that from now on, she would listen to her inner voice and not the voice of her older sister, because Ina was a prime example of what happened to a person who lived in constant fear of everything, and if Evelyn had one goal in life, it was to not become like Ina.

Are you okay? Ina said as Evelyn exited the building and jumped up in the front seat of the embarrassingly yellow postal truck.

Let's just get out of here, Evelyn said.

Chapter Fourteen

Evelyn and I saw each other from time to time during the next couple of months, but it was never the same. Once I stood in line behind her and Anastasia at Video-Nord, we nodded to each other but didn't speak. Another time I saw her with Ina on the escalators in the subway, I was heading down, they were going up, we pretended that we didn't see each other. We never hung out again, not like we did that summer back in 1993, when our bikes were F-14 Tomcats, when my dad had started to disappear without telling us where he went, when my mom started talking about getting a divorce. I never told anyone about why our friendship ended. When my mom asked why Evelyn had stopped coming over, I just said that we had "grown apart" and my mom was silent for a while and then said:

Those poor girls.

I wasn't really sure why she felt sorry for them, because at the time their mother was still alive, Evelyn wasn't sick and Anastasia wasn't doing drugs.

Two months later we noticed that the drapes in their apartment were gone. They had moved. Again. Nobody knew where they had gone. A new family took over their apartment and put up new drapes, they filled their balcony with new sleds, they replaced the naked light-bulb in the kitchen with a lamp. Years passed. Every time I read in the news about a new Jas 39 Gripen crash, in Vänern in 1999, or in Hanö-bukten in 2005, or in Vidsel in 2007, or in Ronneby in 2018, I thought about the Mikkola sisters and wondered where they were now.

Part II

Chapter Fifteen

These were the words that Ina said to her younger sisters, when first Evelyn and then Anastasia came strolling into the kitchen, at 11 a.m. on the second Sunday of May 2000:

Good morning, dear sisters, I hope you slept well, I'm really looking forward to us living together again, wow, this is the first time in many years, it will be so much fun, so awesome, here are some basic rules that apply to everyone who lives here, we put our shoes on the shoe rack, we use the hangers for our jackets, we pull the shower curtain before we take a shower and make sure to only use the shampoo and conditioner that we have bought, this applies to food as well, not all food, no, of course not, that would be impractical and insane, we share things like milk, coffee and tea, and toilet paper, and I would be happy to be in charge of the purchase of these common goods and split the cost between us, just like we will do with the monthly rent, speaking of which, we keep the coffee here, and the filters are in this box, and please only use the metal coffee capsules if you are making one cup or less, if you plan to drink more than one cup, please use this powder and the coffee brewer, filters are located here, as I said, and the microwave is here so you can just heat up your coffee if you plan to drink it later in the day, please take out the filter and clean the brewer when you are done, and actually don't use the coffee capsules, even if you're just making one cup of coffee, thank you for understanding, I have sketched out a preliminary cleaning schedule, Anastasia, you are responsible for bathroom, bathtub and toilet, at least once per week, Evelyn, you are vacuuming and hanging laundry, I'm watering plants, dusting, emptying and loading the dishwasher, planning the laundry, getting common groceries, here's the schedule, we could change responsibilities every week, or every other week, on Mondays we take out the recycling, on Wednesdays I'm doing colored 40, on Fridays white 40, on the weekends white 60, everyone is responsible for changing their own bed linen, Anastasia: no smoking, not in the apartment, not on the balcony, it's not allowed according to the rules of the association, please respect this, and Evelyn: no one-night stands, please, not in my bed, not in the bathroom, not on the couch, not on the balcony, especially if I have an upcoming exam, I don't want this to be like last time, I don't want to find random guys' pubic hairs in my bathroom, I don't want to discover used condoms in the bathroom bin, okay? Are we in agreement, great, this is going to be so much fun, Ina said, attached the printed cleaning schedule to the fridge and left the apartment with her ergonomic backpack and metal water bottle in the special side compartment to meet up with Hector in the Liljan Forest for a walk.

Is breathing allowed? Anastasia said as she reached for a filter to brew coffee.

Let me check, Evelyn said and looked at the schedule. No, sorry. No breathing. No laughing.

Masturbation?

Nope.

I wonder what she will be like when she's old for real, Anastasia said.

She's the world's oldest twenty-five-year-old, Evelyn said.

They looked at each other and smiled. Anastasia made coffee and even though she hadn't smoked for months, Ina's talk about cigarettes made her long for a smoke.

Is she coming back? Anastasia said and nodded towards the door.

Of course she is, Evelyn said.

Keys?

No, I think she has her keys. Something else. Sugar-free chewing gum? An apple?

Gloves? I say gloves.

I think computer cord. Or a book.

Forty seconds later they heard the clunky sound of the elevator stopping on their floor.

Here she comes, Evelyn said. Ina opened the door.

It's really chilly outside, she said, got her gloves and waved goodbye.

Score! Evelyn said.

Excuse me? Ina said.

Have a great day, sis, Anastasia said. We're so grateful that we can stay here. Temporarily.

No worries, Ina said. But from now on you have to help me with Mom. You just have to answer when she calls. Okay? Promise? Great!

Ina disappeared before Anastasia and Evelyn had the time to answer, and the rest of the day Evelyn wondered if Ina had forgotten her gloves on purpose.

Since Evelyn had a job, she offered to pay extra to get the second bedroom, and since Anastasia was between jobs, she offered to pay no rent in exchange for sleeping in the living room. Anastasia didn't care, she was used to sleeping on couches. But sometimes when she couldn't sleep and Ina spent the night at her boyfriend's place, Anastasia snuck in and used Ina's bed. Sometimes she borrowed Ina's pajamas, she tried on Ina's glasses, sometimes she opened one of the many books piled up on Ina's nightstand, and tried to make sense of why a contemporary person would care about some old Russian prince Andrew and some rich countess Natasha who lived hundreds of years ago. Ina loved these kinds of books, and her boyfriend seemed to share her taste, but Anastasia didn't get it, her life was too short to read all these pages, she turned out the lights and tried to go to sleep, surrounded by her older sister's scents, but her head was racing, there were too many ideas in there, too many voices, too much rhythm. She turned on the lights, she checked the time, 2 a.m., the whole world was asleep, except her, and maybe Mathias. She wondered what he was doing, and if he missed her. She was close to texting him, but she stopped herself, no, this was not the time, not now, not ever again.

When morning finally arrived and Evelyn had rushed off to work, leaving the bathroom with steamy mirrors and spills of makeup powder on the sink, Anastasia got up from Ina's bed. She cleared the kitchen of Evelyn's mess, she set a timer to not miss the soap opera that she had discovered at the rental place.

At half past eleven she stood still in the living room, looking at the view, she wondered what would happen if she just remained like this forever, looking at views, letting time pass, without trying to use it. She would turn twenty and didn't have a clue what she wanted to do with her life. Sure, she had rented that art studio at Nya Kontoret, with the idea of applying to Konstfack. But mostly she just wanted a place to stay, which was impossible to find in Stockholm if you didn't have a job, and now she had a perfectly viable reason *not* to apply to Konstfack, and wasn't that in itself a sign that she wasn't supposed to be doing art? Her friends were different, Mathias couldn't live if he wasn't creating something, Fabricia was the same, she was always creating things, when she was poor she made earrings that she sold, and when she sold her first painting, she bought more paint, she never needed an art studio to create anything, when she was sad she created art to survive, and when she was happy she created art to avoid becoming sad again. Anastasia didn't want to apply to art school, she didn't want to do anything, not work, not study, not meet anyone, not do drugs, well, of course one small part of her always wanted to take drugs, there was always a small old percentage of her that hoped she would find a small bag of something forgotten in the lining of a rarely used jacket. But no, not even drugs felt tempting at the moment, she just wanted to stay here, in Ina's apartment, she wanted to look at this view, at 10:45 she was still standing there, the view was unchanged, the timer counted down, she wanted time to stop so she could figure out what the hell she was supposed to do with it.

At 11:10, Anastasia went to the bathroom and looked through Evelyn's makeup bag, big enough to hold a bowling ball, looking for a powder light enough to hide her pimples, but the powder that Evelyn used was too dark, and the rest of the bag was full of utensils that Anastasia had never used, like metal eyelash curlers.

At 11:42, she was back in Ina's bed, with a blanket over her head, and she just lay there, making a point of not reading, not listening to the radio, as if she was rebelling against some invisible pressure. If Ina saw her lying there she would tell her that she was wasting yet another day, not doing anything, not reading, not being productive, not achieving, not producing, not making any money, not changing, she just lay there and refused everything.

At twelve past one, she was still lying there, had she dozed off, maybe, she thought about the differences between her and Evelyn, they were so different, but they had a similar relationship to time, it just passed by them, they didn't make a schedule for it, they didn't try to maximize it, they didn't start every day with making a long list with things that they needed to get done that day and then spend the day ticking items off the list, as Ina did. Ina was a mystery to Anastasia, she couldn't understand how someone could be so organized, so on top of things, and still be so stressed.

A couple of days ago Anastasia had accidentally opened the door when Ina was in the bathroom, and when Ina came out she was more embarrassed than angry, she explained to Anastasia that she had read somewhere that it's more efficient to wipe yourself standing up, and that's why Anastasia had seen what she had seen, and the only thing Anastasia could think of was that her oldest sister was the only person in the world who could even think of making pooping more efficient.

It was impossible to imagine her in love, it just didn't make sense, because love wasn't efficient, her love wouldn't make her finish her dissertation in macroeconomics faster, the love for a freckly historian of ideas wouldn't help her with connections to get a job as a consultant after graduation, but nonetheless Ina seemed to have fallen for the guy she had met on New Year's Eve, Viktor or Stefan or Pascal or Henrik. Honestly, Anastasia didn't care what he was called, and she kept referring to him with the wrong name, just to tease Ina.

His name is Hector, Ina would say.

Sorry, Anastasia would say. And where does he live, this Henrik of yours?

Hector, Ina said.

My bad, Anastasia said.

He lives in Vasastan, Ina said.

Evelyn said he has a huge apartment on Birger Jarlsgatan, Anastasia said. Isn't that technically Östermalm?

He lives right on the border between Östermalm and Vasastan, Ina explained. Anastasia smiled, to show Ina that she understood. Because in Hector's world it was a bit embarrassing to live in luxurious Östermalm, while it was acceptable to live in Vasastan. But in the real world, both Östermalm and Vasastan were equally disgusting, equally full of pedigreed dogs and women in fur coats, Anastasia would never live voluntarily in any of those areas, not even if someone gave her an apartment for free, no way, not her. She despised those rich people with their luxury habits and it was obvious to Anastasia that Hector didn't know anything about real life, he was born with a silver spoon in his mouth, she wasn't fooled by his skater clothes and sneakers, there was something about his confidence that made it obvious to Anastasia that he had grown up with ambassador parents and old relatives who made sure he got the fine china when they passed away.

He's not the least bit spoiled, Ina said. You've only met him, like, three times, and you never give him a chance. Which wasn't true. Anastasia had given him numerous chances, and she knew a lot of things about him, she knew that he had studied literature at university, and that he played squash, and that he was really good at making conversation, at least in that way that people from a certain background are. Ina claimed that she had met her soulmate, just because they could discuss writers who had been dead for years and sometimes when Anastasia heard them in the kitchen, talking about Kawabata versus Mishima versus Mitsubishi, she thought to herself that their hearts weren't in love, but their brains were.

He just gets nervous around you, Ina said. You always make people nervous. They can't stand your silences.

Anastasia tried not to smile.

He's very different when we are by ourselves, Ina said.

Anastasia certainly hoped so, because every time he tried to talk to Anastasia, he asked her polite questions about some recent TV series that everyone watched or some election in France that everyone seemed to know about, and Anastasia knew exactly what she was supposed to answer, but instead she just explained in a friendly or not-super-friendly tone that she didn't watch TV series or follow the news, and she enjoyed seeing Ina moving in to change the subject to avoid yet another long silence.

At 5 p.m., Anastasia was still lying in bed, with her head under a blanket, not doing anything, just lying there, breathing the warm air, watching the small beads of saliva that had formed on the inside of the blanket. Her cell phone vibrated. She hadn't spoken with her mom in several months, but now, without knowing why, Anastasia reached for the phone and answered.

What's wrong? her mom said. Nothing, Anastasia said.

Then why are you answering?

Because you are calling.

But you haven't answered for the last six months. Something must be wrong. Are you okay, my heart's light? Are you sick, my sugar moon? Don't tell me you're dying, my dearest summer breeze?

Anastasia sighed. No, Mom, I'm doing all right.

What a relief, her mom said, and spent the next fifteen minutes telling her youngest daughter how extremely happy she was in the small town that she had recently moved to, the man who owns the Ica store is a real charmer, and they have a local market on the town square on Wednesdays and Sundays, where they sell non-pesticidal greens and the City Park is so much nicer than the park in Örnsköldsvik.

But wait, Anastasia said. Aren't you living in Örnsköldsvik now? Her mom laughed as if Anastasia had told a joke.

Örnsköldsvik? Are you serious? Do you think your mom could stay in Örnsköldsvik? That damn dump. My God, absolutely not, it was impossible, I didn't fit in at all.

So where are you living now?

Her mom said the name of the town that she had moved to. Anastasia had never heard of it. Her mom explained that it was located south of another big town and west of another medium-sized town.

Anastasia hummed.

You still don't know where it is? her mom said. Come by and visit someday? I have a balcony. There's a drawing museum here. Do you still draw?

Sometimes, Anastasia said.

You would sit for hours with your pad, her mom said.

At 8 p.m., Evelyn came home from work, sitting down in the kitchen with a sigh, rubbing her calves, tired after nine hours of standing in high heels.

How was your day? she said.

Busy, Anastasia said and yawned.

Chapter Sixteen

When the Mikkola sisters left our area, my dad changed, and I have tried for years to write about what comes next in Swedish, but for some reason, it doesn't work, so now I'm trying to do it in English, to see if an imperfect language can make it easier, and as I'm writing these words, I wonder if his change had less to do with the sisters' move and more to do with the loss of his daughter, or his sickness, or his money troubles. For years he had dreamed of building a house in Tunisia, all our extra money went to that house, now he had secured a square plot of land in his hometown, he had made a down payment without asking Mom, now he had to start building to avoid losing his investment, but we were out of money and Mom already hated the house, even though it wasn't built yet.

Why are we building a house there, when we live here? And why in Jendouba, of all places, the city you fought so hard to leave?

Dad didn't explain it, he didn't say that he needed to build this house to show to himself and his family and his friends that he hadn't made a mistake when he left, instead he explained to Mom that we would never live in this house, this was just an investment, we build it to rent the apartments to students, and then we can take the money from this house and build another house, maybe by the coast, maybe in Tabarka, maybe in Sousse, no, not in Sousse, "do you think I'm pooping money?" (as Dad always said when we used too much ketchup or too many paper towels), in the second house

Mom and Dad could grow old, but Mom complained that her savings were gone and we hadn't been on a vacation for years and we spent the summers at my mom's mom's cabin, and if Dad wanted to build that house, he had to find a way to finance it by himself, and of course he would do that, but all his business ventures kept failing, one after the other, the watches he imported from Hong Kong seemed impossible to sell for a profit, even when he used me as a salesman, the money he made from bartending and cleaning the restaurant Tre Backar went to rent, when he tried to apply for work as a salesman they laughed at his accent, when he finally finished and sent in a short novel he had written in French, that his wife had translated into Swedish, it came back from the publisher with a polite, thank-you-but-no-thank-you letter attached, they didn't even seem impressed by the fact that he had gotten an op-ed published in *Dagens Nyheter*, in his text he had expressed his concern about the lack of human presence in the subway, new turnstiles were being installed, and my dad claimed that a metal turnstile will never be able to replace the presence of a fellow human being, which seems ironic, since he would soon disappear, without even leaving as much as a turnstile behind.

In the fall of 1993 a new girl started in my class, her name was Radhika and at first I thought she could take Evelyn's place, but soon she started giving things away to get friends, at first she gave away chewing gum and Garbage Pail Kids cards, then she started handing out He-Man figurines, and the more she gave away, the more popular she became, at least on the days when she came to school with gifts in her backpack, when there were no gifts she was just as invisible as before, it was obvious to everyone that she would never be accepted, she had a weird haircut, her Indian parents wore glasses, she was raised in a small town, she spoke with a dialect, her brother had eczema, she wore corduroy trousers voluntarily and once she climbed a tree and got stuck, someone had to run or rather walk to get a teacher to help her down.

When she tried to talk to me on breaks, I avoided her, because I knew how fragile things were, if I was seen speaking to Radhika, she could pull me down to her level, and a few days later one of the ninth graders could land their daily roundhouse kick on my back, instead of Radhika's. But during lunch break, it was hard to avoid Radhika, and once when she sat next to me, she mentioned that she had a bunch of old MASK figurines at home that her brother didn't play with anymore.

Do you want them? she said.

What is MASK? I said, keeping an eye around me, to make sure that the older guys didn't notice us talking.

Haven't you heard of MASK? she said and smiled. Mobile Armored Strike Kommand?

I shook my head.

Radhika told me that MASK are the good guys and they fought an evil crew called Venom, it's a really famous TV series.

I don't have cable, I said, trying to mumble, mafioso style, so that it wouldn't look like my lips were moving.

It's also a computer game, she said.

I don't have a computer either, I said.

So do you want the toys? Radhika said.

I don't play with toys, I told her. I haven't played with toys for years (which wasn't true because I had played my ass off all weekend, helping my brothers to construct a huge underwater war scene with Legos).

Neither does my brother, she said. That's why I'm giving them away. But maybe you want them for your brothers?

A few weeks later Radhika finally brought the MASK toys to school, after having forgotten them at least seven days in a row. She opened the door to her locker and showed me the big brown paper bag.

This is the Condor, she said. It's a motorbike that can transform into a helicopter, look.

And this is the Firecracker, it looks like a normal pickup truck, but look, if you pull here, it becomes a mobile weapon platform.

Our classmates had gathered around us. Radhika spoke with a feverish voice. And this here is the Shark, it's a Porsche 928 that can transform into a submarine.

Even some of the girls seemed impressed by the Shark, they reached for it and tried the transformer button.

And this here is my absolute favorite, Radhika said. It's called the Stiletto, and it's a Lamborghini Countach that turns into . . .

She started pulling out wings and folded the wheels underneath. Wow, an airplane, someone said.

An *assault* airplane, Radhika said. Stiletto belongs to Gloria Baker, who has a mask called the New Collider, that produces her holographic clone.

She handed me the paper bag, with a jerky motion, as if she had to push herself not to cling to it.

Are you sure about this? I said.

Sure, I . . . my brother hasn't played with these in years, Radhika said, and fiddled with the padlock on her locker.

I brought home the paper bag to my brothers, I told them that all these toys were for them, but the Stiletto and Firecracker were mine, they could play with them anytime they wanted, but if we were playing together, I always had first dibs on these two vehicles.

A few weeks later Radhika asked me if my brothers liked the MASK toys. They love them, I said.

That's great, Radhika said.

Why?

Nothing, she said. I just wondered, like if they played with them.

All the time, I said. My youngest brother sleeps with the Shark next to him on his pillow.

Fantastic, she said, but she looked like I had knifed her in the gut.

We still weren't friends, not real friends, not like Evelyn and I had been before she moved, but at least I started saying hi to her and a few weeks later she asked me if I wanted to come over to her place and play after school, and I said yes, because nobody was around to hear when she asked.

After school I waited for everyone to leave before I exited the building and found Radhika on a bench in the school yard, she looked excited, we crossed the bridge towards the apartment building where I knew that she lived with her parents and her brother, it was Graja who had told me she lived there, he had pointed to the building and told me that Ola and William had made a habit out of throwing a few stones at Radhika's window, every morning and afternoon when they passed to and from school, and the first week, nothing had happened, and the second week, still nothing, and they were close to quitting, but halfway through the third week, Radhika's polo-shirted, ponytailed dad emerged on the balcony and started screaming, so now they had continued to throw stones at the window, every day since then.

What did he scream? I said.

I don't know, Giaja said, I wasn't there. He looked at me as if I had asked the wrong thing.

Radhika entered the code to the front door and pushed the elevator button. We rode up to the third floor in silence and when we entered the apartment, both her parents were there, her mom asked if we wanted warm chocolate and sandwiches, her dad took my backpack and jacket and hung them on a clothing hanger, as if I was an adult.

We went to Radhika's room, she switched on her Commodore 64 and we spent the next few hours gaming instead of talking, she had two joysticks, in one game I was Godzilla, and she was King Kong. After an hour or two she wanted to do something else, I convinced her that we should continue playing. We played some more, then she wanted to stop, and I continued playing by myself, while she watched.

Don't you have a computer at home? she said.

I shook my head.

Not even a Nintendo 8-bit?

We don't even have a VCR, I said.

She looked at me with a strange smile.

If you want a computer I have an old one that I don't use.

Are you serious? I said.

Instead of answering she got up from her bed and took out a dusty keyboard from one of the wardrobes. The keys were brown, the function keys were orange, the round body was beige and on the right side there was a logo: ABC 80, made in Sweden, developed by Dataindustrier AB, manufactured by Luxor.

Sure, she said. Take it. But you can't game on it.

She placed the keyboard in my outstretched hands. It was heavier than I expected.

There should be a screen here somewhere, she said. Mom?! Have you seen the screen to the ABC 80?

I prayed that her mom wouldn't hear, because I was sure that her mom would stop Radhika from giving away an actual computer, but her mom heard and said that the last time she saw the screen it was under her bed, and sure enough, underneath her bed, wrapped in two plastic bags, was the screen.

Are you sure about this? I said.

But *of course*, she said, as if she was getting annoyed with me for not understanding that this was happening.

I thanked Radhika and said that I needed to head home, I had to get out of there as soon as possible, before she changed her mind, before her parents realized what she was doing, I almost forgot my backpack, I was just about to enter the elevator with the keyboard and the screen, when her mom appeared in the hallway.

Are you leaving already? she said. I thought you were staying for dinner?

Sorry, I have to eat at home, I said and hoped she wouldn't notice the bags with the computer.

Too bad. Maybe you want to come by and eat dinner here tomorrow instead? She saw the screen and the keyboard.

I gave him my ABC 80, Radhika said. He doesn't have a computer.

I prepared to go back in and leave everything and say sorry. But Radhika's mom just kept smiling.

That's lovely, she said. It was just collecting dust anyway. Don't forget your backpack.

I walked home with careful steps. My mom saw the computer and told me to give it back.

We are not accepting handouts, she said. Right, honey?

My dad looked up from the TV.
I don't care, he said. It probably doesn't work anyway.
Of course it works, I said. But it's not a gaming computer.
So what will you use it for? Mom said.
No idea, I said. Maybe to write things.

Chapter Seventeen

At the end of May, Ina realized that Hector would break up with her, all the signs were there, or at least one sign: They decided a long time ago that she would come with him to his family's house on the west coast this summer, but last night he had started doubting if it was "such a good idea." The house would be full, his newly divorced sister would be there with her crazy kids, and his mom, and he didn't want Ina's vacation to be ruined by his family. At least that's what Hector said. But Ina wasn't fooled that easily, of course he used the house as a reason to break up with her, to let her down easy, probably he had a fling with some girl down on the west coast, someone with skin that never needed lotion, with a body that never needed extra sizes, with a vagina that never had yeast infections, someone with normal parents and well-functioning siblings, someone who didn't fail exams and already had finished her dissertation and . . .

Ina tried to stop her mind from racing, she tried the exercises she had read about, she tried to count her breaths backward, ten to zero, again and again, she tried to take note of five things she saw (bookshelf, shadow of lamp, Georgia O'Keeffe poster, empty wine-glass, opened condom wrapper), four things she heard (his snores, her breathing, birds chirping, bus doors opening), three things she could smell (him, him, him), two things she could taste (him, him) and one thing she felt (I will die if he leaves me, I mean it, I will die, that's not really helping, but that's what I feel, well, stop feeling it,

I will, stop it, I'm trying to, well, try harder, I'm trying really really really hard but right now it doesn't seem to be working).

She wasn't really sure what to call this, it couldn't be love, because if it was love, she wouldn't think of him as her best friend, and it couldn't be anything other than love, because ever since they met at that New Year's party that felt like a lifetime ago, they had been inseparable, how many nights had they slept apart, it couldn't have been more than five nights in total, and it wasn't as if they planned it, it just happened, organically, like everything between them, up until now, when he had started hinting that he was leaving.

She tried the exercise again, slower this time, ten breaths, five things she saw, four things she heard, three scents, two tastes, one feeling. Hector slept next to her and not even his snoring seemed to bother her. When she had mentioned this to Laura and Saskia, her two closest (and only) friends, they had laughed and Laura had said: If that's not love, I don't know what love is, and Saskia had said: I bought an anti-snoring pillow for Peter and he refused to use it, so I gave him an ultimatum: pillow or divorce.

But now it was Ina who was lying here in Hector's bed for probably the last time. The first time she was here was the night after New Year's, she had agreed to come along for "some tea" and before she removed her coat and shoes, she walked up to his bookshelf to make sure that he wasn't a serial killer, the bookshelf calmed her, no serial killer could have Svetlana Alexievich in both Swedish and English, or all the P. O. Enquist novels, or a special section of bookshelf devoted to Toni Morrison.

Have I passed the test? he said from the hallway.

Ina smiled and removed her coat. She couldn't find one embarrassing book to tease him with, so instead she said:

Color-coordinated? Who would have known?

Hector smiled and explained that when he sold his previous place the broker had been firm about the need for him to arrange all his books based on the color of the covers because it would make the broker's work "so much easier." No way, Hector had said, but then the broker told him about a previous client, with "almost as many books," who had chosen not to sort his books based on color, and apparently the price for his flat had been reduced by at least 10 percent and therefore Hector finally went along and sorted the books and when he moved here, he kept the color coordination, because weirdly enough, it is actually easier to find the book you are looking for this way, he said, scanning the shelves with unhidden pride. She asked him about Mishima, he went over to the black section and pulled out *The Sailor Who Fell from Grace with the Sea*. Duras? she said, and he kindly led her down to the orange section where he had *Emily L.* and a bunch of other short novels. There they kissed. Then he asked if she wanted to spend the night. Since then they had barely been apart, most evenings they had spent here, in his bed, especially since Ina's flat had been occupied by her younger sisters.

Ina heard the sounds of a paperboy taking the elevator to the top floor, and descending the stairs by foot, rapid paces, the sound of the newspaper that landed on Hector's doormat. She took note of everything, since she knew that this was the last time she would experience it. The first couple of weeks, she was convinced that it would not last, it just couldn't, there was no way you could feel this for another person for longer than a few days, not without drugs, not without some kind of mental illness. But somehow the feeling remained, and now, after almost six months together, she had started to think of him as her boyfriend (when referring to him), her soulmate (when writing about him in her diary) and her Everything (when thinking of him).

The only thing they never talked about was his ex-girlfriends, he must have had girlfriends before her, but when she asked him he avoided the question, in the same way that she avoided questions about her mom, which was strange because they were able to talk about everything else.

The night before, he had opened a box with old photos, there he was, five years old standing next to a red brook, there he was in a school photo a few years later, the only brown boy in a sea of blond kids, there he was again, as a teenager, with a shaved head, on one knee behind a rusty bike turned upside down, in the process of fixing a flat tire. But there was one envelope with photos that he smuggled away, she noticed that he didn't want to show what was in the envelope, and now, at 5 a.m., when he had told her that she couldn't join him to spend summer with his family, she was convinced that the envelope contained photos of ex-girlfriends.

When it was impossible to go back to sleep, she snuck up to the bathroom, and instead of returning to bed she continued to the kitchen. There was the box of photos, and there was the envelope with the photos he didn't want to share. She opened it and expected to find photos of Hector with a breathtakingly beautiful Italian-French-Ethiopian girlfriend of normal height, with underarms that never needed shaving. But instead the envelope contained five, eight, probably thirty different photos of the same guy. He couldn't have been more than eighteen years old, he stood leaning against a brick wall at a train station, one leg bent, so that the sole of his worn-out sandals rested against the wall, turquoise linen shirt, sunglasses on his forehead, wristbands from music festivals, a large military backpack. He hid his face behind a menu. He sat on a barstool and squinted into the camera. He sat at a table in what looked like a Scottish pub. He kissed the camera. He sat on a mattress and pulled up his shirt to show the ring on his nipple. He became fussy. He got undressed. One garment at a time. Hector was in three of the photos. In one photo they embraced each other. In one photo Hector sat alone in a window and looked out at a passing tram. In one photo they were naked.

What are you doing? Hector said.

She flinched and looked up from the photos.

He stood there on the threshold, his hair was still asleep, he looked at her like she was a snake in a baby's crib.

I just . . . she said. Then she was silent because she wasn't sure what she was doing. It would have been better if he had started shouting, if he had accused her of crossing a line, of betraying his trust, but instead he just looked at her and sighed, before he returned to bed, before Ina had a chance to explain, and even if he would have given her a chance to explain, she wasn't sure what she would have said.

He fell asleep quickly or pretended to fall asleep quickly and Ina lay awake for hours, trying to understand what had just happened. When morning finally came she wanted to apologize, she wanted to blame her past, she wanted to say that she wasn't crazy, at least not as crazy as she seemed, she had a history that made it tricky for her to trust people and hard for her to deal with separations, but she wasn't sure where to start, with her dad's death, her mom's suicide attempts, her mom's crazy ex-boyfriends? Hector woke up, he didn't mention it, so neither did she, during a few wonderful seconds she wondered if she could have dreamed it all, or if he had forgotten it. Then he said that he had some "practical things to take care of," and Ina took her things, even her phone charger, and left his apartment before breakfast.

Chapter Eighteen

A couple of weeks after the Mikkola sisters moved from our area, Mom surprised us with a gift, it was nobody's birthday and the gift was "for the family, but mostly to Dad." The package was so big that she had wrapped it in two black garbage bags instead of wrapping paper, we got to help carry the package from the closet, before we opened it we knew that it was a carpet, only a carpet could be this big and cumbersome, so soft and bristly at the same time. Dad cut the string and pulled off the garbage bags, a dark red carpet with a white-and-blue dome in the center slowly rolled out on our living room floor.

Wow, my brothers said and touched the carpet with their fingertips.

Incredibly beautiful, I said.

None of us dared to walk on the carpet, it was too new, too luxurious. None of them said that the carpet was so elegant that it made everything else in the living room (the white Billy bookshelves from IKEA, the couch with holes in the leather, the ripped rice lamp) look worn in comparison. We looked at the carpet, but it felt as if the carpet looked at us (and felt sorry for us).

Mom beamed with pride, she told us about the carpet's history, the pattern was Berber, the carpet was handwoven in Kairouan in Tunisia and it was actually the Mikkola sisters' mom who had helped her with . . .

How much did she want for it? Dad said.

Mom said that she had received a special price because we had been kind to her daughters and they were about to move and . . .

Combien? said Dad and breathed through his nose.

Mum said that there were things that were more important than money, and she wanted to help the Mikkola sisters get a fresh start at the next place and she hoped that the carpet would give Dad a sense of home.

GEDDESH? Dad screamed and seemed to forget that he was the only one of us who spoke Arabic.

Mom said what the carpet normally costs, and how much reduction she received and finally she told us what she had paid for the carpet.

Dad asked her to repeat the sum. She said it again. Dad repeated the sum. Mom nodded. Dad said the sum again, but this time he yelled the sum, so loudly that the neighbors must have wondered what sport we were watching.

It's handwoven, Mom said.

It's made in a factory in Asia, Dad said.

She said she would send me a certificate of authenticity, Mom said.

Great, it will probably arrive tomorrow, Dad said, sarcastically.

It's really really nice, my brothers said and petted the carpet as if it were a cat.

I was convinced that Dad would roll up the carpet, tie it with the same string it had arrived with and rush out of the apartment with the carpet on one shoulder as if it were a plank. He would find the Mikkola sisters' mom and force her to give us the money back, force her to apologize, who knows, maybe we would even get our money back and keep the carpet.

But instead of rushing out, he sank to the floor and just sat there, as if someone had transformed his spine into sauce. Sometimes he mumbled the price of the carpet and shook his head as if he couldn't fathom that everyone in this country seemed able to make money except him.

Later that fall my younger brothers mustered up the courage to knock on my door, even though they knew that when my door was closed it meant that I was deeply concentrated on programming new games on my ABC 80, while listening to Ice-T in my headphones, and didn't want to be disturbed.

What do you want? I screamed through the closed door.

No response. But I knew it was my brothers who knocked because everyone in our family had their particular way of knocking on the door. My brothers knocked on the door really softly, as if they were afraid that it would explode if they used too much force. Mom knocked firmly, three times with her knuckle when her patience was running low, and she wanted me to be at the dinner table five minutes ago. And Dad, well, Dad didn't knock, he just opened the door, because this was his house, or at least his apartment, or at least his rental (or rather his wife's), so he just walked right in. There was another soft knock and I sighed as loudly as I could, to make sure that it was heard through the door, and then I got up from my desk chair. Both my brothers blinked from the rush of air when I threw open the door.

What?

My younger brother looked at his older brother. We just . . . Are you coding a new game?

No.

Can we watch?

No.

Then why is the screen on?

I was just about to turn it off. What do you want?

We . . . I . . . Can we come in?

I stepped aside and let them in. My brothers were nine and seven at the time, and it took them a few minutes to explain that they were worried about our dad.

Why? I said.

Haven't you noticed that he has changed? my middle brother said.

Well, to be honest, I hadn't really noticed anything. I had been busy with homework, tennis training, ignoring Radhika's calls, coding. Maybe he had been a bit quieter. Maybe he had been working less lately.

He has stopped talking, my youngest brother said.

No, he hasn't, I said, feeling slightly worried by the fact that my younger brothers had noticed changes that I had missed.

And he never goes to bed, my middle brother said.

How do you know?

Because he sits in the armchair when we go to bed, and when we wake up he's still sitting there.

Maybe he . . . Maybe he's watching an exciting TV series, I said, with a voice that didn't even convince me.

Or maybe he has become weird from taking all those syringes, my middle brother said, with a whisper. My youngest brother nodded to show that they had been discussing this possibility before presenting the idea to me and that it made perfect sense. I laughed and shook my head.

He takes those syringes because he has been diagnosed with diabetes, I said. Didn't you listen when Mom said that diabetes is just a normal disease, and not dangerous at all? Not as long as he takes his insulin.

Then why is he so strange? my youngest brother said.

He's not strange, I said.

Can we stay in here? To watch you code? Please?

I let them stay, on the condition that they had to be 100 percent quiet. They lay down on my bed and watched, as I showed them the program I was working on. The first weeks I used the computer to write basic programs that filled the screen with curse words, 10 print cockpussy, 20 go to 10, now I had progressed to creating extremely simple games where the goal was to move the zero symbol from left to right and try to avoid the falling dollar signs. The monochrome screen was full of text, and it took me half an hour to get the computer to draw a straight platform that the zero could "walk" on. I saved the program on a cassette tape.

Can we try it? my brothers said. Please?

I got up from my chair and let them take turns, during the next half hour, they were hypnotized by the screen, trying to control the delayed movements of the zero sign.

Later that night I asked my mom the same thing my brothers had asked me. She was in the kitchen, preparing her herbal tea, when I asked her in a quiet voice if she thought Dad was behaving weirdly.

What do you mean? she said and squeezed the last tea out of the bag.

Well, he barely speaks and walks around in his pajamas and bathrobe, and he looks pale and spends his time glued to the TV.

Mum wiped her hands on the kitchen towel she always kept in the lining of her sweatpants when she was taking care of the kitchen and set me down to explain that Dad had heard some bad news about his firstborn daughter, the one who lives in another country, and maybe that's why he's changed.

What has happened?

She's not well, Mom said.

In what way?

In many different ways.

What about the syringes? I said.

The insulin? Mom said. He will need to take insulin for the rest of his life. But it's not dangerous. Right, honey?

We both looked up and Dad was standing on the threshold to the kitchen. He looked at her and nodded, but it was obvious that he wasn't there, he walked towards the bathroom, his back was bent, his shoulders slumped, he moved slowly and it looked like he had to concentrate to reach for the door handle.

A couple of weeks later he stopped working, and if this had been any other dad, like Isak's dad (who had been in the Iraq-Iran war and been bombarded with missiles, and had a panic attack when a regular car tire exploded down on Långholmsgatan) or Jossan's dad (who read comics and had a collection of Japanese porn that he didn't even try to hide) we might have been fine with it, it would have seemed logical that they stopped working, but this was our dad, with the big biceps, he who never was sick, he who used to tell us about that time when he worked five hours as a bartender on a broken ankle, our dad wasn't weak, but now all of a sudden he was.

The man who had spent all my childhood dreaming of becoming

rich, talking about money as the key that would open all doors, he stopped working. One day the wooden rectangular box that he used to sell watches was gone, when asked about it, he said that he had "returned it," which didn't make sense, because the box had been handmade for us by one of his friends and the watches were impossible to send back to Hong Kong. Dad stopped taking night shifts at the subway and when the boss of Tre Backar called and asked what had happened to his favorite bartender, Dad explained that he wasn't coming back, he had diabetes and wasn't doing well.

In the beginning, Mom almost seemed happy about the change, she had told Dad for years that he had to reduce his work hours and try to be more present with his kids, but she soon realized that he wasn't at home because he wanted to be with us, he was at home because he couldn't go outside, because he couldn't work, because he had to fight just to get out of bed and go to the bathroom. Then she became worried.

You have to get help, Mom told him.

So they can lock me up in an institution? my dad said.

You don't understand. You are going through a crisis right now, and there are professionals who can help you.

Yeah right, Dad said. I'm sure they can help with ruining me, I'm sure they can prescribe some pills that will make me addicted. No thank you, I'm fine, I will make it through this, just you wait.

Chapter Nineteen

One weekend Ina came back to the apartment. She devoted her Sunday to creating a system so that the three sisters could sort their laundry. She explained her new system to Evelyn and Anastasia as if it were a nuclear power plant, colored 40 here, and colored 60 here, and white 40 here and white 60 over here, and refills of liquid detergent here, and softener here, any questions? Evelyn raised her hand.

Hand wash?

Great, I will find a special place for that, Ina said and turned her back to her sisters so she didn't see their smiles.

Evelyn volunteered to make dinner for the three of them.

Good luck, Ina said, as she started going through the empty cupboards, throwing away old crumpled dusty garlic and avocados that had gone from hard to soft and back to hard again.

I'll think of something, Evelyn said. She poured olive oil in a cast-iron skillet, fried some mushrooms in butter, and transformed a sad-looking package of kale into perfectly crispy green chips. She poured so much salt in the boiling pasta water that Ina couldn't help but clear her throat.

What are you making? Ina said.

Not sure yet, Evelyn said.

Do you want me to look up a recipe? Ina said. Or go grocery shopping?

I'm good, Evelyn said.

Are you sure?

I'm sure.

When the three sisters sat down to dinner the flavors of the food seemed to fill the whole room. Ina didn't understand how Evelyn did this, it was just pasta, garlic and tomato sauce, some fried mushrooms on the side, kale with sea salt as a starter, some nuts on top, tomatoes with basil, but it tasted heavenly.

How do you do this? Ina said.

I've taught her everything I can, Anastasia said.

You haven't cooked once since we moved here, Evelyn said with a smile.

Food is overrated, Anastasia said and served herself a second portion.

Evelyn told them about her job, she mimicked her bosses' voices, she said that she really had to quit before she turned into Kattis, who had worked there for years.

How long have you been there now? Ina said.

Come on, I haven't worked there for as long as Kattis, said Evelyn. Not at all. She started two years before me.

It's not good for a person's soul to spend eight hours per day selling stuff, Anastasia said.

. . . says the person who has never had a job for longer than three months, Ina said.

I'm a restless soul, Anastasia said with a smile.

For a couple of minutes, Evelyn felt as if they were a perfectly normal family, three sisters who were having dinner early on a Saturday evening, no drama, no piercing jabs, no deep conversations about a painful past, no crazy mom who calls twelve times in fifteen minutes to let you know that she has become best friends with her mailman or has been treated to a free cinnamon bun at the local café. Just a perfectly normal dinner, where their oldest sister told them that some of her colleagues at university were jealous because she would soon publish an article in the *Journal of Political Economy*.

So what are you and Henrik doing this summer? Anastasia said.

Hector, Ina said. He's going to his family on the west coast. I don't have any plans.

Wait, weren't you both going there? Evelyn said.

I could go if I wanted to, but you know. I have a lot of things to do here.

Sure that laundry system wouldn't design itself, Evelyn said and Ina nodded. It wasn't until she saw that both Evelyn and Anastasia were laughing that she realized that it was a joke, and instead of showing that she had misunderstood, she tried to show that her head nod had been sarcastic.

Exactly, Ina added, who would organize the laundry if I didn't do it, nobody, right, and that would be disastrous, haha right, as if that would matter at all.

Evelyn and Anastasia looked at Ina.

Are you okay, sis? Evelyn said.

Sure, Ina said and tried to hold her tears back.

They ate in silence. Ina felt lonelier than she had in years. It was always like this when the three of them hung out. Anastasia and Evelyn shared so many similarities, they were closer in age, they had the same kind of humor, all three of them had different complexions, but at least Evelyn and Anastasia were of medium height, and they always made references to sitcoms or movies that Ina hadn't seen. Sometimes she tried to watch whatever they were watching, just to understand why it was supposedly funny when Evelyn came home from a one-night stand yelling "Jerome in the house" or why they both cracked up when Anastasia said "No soup for you" just before they sat down to eat soup, but whenever Ina sat there, in front of the TV shows to which they willingly gave endless hours of their lives, she just didn't get it, she felt that there was something wrong with her because she couldn't enjoy it, she didn't laugh out loud like the studio audience, she wasn't moved when the main character and that girl with the hair whom he supposedly was in love with finally kissed, Ina just saw how every episode was built up according to the exact same formula, and she wasn't amused, she didn't laugh, she was just bored and felt that her life was trickling away, and after a few epi-sodes she turned it off and returned to her books.

So let me get this straight, Anastasia said. You spend the spring with this Enok dude . . .

Hector, Ina mumbled.

And now you're not going to see each other over the summer?

Speaking of which, Ina said, in a desperate attempt to change the subject. When are you going to start contributing to the rent?

I'm broke, Anastasia said.

Getting a job usually helps, Evelyn said.

I won't need a job when I'm a famous artist, Anastasia said.

Well, in order to become a famous artist, you have to work, Ina said.

I *am* working, Anastasia said. I'm collecting ideas. Finding inspi-ration. I'm preparing my application for . . .

Sure you are, Ina said. But in the meantime, it would be great if you could collect ideas *and* pay some kind of rent. Now it's been over six months and you're not paying for groceries, not paying for rent, and I don't get how you became this spoiled.

Ina noticed that she was clinging to the knife and fork way too tightly.

Are you okay? Anastasia said.

No, I'm not, Ina said and slid down from the chair to the kitchen floor. Anastasia and Evelyn crouched down and hugged her.

What's happening?

Nothing.

Tell us.

No, I'm just . . . I know that Hector will break up with me.

Well, if he does, it will be the most stupid thing he ever does, Anastasia said.

With the tears burning in her eyes, Ina told her sisters about his changed summer plans and the envelope with photos that she had looked at while Hector was sleeping, even though it had been obvi-ous that he wanted to keep them secret.

It's his fault for not having hidden them better, Evelyn said.

And it could have been so much worse than photos of an ex, Anastasia said.

He has never even mentioned that he has been with guys, Ina said.

So? both sisters said.

It just seems like an important thing to tell the person you're dating. I mean, what else has he been hiding?

Nothing, Evelyn said.

He doesn't have to tell you everything, Anastasia said. Have you told him everything? Have you told him about Mom?

Now I've destroyed it all, Ina said and started crying.

Evelyn helped her older sister up from the floor, Anastasia brewed some tea and turned on her new favorite soap opera. She spent the next hour trying to explain who was in love with whom, who had had a brain transplant and who was a secret son to whom. Three sisters on the same couch, sharing one blanket, watching the same brain-dead (Ina), slightly predictable (Evelyn), amazing (Anastasia) soap opera, eating popcorn, drinking herbal tea, booing in unison every time the evil drug lord appeared on-screen, cheering when the secret son finally got his revenge.

The day after, Evelyn called Hector, without saying anything to Ina. Two days later Anastasia started looking for a job, even though Ina had stopped complaining about her not paying rent. Three days later Hector reached out to Ina and asked if she wanted to join him and his family on the west coast.

But you said it would be too crowded? Ina said and wondered if there was something seriously wrong with her tongue.

We can stay in the Frigga, Hector said. And I want to introduce you to my family.

Ina wasn't sure what a "frigga" was, but she said yes immediately and when Evelyn heard what had happened, she wondered if she and Anastasia were doing Ina a favor by staying here, rather than the other way around.

Chapter Twenty

n November 1993 I convinced my dad to come and watch a tennis game I was playing in Åkersberga. I had been playing tennis since I was seven, I had hated it since the beginning, and now I was fourteen and had no idea why I played, but both my Swedish uncles played tennis, and my mom had been a good player when she was young, and when my dad moved to Sweden and heard that his future wife came from a tennis family, he made sure that I started tennis school, for him tennis was something ultra-Swedish, it was overclass, it was the French Open and Wimbledon, it was the ice-cold Björn Borg, the attractive Mats Wilander, grumpy, always-looking-like-he-had-a-potato-in-his-mouth Stefan Edberg. When I started playing dad always came with me to practice, we went together to the Royal Tennis Hall, located in fancy Östermalm, we took the subway from Hornstull to Tekniska Högskolan, and every time we exited the subway Dad looked at the huge brick KTH university building and asked me the same question:

How many bricks do you think they needed to build this thing?

And I always shook my head and said that I had no idea, and Dad said: We'll have to ask Grandpa.

Not because mom's dad was an architect, but he was an engineer and he surely knew some smart way of calculating how many bricks were needed to build this huge campus. We continued towards the forest, we walked along the gravel path, we passed the hospital on our right side and the illustrated map on our left side, I don't remember what we talked about, but I remember that it felt amazing to be walking there, next to him, feeling so proud that he was my dad and nobody else's (except my brothers'). We arrived at the tennis school, all the other boys were blond and blue-eyed, I wasn't aware of it, not until Filip started, Filip was brown, like me, maybe he was from Latin America, maybe he was Asian, I don't know, I didn't care, I just noticed that he was brown and that he played tennis like he was from another planet, his backhand was not one-handed, nor two-handed, instead he sliced the ball, again and again, on the forehand side he used so much topspin that our trainer had a hard time getting the ball back, Filip rarely hit the ball in the court, but he always, always got the ball back over the net, nobody understood how he did it, he was seven years old and ran after each and every ball like his life depended on it. When Filip started playing, I felt that my place in the tennis club was unclear, before I was the brown one, who was potentially bad because I was brown, because we were the only ones without a car, because the other boys had Prince rackets and I had an old blue-and-yellow Yonex (that I loved because it sort of sounded like Younes (and it sort of felt as if I was sponsored)). But with Filip it became obvious that the racket didn't matter, nor did the skin color, Filip also came to practice via subway and his racket was worse than mine, still he was better than all of us, he had that spark in him, I saw how my dad looked at Filip with longing eyes, as if he dreamed that he was there as Filip's dad rather than mine.

Eight years later, I was still playing tennis, even though I really didn't know why, or rather I knew exactly why, because I wanted my dad to love me and look at me like he had looked at Filip.

We took the commuter train to Åkersberga and walked from the station, I felt nervous, I normally didn't care if I won or lost, but now, today, with Dad present, I really wanted to show him that all his dedication, all those times when he brought me to training when I was young hadn't been in vain. We signed in at the office, I said my surname, twice, the third time I spelled it using Swedish forenames,

"Kalle Harald Erik Martin Ivar Rickard Ivar," they finally found my name, the organizers informed us that my game was on another court, they explained how to get there.

Is it far? I said.

No, just ten minutes, they said and described the way.

We don't have a car, Dad said.

Oh, the organizers said. Okay. We will find you a car.

They arranged so that we could hitch a ride with my opponent's dad, he drove a dark blue shining Saab, both Dad and I were in the back seat, my opponent sat in the passenger front seat, nobody said a word during the ten-minute trip, it had started to rain.

We said hello to the young, very nervous umpire, we started warming up, ground strokes from the baseline, volley, then an index finger towards the sky to signal that you wanted some lobs, then back to the baseline to practice some serves. I heard my coach in my head, bend your knees, focus on the ball, follow through, but I had a hard time concentrating, I kept thinking of other things, the car ride here, Dad, Dad's hands as he stroked the interior of the car, my opponent, his red hair, his grunts every time he hit the ball, I told myself that if I were to win one game in my life, it was to be this one.

I won the first two balls, then I lost 6–0, 6–0, I started to cry, Dad walked out into the rain, afterwards the father of my opponent asked if we wanted a ride back to center court.

No, we are fine, my dad said.

I could drive you to the train station if you prefer? the other dad said.

Thanks, but no thank you, Dad said. We are being picked up by my wife. She needed the car.

Okay, the dad said. Good game today, son.

I looked up, he had actually said it to me, I smiled, Dad and I got up and left the tennis court, we started walking back to the train station, the Saab passed us without stopping, after a while we saw a bus stop. Dad checked the timetable, the bus only ran Mondays to Fridays, we kept walking in silence, the rain poured down. I wanted to ask him if he would rather have another son, a better son, a stronger son, a son who didn't break down in tears when he lost a tennis match, a son who was more like Filip and less like me, but I didn't say anything and Dad didn't turn around, we kept walking and didn't say a word the whole way home.

Chapter Twenty-One

The next morning Anastasia woke up on the couch in the living room, popcorn crumbs in her hair, she knew from the silence in the kitchen that her sisters were off to work and university. Instead of getting up, Anastasia closed her eyes, and for the first time in many years spoke to Maktoub, the almighty Goddess of Destiny, to whom her mother used to refer. Their mom wasn't religious, she didn't read any holy scriptures, she never fasted, she never wore a hijab, she drank alcohol and ate ham, and when other Muslims referred to maktoub as that which is fated, the already written, that which we normal humans can't change, Anastasia's mom referred to Maktoub as if it were a personal friend, an ex-colleague that she had worked with many years ago and who now had reached an influential CEO position, a local politician who had become prime minister, it was important to be on good terms with Maktoub, but it was even more important to remember that the worst thing Maktoub knows is to be ignored, Maktoub always sends out signs and the person who misses these signs will be punished, so when Anastasia had eaten breakfast she left the apartment with her senses on full alert, looking for signs of what kind of job she could find to start paying rent.

She saw an older woman with two dogs, should she try to become a veterinarian? Should she start a daycare center for dogs? Should she become a dog walker? She saw two men working with leaf blowers, was that a potential job for her? A leaf blower person? Or a gardener? She saw a taxi driver slow down, was that something? Could she drive a taxi? That could actually work, she was comfortable with silences, she was great with addresses, she liked sitting and waiting.

The only thing between her and a career as a taxi driver was the fact that she didn't have a license. She continued down towards the water, a bunch of kids in yellow neon vests were crossing a lawn glittery with dew, they looked incredibly happy, even though it was windy and they were just walking, everyone holding on to a rope that one of the preschool teachers was holding.

Anastasia, is that you?

She turned around and looked back at the group of kids. One of the teachers was waving to her, at first she didn't recognize him, but then she saw that it was Dino, a friend from the past, or maybe not a friend, but an acquaintance, when she knew him, he was a heavy user, needles and heroin, now he was standing there in the sun, handing out field hockey clubs to a bunch of kids, sure his tattoos were still visible underneath his T-shirt, and he had those jittery hands that reminded her of his past, but now he was here, standing next to the glistening water, smiling and waving, with sunlight in his beard and a functional backpack and a bunch of kids surrounding him.

Under normal circumstances Anastasia would have just waved and said hello from afar, but since she had explicitly asked Maktoub for a sign, she approached him and asked him how he was doing, and if he had heard anything from Peter or Alessandro or Mathias lately, he said that Peter was back in Östersund working as a plumber, but Alessandro was . . . he raised his eyebrows and shook his head, which Anastasia interpreted as if he was dead or in jail, or possibly had died in jail.

And Mathias?

No idea, Dino said and handed out the last club. And you?

I'm great, she said and wondered if that was true. How long have you worked as a . . . Anastasia wasn't even sure what to call it. Teacher? Babysitter? Field hockey coach?

These kids are adorable, he said. I have been doing this for almost two years. It's the best thing ever. We're really understaffed if you are looking for something?

Four days later Kerstin Holmström, the boss of Gullvivan Pre-school, called Anastasia and asked if she could come in for a quick interview.

It's nothing to worry about, Kerstin said when she heard Anastasia's reluctant silence.

Just a standard procedure, Dino has told me that you worked together at . . . what was it called . . . Dockan Retirement Home?

Yes, Anastasia said, and smiled, because Dockan was what they used to call Docklands, the rave club in Nacka that politicians had been trying to close down for years.

Taking care of old people and young people is more similar than you may think, Kerstin said. You will recognize a lot of things from your time at Dockan. The changing of diapers, the cutting up of food, the stopping of occasional runaway attempts.

Anastasia heard that Kerstin was joking and tried to make a sound of approval to signal that she found what she had just heard amusing so that things wouldn't be as awkward as they usually were when Anastasia had to interact with people she didn't know.

Two days later she descended the hill to meet Kerstin at her of-fice, Dino was standing in the yard of the preschool, he smiled at her and gave her a hug and whispered that she just had to say yes to whatever Kerstin was asking. He was right, Kerstin asked her if it was true that she had worked at Dockan for two years, yes, and was this the right person to call for references, a certain Alfredo Pessoa, yes, and Kerstin asked if she had any plans for the summer, yes, and Kerstin said, what kind of plans, and Anastasia said: Well, I hope to be working here. Kerstin smiled. When Anastasia left her office, she saw Dino again, he was on his knees trying to convince a stubborn three- or five-year-old to put on her sweater.

How did it go? he said.

Who's Alfredo Pessoa? Anastasia whispered.

It's Affe! Dino said. He has the best phone voice, he sounds like a fifty-year-old CEO when he wants to, he will give you amazing references, he always comes through.

Two days later, Kerstin called Anastasia and asked her if she could come in with short notice, one of the teachers had called in sick, and Anastasia said yes, got dressed, ran down to the preschool to meet Åsa and Axel and Filip and Charlie and Nahom and Saga and Florence, and they were all four to five years old and they asked her why she had such yellow teeth and how she had received the scars on her wrists and why she had that red stone around her neck and if she was good at drawing bears and if she knew how to wolf whistle and why she had different-colored socks and which fruit she liked best, apples, oranges or pine cones.

Chapter Twenty-Two

n January 1994 my mom suggested that my dad and I should take a computer course together, she had heard about it through a colleague, it was a subsidized course, primarily for parents who wanted to take the course with their kids and retired people. My dad wasn't interested. Mom tried to convince him by telling him that there was big money to be made in computers.

I don't care about money, Dad said.

Mom's lower cheek dropped. For the first time she looked really worried. Despite his protests, Mom signed us up for the course. The following Saturday morning, we took the red line to Slussen and then the green line to Rådmansgatan, then the stairs up to Sveavägen and turned right, it had been a long time since we did something together, a long time since we actually spoke to each other, and we weren't about to start now. We chose the wrong exit and came out close to the main library, so we turned right and walked back towards the city center, we passed the Stockholm School of Economics, where I would study international economics for two and a half years with the hope of getting my father's approval, we passed an empty gym, we passed the RFSL headquarters, where there was a rainbow flag in the window and posters reminding people to practice safe sex and my dad said: Bögmusik (faggot music), which lingered in my mind because I hadn't even heard any music as we passed the organization.

Then we passed the cinema where Prime Minister Olof Palme

saw his last movie with his wife before he was gunned down in the street, and when Dad saw the cinema, he sighed and said that Sweden will never be the same, I asked him why, and he said:

It just won't be the same.

We continued past the cinema and a pharmacy and entered the ABF headquarters. On the second floor, in what looked like a normal classroom, there were brand-new top-of-the-line PC computers. Our teacher was from Greece, I don't remember his name, but I remember I had a hard time understanding his accent, and I wasn't alone, the first time he welcomed us to the course and told us that we were allowed to turn on the computers, one of the elderly ladies raised her hand and asked him if he could teach this course in English, simply because she didn't understand his Swedish. The teacher looked sad and said that unfortunately his English was not very good. But his Russian was great, he said with a smile. Does anyone speak Russian?

I speak French, my father said, not mentioning that he also spoke Arabic.

Not Russian?

Everybody shook their heads, so we were forced to use Swedish.

The course was for beginners, but the computers that the workers' association had invested in were blazing fast. When we turned them on they booted up in less than five minutes, first they checked extensive RAM memory (640 kb), and then they checked the hard drive memory of a whopping 20 megabytes, then there was a loud clicking noise as the motherboard made sure that the 3.5 floppy drive and the large 5.14 floppy drive were in use, because yes, these bad boys had both kinds of floppy drives. I had never seen anything like it, my friend Martin who was from Bromma had an Atari and a Commodore 64, which was just insane, but this was something else, these computers were bigger than a small fridge, and there were no games on them, just MS-DOS and GW Basic. When the log-in process was done the computer welcomed us with a friendly prompt:

C:\>

Now this, our teacher said, this is the start of everything. From here everything is possible.

What did he say? one of the ladies said.

My dad told them what the teacher had said.

I don't understand him either, the lady said.

I told them what both the teacher and my dad had said.

Finally someone who speaks proper Swedish, the lady said. No offense, she added and looked with a smile at my dad.

None taken, my dad said and looked like he was ready to smash her head in with a keyboard.

During the following hour, we learned the basic commands of MS-DOS, it was really easy, "dir" showed you the content of the directory, "chdir" meant changing the directories, "cls" cleaned the screen, "mkdir" created directories, the current startup file is autoexec.bat and the old one is autoexec.bak. My dad looked at the blinking prompt on the screen and looked like a question mark.

He's not a good teacher, he whispered in French.

Any questions? the teacher said with his Greek accent.

During the rest of the class, the teacher showed us how to create a simple code program in GW Basic. I followed his instructions, 10 CLS to empty the screen, 20 INPUT to ask for the code, 30 "IF NOT" to specify what would happen if the code was wrong.

I don't understand how you understand this, Dad said.

It's simple, I said, beaming with pride because I had finally, after all these years, found something that came easily for me.

Now we just need a password, I said.

What password?

Just invent one, I said.

Evelyn, he said.

Evelyn? I said.

Evelyn, he said.

Like Evelyn Mikkola?

It's just a name, he said. A password.

Is it true that you and their mom were in love in Tunisia? I said.

Dad looked at me.

Their mom has not had an easy life, he said. I just tried to help.

Do you know where they are now?

This is pointless, Dad said in French.

What is? I said.

Everything is, he said and left the classroom.

I stayed at the computer, the fan system whizzed like a jet motor.

Dad never returned to the computer course. I kept going and in the beginning, I made up reasons as to why he was absent (he was sick, he had a lot of things at work, he had jammed his toe in a door). When he wasn't back in February I started telling the truth, or almost the truth, I told the teacher that my dad had gone to his home country, I explained that there was a family emergency. When he wasn't back in March, I kept saying that Dad was in his home country, and that I wasn't sure when he would be back, which was 100 percent true. The teacher kept calling his name at every roll call. I kept explaining why he wasn't there.

In April the course ended. The teacher called my name and I got up from my desk and approached him to get my diploma. He shook my hand and congratulated me while handing me a large white envelope. When I returned to the desk, my classmates applauded, just as I had applauded when they received their envelopes. I looked at the diploma to check that my name was spelled correctly, which it was. It said that the thirteen-week-long course had given me knowledge in MS-DOS and basic programming skills.

After the last class, the teacher signaled to me to approach his desk. He asked if my dad was okay. I said that I wasn't sure, he had been sick, and then he had gone abroad and now my mom was threatening him with divorce and I don't know what's going on, or when he will be back.

Okay, the teacher said, looking a bit overwhelmed by the amount of information.

You do understand that I can't give him his diploma, right?

Yes, of course, I said. He was only here once.

Exactly, the teacher said. I saw that he held an envelope in his hands with my father's name on it. I wondered if he was considering giving it to me. Then he took the envelope, tore it into two pieces, and put it in the paper bin.

Good luck in the future, he said.

Thank you, I said and left the classroom.

Chapter Twenty-Three

And so there Ina was, standing with her packed bag under the blue sky, checking the time, waiting for Hector, in the strangely straight and already warm shadow of the tall building where she had bought a flat with two bedrooms, so she would never need to move, so that she would have room for her sisters, *if* or rather *when* they needed her help. She would never become like their mother, whose whole life seemed dedicated to moving from one area to the next, and then, a few months later, getting ready to move again, there was always something wrong, the local grocery store was disgusting, the hill to the subway station was unbearable, the view from the balcony was depressing, the neighbors were too noisy, or too nosy, or too alcoholic or too white trash or too overclass or too something else. No, Ina told the broker when she signed the contract that she would stay here forever, if she ever had kids she would live with them here, there was a storage area for strollers and kids' bikes, if she lived until she was one hundred, she would die here, the elevator was large enough for a wheelchair, she could roll down to the water and watch the sunset. She would tell Hector's parents that she was proud to live here. Sure the area didn't have a great reputation and it was located south of the city, there were drugs being sold at the square and the houses were a bit brown, the high-rises created courtyards that her friend Saskia jokingly referred to as "prison yards" when she was visiting from Malmö. But Laura and Saskia didn't see the beauty of this area, they didn't notice that every brown high-rise had its own particular shade of brown, and yes they were all eight stories high, and had been built quickly in 1967 to house an influx of new inhabitants, but these buildings were not like the other high-rises, built farther south, with asbestos in the balcony and plastic moldings, that turned into lethal smoke chimneys if there ever was a fire. No, these houses had wooden moldings and window-sills made out of actual marble, that's why she fell in love with the flat, and that's why she bought it, and sure, it had also been severely underpriced, and the sellers really needed the money quickly and it was the safest place to buy an apartment if you wanted to make sure to get your money back, but that was not why she had bought it, she had bought it because she needed something stable, something that was hers, something to trust when everything else, including her mom, felt unsafe.

Hector was supposed to be here by nine, they had a long drive ahead of them, she looked at the cars that came sliding down from the roundabout, she saw a black taxi and then a red sedan, and then a dark blue hatchback, it looked like a rental because of the logos on the windows, but the car turned right and continued towards Mälar-höjden. Had he forgotten her? Had he changed his mind (again) and gone down to the west coast by himself?

After a few minutes, Ina got tired of waiting, she pulled out her book and sat down on a surprisingly warm stone nearby, to make sure that Hector would see just how late he was (in reality he was not more than ten minutes late and Ina had gone down to the side-walk five minutes early). When she looked up she saw him, he came down the hill in a shiny silver-gray car, his smile was the size of the steering wheel.

May I offer you a ride, ma'am? he said, leaning his head sideways out the open window.

Depends, she said, getting onto her feet, putting the book in the backpack. Are you heading south?

Sure am. South and west.

What an incredible coincidence, she said, as she leaned forward and kissed him, his lips, the warmth of the car's metallic paint, the cold of the AC, Lauryn Hill's voice from the stereo.

For a moment I thought you'd changed your mind, she said, and instantly regretted saying it.

About inviting you to come? Are you kidding me? I wouldn't survive down there without you . . . Just remember . . . I warned you . . . These people are crazy. Crazy, he repeated, as he helped her to put the bag in the trunk.

Hector turned the car around and drove towards the freeway. Ina wondered how many cars she had been in during her lifetime, how many times had she sat in a passenger seat after a basketball game or after a late dinner with friends, everyone always offered her the front seat because of her long legs, but she had never, ever sat in a seat like this, it was both hot and cold at the same time, and it felt like it wrapped itself around her and wouldn't let her go, and maybe it had something to do with the fact that she was about to go on vacation to the west coast, with the first person she could see herself spending her life with, but it was something else as well, it was something about the materials, how the seat belt gently pulled itself around her body with a smooth jerk when she fastened it, the soft-touch leather of the dashboard. When she put her water bottle in one of the cup holders, there was a gentle clicking sound, and it was nothing, it was just a click, but on that day, in July 2000, that clicking sound meant the world to her.

She pulled the bottle out and put it down again, just to hear the sound.

I know, Hector said and smiled.

She stopped herself from asking him how much the rental was, if they should split it, how it was possible for him to walk around in a world where you don't research for hours to find the most practical and cheap car, and instead choose a car that has clicking bottle holders, and smooth cool warm leather seats, magical seat belts, and a magnificent sound system, but actually, this is just a normal car, she tried telling herself, it has four tires, a steering wheel, doors and mirrors, and the back seat is ridiculously small, it's just stupid to pay extra for unnecessary things, Hector could just as easily have contacted that rental place in Midsommarkransen where she found the rental truck, and they would have gotten away with a third of the cost and then she wouldn't be sitting here in this passenger seat, worrying about the cost.

Push that round button, he said.

This one?

She pushed it, there was a smooth metallic sound, and the roof disappeared.

Chapter Twenty-Four

When Dad disappeared Mom started developing strange symptoms, this was in the summer of 1994, the summer of endless sunlight, the miraculous summer when Sweden's crappy soccer team somehow scored more goals than any other team in the World Cup in the U.S. and secured a bronze medal. While everyone was celebrating the soccer team's unlikely success, Mom sat in the waiting room at the local hospital, her allergies became worse, she had sudden migraine attacks, she started having stomach cramps, she went to the ER multiple times, she explained to the doctors that she was a physiotherapist and that she had studied the body in detail for so many years and she had worked with alcoholics and she could write a book about psychosomatic traumas, but this was something else, this was her body, not her worry about her disappeared husband, not her sadness about him not returning her calls, not her loneliness, not her anger about him taking her money to build a house that she never wanted, not her stress about being a sole provider for three kids, and the doctors nodded and followed her advice, they ordered X-rays, they gave her gastroscopies, they sent her to multiple experts, but nobody could find anything wrong, the pain persisted, she went home and then returned to the hospital, once they kept her there over the weekend, I brought my brothers in to visit, we took the bus and walked up the hill to Södersjukhuset, she lay on her side when we came, she looked so young, like a little girl with a few strands of gray hair, she had a medical plastic band around her wrist, I checked the spelling of her name to make sure it was correct, she smiled when she saw us, she said that we shouldn't have come, she said that there was food in the freezer at home, she told me to get the handbag in her locker and gave us money for takeout, she said she would be back soon, in a couple of days, we shouldn't worry.

I can't believe how grown-up you are, she said. You are old enough to get by on your own, right? We don't need to tell Grandmother about this?

And we agreed, no need to tell Grandmother, no need to worry her, especially since Grandmother had been saying for years that Mom had chosen the wrong husband, she should have chosen someone Swedish, someone from a more similar background, someone with richer parents and fewer siblings. One of my brothers started crying when we were about to leave, he wanted to stay here, at the hospital.

We have to go, I said, gripping his arm tight to make him pull himself together.

My other brother nodded, he understood the situation, he was already heading towards the corridor, he held himself together.

I'm not going to die, Mom said. I promise I won't die.

We left the hospital and walked home to Hornstull in silence, three brothers, I was fifteen, my middle brother nine, our youngest brother eight.

Chapter Twenty-Five

When they arrived it was late afternoon, they had driven for six and a half hours, they had stopped for a quick lunch at a restaurant just before Jönköping, Hector had left the highway and taken a bunch of small roads to find a place where he had been as a kid, they stopped at a hotel to ask for directions, the hotel was closed for renovation but one of the carpenters knew the restaurant, Take a right, then left, then right, right, the sign outside claimed that it was a tavern, but the restaurant looked more like a school canteen, dark green plastic plates, an odor of chlorine.

Today's special is meatballs, the lady behind the counter said with a drawling voice.

Their special has been meatballs the last twenty years, Hector said when they sat down at a table with their meatballs.

Then they continued south, past the breathtaking views of Vättern (Mom always said this looked like Italy, Hector said), past the strangely straight highway towards Ljungby (Mom always said she could drive this part with her eyes closed, Hector said), then they turned right towards Halmstad, Route 25, and as the hours passed they continued to talk, they talked about Hector's teaching and Ina's dissertation, they talked about Saskia's longing for children and Laura's ex-boyfriend, they talked about Hector's sister's divorce and Evelyn's fear of long-term relationships, they talked about Tolstoy's ability to zoom and Mishima's bodies, and Duras's details and Chamoiseau's voices.

What is this magic? Ina kept thinking to herself. How does this work, how is it possible for two people to sit in an enclosed space for six-plus hours and not be bored, not start hating each other? Hector seemed just as surprised, when they passed Halmstad he told her to look in the glove box, and when she opened it, a bunch of audiobooks fell out.

I wanted a backup, he said. In case we ran out of subjects to talk about.

But they would never run out of subjects and Ina touched Hector's hand when he changed gears, and Hector accidentally brushed her breast when they stopped for gas, and then they locked the rental and snuck away from the road, just to touch each other without being seen by passing cars. After almost seven hours in the same car, it was obvious that they wouldn't need any audiobooks, all they needed was time and themselves and some gas and today's special meatballs and a rented BMW 318i convertible. The only thing they didn't talk about was Ina's mom, and when Hector asked why, Ina said:

I don't have the energy.

For what?

To talk about her. To talk with her. I need a break from her. Lucky you, Hector said, because we are almost there.

Ina had to suppress the impulse to tell Hector to keep going, don't leave the highway, let's continue down the continent, Denmark, Germany, Greece, Istanbul, the world. But Hector had already started pointing out landmarks.

That's Ica Maxi, he said, nodding towards a red strip mall that swooshed past on their right side. That's the nearest big grocery store. Ina nodded.

And that's the exit towards Laholm, he said. Where they have a great library. Ina nodded. He continued driving, Ina noticed that there was a shift in his tone of voice, he felt tense, as if the nearness to the family house made him stressed.

This is our exit, he said and signaled to the right. They left the highway and approached a stop sign with too much speed, Hector pushed the brake and pushed it again, after so many hours on the highway both their bodies and the car had been so accustomed to high speed that Hector had to stop the car with a jolt to avoid driving into incoming traffic. The motor stalled.

Hector swore and turned the key. Green fields, yellow fields, a horse farm and a small stone church in the distance.

Is that it? she said.

No, he said with a smile that made her feel silly. That's a nearby village. We are heading this way.

He turned right and the car slowly approached a sign where it said VÄLKOMMEN, the corner of the sign was decorated with a big sun.

I always hated that sign as a kid, Hector said.

Why?

It seemed ironic somehow. It rains more here than anywhere else in Sweden.

She nodded.

Because of the ridge, he said, nodding towards what looked like a nearby mountain.

Ina didn't answer. She wondered about this new sharp voice of his, where it came from, and if she had done something wrong when she thought the neighboring village was his village, or when she didn't want to talk about her mom.

Here we have two alternatives, he said. We can either go left, past the cabin area, it's a bit shorter, or go right, past Svens Livs.

Let's go left, Ina said.

We always go right, Hector said and went right.

It's like a tradition to go right when we arrive the first time, he explained. They drove past a permanent flea market, a recycling station and a sign indicating tennis courts. They passed by a grocery store and a bakery.

It's getting a bit chilly, right?

He pushed the button and the roof of the car came back up.

This is the main street, he said.

It was just a street, with small houses lining both sides.

That's the Centrumkiosk, he said, pointing to a yellow kiosk. And the camping area is behind there. And this . . . He gently turned the steering wheel to the right . . . This is the sea.

He was completely correct, at the end of the street was the sea, a raging blue, wavy white sea, it looked like the street ended with seashore, and in a way it did, you could actually drive down to the water, and since this was what they always did when Hector was a kid, this is what they did this time around as well, black asphalt was replaced with dark wet sand and Hector sighed.

We made it, he said.

Ina opened the door and got out, the wind got a hold of the door, she had to struggle to shut it again. She stood in a breeze of seaweed and salt water and even though she had never been here before, she felt weirdly at home, as if she had been searching for this road, this sea, this beach, this cloudy horizon her whole life. She noticed that the car was still running.

You're not coming out? she said. Hector was about to say something, maybe about how they normally do it, normally they only drive down to the water for a quick glance and then they take the car to the house and then they descend on foot, but he didn't say it, he looked at her, turned off the engine, got out into the wind. He took her hand and they walked down to the shoreline, the wind was so strong that it felt like they could lean towards it without falling, and for a moment they tried it, they leaned towards it and fell and leaned and fell, and seagulls kept laughing at their attempts to challenge gravity. The beach stretched for as long as she could see in one direction, and just as long in the other.

This is the longest sand beach in Sweden, he said, as they got back into the un-windy car.

Again he used that tone of voice that she hadn't heard before, as if he was quoting a tourist brochure. They drove back up the street, took the first right and parked in front of one no two no three no four blue houses. His mother was standing in the window watching them as they got out of the car.

Chapter Twenty-Six

n the spring of 1995 Mom sent a letter to my father saying that she wanted a divorce and we still didn't hear anything, Dad was gone, nobody knew where he was, by now the whole family knew, my uncles, Mom's friends, even Grandmother, and for some strange reason she didn't say "I told you so," instead she came by with pizzas and asked if we wanted to spend the weekend at her house, we could help her in the garden, Mom could get a break and heal her gut. One evening my grandmother called me and asked if I had heard anything from Dad.

No, I said. Why?

I just had a feeling that he would be back soon, she said.

He's been gone for over a year, I said.

I know, she said.

Later that evening the door opened and there he was, back with his suitcases, he had brought dates and shisha tobacco and brik ingredients and toys for my brothers and a postcard with a smiling Michael Jordan for me and a red coral necklace for Mom. He hadn't called, he hadn't answered the letter, instead he just stood there in our hallway, with a broad smile, his eyes looked sadder, his waist was bigger, he had lost some hair, but my brothers didn't care, he's here, Dad's back, they dropped whatever they had been playing with and ran towards him to hug him, and I did the same, hugged him, only to realize that I had to crouch down because I was now taller than he was.

Where have you been? I said.

I've been working on the house, he said. Our house. In Jendouba.
Is it finished?

Instead of answering he held up a glittering new silver key.

Is it finished? I said again.

Almost, he said. The foundation is in place, the walls are up, and
the roof. Now we are just waiting for the windows and then I have to
bribe some local politicians in order to . . .

He stopped mid-sentence. Mum walked in from the kitchen, drying her hands on the towel that she kept in the lining of her pants.

I got your letter, he said in French. Mum kept drying her hands.

We can't get a divorce, he said.

Mum just stood there, drying her hands.

Je t'aime, he said. It can't end like this. He reached out his arms.
I need you.

He hugged her.

I can't get by without you.

Mom's arms were still holding the kitchen towel.

We can heal this, he said. We can get through this. We are stronger than this.

He backed away. Mom slowly put away the kitchen towel.

I thought she would scream. I was convinced that she gathered
force to curse him out.

Where have you been? she whispered.

The house, Dad said and held up the key. As if a soon-finished
house, built with her savings, in a city they both hated, would make
everything okay.

And now I'm back, he said and tried to put the necklace on her as
if it were a gold medal.

She recoiled.

It's too late, she said in French.

I had to help a friend.

What friend?

A friend.

Her?

Dad looked at us and sighed.

She doesn't have anyone else, he said.

It felt like a strange relief when Mom finally started screaming. I took my brothers to the living room, closed the door and put on the TV extra loud to drown out the curse words.

Chapter Twenty-Seven

You must be Ina, Hector's mother said and stretched out her ring-filled hand. Ina nodded and shook her hand, feeling slightly nervous all of a sudden, when she saw the amount of people that came pouring out of the houses to look at her or the car or both.

I'm Ingrid, his mother said, that one over there with the big belly and hairy back is my brother and these are his sons, and this is their mother, and this is my friend Astrid and her two daughters, and these are the kids of the neighbor and this one . . . I have no idea who this is, Ingrid said with a smile.

I'm Sanna's friend, the child said.

Oh, so *you're* Sanna's friend, Ingrid said as if she had been looking for Sanna's friend all day long without being able to find her.

Sanna is Hector's sister's eldest, Ingrid said. But where's Esmeralda? Esmeralda! Come and say hello!

Hector's sister walked over with a baby on her arm and a toddler in her hand.

Welcome, she said. How was the tri—

As you can see, it's a very relaxed atmosphere here, Ingrid said. People are coming and going as they want. My dear husband is here somewhere, Enzoooo. Enzooooooo!? Come now, where are you, ENZOOOOOOO!? Well, he's bound to be somewhere.

Ingrid instructed some of the kids to carry Ina's bag to the Frigga and took Ina's arm to lead her into the garden and give her "the grand tour."

So this is the Blue House, she said, pointing to a blue house, and this is the Small House, she said, pointing to another house, in the exact same color as the previous house, and this here is the Dorm House and that's the Frigga and that over there is not really a house, it's just for laundry and showers, and there's a sauna in there as well, do you like to sauna? I've never liked it, but when it's raining, which it rarely does, we dry our laundry in there, Enzo, where are you, ENZOOOO, they're here now, I don't understand where he is, he knew you were coming, please excuse the state of things, when we are here by ourselves things look very different, but now it's vacation and we haven't gotten around to doing anything, except basking in the sunshine, it's vacation, after all, she said as if she was trying to convince herself, still holding Ina's forearm in a firm grip.

Mom, let her go, Hector said when they came back to the patchy grass between the Blue House and the Small House.

I'm just showing her around, Ingrid said. Esmeralda asked Ina if she had been to the west coast before, and Ina had just enough time to shake her head before Ingrid declared that she hadn't been here either, not before they bought this plot of land, she had a lot of stereotypes about the west coast, rich people from Gothenburg with sailing boats, irritating Stockholmers who spray champagne during the tennis week in Båstad, but then she came here, to this plot of land in between the sea and the forest, and realized that it was heaven on earth and now she never wanted to leave. During a couple of seconds Ingrid's face relaxed and Ina could see a younger and much less confident version of Ingrid standing there in the garden, trying to convince herself that she hadn't made a mistake when she moved down here a couple of years before her retirement.

Please don't mind the guns, Ingrid said, and Ina suddenly realized that there were neon plastic water guns everywhere, on the ground, in the bushes, on the gray steps leading up to the house.

Someone . . . I'm not going to say who, Ingrid said and pointed to one of Esmeralda's children, started a water war a few days ago and nobody has bothered to put the toys back, this is what we do here, we relax and take it day by day, we don't make plans, it's vacation, she said for the third time.

I'm really happy to be here, Ina said.

And we are so happy that you decided to come along, Ingrid said. Hector! Why don't you take her down to the sea? But first you must eat something. Enzo? ENZO?

A man got up from a lounge chair on the patio, he wore a polo shirt and round yellow glasses. He looked like a shrunken version of Hector, it was Hector with thinner shoulders, shorter legs, darker skin and more freckles. With a worn-out sun hat on his head.

But there you are, have you been there the whole time? This is Enzo, Hector's dad, Enzo, say hello, greet them.

Enzo looked at Ina and nodded and smiled. He was just about to say something, maybe ask about the trip, when Ingrid interrupted him.

They are hungry, they must eat something, she said and directed Ina and Hector to the kitchen. Take what you want, it's all yours, there's no particular system, here's bread, here's cereal, here we have protein, we always keep the milk here, so we know where we can find it, and are you sure you're not hungry, a hundred percent sure, well, okay, then you might as well go down to say hi to the ocean, you can use this door.

Ingrid opened a door on the other side of the house and pointed towards the sea. Ina looked back towards the patio, Enzo returned to the lounge chair, moving slowly as if he had just woken up and still wondered if this was all a dream.

Chapter Twenty-Eight

After the divorce my dad disappeared again, I saw him once, a few months after he moved out, he was living in temporary housing close to Södra Station, it's for "thieves and drug addicts" he said when we spoke on the phone. I went there with my brothers, I convinced myself that we went for their sake, I told myself that I didn't want to see him, not after what he had done to Mom, first he disappeared, then he reappeared when Mom wrote that letter, and when Mom didn't want to forgive him, he started screaming that it wasn't right for a woman to leave her husband when he was sick, Mom said he wasn't sick, he just had diabetes, and Dad said he didn't accept a divorce, Mom said he didn't have a choice, finally he left the apartment, then he came back a few days later when nobody was home and stole her jewelry, it took Mom a few days to notice that her wedding ring was gone, and that necklace that he had just given her.

When I came home from school there was a surprisingly thin man on his knees changing our locks, I had always imagined locksmiths to be broad and strong, but this guy looked more like a weasel than a bear. He gave us a new set of keys and a few months later my brothers and I went over to see Dad, this was the fall of 1995, did we take the bus there, did we walk, no, it was a bit too far, we must have taken the bus, probably the 66 line, leaving from below Högalidskyrkan and then trickling east in a more haphazard way than the more efficient and goal-oriented 54 bus, past Zinken, past Mariatorget, there was a stop just next to Södra Station, on our way over there I told my brothers that I used to think of our mom as the 54, all systems and efficiency, lists and perfect timetables, and our dad was the 66, a kind of random haphazard system of thought and movement, but it took you to places that you wouldn't see otherwise. Though actually, now that I think of it, I think we took the subway, yes, we took the red line to Mariatorget, and then we walked down Swedenborgsgatan, and it was there, by the bus station, that I said that thing about the differences between our parents, I guess I wanted them to understand that we needed both our parents, that we couldn't say that one of them was kind and the other one evil, but in reality I guess I was the one who needed to hear that, I don't know why I'm crying when I'm writing this, it's really nothing, just three sons going to see their father for the first time since the divorce, since he stood there on the threshold and said those things about our future, spitting them out like a snake spits venom.

They will fail, he said.

Go now, she said.

You're nothing without me, he said.

Go, she said.

You will see, he said. Your sons will become drug users and failures without me. When Mom finally closed the door I thought about the Mikkola sisters and that this was another kind of curse, and now we were heading over there to see him. He waited for us in the lobby, there was another man behind the counter, he looked more like a security guard than a receptionist. You had to sign in and show your ID card to be allowed in as a visitor, I had just gotten my own ID card and was proud to finally be able to use it, but Dad gestured to me to put it back into the wallet.

These are my sons, he said to the man behind the counter. He looked at Dad, he looked at us, he nodded and pushed a button so that we could pass through the gate, and I remember thinking that if things were different, if it was our mom who was living in temporary housing and we turned up, three sons with brown skin and black hair, we would need to show ID, because it wasn't obvious that we were hers, and without our dad present in the family pictures, our existence in our white middle-class tennis-playing piano-practicing psalm-singing Swedish family would become a mystery, we looked like we were adopted, we looked like we were supposed to be somewhere else, and from this moment on, we wanted to be somewhere else, at least I wanted to be somewhere else, I still want to be somewhere else, no matter where I am there's another place where I would fit better, another country, another city, another book, another world. There was a loud sound and a red light turned green. We were allowed in through the metal gate, my brothers treated the turnstile as if it were a roller-coaster ride, and while we mounted the stairs my youngest brother kept asking me if we would be able to use the turnstile again when we left, and I nodded and said that we would. Dad opened a glass door to his corridor and we entered a boat, or rather a submarine, we were deep under sea level, it was dark and damp like in a closet, hundreds of identical dark brown doors, no names on the doors, just numbers, and we walked in silence, under yellow lightbulbs, for what felt like forever, my brothers didn't play tag, my father didn't ask us about school, I didn't ask him about Mom's jewelry, we just walked and walked, past one door with music and another door smelling of smoke and then another door that had both smoke and music and this time the music wasn't rock or pop but it sounded like a weird kind of slowed-down, super-sad tango, the Spanish or possibly Portuguese singer sounded like he was close to tears, then a door that had a name written on a Post-it note, and then a door that had signs of a burglary gone wrong, or possibly a police breakdown, there were big chunks of the door missing, and my brothers looked at the door and didn't ask what had happened to it, they didn't touch the damaged wood, they didn't say that it looked like someone extremely strong, like He-Man or Spider-Man, had kicked in the door. No, instead they just looked at the door and kept going, and I remember thinking that they were finally growing up, they were finally realizing that being an adult was all about not pointing out the obvious in situations where the obvious was too painful to take in. Finally we reached our dad's door, this was his life now, or at least for another two months, nobody could stay here longer than two or maybe three months, this was his room, this was his green wall-to-wall carpet with cigarette burns, this was his small bookshelf attached to the wall, containing only an instruction manual to the fourteen-inch TV and my dad's three favorite books (Machiavelli, Pär Lagerkvist and Kahlil Gibran). A small table, also attached to the wall, two folding chairs not attached to the wall and a bathroom that seemed smaller than the bed. My brothers entered the room and kept walking, opening the door to the bathroom, then opening the door to the closet, as if they couldn't believe that a room this small could contain their father. We sat on the couch, except there was no couch, so we must have sat on the bed, Dad opened the tiny refrigerator, he took out three bottles of high-sugar fruit juice, one of them was called Safari. We poured the juice into white plastic cups and drank the juice. My dad asked how Mom was doing. We said she was doing fine. My dad asked how school was going. We said it was going well. I concentrated on drinking my fruit juice, trying not to cry. My brothers started playing with something, I think they brought toys, maybe they had their beloved Turtles in their backpacks, Donatello and Rafael, Michelangelo and a fourth one who I've forgotten the name of. I told Dad that the Turtles had been impossible to find before Christmas, especially Rafael, and I had spent weeks calling different toy stores, going from mall to mall, digging through mountains of Splinter (their rat mentor) and April (the female journalist) in a desperate attempt to find Rafael before Christmas Eve and finally I found him, in Skärholmen Centrum, under a pile of Donatellos, and I bought him and brought him home to Mom to wrap. Dad looked at me as if he hated me.

How much was it? he said.

I don't remember, I said.

I just wanted to show him that I had taken responsibility for the family when he was gone, but he looked at me as if he was disappointed and in the silence that followed I wondered if I also had looked for that Rafael to show Mom and my brothers that there was no reason for worry, Dad was gone, but I got this, I'm sixteen and more or less adult, I was born old and will die old, and once again I start crying when I'm writing this, I don't know what's going on, but I know that I will go through this text in the future and edit these things out, I will carefully remove every sentence where it says that I'm crying, because I don't want to come across as manipulative, or weak, or as a crybaby, but before I remove this, why am I crying, why do these old memories create such a strong bodily reaction, why do my forty-two-year-old eyes, that have seen the birth of two kids, the death of all my grandparents, produce saline liquid just because I'm thinking of a memory from when I was sixteen, I don't know, and still I'm sitting here crying my eyes out, resisting the impulse to take out my phone and take a photo of my tears, as if I want to document them, as if I want to be able to show them to someone, in order to understand them, maybe because they show me that I'm real, that I can feel things, that there's nothing wrong with my empathy, at least not my empathy with a young version of myself (which can't really be called empathy, can it).

We sat there in silence, my father and I, while my brothers were playing on the bed with their Turtles. My dad got up and opened the curtains, there was a shiny metallic building on the other side of the street, office cubicles, conference rooms, plastic plants, people in shiny shoes making client calls, the office was well-lit but deserted, it looked like an aquarium, a woman sat at a desk talking into a headset, she had gold picture frames on her desk, probably photos of her kids, maybe her kids with her pets, maybe her parents with her kids and her pets. She looked out the window, it felt like she looked straight at us, but she didn't seem to see us, she turned her head and smiled as if she wanted to check the bounce in her ponytail, she smiled as if she was trying to charm her reflection, she kept talking into the headset. Dad stood there and looked at the woman, then he drew the drapes and told my brothers to put away their toys and listen, because he had something important to tell us. They put their toys back in their backpacks and sat on the bed.

Then we were all quiet, for a very long time. We just sat there in the small room, we drank fruit juice, we listened to the steps from someone who passed in the corridor, we heard random voices from Dad's new neighbors.

Many people who live here are alcoholics, Dad said. We were quiet. My brothers smuggled out their toys from their backpacks. Dad didn't seem to know how to proceed.

Last week a guy died here, Dad said in French, so that my brothers wouldn't understand. I saw his body when they broke down the door. He was lying on his back and the top half of him was light, and the bottom half was dark, can you guess why?

Because he had drunk wine? I said.

No, of course not, idiot, Dad said, and I thought about all the words he had used to describe me, *idiot* when I said something stupid, *Einstein* when I forgot or lost something, *sakkerfamek* when I read books and was so lost in the story that I forgot to keep my mouth closed, *Stalin* when I tried to break up a fight between my brothers using my fists.

Dad sighed.

What is similar to wine but in your body?

Blood? my youngest brother said.

Exactly, Dad said. Even kids know this, he added in French. The man was on his back and when his heart stopped beating his blood gathered in the lower level of his body, so when they noticed the smell they broke down the door and it looked like he was split in two.

Why did they break down the door? my middle brother said.

He had locked it.

But didn't they have extra keys? my youngest brother said.

Here are two people with well-functioning brains, Dad said with a smile. They will go far. People who can think for themselves are very rare. You are so right, they do have extra keys, but he had bolted the door, so they had to break down the door to help him.

But wasn't he already dead? I said.

Yes, Dad said.

We were silent for a few seconds. My brothers asked if they could turn on the TV, and my dad said: Of course, and with a sigh of relief we spent the rest of the visit watching one or maybe two episodes of a TV show for kids in Serbo-Croatian.

When we had finished the juice and Dad had thrown away our plastic cups we got up and left. Dad walked with us to the reception. He told us to say hi to Mom, he said he would call the day after, he said we should do our best in school and listen to our teachers and continue playing soccer and tennis and do our homework and take care of our mom and next weekend we could go to the movies together. My brothers asked if we could go to see the new Disney movie.

Absolutely.

My brothers asked if we could get popcorn.

Absolument.

My brothers asked if we could get butter-flavored popcorn, it was a bit more expensive, but a lot more tasty.

Do you think I'm pooping money? Dad said, but smiled to make sure that we understood that it was a joke and of course we could buy popcorn with butter flavor if we wanted to.

Can we get one each instead of sharing one big?

Whatever you want, Dad said. I will call you tomorrow so we can make a plan.

We hugged him goodbye, he kissed our cheeks, the security guard opened a door so that we wouldn't need to pass through the turnstile. On the way out I saw a big sign that warned visitors against bringing in any kind of weapon, there were crossed-out symbols of a gun, a baseball bat and some kind of tear gas or pepper spray, and on our way home I couldn't stop wondering why that sign had been placed so that it was easier to see it when leaving than when entering, as if it was okay to have weapons in the room but not to bring them out into the street. We walked to the 66 stop and took the bus back to Hornstull. When we got home, Mom asked how it had been.

Good, said my brothers. They told her that we would go to the movies next weekend, I said that Dad seemed okay; he had bought fruit juice, three different kinds, he says hi.

He didn't call the next day, and we didn't go to the movies the following weekend. The next time we saw him, five years had passed.

Chapter Twenty-Nine

The first day was warm and cloud-free. Hector and Ina had slept in the Frigga, which turned out to be the smallest house, where Hector's parents normally stored their lawn mower. They woke up early, since Ingrid had taken out the chain saw and decided to cut some wood at seven in the morning.

I'm sorry, did I wake you? she yelled with sawdust in her hair, when Hector stumbled out of the Frigga.

After breakfast Hector took Ina to the nearby forest to be alone with her.

I tried to warn you, he said when they walked next to each other on a path that was just wide enough for Hector to put his arm around her.

What do you mean? Ina said. They are great. A real dream family.

Sometimes I wish my mom had an off button, Hector said.

She has a lot of drive.

The forest path was full of pine cones and needles and everything looked just as she had imagined, it was quiet except for the low, intense murmur of the sea.

It's impossible to get lost here, Hector said. If you get lost you can just follow the sound of the sea.

The forest opened up to a field, Ina felt as if they had been walking in a fist that all of a sudden turned into a palm. They stood in the blinding sunlight, facing a jumble of small trails that all led down to the wavy sea.

Are those blueberries? Ina said.

Crowberries, Hector said.

Are they okay to eat?

Yes, but they don't taste like much.

Ina ate one, and then one more.

We used them to build traps when I was a kid, Hector said. We hid in the forest and used air pumps and hoses to shoot crowberries at passersby.

Did it work?

Never. But in our imagination, we had created the world's first crowberry AK-47. In reality the berries barely made it out of the hose.

It doesn't sound like a trap.

It was just something we did, Hector said. To pass the time. And you see the brook over there?

He pointed towards a stream of red muddy water that slowly trickled towards the sea.

I don't know how many hours we spent trying to build dams there. In the beginning we used sand and then rocks and planks. Once a friend of mine came down to the beach with a wheelbarrow and a block of cement.

But . . . why?

It was just something we did, he said again. To . . .

Pass the time, Ina said.

He nodded. They had come down to the ocean, the sand was hard, it almost felt like walking on asphalt, except for the white seashells that cracked with every step.

Do you want to go north or south? Hector said.

This way, Ina said, and started walking, without knowing if she walked north or south.

Ina been here less than twenty-four hours and wondered why she felt homesick. Everything here was perfectly arranged, so normal, so structured, all family members spoke with one another, all stories had continuity, no moms tried to commit suicide, no aunts had mental problems, no sisters were taking drugs, still it felt so hard to breathe and she had a nagging worry that this was how her sisters felt in her presence.

Is your dad always this . . . quiet? Ina said.

Not at all. Only when Mom is around.

Do you two ever hang out?

Very rarely. He talked a lot more when I was young. He has been through so much shit.

What kind of shit?

Just crazy shit, Hector said. He picked up a stick from the ground and started peeling off the bark, while he told her about that time when his dad tried to go back to his country, believing that his Swedish passport would protect him, the police took both passports at the airport, they locked him up, they kept him for seven months, Enzo never talked about what happened in there, but Hector had read about the torture in that prison, the "wet submarine" when the head of a prisoner was pushed into a bucket with water, vomit, poop and blood, the "dry submarine" when a plastic bag was wrapped around the prisoner's head, the guards extracted nails and arranged mock executions, they used car batteries to give electric shocks . . .

How did he make it? Ina said.

Somehow he survived, Hector said. But I'm not sure he made it. Should we turn around?

Where have you two been? Ingrid said when they came back from their walk.

I showed her the sea, Hector said. And then we went for a walk.

You poor thing, she said, turning to Ina. You've been gone for three hours. Did he convince you to go all the way to Storån? Here, come, sit down, have a breather, do you want some cold lemonade? There are waffles. You must be so tired, walking three hours in this intense heat.

Enzo sat in the chair as the day before. He looked up from his crossword and waved.

It's not *that* warm, is it? Ina said.

The whole family froze. She had made a mistake, but she wasn't sure what it was.

What? Ingrid looked at her as if she was insane. It's almost *twenty-three* degrees, Ingrid said and looked at the thermometer to verify that her number was correct.

Twenty-three degrees, Ingrid said. In the shade! No, this heat is too much for me. Who's up for a swim?

They all went down to the sea, the young kids rode in a wooden cart that everyone referred to as a "skrinda," and Ina repeated the word silently to make sure she remembered it, *skrinda, skrinda,* and when they came down to the sea everyone put their towels in the wagon and Ina heard herself saying:

Is it okay if I put my towel in the "skrinda" as well?

Of course, you are part of the family, Ingrid said and smiled.

They started walking towards the horizon, first they had to get through a few meters of jellyfish and seaweed, then they walked for one minute, two minutes, after five minutes the water barely reached their knees.

Is it always this shallow? Ina said.

It's so great for kids, Ingrid said. Incredibly safe.

After ten minutes the water was almost up to their waists and everyone started diving, Ina looked back towards the beach, they were so far out that the skrinda looked like an insect. She took a deep breath and jumped headfirst into the salty water, trying to cleanse away the strange nervousness that wouldn't let go of her.

Did you tell her how we ended up here, Hector? Ingrid said as they were walking back towards the shore.

Not yet, Mom, Hector said with a sigh.

So let me tell you the story, Ingrid said, and she started telling Ina the story. The story lasted all the way to the beach and up to the house, there were many details, Enzo had worked as a consultant for the water treatment plant nearby, they had driven down, it was night, it was a full moon, they had stopped by the ocean, Ingrid and Enzo were young, they had snuck out of the car and swum in the ocean, and even though they had no idea what the area looked like, she knew that this was her place, she would live here, she would die here, and then they had found this plot of land, both these plots were for sale, but they bought this one, higher up, to avoid the wind from the ocean, sure the other plot had a better view of the ocean, but it's better with no wind than a view, right?

Ina nodded.

I think we made the right choice, Ingrid said.

Ina took a shower in the house where there was a sauna, a rusty water heater and spiderwebs in the corners. The warm water quickly ran out, but she kept showering under cold water, there were a bunch of old almost run-out packages of shower gels, she tried one package and then another, she kept thinking of the difference between Hector's family and hers, maybe it wasn't true that her family was chaotic and his family was proper, the biggest difference seemed to be the story, Hector's family always had a story, a perfectly neat, organized story, with a beginning, middle and end, with a main character and an obstacle and an enemy, with a complicated Before and a happy After, and in their presence, her own past seemed even more messy and complicated than usual.

When she left the shower and dried herself she wondered what a story about her family would look like, how impossible it would be to recount everything in the same unthreatening, contented way that Ingrid did. Or maybe it was only possible for someone like Ingrid, who seemed to turn everything that happened into neat packaged stories.

There was a knock on the door. Hector asked if she was done. He opened the door and let himself in, her towel fell to the floor, when they were done the water heater had filled up again.

In the evening they had oven-baked fresh salmon in the big house, salad and fresh potatoes, one big table for grown-ups and a smaller table for the kids and a blanket called "hästtäcke" for the kids who didn't fit around the smaller table. Ingrid asked Ina to sit next to her and as she sat down, Ingrid informed her that she really wanted Ina to feel at home here, everything in the fridge was hers, just come and go as you please, we really want everyone to be able to relax and be themselves here.

You have already said that, Hector said.

Ina smiled and thanked Ingrid. I do feel at home here, she said, and Ingrid beamed.

Everyone started serving themselves and as soon as they started eating, Ingrid said:

Now . . . Ina. Tell us a little about yourself.

Mom, Hector said. Let her eat.

I'm curious, that's all, Ingrid said with a broad smile. Let's start with your name. Why did your mom call you Ina and not a beautiful Arabic name, like Fatima? How did your parents meet? So I understand your father is or was a musician, is that correct? And your mom worked as a . . . salesperson? And your sisters, are you in close contact with them? Hector told me that you are studying international economics? At the university or Stockholm School of Economics? How long to graduation? Have you chosen a field of expertise? Hector mentioned that you played semi-professional basketball? What university did you play for in the U.S.? What do your younger sisters do? And how long has Evelyn owned a clothing store? And Anastasia is studying law, did you hear that Esmeralda, just like your friend Karolina, so exciting.

Mom, that's enough, said Hector. You must be thirsty, Ina, after all that talking. Water? Beer? Wine? Why don't you tell Ina about why we don't have any bottles on the table?

Ingrid smiled and started telling the story, Ina sent a thankful glance Hector's way, this seemed to be the only way to get Ingrid to change focus, and while Ingrid told the story of someone in her family's past who had been a drunk pastor and gambled away his farm on cards, Ina felt Hector's foot brushing against hers under the table, and even if it was just a few seconds of touch, through two layers of cloth, that touch meant the world for Ina, because it reminded her that she wasn't alone.

And that's why we never have bottles on the table, Ingrid said and looked like she was expecting applause.

Cheers, Enzo said and raised his glass. It was the first time Ina heard his voice.

I don't drink myself, Ingrid said, but I don't have anything against people who drink, my brother drinks, Enzo drinks, Esmeralda drinks, she drinks almost every day and I don't judge her for that.

Refill, please, Esmeralda said

One glass of wine per day keeps the doctor away, Ingrid's brother said. Would you like some wine, Ina?

Everyone looked at her to see what she would answer. Her body preferred to drink water, but she didn't want everyone to think that she was too afraid to ask for wine.

I would love some wine, she said. Just half a glass. And some water.

Ingrid looked at her as if she tried to decipher whether or not she could be trusted.

Back in the Frigga, when they had brushed their teeth and had silent and rather uncomfortable sex on two twin beds that kept sliding apart, Hector said sorry for his mother's cross-examination.

I'm flattered that she's so interested, Ina said.

She was seconds away from asking for your dental records, Hector said.

I just wish I knew more answers to her questions.

I thought you were just avoiding her questions.

No, I answered her to the best of my ability.

Come on.

At least I didn't lie, Ina said. Evelyn *has* been thinking of investing in that store, which would technically turn her into one of the owners.

And Anastasia as a law student?

Okay, that was a tiny white lie. I just couldn't tell them that she's a recovering drug addict, working at a preschool.

You could have said that she's a young person with artistic dreams.

Yes, but I choked, Ina said. I drew a blank.

Now you're speaking English again.

Sorry. I don't know why our mom left Tunisia. Or how my parents met. Or why they named me Ina. My parents weren't like yours, they didn't dress everything up in perfectly neat stories, they just lived their lives.

What happened between them? Hector said.

I will tell you tomorrow, Ina said and yawned demonstratively.

Chapter Thirty

n the fall of 1996 my father had been gone for a year. Sometimes I thought about contacting some friends of his to ask where he was, why he didn't call his sons, why he didn't love us, but then I realized that I didn't know his friends, I wasn't even sure if he had any friends. Before the divorce, when Dad had met up with a friend of his, there was always talk of favors and business opportunities, one friend was a person who worked for an embassy, and maybe he could help us to get a secondhand IBM computer at a reduced price, another friend was the person who introduced my dad to the idea of selling watches, he showed my dad the catalogs from Hong Kong and gave him a special referral code that made the watches cheaper, only later did my dad understand that his friend received even better prices, since he had brought them a new customer. When Dad started selling his watches at Hötorget, where his friend also sold his watches, their friendship ended. Still I reached out to him, he was the only person whose number I had, I called his home number, his wife answered, when I heard her Finnish accent I thought about the Mikkola sisters, I wondered where they were now, if Ina still believed in the curse, if Evelyn still dreamed of becoming a pilot, if Anastasia still used that orange bike, if they ever thought about me as I thought about them. The wife informed me with an eerily calm voice that her husband was dead, he died six months ago, he had been walking home from a bar, he had collapsed on the sidewalk, someone called the cops, not an ambulance, she said, with a faint tremble in her voice, but the cops, the cops came, her husband couldn't walk, he slurred, the cops felt the odor from his breath, they put him in a drunk tank with a rubber mattress, the morning after he was dead.

The autopsy showed that he had had a cerebral hemorrhage.

He wanted to be buried in Tunisia, his wife said. But we didn't have the money, so we buried him here.

I cleared my throat. I didn't know what to say, but I tried saying what I thought my future adult self would say.

I'm sorry for your loss, I said.

Thank you, she said. I still can't understand that he's gone. We were silent.

And you haven't heard anything from my dad? I asked her.

No, she said. Nothing.

We hung up.

When Dad disappeared I stopped playing tennis and started playing basketball. I tried to distract myself from the thought that he might be dead, that he had jumped from a bridge, that he had stepped in front of a train, by playing basketball until my hands grew calluses, at first by myself in Draken or with Juan, Andreas and Julius at Södermalmsskolan, or with Ellet at the Åsö gymnasium.

That summer, as part of the Water Festival, there were basketball courts on Sergels Square and we went there to play three-on-three, to look at girls, to eat ten-krona hamburgers, most people were from the poor suburbs, there was the red line crew, from Fittja, Sätra, Bredäng, Norsborg, there was the green line crew, representing Farsta, Bagarmossen and Dalen, there was the blue line crew, with Akalla, Kista, Husby, and everyone who came from the same area seemed to know each other, they gave dap, they nodded, they asked how their brother was doing, is your mom still in the hospital, is your dad back out, but Julius and I were by ourselves, we didn't have a crew, we were the only ones repping Hornstull, but we both had fathers from Africa who had left and never called, and we talked about everything, except our dads.

One day a short guy with shock-absorbing plastic glasses approached us and asked us if we were from Hornstull, I confessed, but quickly added my standard thing: "Yes, we grew up in Hornstull, but in the area of Drakenberg, which is part of the miljonprogram, and our dads are from Tunisia and Congo," which was my way of making sure that people knew I was real, I was down, I was not just a middle-class kid, just because I had grown up in the posh inner city, no, did I mention that I cleaned a restaurant with my dad when I was twelve (how many weekends did we actually do that?), I sold watches on Drottninggatan (again: how many times did we do that?), have I told you that I sold weird fake perfumes at the Skärholmen flea market with my dad (yes, yes, you keep repeating this, but again, was this a recurring affair or something you did once or twice or maybe five times (and does it really *count* as doing it when you were 100 percent *aware* that this increased your street cred (that somehow this activity *fit* (not with the person you were (but rather with the person you tried to be? (you were on your knees scraping dried-up puke at the restaurant (you folded up your leather suitcase full of watches at Drottninggatan and ran when the cops came (you were a kid, but already totally *aware* that this was good for your myth (it fitted your story (one day you would capitalize on this (you could use it as motivation when you tried to convince yourself (and the world (that you had started on the bottom and gotten yourself all the way up (that you were real (that you weren't a part of this society (but actually a part of something different (a parenthesis (an outcast (and if that's not the definition of middle-class (a person who is so comfortable in his status (that he's able to romanticize the working class (I don't know what middle-class is)))))))))))))))))))))).

Here are some things that I never admitted when people asked me where I was from: that my mother's father had been a really talented civil engineer, he had a well-paying job at the city planning office, for years he was responsible for creating an efficient system for handling the city's garbage, that my mom's mother was a teacher at Mariaskolan, where she had the famous singer Carola as one of her students, that both my Swedish grandparents loved to play tennis, that my mom had gone to the music school Adolf Fredrik, that my mom's parents lived in a big house in Älvsjö, it had three floors, a table tennis room, a TV room, a living room, where we celebrated our Christmases, big rugs on worn wooden floors, a huge-ass tree, a piano, a rocking chair and every Christmas, before we handed out the gifts, one of the elder men read an excerpt from the Bible, that part about Josef and Maria who were going to get taxed, my grandmother was a devout Christian, she kept giving me Bibles, every year, I have two of them on the bookshelf that is mounted to the wall where I'm writing this, one of them is on the bookshelf at my office, my grandparents had a summerhouse on the west coast, whenever I referred to it, I said that it was a "stuga," which is the Swedish word for "cabin," but no, it wasn't a cabin, it was three separate houses, that my grandfather had built "with his own hands," and I grew up ashamed of all these things, ashamed for having been born in the wrong area, ashamed of my privilege, ashamed that my grandparents had money, ashamed of being one of the kids with a summerhouse, just because I on some level felt that the summerhouse and the tennis and the Bible Christmases made me less what? immigrant? less street? less svartskalle? less real? Svartskalle was the only identity I had back then, if I wasn't a svartskalle, then what the hell was I, I wasn't a Christian, I wasn't a Muslim, I wasn't Swedish, I wasn't Tunisian, I had the genitals of a boy, but I looked like a girl, I had the age of a teenager and the height of a grown man, I had the shoulders of a seven-year-old and the acne of a fifteen-year-old, I listened to straight-up muddafucking gangsta rap, kill that bitch, suck that dick, and had the best grades in school, I claimed to be a womanizer and was a virgin, I claimed to be left-wing while planning to apply to the prestigious right-wing Stockholm School of Economics, Monday to Friday I was in school, making sure to never miss one class, especially now that Dad was gone, since our teacher had said that all unexcused absences would be counted against our final grades, and therefore I made sure not to be absent one single hour the first year, and then I managed to do it the second year as well, and the third year I missed one class, a morning session in chemistry (the same morning that Emma and I got together) and then I convinced the chemistry teacher to let me switch groups and take the same chemistry lesson with another class, just to avoid being absent (when we graduated in 1997 there was no mention of the absence on my report card and when I asked my teacher about it, she smiled and said that she had just made it up, so that we wouldn't play hooky), I read Nietzsche and Kafka and Camus and hated humanity while spending my days walking around the city with a smile on my face, holding doors for old people, helping mothers to carry strollers upstairs, not because I wanted to help but because I had such a strong negative image of myself and was so afraid that Dad's curse would become true that I had to prove to them (and myself) that it was possible for a person looking like me to be different than the person that I imagined they thought I was, so when someone on the basketball field at Sergels Square, the summer of 1996, asked me if I was from Hornstull, I had a wave of counterarguments to prove that I wasn't who I was, but the guy who asked didn't seem the least interested in me, he just looked up at me and asked me if I knew how to dunk.

Sure, I said. But only with a small ball.

Show me, he said and I took a small ball and ran towards the paint, one step, two steps, three, I jumped, I used my arms to get momentum, I reached towards the rim and barely managed to dunk the ball.

You really should be able to do it with a big ball, he said.

I know, I said.

You're so tall.

I know, I said again.

Like this, he said, and ran towards the basket with a big ball, jumped up in the air and dunked the ball over his head.

Two days later I saw Ina on the third court from the left, her hair was long and black and in a ponytail, normally people look shorter than they actually are on a basketball court, but she seemed to have grown even taller, she was the only player out there who wore a mouth guard, so every time she wanted to trash talk an opponent she had to take out the glistening plastic. She was playing with two short guys in matching red shorts, they were good, but Ina was better.

I know her, I told Julius.

Are you sure? he said.

Mmm, they lived in Draken a few years ago.

During a water break, I approached Ina, I walked slowly so that everyone seated on the wide stone staircase towards Drottninggatan would see that I was about to say hello to an old friend, that I also had pals here, that Julius and I weren't as lonely as we looked.

Ina! I said. Remember me?

She looked me up and down.

Sure, she said. You used to play in Akropol, right? With Maki?

No.

Are you Sami's brother?

No, I was a friend of Evelyn's. When you guys lived in Drakenberg.

A smile spread on her face.

I didn't recognize you with all those pim . . . Wow, you have grown. Look, it's Jonas from Drakenberg!

One of the guys in red shorts looked up from the bench, and I realized that it was Anastasia, her hair was shaved, I wondered what had happened, had she been sick, had someone torched her hair?

Want to play? Anastasia said, and nodded towards Julius, who was standing behind me. We took off our backpacks and joined one team each. Ina's team won easily, she played center, but shot three-pointers like a guard and grabbed rebounds like a power forward and played defense as if her life depended on it. When she was guarding me, I had the feeling that she had four arms, one arm touching my back to make sure that I didn't drive to the basket, another arm poking my ribs to make sure that I didn't go up for an easy shot, two extra arms constantly reaching in, trying to steal the ball.

Even game, Ina said, when we took a water break and they were up 21 to 5. I didn't care about the result, I just wanted to find a way to ask about Evelyn. I wanted to ask how she was doing, where she was living, what school she went to, what she read, what she listened to, who she dated, but the only thing I could come up with was:

So . . . How's Evelyn?

I took a sip of water after I had asked the question to show that I didn't care that much about the answer.

She's doing . . . good, Anastasia said. But there was a long pause between "doing" and "good."

Are you still in . . .

I became silent because I didn't know where they were staying at the moment, and I hoped that one of them would tell me, but neither Anastasia nor Ina said anything.

Ina is going to the U.S. to play in the fall, Anastasia said.

You're kidding me, I said.

No, it's true, Anastasia said. Tell him, Ina.

It's true, Ina said and bent forward to stretch her thighs in an attempt to hide her happiness. I got a scholarship to play for an American school.

Wow, that's incredible, I said. Congratulations.

Thank you.

What team are you playing in? Julius asked.

KFUM Söder, Anastasia said.

You're pretty good, no?

Not us. I play in the C team. It's a mixed team, boys and girls together. Different ages. We have never won a game.

But you have the league's coolest coach, Ina said. He played in the NBA.

I wanted to know more details about Evelyn, I wanted to ask for her phone number, I wanted to say that there was something about the Mikkola sisters that made me feel less alone, I wasn't in love with Evelyn, not at all, not then, not later either, this was something else, something that I couldn't find words for back then, and that I can't seem to find words for now either, maybe I wanted to stay close to them because my own older sister had been lost, maybe it was something else, but just as I was about to ask Anastasia for Evelyn's phone number, we were interrupted, a big fight erupted on the court behind us, shoves and your-mama insults, roundhouse kicks and slaps, flying kicks and hammer fists, someone fell, someone threw a fire extinguisher, someone folded a chair and used it as a weapon, security guards and batons, police officers and sirens, red line versus green line, or blue line versus green or everyone versus everyone, some ran towards the fight to help a friend, to not chicken out, Julius took my arm and pulled me backward, towards the subway, away from the chaos.

Chapter Thirty-One

The days passed and somehow Ina never told Hector more about her parents, sure it was vacation, but there was constant activity, everyone was playing board games or playing cards and if the sun came out everyone was swimming and if it was raining everyone should sit in front of the fire and if Sweden was playing everyone had to gather in front of the TV and when the antenna wasn't working everyone should tell Ingrid's brother to go up on the roof and fix it.

Every night Ina and Hector went to bed in the small cabin called the Frigga, which smelled of paint and turpentine. Every morning they woke up early when someone, always Ingrid, was making sounds with a rake or a hammer or an axe just outside their house.

Please, Mom, Hector yelled.

Oh sorry, I had no idea that you were *still* asleep, Ingrid said, as if she had never met anyone who had the ability to sleep until eight thirty on a sunny Thursday.

They had breakfast in the big house, Ingrid asked them what they had planned for the day, Hector said that they didn't know, and Ingrid gave them three or four ideas of what they could do, Hector reminded her that they were here on vacation, and then they normally ended up doing one of Ingrid's suggestions. Ina spent ten days trying to be the perfect girlfriend, she offered to help in the kitchen, she did the dishes, she made her special salad dressing, she went to the forest that everyone called the Enchanted Forest and walked a trail, without questioning what was enchanted about this particular forest, she went up the hill to a café and was amazed by the view, she went to an ice cream place and ordered the same ice cream as everyone else, she laughed at the story about Ingrid's brother who had managed to eat eight no nine no thirteen of these ice creams in a row, she agreed every time Ingrid explained that this summer's weather was extremely rare.

It's a bit breezy, Ingrid said when the wind was so strong that a birch next to the house looked like it was crouching to avoid getting ripped up with its roots.

Tomorrow it will change, Ingrid said when it had been raining for three days straight. Today we can eat outside, Ingrid said when it had rained for five days straight.

Ina didn't mention the appalling weather, she didn't complain that it was tricky to find a spot to read when people continuously tried to make conversation (what are you reading, is it good, it looks thick, is it Russian, there's food in the fridge, just take, feel at home). Ina didn't mention that she sometimes felt exhausted by all the words that Hector's family filled their vacation with, or that she was surprised to find herself thinking about her mom's wordlessness and missing it.

One night Ina decided to go to the Frigga after dinner to read and be by herself for a moment, Hector's family was playing a special card game that they always played, but Ina still wanted to go to the Frigga. The day after, Ingrid asked her if she was okay, was she sick, did she need some painkillers, as if this was the first time in this family's collective history that someone wanted alone time.

I'm fine, Ina said.

We were just worried, Ingrid said, as if Ina's alone time had destroyed everyone's evening.

When Hector wanted to make love, Ina tried to divert him, she didn't want to, she was too tired, maybe it was the ocean air or all the energy it took for her to stay somewhat normal in the closeness of his family, because every day it became harder to find things to say, especially when Ingrid asked her questions about her background. Ina felt more and more empty every day that passed, more lonely, more isolated, and all the things that were left to tell about her past felt unfitting to share (like that time when Evelyn came home and had been followed by four guys on two mopeds or when Anastasia overdosed on mushrooms or when their mom climbed up on the balcony railing and threatened to jump). One morning Hector woke her up and whispered:

You don't really want to stay here, do you?

I just woke up.

You are aware that we can go home whenever we want.

We have told them that we would stay until the . . .

We can go home tomorrow. Should we? Should we just go? Let's get into the car and go somewhere else. Do you want to?

Ina looked at Hector and realized that she loved him. They announced the news over breakfast.

We will leave earlier than planned.

Ingrid choked on her coffee. Enzo looked up from his crossword puzzle and smiled.

But why, Ingrid said. Why?

We just feel like it, Hector said.

But you just came? Is it the weather? Is it too cold in the Frigga?

Not at all, it has been lovely, Ina said. We just need a change of air. And we are visiting my mom also, on our way back to Stockholm.

Hector looked at her, they hadn't talked about this, but he played along.

Exactly, now we have been here and then we are visiting Ina's mom.

Ingrid looked at Ina as if she had strangled a cat. Enzo looked at Ina and appeared proud.

Esmeralda looked at Ina and gave a thumbs-up.

At the last dinner, Ina took command of the conversation, she told them, randomly, that her father had told them when they were small

that their great-grandfather had left his wife and children and emigrated to the U.S., he had arrived at the height of the Depression,
he stood in line for construction sites to get a job, when someone
was hurt they waved forth her great-grandfather, he built a number
of famous skyscrapers, including Rockefeller Center, he was actually
one of the steelworkers depicted in the world-famous photo *Lunch
atop a Skyscraper*. And suddenly Enzo opened his mouth and started
talking, it was the first time Ina heard him say more than monosyl-
labic words, he had also heard that there were Irish, Italians and two
Swedes depicted in that photo, there had been an article about it in
a local newspaper a few years ago, one of them had apparently come
from a village not too far from Falkenberg, Okome was the name of
it, Hector looked surprised, Ina as well.

That's probably one of my relatives, Ina said.

For a short second Ingrid lost control over her face. Then she
smiled and said: What an incredible story.

During the rest of the dinner Ina thought about that look that
had fluttered across Ingrid's face, and then quickly disappeared like
a cloud blowing past the sun. Was it irony? Or sarcasm? No. It was
disgust.

The following day, they shoved their luggage into the minuscule
trunk of the rental car and waved goodbye to the uncles and cousins and friends of cousins' kids, and drove towards the highway.
Ingrid had gone grocery shopping, she would only be away for
a few hours, but she had told Esmeralda to tell Hector to drive
carefully.

I can't wait for next summer, Hector said as they reached the highway and they both started laughing, they couldn't stop, Ina wasn't
even sure if Hector had been serious or not, but they laughed for
several minutes, they laughed without knowing why, they laughed
because they were low on sleep, they laughed because their families
were so different, they laughed because all families are so different,

and no matter how their families behaved, Hector and Ina would always be around, and they would build something new, and they would never become like their parents.

When are we meeting her? Hector said.

Who?

Your mom.

I just said that so we could . . .

I know. But it would be great to stop by. Can't you call her and see if it would be okay?

Ina took out her phone. She hadn't spoken with her mom for a couple of months, it had felt impossible to connect Hector and her, it just wouldn't work. She knew she was making a mistake, or maybe not, because Hector was sitting next to her, and there was a button that could remove the roof of the car and if you didn't like a place it was always possible to get into the car and drive somewhere else, and with tingling fingers she called her mom and asked if she wanted to be invited to lunch.

Where? was her mom's first question.

You choose, we have a car.

Who are "we"?

Hector and I.

Who's Hector?

Hector is my . . . Hector is my sweetheart, Ina said. Her mom was quiet for a couple of seconds.

There's a city hotel here with decent food actually, her mom said and Ina heard her speaking loudly and suspected that she was on speakerphone. We could meet there, maybe at one p.m., how does that sound?

That sounds great, Mom. See you soon.

Ina hung up and Hector smiled, which wasn't too strange, because he had no idea what he had gotten himself into.

Over the next few hours, Ina did her best to prepare him. She used the same strategy she used when correcting students' essays at the university; she started with the good things. She told him that her mom is incredibly generous, charming, and has a magical ability to enter a room and make everyone in the room like her, even before she says anything.

I don't know how she does it, said Ina. Evelyn has inherited some of that, but not all. And she's incredibly funny, quick-witted and a *fantastic* salesperson.

Evelyn? said Hector.

Mom, said Ina, with unnecessary sharpness because she instantly became jealous of her sister.

Gradually, Ina began mentioning the things that were harder to like, and just like when she corrected essays, she did her best to signal that what she didn't like was less important than the effect of the whole.

Mom had some delusions when we were growing up. She really liked moving. She talked quite often about a sort of curse that someone had put on her and her daughters, and as soon as she felt that bad energy had caught up with us, we moved.

Moved where?

To the next place. But the good thing about it was that we got to see so many different parts of the country, said Ina, wondering why she felt like an advertiser.

But wasn't it difficult not to have a sense of belonging? To never have friends? To constantly start over?

Ina thought about all the times she entered a new class and saw everyone's glances, from top to bottom and then up again.

We didn't need friends, she said. We had each other.

And your dad? said Hector.

He died, said Ina, without providing any more details.

Okay. Anything else I should know?

Yes. She's a bit crazy, said Ina.

Crazy?

Yes. A little crazy. Beautifully crazy. Unstably crazy. I mean, she has different episodes, and sometimes she's up, and sometimes she's down, and . . . we'll see.

Does she have a diagnosis?

If she does, said Ina, she probably has about seventeen different diagnoses. Just one thing: whatever you do, *don't* mention the curse.

Hector swallowed and looked as if he longed to return to the security of Ingrid's kitchen.

Chapter Thirty-Two

n the fall of 1996 I took the bus to my first practice with KFUM Söder. Anastasia had told me that they were always looking for players, and that most guys were unwilling to play in a team with girls on it, but when I arrived at my first practice there were only two girls there: Anastasia and a red-haired girl who I don't remember the name of, the rest of the players were chubby boys my age. Anastasia didn't seem too surprised to see me, her hair had grown out to a short stubble.

After a few practices, I realized that the real reason we had a hard time finding players was that we were the worst team in the league. We lost every game by at least thirty points and it didn't help that our home court was located in Fryshuset, a youth center infamous for housing a meeting place for racist skinheads in the basement.

But we didn't care, because Anastasia was right about the coach: Terrance Branford was the coolest coach in the league. He was American and had played in the NBA, he was tall as a tree and during warm-up Anastasia told me that his feet were so big that he kept his wallet in his shoes. And I remember thinking a lot about the practical challenges of having your wallet in your shoes, did he have to take his shoes off every time he bought something, or did he keep loose change in his pockets and the wallet in his shoes as protection from robbers, maybe it was a routine he had started when he was in the NBA, to confuse potential pickpockets. I couldn't fathom that I would be coached by someone who had played in the holy grail of basketball leagues and that he would coach thirteen teenagers who were too bad to play in KFUM Söder's B team (a team that was way weaker than the A team). It was just too good to be true. Before my first practice, I doubted that Terrance even existed. Maybe Anastasia and Ina had just made him up. Then I saw him and immediately realized that they had been telling the truth, he looked like an NBA player, he walked like an NBA player, he talked like an NBA player, and those shoes, they definitely looked big enough to carry his wallet and keys and a paperback edition of *Moby-Dick*.

During our first practice we worked on layups and screens, it was a normal basketball practice, but everything felt different, because Terrance spoke English with an American accent, and had played in the NBA, and kept his wallet in his sneakers. Everyone who played basketball dreamed of playing in the NBA, or actually, most of us just dreamed of being able to see a game courtside or just see a game live, or now when I think about it, back then, in the mid-nineties, most of us would have been overjoyed just to see a live basketball game on TV because the only way we could stay updated on the latest results in the NBA was to scan the notices in *Dagens Nyheter*, in the smallest font possible they summarized last night's results, they didn't mention any stats, we never got to know if Hakeem Olajuwon had made ten blocks or how many assists John Stockton had fed to Karl "The Mailman" Malone, no, the only thing they printed was the results, Houston Rockets, Utah Jazz 91–89, and we had to add everything else, the nervous time-outs, the cheerleaders, the kiss cam, the car commercials, the trash talk, the elbows, the technical fouls, the free throws, and then, as only a handful of seconds remained of the final quarter, four on the shot clock, last time-out, the players in a circle around the hoarse head coach, deciding which strategy to use, pass, pass, screen, shot, and now they are back on the court, the referee hands over the ball, inbound pass, the clock counts down, four, pass, three, pass, two, and time stops when someone, probably Hakeem, gets the ball and attacks the basket, he draws a double team and passes the ball to a point guard who is ready to unleash a three-pointer, and with half a second to go his fingertips release the ball and the mechanical sound of the buzzer echoes in the stadium, but nothing is over even if time is up, because the ball is still traveling through air and as long as nobody touches it after the buzzer, the game can go on for all eternity, the audience on their feet, their open mouths, the ball still moving towards the rim, it's a planet with a predetermined orbit, a heat-seeking missile, it reaches its peak and slowly descends, as a setting sun, gaping commentators, smiling mascots, sweaty referees, it's all over, but everything keeps going, because nothing is over until the ball actually touches the rim, and now it happens, finally, after a journey of a couple of years the ball lands in the hoop and with a slurping swoosh sound the Houston Rockets have defeated the Utah Jazz with a buzzer beater, but none of this was in the paper, we just had the result, and the rest we had to create ourselves with the help of NBA playing cards and our imagination and the VHS cassettes that Ina had started sending home from the U.S. to her sisters.

We could barely fathom that Ina was actually there now, in the United States, in that magical world of Coca-Cola and Nike, of Chryslers and McDonald's, of Skittles and Kentucky Fried Chicken, of strip malls and talk shows and drive-in movies and drive-thru restaurants, and once Ina had told Anastasia that she had actually seen a drive-thru funeral home, and at first we didn't believe her, but then Anastasia said that she had seen photos of it, it was true, they had a place where you could bury your dead without leaving your car, and to us it sounded like heaven, in the U.S. there was no jealousy of people who dreamed big, no rules that made it impossible to become a better version of yourself, the Americans had immigration in their blood, they welcomed everyone, or wait, maybe not everyone, but still the USA was the USA and even if we weren't good enough to dream of playing in the NBA, we could dream about going there one day, and checking into our motel and sitting there in our water-damaged room and watching actual NBA games live, but instead we were stuck here, in this small frightened country where everyone begrudged people who dreamed too big, where everyone tried to transform themselves into the smallest possible version of themselves, and instead of the NBA we had Basketligan, and instead of

Utah and Houston, we had teams from Södertälje and Köping and it didn't matter that they tried to change their names to Södertälje Kings or Köping Stars, it didn't matter that they tried playing hip-hop during their time-outs, it wasn't the same thing, it never would be.

Instead of going to games at Basketligan we went home to Anastasia's after practice, to a three-bedroom apartment in Kista where she lived with her mom and Evelyn. I always hoped that Evelyn would be home, I glanced into her room to see what posters she had on her walls, I used their restroom and wondered which of the toothbrushes was hers. Sometimes I asked Anastasia if Evelyn would be home soon and Anastasia always shrugged her shoulders as if she didn't know or didn't care, or both. Their mom wasn't working as much, she was mostly at home, the kitchen was full of dirty dishes, the living room was full of smoke, the plants had cigarette butts in the soil.

We gathered in front of Anastasia's fourteen-inch TV, not the whole team, but we who were part of the starting five, to watch the latest VHS cassette that Ina had sent. Anastasia had explicitly told Ina not to pause the recording during the commercials, because we loved the commercials too, almost as much as we loved the game, we had two national TV stations and they never showed commercials, the only time we saw commercials was before a movie started at a cinema, but here there were commercials nonstop, for cars and soda and insurance and medicine, but we preferred the game, how it made us feel, how it gave us alternative lives to lead, far from our reality in Stockholm.

I was Hakeem, since I was tall and had a Muslim second name and played center and was better at blocking shots than making them. Stanimir turned into Scottie Pippen, mainly because they shared so many similarities (their names started with an S, they were both forwards, they both had big flat noses). Erik became Horace Grant because Erik wore diving-mask-thick glasses and Horace Grant did too. Kristoffer wanted to be Jordan because he said that Jordan was the greatest, and we just looked at him as if he didn't understand the game, of course Jordan was the greatest, that wasn't even a question, the challenge was to find a player who matched your playing style, that's why Sami was Clyde "The Glide" Drexler, because he moved like a wave when he went up for a layup (but always shot air balls when he was outside the paint), and Simret was Robinson in the Spurs, because they were both calm and wide-shouldered (even if Simret was incredible during practice and a nervous wreck whenever we played games). Marco was Charles Barkley, just because they both got extremely angry, angry at the refs, at their teammates, at their coaches, at the too-bright lighting in the stadium.

The strangest thing was that Anastasia voluntarily chose to be Reggie Miller, even though Miller looked like a skeleton and was a much better trash-talker than he was a player, at least that's what we thought until he started winning over everyone. I used to think that Anastasia wanted to be Miller because Miller was the underdog, he was seen as a joke, and Ina had said that Miller's sister was one of the best female ballers in the world, and that compared with her, Miller was a nobody, and when I heard this I kind of understood why Anastasia wanted to be Reggie Miller.

Anastasia was also an underdog, she was one of two girls on the team, she was younger than most of us, she didn't live south of the city like the rest of us, she lived north of the city, and it would have made more sense for her to play on another team, a better team, a team closer to her neighborhood, like BK Järva, or Tensta BBK, she wasn't that far from Alvik territory, and Alvik was the classic basketball club that had more victories than any other team, Alvik was our Boston Celtics, their team was blonder than all other teams and they even had a green logo. But still Anastasia took the subway down to play with us, and even though she never said it to anyone, I always had the feeling that she had a hard time in her school, she kept coming to practice with strange bruises, her legs were covered with the kind of contusions you get when someone in your class spends the fifteen-minute break aiming their kicks at your thighs, once on a Tuesday practice she had multiple burns on her left arm, it looked like they came from cigarettes.

What's that? I asked her.

It's nothing, she said.

Once when Sami and I went to pick her up at her school, she was nowhere to be found.

We asked some girls who looked like they were our age if they knew where Anastasia was.

Anastasia? one of them said.

You mean the Crow, another one said and two of the three girls started laughing and the third girl just looked at us as if we were aliens.

Who are you? she said.

We play on the same team as Anastasia, Sami said.

They left the courtyard laughing, as if it was inconceivable that Anastasia, Sami and I were basketball players, even though we had the outfits of basketball players, sure we were rocking LA Gear sneak-ers instead of Nikes, and our shorts were no-brand size XL from Sta-dium, and our caps were fake Korean imitations of real Starter caps, but at least we tried. We hung around the empty school yard for fifteen minutes, waiting for Anastasia, sometimes practicing jumping up and touching the basketball hoop, sometimes setting up some in-visible plays, like an advanced alley-oop and behind-the-back dunk, with our invisible basketball. Then Anastasia appeared, she came running down the stairs.

Hurry, she said and we ran after her, behind us I saw a group of guys, they weren't running, they were just strolling down the stairs, pointing at us and laughing, one of them held a stick that looked like it could have been connected to a broom, another guy carried a backpack that looked just like the one Ina had sent to Anastasia from the U.S., he wore it on his stomach, so that it kind of looked like he was wearing a bulletproof vest.

Isn't that your backpack? I said.

No, he has a similar one, Anastasia said. I forgot mine at home.

We kept running, without really knowing why, and didn't stop until we had reached her apartment. We didn't talk about the guys in her school, I didn't ask her why her backpack wasn't at home, instead we inserted the latest VHS cassette that Ina had sent, and I hoped that Evelyn would come home, and I kept thinking that we would become better just by watching these games, but when the league started we still lost every game.

We lost against teams that turned up with five players and no bench players, we lost against teams younger than we were. Once we lost a training game against a team of girls, and when we returned on the subway even Anastasia aka Reggie Miller was quiet, we were bad, but we weren't that bad. There was just something that made us incapable of winning matches, and Terrance said that we had to work on our mentality. Next practice he started telling us about his time in the NBA, it was the first time he mentioned it, and I remember Anastasia's open mouth and Sami's irritated gaze directed at some kids who were bouncing a ball on the other end of the court.

Terrance said that all the best trainers in "the league" focused on mental training in combination with physical training, and we had the basics, we knew how to do layups, we could score in the paint, we weren't that bad at taking rebounds, but there was something in our minds that held us back.

We needed to work our brains instead of our feet, he said, and everyone nodded. If this would have come from anyone else, like our normal gym teacher, or a random coach who hadn't played in "the league," we would have just laughed. Our mentality, screw that, the mind is what it is. But our coach wasn't anyone, our coach knew what he was talking about, and he said he had cassette tapes that we could buy from him if we wanted to broaden our minds. He called them motivational tapes.

They are huge in the U.S., he said and all the big stars in "the league" listen to them and if you want to try it you can bring some cash to next training. Any questions?

I could see that Anastasia was itching to ask our coach if he had ever met Reggie Miller, and if Reggie Miller listened to these kinds of tapes, and if Reggie Miller seemed nicer off court than on court, and what kind of car does Reggie drive, and does he have a wife, and does she also play basketball, and is she super tall or of normal height and where do the basketball players get those ill-fitting suits with really long legs, or maybe these were just the questions that I wanted to ask about Hakeem the Dream, but nobody raised their hands to ask a question, and next practice most of us brought money to buy a cassette tape. They were a bit expensive, especially considering that they were bootlegs, they weren't even official bootlegs, it was just empty store-bought cassettes, some were TDK, some were Sony, ninety minutes in length, forty-five on each side, filled with material that our coach must have received from his coach in "the league."

Get ready for change, Terrance told us as he handed over the cassettes. You will remember this day forever, he said as he collected our money.

This cassette will change your life, he said as he put the money in his too-short cuffed sweatpants and not in his shoes.

I went straight home after basketball practice to listen to the tape. A man was speaking, at first I imagined him alone in a recording studio, howling to himself with that growly voice of his, then he asked the audience something, and I realized that he stood on a stage, he told the listeners that they needed to understand that they were in control of their own destiny, it will be hard to attain success, but that's what makes it interesting, he told them that true success comes from not giving up, from pushing through, from developing a strong mindset, from having the courage to persist, controlling your thoughts, getting up every day to work even harder for your dream.

Say AAHH if you're with me, the man said, and the audience answered, AAHH.

He told a story about a man who wanted success and his master took him down to the sea and pushed his head underwater and kept it there until he was close to passing out, and when he finally came up, gasping for air, his master said that when you want success as much as you want air, you will succeed, otherwise you will never make it. After forty-five minutes his speech was interrupted mid-sentence, I turned the tape over, on the B side another hoarse man spoke about the value of creating a meaningful life and the necessity of visualizing your goals.

Next game we came out swinging, we still lost by twenty points, but we played better, at least it felt as if we played better. At halftime we were only down by seven, and we were more focused, we didn't give up, and when Terrance gathered us in the locker room after the game, he said that this was the first time he had seen us play like an actual team. If we just continued to listen to the tapes and kept practicing we would soon win our first game.

We kept practicing, we kept listening to the tapes, and whenever we finished one tape, there were always more tapes that Terrance could sell us. One was dedicated to the power of God, one was more focused on the mechanics of the brain, but ultimately the message was always the same: If you want to change, you can, nothing can stop you, just visualize where you want to end up and you will reach your goal.

We kept losing but now we only lost by five points, seven points, three points. Teams that we had met before stopped joking around during warm-up, not because they were afraid of losing, they had lost games in the past, but nobody wanted to be the first team to lose against a team that had never won a game.

Chapter Thirty-Three

A waiter welcomed them and led them to a table in the middle of the restaurant, but Ina knew that her mother wouldn't feel comfortable there, too many potential eavesdroppers. So instead she stood up and asked another waiter if they could have one of the corner tables.

Absolutely, said the waiter, just give me two minutes. Three people, right?

Ina nodded.

Yes, three, she said, as if trying to understand it herself. Three people. Hector, Ina and her mother. She had never introduced a boyfriend to her mother and could hardly believe it was happening like this, spontaneously, in a city she had never been to before, at a lunch restaurant overlooking a sparkling river with a stuffed moose head on the wall.

The lunch rush was just over, several tables were covered with plates and breadcrumbs, used napkins and glasses with lipstick marks. They were a few minutes early. While waiting for the waiter to finish preparing their table, they got drinks from the self-service cooler and when they sat down they ate bread and butter to calm some of their nervousness. Hector seemed to want to be in the middle of a conversation when her mother arrived, and he was probably right, it would make everything easier. He looked out at the river and asked if she had ever tried fly-fishing, he said that he was looking forward to trying the food, did she know if the restaurant had any specialities, and Ina knew she should respond, she should say something, but despite talking nonstop throughout the trip, she was strangely incapable of uttering a word now.

The time arrived.

The time became five past.

She's not coming, Ina said with sudden certainty. Should we leave?

What do you mean?

I know she's not coming. This is so typical. We make plans, and she doesn't show up. Unbelievable. I knew it. Come on, let's go.

Ina, breathe. It's six minutes past. She'll come, Hector said, hoping he was right.

Twelve minutes past, Selima walked in from the town square, wearing black sunglasses, a checkered gray-black scarf over her shoulders, high-heeled shoes, with her gaze fixed firmly on Ina. Hector got up in an attempt to be polite, but Ina's mother didn't see him, she only had eyes for Ina. She walked straight in, past the waiter who wanted to show her to a table, straight through the team of middle school teachers who had finished their lunch and were lining up at the self-service coffee table.

My beloved daughter, she said, leaning forward for a cheek kiss. What an honor to see you here. How I have waited. HOW I have WAITED!

Hi, Mom. You're dressed up. This is . . .

Her mom turned in slow motion towards Hector. She moved as if she were on a stage and trying to be seen in the very last row of the theater.

And you must be Hector? What a pleasure to finally meet you!

Hector extended his hand through a cloud of perfume. She took his hand and pulled him towards her for a cheek kiss.

Please, sit sit sit sit sit sit! the mother said, sitting down. Have you ordered already? Monsieur? Please? Can we get some service here, please?

It's self-service, Ina whispered.

I'm a woman, not a cow, her mom replied. A reluctant waiter approached their table.

What are your specials today, young man? Selima said, switching to English.

They are . . . The waiter gathered his thoughts to find the English word for *torsk* (cod).

It's okay, she speaks Swedish, Ina said.

The waiter breathed a sigh of relief and recited the daily specials in Swedish.

I'll have the fish, Selima said in English.

It's self-service, the waiter said.

Selima nodded.

The fish, please. Torsken.

It's . . .

Look at me, I'm an old woman. I'm sick. My legs are hurting. I can barely walk.

Okay. Do you want potatoes or rice with that?

The waiter brought food to Selima, while Ina and Hector got food for themselves. On their way back to the corner table, they exchanged glances, a quick smile that whispered, "We'll handle this, just like we handled the car ride and Ingrid's interrogation and that misunderstanding when one of us accidentally went through the other's secret photo collection." They sat down, and Ina prepared to be overwhelmed by her mother's personality. She braced herself to listen to talk about energies and crystals, horoscopes and tarot cards. First, Selima would spend fifteen minutes talking about how incredibly popular she was in the neighborhood (the neighbors loved her, the children on the street always wanted to play at her place, the local politicians were so proud that she had moved here), and then she would spend the next fifteen minutes explaining why this particular place was not right for her. It was an uphill walk to the town square, the waiters at the City Hotel refused to serve her and sometimes, at night, when the wind was blowing a certain way, you could hear the sound of the nearby highway. But no. Instead, Selima turned to Hector and said:

How are you, Hector?

Good, thanks.

That's nice to hear. What a day we're having, huh? What weather?

Indeed.

Earlier this morning, it was cloudy, but now it seems to be clearing up, right?

Yes, it seems so.

Hector didn't seem surprised at all, but Ina couldn't touch her food. When would she take his hand and try to predict his future? When would she look at his lifeline and whisper that he should be very careful the next time he opens an avocado? When would she say: "I wouldn't go on a long trip for a few years if I were you"?

Selima didn't do any of that. She just sat there, in a half-empty lunch restaurant, and . . . conversed. Like a normal person. In a way she had never done when Ina lived at home. Hector and Selima discussed the weather for ten minutes, then they talked about the advantages of driving an automatic compared with a manual car. Selima said that new potatoes were still new potatoes, and Hector agreed, he also thought fresh potatoes were fresh potatoes, and Ina agreed too, without being entirely sure what she was agreeing to. Who was this person?

Do you like it here? Ina asked, almost in an attempt to bring out that old personality, the mother from before, the one who could never stay in one place for more than six months, who was convinced that everyone from librarians to pizza bakers to parking attendants were part of a larger conspiracy to make her life difficult.

Yes, said her mother. This is my place on earth. I'm going to stay here. But what about you, Hector? Where are you from? What do you do? How did you two meet?

Ina drifted further and further away from the conversation around the table. She saw her mother and Hector socializing, smiling, conversing. Selima signaled to Hector when he had white fish sauce in his beard, and when he missed a spot, her mom took her napkin and wiped it off.

Did you eat too much bread? Hector asked.

What? No, I . . . said Ina. They were almost done, and she still hadn't touched her food. She tried to understand what she was feeling. They were getting along, talking to each other, no outbursts, no paranoia, they were spending time together. Why did she feel so . . . deceived?

Coffee? Hector said, getting up. Milk, sugar? Ina went with him to the coffee trolley.

This is going really well, Hector whispered.

Absolutely, said Ina.

She's really nice, said Hector. Very easy to talk to.

They returned to the table. Selima smiled.

I'm so happy for Ina, she said. Young love. There's nothing more beautiful.

I'm happy for myself, Hector said. How did you and Raimo meet?

Selima cleared her throat. Ina smiled inwardly. Now it was coming. Now he was trying to dig into her mother's past, and she would close up like a bank vault. She would give her usual answer: "How do you think we met? We just met. First, we didn't know each other, then we got to know each other. What else do you want to know?"

But Selima signaled to the waiter to remove their plates, and then she began to tell the story. She said that Ina's father had been a musician, a young and Swedish-speaking man with Finnish roots, boyish and handsome, with a smile that set hearts ablaze from Haparanda to Ystad. He came from a small town in Blekinge and moved to Stockholm to get away from a family full of accountants. He was discovered on a dance floor; a promoter named Axel Stensvik asked if he could play the piano. Raimo shook his head and continued dancing, but the promoter came back later that evening and gave him a business card anyway. They hired Raimo to play the keyboard, it didn't matter that he couldn't play, everyone was lip-synching anyway, they wanted him for his incredible energy, his smile, his liveliness, his ability to ignite the audience. He pretended to play his keyboard in basements, TV studios, as an opening act for Tina Turner, and after a while he learned to play. He became really good, in fact. They started plugging in his keyboard, and for a while, he was one of Sweden's most respected keytar players.

Keytar? Hector said.

Guitar plus keyboard, Selima said.

So you met at a concert? Hector asked.

No, not at all, Selima said. Concert, haha, you're funny. No, we started talking to each other in a grocery store. He complimented my shoes. Then we had three daughters, then he died, snip snap, and that was the end of the story.

Selima smiled as if she had given a comprehensive answer.

Why do you always do this? Ina said. You talk about anything except your own story.

I'm uninteresting, said Selima. The sole purpose of my existence has been to give life to my fantastic daughters. Nothing has been more important to me than being a good parent. Providing my children with security and stability and . . .

Ina chuckled.

Mom. You gave us many things, but security was not one of them.

What do you mean?

We moved around our entire childhood.

Yes?

Every time we settled somewhere, made friends, found a basketball team, you uprooted us and forced us to move on.

Yes?

That doesn't provide security, does it?

But Ina . . . Selima smiled. I gave you the security that you would always manage. Regardless of the circumstances. Regardless of the idiots surrounding you.

But you were never there?

What do you mean?

You were never home? We moved to a new place, and then you went off to work, leaving all the responsibility to me?

You were always very responsible.

No, I was forced to be responsible because you were so damn . . . so damn . . .

Ina wanted to say "childish." She wanted to say "naive." She wanted to say "unstable." Instead, she said:

Absent.

More coffee, anyone? Hector said in an attempt to lighten the mood. Selima sighed.

You're right. I was absent. I loved you, but I never loved you more than when I was away for work. I don't know why it turned out that way. But it did. When I was away, I missed you, and when I was with you, I longed to be away. And I preferred longing for you, so I stayed away.

For years, Ina had imagined how this discussion would end if she ever dared to bring it up. In her version, Selima always raised her voice, rushed away with tears streaming, overturned the table, accusing her daughters of being too fragile, too sensitive, too Swedish. But now she had said something that almost resembled an apology.

I told Hector about the curse, Ina said.

Curse? Selima said, looking as if she was trying to remember the name of an old supporting actor. What curse?

Stop it, Mom. The curse you threatened us with throughout our upbringing. Have you forgotten about it, perhaps?

Selima swallowed.

Oh, that old curse.

Who was it who put it on us?

I don't remember.

But what was it about?

I don't remember that either.

That everything we love too much will be taken away from us, right?

Perhaps that was it, her mom said. But now I want to know more about you, Hector. Do you play any instruments?

There had been a glimpse of honesty in their conversation, and now it had disappeared.

When the coffee cups were empty and the waiters circled the table to signal that only their table remained to be cleared, they got up and headed towards the counter. All three of them tried to pay, Selima handed over cash, Hector and Ina presented their respective cards.

Their cards are stolen, said Selima and smiled. Cash is king.

She paid for all three and left a tip for the waiter who had served her cod.

When they stood on the square, it was cloudy again. They talked about it for a few minutes, this morning it was cloudy and then it cleared up, but now it seems to be getting a bit cloudy again, really, what strange summer weather we've had, really, we certainly have. Ina noticed that her mother's shawl was full of holes. Her high-heeled shoes were worn out, the leather on the left shoe was bubbly, as if the shoe had goose bumps. When they hugged goodbye, Ina could smell sweat beneath her mother's perfume.

Don't hold on to him too tightly, her mom whispered before they let go of each other.

They parted ways with promises to see each other again soon.

Chapter Thirty-Four

n November 1996 we had a home game, scheduled on the court in Fryshuset, by now we had gotten used to the racist graffiti on the walls, in the elevator, in the bathrooms, we knew that the skinheads had their meeting place in the same building, while we were doing layups on the fourth floor a bunch of teenage skinheads played pool in the basement, most of them were young, which was the most dangerous kind. They had shaved heads and black or military green bomber jackets with Swedish flags on the shoulder and fake Nazi tattoos on their hands. They had snuff under their upper lips and their girlfriends also wore bomber jackets and steel-cap boots but they kept their hair. Of course we were scared of them, but they knew that if they touched us they would lose their meeting spot, and we knew that if we touched them, well, actually that was never an option, they were young skins but still older than us, and when we came walking from the bus stop with our basketballs in our hands, the skinheads were standing outside, smoking and greeting us with a Nazi salute, shouting "Out with the scum!" and I always wondered if they did the same thing to Terrance.

The home game was against BK Järva, probably their fourth or fifth team, so technically we should have had a chance, maybe not to win, but at least not to lose by more than fifteen points. We were on the court warming up when the opposing team arrived. I heard someone yell "The Crow," and I saw Anastasia react as if someone had hit her in the face. On the other side of the court, I saw the guys from Anastasia's school. The one who had carried Anastasia's backpack on his stomach was smiling and waving, gripping an invisible penis that he slowly pushed in and out of his mouth while letting his tongue push out one cheek. His friends laughed, one of them cracked his knuckles.

This is going to be fun, one of them said.

Let's get ready to ruuuuuuuumble, the backpack guy said.

The referee arrived, he had forgotten his indoor shoes, so he officiated the game in his socks. Terrance gathered us and reminded us that we were special, that we had nothing to lose and everything to win. Maybe they are better on paper, but we are better prepared mentally, right? We nodded. Anastasia looked like she had swallowed an aquarium.

Are you okay? Terrance said.

Anastasia nodded and went out onto the court.

Oh, the Crow is in the starting five, one of the guys said, and the opposing team's bench started chanting, CROW CROW CROW, and I remember wondering if they called her the Crow because she liked black clothes, or because she had dark energy, or because she had short black hair, or if it was the Crow for mythological reasons.

The referee took the ball, and we were ready for the tip-off. I was the tallest and responsible for getting the ball. The referee leaned forward, he had yellow socks, and one of the socks had a hole, not in the front, strangely, and not on the heel either. I remember thinking about that, just before I jumped up for the ball, how come he had a hole on the side of his sock. Then he blew the whistle and threw the ball up, and I jumped like I had never jumped before and tapped the ball to Anastasia. When she caught the ball, she bounced it a few times, as if to make sure the ground was still there. Her eyes were focused on the defense, on her opponent, on the basketball hoop. She faked right and went left, running all the way to the basket, an easy layup, and we were in the lead.

That day, I realized that it didn't matter why they called her the Crow before because from now on they would call her the Crow because she could soar, because she could single-handedly score twelve points in the first five minutes, because she played such intense full-court defense that the guy who had taken her backpack started complaining to the referee, who told him to "man the fuck up," which was extra funny coming from a referee with yellow socks, gliding back and forth on the court as if he had skates on. After three turnovers, we were leading by twelve, something that had never happened before. The opposing team's coach made some substitutions, and now the backpack guy's buddies came onto the court, and it turned physical.

They played rough against everyone, but especially against Anastasia. They elbowed her in the stomach, they tripped her and raised their hands in the air to show it was an accident, they kneed her when she approached the paint. Once when she went up for a three-pointer, one of the guys hammered her down, he just rushed at her and pushed her so hard that she landed on her back, and I heard Terrance roar from the sideline. But no matter what they did, they couldn't stop her.

Somehow, she kept making her shots. The referee called a flagrant foul first and then a technical foul when the opposing team started complaining, and Anastasia went to the free-throw line. She missed the first free throw.

How are you doing, Crow? one of the guys shouted. Nervous?

Anastasia didn't look at him. She bounced the ball and made the next free throw. Then she closed her eyes and made another free throw.

Stop clowning, Terrance shouted from the bench, but I could see that he had to make an effort not to laugh because Anastasia was on a different planet. I had never seen anything like it. She was always better at talking than shooting, but on this day, she was on fire. She had twenty-three points at halftime, and with three minutes left in the game, we were leading by nine points. We could hardly believe it, but we actually had a chance to win our first game.

Then I heard one of the guys say something about Ina. It was the backpack guy, and instead of the usual trash-talking, like "Your sister Evelyn sucks dick" or "Your mom is a whore," he shouted:

Anastasia! Things didn't go so well for Ina in the USA, huh?

Anastasia looked at him.

Do you know how I know? I saw her collecting bottles for recycling at Kista Centrum yesterday.

Even the referee seemed surprised by this kind of trash talk.

Anastasia took a breath. At first, it seemed like she didn't care. Then the guy said it again, describing how Ina looked while picking up the bottles. He said it wasn't surprising that she needed to collect bottles with a sister who was a whore and a mother who was . . . Anastasia roared and kicked the basketball at him, she rushed at him, tackled him to the ground, punched him in the face, headbutted him. When our team came running to try to pull her away, she bit him on the leg.

The referee sent Anastasia to the locker room, the opposing team got free throws, and since Anastasia wasn't there, we immediately lost possession, and in the end, they won by three points.

We gathered in the boys' locker room afterwards. Simret was close to tears, Sami said we should go down to the skinheads and ask them to kick the shit out of our opponents, Marco slammed his hand so hard against one of the lockers that his knuckles were still purple at the next practice. There was a knock on the door. Anastasia came in. She had showered and changed.

Terrance came in after her, always with that graceful sideways bow he had to perform to avoid hitting his head on the doorframe.

I just wanted to say that I'm proud of you, he said. You won this game. Then he left. I looked at Anastasia. She was the only one smiling.

Chapter Thirty-Five

For the next half hour, Ina sat silent.

Is everything okay? Hector said. Wasn't it how you imagined? Did I do something wrong? Are you angry at me, Ina? Or angry at her? Should I have paid? Did you want to stay longer? Hello, I'm talking to you, can you hear me? Are you planning to stay silent all the way to Stockholm? Mature. Very mature. Well, I'll keep talking, then. I can talk to myself if that's what you want. I thought it was really nice. I enjoyed talking to her. I find her fascinating. It was lovely to hear more about your father. I'm really glad we stopped to see her. Aren't you? Hello, can you hear me or not? Did you notice she only used her left hand while eating? She looked a little pale. Did you notice she smelled a bit . . . I don't know what to call it. Stuffy? Like she hadn't been outside in a while?

Ina didn't know what to say, so she stayed silent. She wasn't angry or sad, she was just amazed that the mother she had wanted her whole life had been there all along. It had only taken a stranger and a lunch restaurant at the City Hotel to reveal her.

Chapter Thirty-Six

ater, when I had stopped playing for KFUM Söder, when TV3 had started showing NBA highlights on Saturdays, when there were actual stores where you could buy official Starter caps, I ran into Sami at Åhléns. He told me he had seen the collector's card for our coach. Terrance Branford had apparently only played one season in the NBA, averaging two points and three fouls per game. We laughed a little about it, that the person who meant so much to us had only played one season and averaged two points.

And even later, as I'm writing these words, in the spring of 2021, when the world has shut down due to a pandemic, when the fellowship I received to go to New York and write a novel has been postponed, when it is uncertain if we will ever get there, when all NBA games are played in front of empty stands but can still be streamed online to the whole world, when all knowledge is available, I begin to wonder about that statistic. I search for "Terrance Branford" and "NBA statistics" and it turns out he was drafted three times by three different NBA teams, first by the Cincinnati Royals (as the 51st pick), then by the Lakers (as the 212th pick), but he never played a single game for any of these teams. He played in Italy and then in Switzerland, and then he returned to the NBA in 1972 to play for the Dallas Chaparrals, but he only played one game for them, and during that game, he totaled no points, no free throws, no three-pointers, no dunks, no rebounds, no blocks, no steals. His entire NBA career is summarized by a long series of zeros and a one (a foul that probably led to him being substituted again).

The last time I saw Terrance was in the subway at T-Centralen. He was going down the escalator, I was going up. He was wearing a yellow reflective vest, I was with my children. He didn't look at me, I didn't look at him.

Part III

Chapter Thirty-Seven

When Anastasia received her first paycheck, she went into town to buy gifts for her sisters, a symbolic way of saying thank you for the past six months when they had paid for everything for her. She emerged at T-Centralen, took the escalator up to street level, and crossed the black and white triangles at Sergels Square. Maybe she thought about that summer when she and Ina played basketball here, maybe she thought about the huge fight, maybe she thought about me, maybe she just remembered me as that "clingy guy who joined her basketball team because he was in love with Evelyn," but most likely she just crossed the square without remembering any of that. It was so long ago and didn't matter today. She entered the tunnel to the luxurious department store that she hated but still visited occasionally, just to be reminded of everything she disliked about this money-hungry city. She passed the luxury pen section, luxury chocolates and luxury tea. In the kitchen department, she spent fifteen minutes feeling the handles of various luxury frying pans and testing the weight of different knives. She was there just long enough for the sales staff to call the guards, but when the guards arrived, Anastasia chose one of the most exclusive Japanese knives and signaled to the surprised and suddenly very friendly saleswoman that she wanted it wrapped.

Anastasia moved towards the perfume department. The security guards weren't sure what to do now. She looked as she always did (torn tank top, ripped jeans, piercings, and self-cut hair), but now she carried a bag that signaled she had shopped here and potentially could shop more.

Anastasia spent fifteen minutes trying out different perfumes, enough time for the security personnel to leave her alone. She wanted to buy something for Ina that she wouldn't buy for herself, something that was 100 percent impractical, not a knife, not a frying pan, but rather . . . She asked one of the painfully face-lifted women to fetch the most expensive soap they had and wrap it up.

What's this? Ina asked when she returned home from her road trip with Hector.

It's for you, Anastasia said.

Ina opened the package.

Wow, Evelyn said, recognizing the logo and knowing approximately how expensive the soap was.

How much did you pay for this? Ina said.

It's a gift, Anastasia said.

Thank you, Ina said. How expensive was it?

Please take the gift and don't worry about how much I paid for it, Anastasia said.

Look, I got a kitchen knife, Evelyn said, looking as if she had wanted the soap.

Thank you, Anastasia, Ina said, gazing longingly at the shiny knife.

Evelyn placed the knife in a kitchen drawer. Ina took the soap and put it in her wardrobe.

Aren't you going to use it? Anastasia asked.

Absolutely, Ina said, placing it reluctantly in the bathroom.

Anastasia smiled when she saw how difficult this was for Ina. She knew that if Ina had lived alone, she would have asked for a receipt, gone back to the store and exchanged the soap for money. It wasn't because Ina was broke, far from it. She had study grants and student loans, and she worked part-time at some kind of financial office near Thorildsplan. She might not earn as much as Evelyn, but she still earned enough to set aside a little money each month and invest in index funds. It was all thanks to planning, Ina used to say. The planning that made her unable to make a purchase without reading consumer reports beforehand, the planning that made her regret every purchase, especially if it was something that brought her joy, something that wasn't an absolute necessity. She felt anxious, found faults in the product, tried to return it or give it to one of her sisters. Anastasia was sure that the luxury soap would soon go back into the wardrobe; it wasn't possible in Ina's world to use luxury soap every day. Her hands weren't worth it. If she surrendered herself to such simple pleasures, she wouldn't know where it would end. Soon she might spend all her money on soap instead of investing in index funds. Anastasia counted down the days until the soap would disappear, to be saved, to be used on special occasions, to be brought out when they had guests or something to celebrate. To stand on a shelf in the wardrobe for ten years and then be taken out, smelled and, realizing it had gone bad, thrown away. But the strange thing was that the soap remained there, day after day, week after week, and Ina used it. She enjoyed it, and when the soap ran out, she filled the bottle with generic soap from a refill bag and insisted that the scent from the original soap was still there. She just had to close her eyes and smell properly, and it was there underneath everything else.

Chapter Thirty-Eight

n spring 1997, Anastasia stopped coming to practice. No one knew why. This was before mobile phones, and she didn't have a pager. The only way I could contact her was through her home number, and I remember calling it again and again from our landline phone, but I never got a response. There was no answering machine, no clicking sound disconnecting the call after thirty seconds. The phone just rang and rang. When no one answered, I decided to go to Kista myself. I took the red line to T-Centralen and then the blue line northwest. I got off the subway and walked towards the exit with that shameful nervousness I always felt when I was alone in a suburb where I didn't belong, which basically meant all suburbs, both rich and poor ones. But the square was empty, and the only people I saw as I walked towards the sisters' building were a few drunk men on a bench.

I entered the building and took the elevator up. The sisters' last name, which had been written by hand on a piece of white masking tape on the mailbox, had been removed. Next to the sticky residue from the tape were the stickers Anastasia had pointed at and said, "These were here when we moved in," as if she was embarrassed by them. One sticker said, "Give blood, play hockey," and the other said, "Be the best with *Buster Sports Magazine*." The doorbell had been broken the last time I was here, and it was just as broken today, the black round button was stuck, and when I pressed it, there was no sound. So I knocked instead. I knocked three, four, five times, and when no one answered, I waited and looked at the stickers, wondering if they had some secret meaning. Maybe I could figure out where they had moved by deciphering the code they had left behind. I wondered if many hockey players were blood donors. I wondered what it was about *Buster Sports Magazine* that made its readers the best.

Before leaving, I looked through the mail slot, I felt a gust of wind from the apartment, I saw a stack of advertisements but nothing else, no shoes, no carpet, no trash bag waiting to be thrown away, no signs that they still lived there (but no real signs that they had moved either, I convinced myself). As I left the building, an old lady with a metal cane entered. I held the door open for her, and when she thanked me, I asked her if she knew what had happened to the three sisters who lived on the third floor.

You mean the two sisters? she said.

No, there are three sisters, I said. But one of them has been playing basketball in the U.S., so maybe you haven't seen her.

Oh, there were only two girls, she said. Two girls. And their mother. And another woman.

Yes, I know, I said, speaking louder because I thought she had hearing problems. But the other woman is their sister. She has been playing basketball in the U.S.

The U.S.?

At UCLA, I added, which was an utterly unnecessary lie because I knew Ina was attending some small, unknown university near Austin, and the chances of the old lady being familiar with UCLA were nonexistent.

Poor girls, she said. I don't know what happened to them. Not after their mother went crazy and jumped from the balcony.

Chapter Thirty-Nine

n September 2000, when everyone else had already had their vacation, Anastasia took a few days off and bought a last-minute train ticket to Gothenburg to visit her friend Fabricia, who had moved there the year before to attend Valand, the second or third most prestigious art school, depending on who you asked. Despite having lived in many different places, this was Anastasia's first visit to this bizarre city. She walked out of the train station and was almost hit by a chiming tram. The city claimed to be the second-largest in Sweden, but as she walked around the city in the afternoon, went into a large shopping center, followed a pedestrian street, passed an apparently famous statue, she kept seeing the same people, not just people who looked alike, but exactly the same individuals, again and again. She couldn't understand how Fabricia could voluntarily live here. But then again, she had gotten into an art school, which was much more than Anastasia had achieved since high school.

They had arranged to meet at a place called Järn Square, and when Anastasia asked a lady with a dog for directions, the lady spent at least five minutes trying to explain the way.

First, you have to cross the canal, then follow that street, and then keep going, and then you go straight ahead, and when you reach a church, just continue forward.

So, essentially I should just go straight ahead? said Anastasia.

Yes. Straight ahead. Just keep going and you'll see it.

Ten minutes later, she reached the square, and despite her being early, Fabricia was already there, with her big smile and dangling earrings. They screamed, hugged each other, and passersby couldn't help but smile. Fabricia wiped a tear from her eye, and Anastasia was reminded of one of the things she missed most about her friend: her ability to experience her emotions without shame or guilt. It was a rare ability in people, and even rarer in the art-oriented high school where they had first met, where Anastasia had sought refuge from the group of boys who put gum in her hair and called her the Crow.

Before starting, Anastasia had a clear image of her future classmates: parading around in black berets and black makeup, both boys and girls, quoting Russian poetry, having been to art exhibitions since they were children, their parents knowing gallery owners and museum directors. They would come to the first class with an easel under one arm and a guitar under the other, or no, the guitar was too modern, a lute, they would play the lute. But when she started high school, she was struck by the fact that most of her classmates looked and spoke like small accountants. They didn't smoke, they didn't paint, all they did was theorize. They read postcolonial thinkers and quoted feminist scholars. They had cats named Žižek and planned interactive performances or installations that required a lecture to be understood. At the same time, they were well-informed about whose artwork was being sold for what price. This and that piece was bought by the Moderna Museet for so much, and this and that artist had just been invited to the Venice Biennale. There were two students who were different, who didn't prioritize career first and creativity second. One was Fabricia, the other was Mathias, and Anastasia became friends with both. Fabricia continued to create, Mathias stopped. Fabricia moved away from the city, Mathias stayed. Fabricia had made contact with a gallery, Mathias convinced himself that his gender, skin color and creative practice were so outdated that he switched brushes for needles.

On the way to an anarchist café, Fabricia told Anastasia about her classmates and teachers, and then said that they had to try the local specialty.

What is it? Anastasia asked.

For some bizarre reason, their thing here is sandwiches, Fabricia said. Everyone sells these fairly cheap, pretty disgusting sandwiches. You have to try one.

They entered the café and ordered coffee and two sandwiches, one with hummus for Anastasia and one with shrimp salad for Fabricia. Sitting at a corner table, Fabricia leaned forward and asked about Mathias.

Before she answered, Anastasia fetched some paper napkins because she knew what was coming. She hadn't talked to Mathias since New Year's.

Is everything okay? Fabricia asked.

Anastasia told Fabricia everything she knew about Mathias, how he had lost control after the recent rejections, how he started doubting his talent, how he had gone from taking a little on weekends to buying larger packages and starting to sell. At first, she had tried to save him, then she had tried to go along with him, and then New Year's came and she realized he was beyond saving.

Fabricia cried, and Anastasia handed her some paper napkins. It's terrible, she said. He was the best of us.

Not better than you, Anastasia said.

But he had something else, Fabricia said. There was something raw and unfinished in his work. Didn't he get accepted anywhere?

Anastasia shook her head. But hey, neither did I, she said.

It's not the same, Fabricia said. You only applied to one place, and how many hours did you spend on that application? Three? Barely?

I don't care, Anastasia said, but she wasn't entirely sure if she was being honest.

What are you afraid of? Fabricia asked. I promise, if you really make an effort, you'll get in.

At Konstfack?

At whichever school you want, Fabricia said. Mejan, Konstfack, Beaux-Arts. But there's something holding you back, and you have to figure out what it is.

When they left the café, the sky had turned dark. They had been talking for three and a half hours, time had disappeared, as it does when you meet an old friend who knows you better than you know yourself. It was painful to realize that this was how it would be from now on. Fabricia would stay here for at least three more years, maybe more if she did a postdoc here, maybe forever if she met someone and decided that this windy city full of deadly trams and soggy sandwiches was her new home.

As they hopped on one of the trams and headed towards the apartment Fabricia shared with some of her classmates, Anastasia wondered if she could ever move here, what life would be like, so far from her sisters. She wondered to herself why she didn't feel more jealous when Fabricia talked about her courses. She wondered if the reason she hated this city so much was that it had taken Fabricia away from her.

When they arrived at the apartment, Fabricia's friends had prepared a vegan stew, and they had three boxes of wine for nine people. They ate, went out to smoke, drank, started smoking indoors, talked about going to a club, decided to stay at home, hated on contemporary artists, showered love on dead artists, criticized the Venice Biennale, showered love on the Berlin Biennale.

As the clock approached midnight, one of Fabricia's friends leaned forward towards Anastasia and asked if she knew Arabic. Fabricia looked at her friend as if he had uttered an insult. Anastasia felt flattered instead, as it was rare for people to pinpoint her ethnicity, and it was always Evelyn and Ina who received those questions.

Shwaya shwaya, Anastasia said, which was Evelyn's standard response, meaning she knew "a little, little" Arabic. Which wasn't entirely true, as neither of the sisters spoke their mother's native language; they only knew scattered things like *money* ("flous"), *thank you* ("shukran"), *hello* ("aslema") and *goodbye* ("beslema"). The guy who asked the question switched to Arabic and spoke for at least ninety seconds before Anastasia interrupted him and explained that she hadn't understood a word.

Sorry, she said. We never learned Arabic, even though our mom is from Tunisia. She thought it was more important for us to learn other languages.

The guy told her that he had learned Arabic in Tunis, five years ago, but unfortunately, he had forgotten most of it now. Then he said a few more phrases with such beautiful pronunciation that Anastasia felt like kissing him. He mentioned that the school had been great, a nice mix of Tunisians and foreigners like him.

Aren't you Arab? Anastasia asked.

I'm from Colombia, he said, smiling. You do know that the Tunisian government offers scholarships to all Tunisians living abroad who want to learn Arabic, right? They pay for the flights, school fees, and I think you even get free meals.

Anastasia had no idea about this, yet she nodded and thought about her mother, why it was so important to her that they learned any language except Arabic. English, yes. French, mais oui. Chinese, shì de. Arabic, well, inshallah, when you have time, it's not a language for the future, her mother would say. It's a historical language, and sometimes Anastasia wondered whose past she was referring to.

Around two in the morning Anastasia and Fabricia changed their minds and decided to go out, everyone else stayed at home, they took a taxi, and the club was gigantic, one floor was decorated like a living room, with sofas along the walls and an indifferent moose head above the DJ booth, a crowded dance floor. Anastasia and Fabricia danced, and a guy kept creeping up behind Fabricia, she moved three times, but the guy continued to follow her, always behind her, grinding and smiling at his friends.

Finally, Anastasia lost her patience. She asked Fabricia to go and fetch two glasses of water from the bar. As soon as Fabricia turned her back, Anastasia reached out her hand towards the guy. From a distance, it probably looked like she wanted to shake his hand. Maybe she was jealous of all the attention he had given her friend, or perhaps she wanted to propose a threesome or a quick blow job in the restroom, but when he smiled and tried to shake her hand, she grabbed his elbow and locked it in a firm grip, she took out the butterfly knife she still carried out of habit and showed him exactly where she would cut him: here, here, here and then here, she told him to nod if he understood, and he nodded and nodded again and when he returned to his friends, he looked pale and had four holes in his polo shirt.

Fabricia fell asleep in the taxi on the way home. Anastasia woke her up and half carried her to bed. Then she took her toothbrush from her backpack and brushed her teeth while thinking about the French guy she had met one night at Tegel Airport. Laughing, he had said that all the Swedish girls he had met (he made it sound like there were hundreds) had two strange things in common: a) they drank more alcohol than French girls, and b) they always ended their drunken nights by brushing their teeth.

Anastasia checked her phone. No message from Mathias. But two messages from her sisters. Ina asked if she had heard anything from their mom, expressing a bit of worry as she hadn't answered her phone for several days. Evelyn messaged that Ina apparently wanted to take them to an "aquarium with Hectore" (Anastasia wasn't sure why she called Hector "Hectore"). Anastasia put her phone away, put on a large sleep T-shirt, took off her jeans, and crawled into bed next to Fabricia. As she lay there, between her warm friend and the cold cement wall, in the sounds of a slowly awakening city, birds chirping, footsteps from newspaper delivery boys, she felt a sudden urge to cry. She quickly pushed the tears away and reminded herself that she wasn't one of those people who cry for no reason.

Chapter Forty

According to the neighbor, it happened a few days after Christmas Eve, she had been at home and heard people screaming, but she had grown accustomed to the screams, she had been living here for twenty years, and ten years ago, you could leave your bike unlocked on the street, now it gets stolen even if you lock it, it's true, it happened last year to one of her grandchildren, they came to visit her, she locked their bike outside the building, and an hour later the bike was gone, there are gangs selling drugs, people grill food on balconies, they smoke in elevators, and if she could move, she would, but she can't because at the same time she loves this area, she has lived here too long to move, she loves the forest and the growing shopping mall and the proximity to the subway and the people, the people are fantastic, they help her carry groceries home, they stop by and knock on her door if they haven't seen her in a while, they genuinely care about us, the elderly, they respect us, it's just a shame that they're so criminal, that they can't keep their hands to themselves, that they don't understand that they live in a country with law and order, she tries to be a good neighbor, when the two sisters moved in with their mother, she welcomed them to the building, she knocked on their door and kindly informed them about the rules, she told them about the ban on grilling on balconies and the no-smoking rule in the elevator and she immediately noticed that the two daughters were completely different, one daughter politely thanked her for the information and wished her a nice day, the other daughter shrugged her shoulders and tried to close the door in her face, the polite daughter said she could knock if she needed help with anything, the rude daughter asked if she got paid to be the building's police, and the woman was convinced that it was the younger daughter's rudeness that made the mother jump from the balcony, the mother was sick, there was something wrong with her, she needed medication, she never went out, the children did the shopping, cooked the food, bought Christmas presents for themselves, wrapped the presents and opened the door when someone from social services came to check on them, the children assured them that everything was fine, everything was going well, their mother had a job, she just had some difficulty managing it right now, the neighbor didn't know that Ina had wanted to stay in the U.S. for another six months and that's when the mother started threatening to jump from the balcony, she didn't know that Ina had cut her semester in the U.S. short and come home earlier to take care of her mother, she only knew that Anastasia was rude and that Evelyn was being pursued by older men in cars and on December 29, 1996, the mother had climbed onto the balcony railing and jumped, it's true, go outside and look at the bushes under their balcony, if it wasn't for those bushes, she would have died, the neighbor said and nodded as if she had been responsible for planting the bushes.

Chapter Forty-One

When Anastasia came home, she started looking through her moving boxes in search of her Tunisian passport. She knew it had to be somewhere, just not where, she found old letters from boyfriends, old diaries, old SIM cards. But no dark green Tunisian passport.

Why do you need it? Evelyn said.

I heard about a language course in Tunisia, Anastasia said.

Since when are *you* interested in learning *Arabic*? Evelyn said, with a tone signaling that the combination of Arabic and Anastasia was impossible to reconcile, like orange juice and toothpaste, like water and oil.

What do you mean? Anastasia said. I've always wanted to learn Arabic. And they pay for everything, she added when Evelyn looked like she questioned her sanity.

I wouldn't go down there if they paid me, Evelyn said.

Anastasia was close to saying that Evelyn has indeed done quite a few repugnant things for payment, but chose to focus on searching through her boxes. When she couldn't find the passport, she started wondering if Mathias could have stolen it. But what would he use it for? Maybe sell it to someone? But who?

A few days later, Ina came home from Hector's, and since Anastasia still hadn't found the passport, she asked her older sister if she had any idea where it could be.

I have mine here, Ina said and walked up to the large wall-mounted bookshelf in the living room and pulled out a perfectly organized binder with plastic pockets, where one of the first ones contained her passport.

And you haven't seen mine? Anastasia said.

Ina shook her head.

Mine is here, Ina said. In this binder.

I see it, Anastasia said. You're so organized.

Sorry. Why do you need it? Ina asked.

I'm considering applying for a language course, Anastasia said. In Tunisia.

Yet another application? Ina said.

What's that supposed to mean?

Maybe Mom has it? Ina said, trying to change the subject. Have you heard from her?

Anastasia sighed. She hadn't seen her mom all year, and she knew that if her mom started calling, she would never stop. But now she dialed her mother's number anyway and heard the call connect. She called once. Twice. Three times. Still no answer. On the fourth time, her mother answered. She sounded out of breath. She immediately said that she didn't have any of their old stuff, she threw away all the junk with every move.

We're talking about my passport here, Anastasia said. Not some old childhood drawing. Are you sure you don't have it?

I'm sure, her mother said.

Have you checked in the basement? Anastasia said.

Are you crazy? she said. I'm never going down there again, not after what happened last time.

Chapter Forty-Two

When Anastasia stopped playing basketball, I did too. That same spring, I noticed that Mom started worrying about me. I had developed certain physical tics, nothing major, but I knew that she saw them. Every time I had a good thought, I touched my earlobe, kissed my knuckles, knocked three times on wood and touched my earlobe again. Every time I had a bad thought, a thought that said Dad was dead, that Mom's recurring stomach pain was cancer, that the Mikkola sisters' mom had been locked up in a mental hospital, that Anastasia had been placed in foster care, that Evelyn was dead, I took a deep breath and held it for at least thirty seconds to prevent it from happening, then it became forty, then fifty, then sixty seconds. Before answering the phone, I had to blink hard five times to ensure the call didn't contain bad news.

Mom suggested that I call Julius, but I explained that we had drifted apart, he used to be my best friend but now he was studying electrical engineering at Sankt Eriks, and I was studying social sciences at Södra Latin, his classmates smoked weed and walked around with replica pistols, while my classmates recited poetry and wore clogs, when Julius called and invited me to a "possible house party" in Hagsätra at a friend of a friend's sister's boyfriend's place (whose parents might be out of town), I told him that I couldn't come, that I was invited to another party or that I had to study, then we hung up, and I spent the evening at home with my headphones and library books, I listened to Brand Nubian and Oum Kalthoum, I read Ghassan Kanafani, Naguib Mahfouz and Kahlil Gibran, whenever I went out I always carried my modified airsoft gun, it was a silver Colt 45, and from a few meters away, it looked completely real, no one could suspect that it could only shoot small yellow plastic balls, and it gave me a sense of security to have it tucked into my waistband when I went out, if I were attacked by a skinhead gang I might have a chance to scare them off, it made me feel less lonely than I actually was.

Later that spring, I stopped eating, Mom noticed that something was wrong, I explained that it wasn't a diet, I had just decided to reduce my calorie intake, I pulled up my T-shirt and showed her my trembling stomach, the love handles overflowing my waistband, I said that Dad was actually right when he said I needed to think about my weight, and Mom just shook her head.

When did he say this?

Before he moved out.

Your dad was depressed. He was disappointed that life didn't turn out the way he had hoped. You're not overweight. If anything, you're undernourished. Please try to forget what he said to you.

But the longer Dad was gone, the stronger his voice grew inside me, I heard him from the moment I woke up (Why did you sleep so long?) until I went to bed (Why are you so lazy?), I heard him when I stood in front of the mirror (Look at all those pimples), when I went to school (Take off your headphones, listen when I talk to you, you're fat, you have too much acne), when I exercised (Why don't you exercise more? Why are your arms so skinny? Why didn't you learn karate? You need to practice kung fu. Why aren't you at home doing your homework?), when I did my homework (Why are you always at home doing homework? Why aren't you out socializing with others your age?), I heard him during school breaks (Why don't you have any friends? Is it because you're so tall, fat and skinny at the same time? Your shoulders are too narrow compared with your lower body), I heard him when I was having lunch in the cafeteria (It's the food that makes your face look like that. Maybe you're allergic to something, maybe it's milk, maybe it's bread), I heard him as I walked home from school (Why do you read all the time? You read the wrong kind of books, read science, read Einstein, read Plato, read Machiavelli, they write real books about real things, not imaginary stories, cut your hair, look at me when I talk to you, lower your gaze when I talk to you, I'm still your father, and you should respect me, listen closely, one day I'll be gone and you'll regret not listening to me, do you hear that, good, are you listening carefully to what I'm going to say, good, why are you so fat?).

The only time I didn't hear him was when I listened to music or read a book, so that's what I did, I read and listened to music and tried to get used to living with this self-hating voice, and when that didn't work, I tried to appease the voice by stopping eating. One week, I only ate cornflakes and milk, I felt great, I flew high above the city, then I collapsed in a record store, I stood at the information counter, listening to a CD, trying to decide if it was good enough to buy or not, when the world started spinning and I fainted.

When I woke up, I saw a circle of worried faces looking at me, behind them were the store's spotlights, behind the spotlights the ceiling, behind the ceiling the sky, behind the sky the universe and eternal darkness.

Are you okay? one of them said.

Yes, I said, trying to get up.

I untangled the headphones that had gotten stuck around my neck and said I had to go, I went straight to McDonald's and ordered a combo meal, it's still the most delicious thing I've ever eaten.

When the voice focused on my pimples, I tried to treat them with my grandmother's Vademecum mouthwash, my acne was a sign that I was rotting from the inside and that there was something seriously wrong with me, why else would my dad choose to leave me, I had tried everything else, Clearasil, Basiron, Aco Acnegel, and now all that was left was this incredibly strong mouthwash, it burned when I dabbed it all over my face, I was as red as a lobster for a few days, the pimples dried up, then came back with a vengeance. At school, I made up that I had had an allergic reaction to some food, but in reality I punished my face because of how it looked, and even today, I'm unsure of how I even came up with the idea that Vademecum would help, there was no logic in dabbing corrosive mouthwash on your face unless there was something in the pain and burning sensation that gave me pleasure, there was a correspondence between the pain and self-hatred, not only because I was afraid my father was right about all the things he said about me, but also because I hated myself for feeling relieved that he was gone.

And all the while Mom was there, without her voice I would have been lost. Dad's voice pointed out my faults, but Mom's voice claimed that anything was possible. She listened and asked follow-up questions, she encouraged and helped with homework, she packed lunches and cooked dinners, she attended my youngest brother's soccer games and my middle brother's theater performances, she bought Christmas presents and filled Easter eggs, she was a class parent and volunteered as a cat sitter for neighbors she barely knew, even though she was allergic and never understood the point of having pets. She bought new clothes for us and secondhand clothes for herself, she shopped at three different grocery stores to take advantage of special offers, she carried groceries home in an old stroller, she declined party nights, and somehow she managed everything, without support from Dad, without a partner, without help from friends, without money from her mom. She raised three sons on one salary, and her only luxury in life was a newly borrowed library book, two squares of dark chocolate and a cup of herbal tea on Saturday nights.

Only once did I see her wobble, it was that time when she slipped on an icy patch on her way home from work, she came home and sat on the stool in the hallway and said:

I slipped. I slipped. I slipped on the ice.

We helped her with her shoes, we guided her into the living room, we cooled her scraped temple with frozen peas.

I slipped, she said, again and again. On an icy patch.

As if it were inconceivable that she, who had control over everything, could lose her balance because of something as ordinary as an icy patch.

When spring approached summer, Mom invited me and my brothers to a dance show at the Re:Orient festival.

I don't like dancing, I said.

You'll love this, she said. It's the dancing dervishes!

She said the name as if they were world-famous, and maybe they were, but I had never heard of them. They were visiting from Istanbul, and I had never been to Turkey, but I knew it was a Muslim country, and the flag resembled Tunisia's, both were red, both had a star and a moon and so I promised Mom I would go.

We took the subway to T-Centralen and crossed the bridge to Skeppsholmen, the tent was big and white, we sat on a wobbly wooden bench and waited, Mom took out the program and whispered that we were about to experience an eight-hundred-year-old tradition.

It's starting soon, look, here they come!

My brothers sat up as the music began, the lights went out and ten men in black coats and beige tall hats came out onstage. They walked very, very slowly, one step at a time, they bowed to each other, they walked in a circle, still one step at a time.

When does it start? my youngest brother asked.

Soon, said Mom. Just wait.

The ten men leaned forward and prayed, they bowed, they bowed again, they prayed, they knelt down and prayed some more, and then, after ten minutes of different bows and prayers, they took off their black coats and stood ready in heavy white costumes to begin spinning.

Are you ready? Mom asked.

My brothers nodded, and so did I, fully prepared to connect with something that may not have been from my homeland or even my father's homeland, but still, a connection to something.

One by one, the men began to spin, they extended their arms, tilted their heads, their long costumes swooshed through the air as they spun around and around.

When does it start? my youngest brother whispered.

I think it's already started, I said.

Their hats look like beehives, my middle brother said.

Mom hushed him. People on nearby benches looked at us and smiled. My middle brother noticed and spoke louder.

But they really do look like beehives, look, Mom, they have beehives on their heads!

Mom looked at him as if he wasn't her son.

Or giant baguettes!

Thirty minutes later, and the dancing dervishes were still spinning, around and around and around. My youngest brother had fallen asleep, my middle brother had stopped trying to come up with funny things their hats resembled (thimbles! rolls of paper towels!) and looked like he was about to die from boredom. Finally, we gave up, we left the performance and went out into the warm spring air, my youngest brother was still asleep, I carried him because Mom had a stomachache.

That was the worst thing I've ever seen in my life, I said as we crossed the bridge back to the city.

Mom had one hand on the railing and the other hand over her stomach. But cool hats, my middle brother said and looked like he meant it.

Chapter Forty-Three

That weekend, Anastasia took a long-distance bus to the city where their mom lived. As Anastasia walked from the bus terminal towards the address she had looked up in advance, she had the feeling that she had been here before, there was something about the main street, the hot dog stand, the hairdresser, the fabric store, the cobblestones and the bridge over the small canal that made her remember other cities they had lived in. Ina and Hector had visited here a few months ago, and according to Ina, Mom was unusually well, everything seemed stable, she had even gotten a cat.

Mom's apartment was on the ground floor, the windows were so dirty that they didn't need their dark curtains, but the curtains were still drawn, and Anastasia wondered if there were sunrays strong enough to penetrate that kind of dirt. She opened the door and rang the doorbell. The doorbell didn't work. Of course not. She had probably unscrewed it from the inside to avoid visitors. Anastasia knocked. An angry voice from inside.

What do you want?

It's me.

Who?

Me!

Who?

Anastasia!

Her mom opened the door without removing the security chain. Are you alone?

Let me in, Mom.

Nobody followed you?

Please just open the fucking door.

Her mom closed the door, and for a moment, Anastasia thought she wouldn't open it again. But then she heard a metallic sound and some steps, which she knew meant her mom had removed the security chain and backed into the darkness of the hallway, probably ready with a baseball bat, in case Anastasia turned out not to be who she said she was, if Anastasia was, in fact, a secret agent equipped with an Anastasia-like silicone mask and a special voice-modifying machine that perfectly imitated Anastasia's voice. Anastasia opened the door and hung her jacket on one of the five hangers, all of different brands and materials, two wooden, two plastic, she chose a thin hanger made of wire, the kind you get from the dry cleaner's, and it looked as if the hanger struggled to hold up her jacket. Her mom looked at her and whispered her control questions.

What animals did the Ivarsson family have in their window on Drakenbergsgatan?

Bears, she said, with a tired voice. A lot of carved wooden bears.

Who took care of you on your first day at preschool?

Nina and Agneta, Anastasia said. But mostly Nina.

What route did we take to school when we lived in Blackeberg?

Come on, Mom, Anastasia said, trying to lean in for a hug.

Selima raised the baseball bat and repeated the question. What route? If you're my daughter, you definitely know the answer.

The shortcut across the field, she sighed.

Selima put away the baseball bat and smiled.

My beloved child! she said, stretching out one of her arms. How I've been waiting for you to come home.

They tried to drink coffee in the kitchen, but after a few minutes, Anastasia couldn't stand the smell, so she persuaded her mom to go out onto the balcony.

Don't you like my coffee? her mom said.

Well, your coffee smells good, Anastasia said. It's the smell of corpses that I can't handle.

It's not a corpse, her mom said, smiling. It's Priscilla. She knows that something bad is going to happen, and then she can't control her bladder.

Priscilla was her mom's cat, in cat years she must have been around two hundred, she was already old when Selima found her, and somehow she was still alive. Anastasia walked towards the balcony, and when she opened the door, the rubber seal between the wall and the door creaked and cracked.

How long has it been since you sat out here? she said to her mom, who stood still in the darkness of the apartment. Come out now.

I can't.

Come on.

Selima bent down and crawled out onto the balcony, to make sure she wasn't seen by any long-range snipers hiding in the bushes on this particular day, the balcony was full of junk, empty bottles, a dead plant, some loose planks, an empty aquarium with a crack in one of the walls, but no chairs. Anastasia sat on the floor. Her mother approached slowly. Anastasia noticed that she crawled with one arm, the other hanging down towards the floor. Now they sat there, next to each other, leaning against the secure cement wall that provided protection against bullets. The mother looked up at her daughter, adjusted her morning robe and spoke with an aristocratic tone:

So how is my princess doing on this wonderful day?

She was only fifty-five years old, but she looked like she was seventy, she had led a hard life, fighting through depressions and setbacks, she had learned Swedish bureaucracy and grammar, sold vacuum cleaners and hand-knotted rugs, she had been pursued by authorities and debt collectors, she had been on the run from a curse for thirty years, and now Anastasia saw the consequences of this constant fleeing, her mother's teeth were brown, her hands were sore, her face full of wrinkles caused by a life of fear, and despite all this, she had the ability to look at her daughter and speak to her as if Anastasia were the most important person in the world, with that fake British accent she used when she picked up their keyboard-playing father in a supermarket more than thirty years ago. And when she said the words "this wonderful day," Anastasia saw what their father had seen in her, just for a few seconds—the raging uncontrollable charm that Anastasia recognized in Evelyn and that her mother could have used for so much more than just selling things if she had only found her greater purpose in life.

I need my Tunisian passport, Anastasia said.

You were born in 1980, my daughter, her mother said. In April.

I know, she replied.

I remember it like it was yesterday, Selima said. You came into this world early in the morning, with the first rays of sunlight.

Are you sure? Anastasia asked.

Yes.

Dad always used to say that I was born just before lunch, and that's why I was always so hungry.

He wasn't there, Selima said.

Wasn't Dad there when I was born?

Of course he was there. But he wasn't there like I was. He came and went. He was free. Men don't know what it means to bring a life into this world. Why do you want your passport?

I want to go to Tunisia, Anastasia said. I want to learn Arabic. Maybe I can meet some relatives while I'm at it.

A roller blind closed in front of Selima's face. She leaned forward and whispered, covering her mouth with her hand so that the security police hiding on the nearby balconies, filming them and trying to read their lips, couldn't see what she was saying.

On whose behalf? she whispered.

On my own behalf, Anastasia said.

Have they sent you? Is that why you're here? For revenge?

Who are "they"? Anastasia asked, unable to hide her irritation this time.

You'll know who they are when you see them, Selima said, smiling. In a matter of seconds, she had gone from crazy to queen and then back to crazy, and Anastasia wondered if it was only a matter of time before something similar happened to her or her sisters.

Can I ask you something? Anastasia said.

Sure.

What happened to you? How did you end up like this?

Both Anastasia and her mother seemed surprised by her honesty. What do you mean? her mother asked. I haven't changed a bit.

You were always a bit different, Anastasia said. But this is something else.

Well, for starters, she said, they brainwashed my husband . . .

No, "they" didn't brainwash anyone, Anastasia sighed. Because "they" don't exist. Dad had bone cancer and died. It wasn't anyone's fault, not "theirs" or "the curse's" fault. It was life's fault.

Haha, "life's fault," that's a good one. You weren't there. You don't know what happened. Go down to the basement and you'll see.

Thirty minutes later, Anastasia stood in her mother's basement, going through another set of moving boxes, hoping to find a dark green binder with her name on it. That's where her mom kept important documents such as diplomas, vaccination records and (perhaps) their Tunisian passports. Her mother had been in charge of the practical matters in the family—the paperwork, the shopping, the cooking, the finances, the cleaning—while their dad had been . . . well, what had he been doing actually? Anastasia barely remembered him, but according to Ina, he was the visionary, the man with a dream, the most talented keyboardist in Stockholm, the most optimistic man who had ever lived, it was he who told them that their great-grandfather had built skyscrapers, it was he who continued to decline job offers that were "beneath his dignity," such as performing playback in a senior citizen TV show or going on tour with a children's play, the years passed, the job offers became increasingly undignified, finally he couldn't say no any longer, he went on tour with a puppet theater and provided the sounds for the performance with his synthesizer, he was called in to play keyboard on a demo with a girl whose only claim to fame was being the sister of a guy in a somewhat famous boy band at the time, then they discovered the cancer, and three months later, he was gone.

Finally, Anastasia found the right binder, inside all her papers were neatly sorted in plastic folders, Ina couldn't have done it better, their mother's free-flowing handwriting indicated where in the binder Anastasia could find her grades, insurance papers and yes, there it was, in a plastic folder that had become stiff and yellowed with age, she found her dark green Tunisian passport, with handwritten letters on the photo page.

In another box labeled "TRASH," she found piles of letters, they were handwritten or typed, sent from Ystad or Haparanda, Strömstad or Kongsvinger in Norway, a firefighter in Örebro had changed his mind and wanted to cancel his purchase, an archivist in Edsbyn "loved her carpet" but wanted it in blue instead, a physiotherapist in Stockholm used her employer's letterhead with the official logo at the bottom when trying to get an answer as to why her carpet was supposedly "manufactured in an Asian factory" according to "several sources," and not "hand-knotted" in Tunisia, some letters used a respectful tone, others threatened legal action, most of them wanted the same thing: they reminded Selima to send the "promised certificate of authenticity" for the carpet they had purchased, they looked forward to receiving the certificate within three weeks, if it did not arrive within seven working days, they would take legal action, their next step would be to contact the police.

Anastasia couldn't understand why her mother had kept all these letters and she was just about to close the box when she noticed a dusty bag containing her mother's old notebooks.

Anastasia put the bag in her backpack, not because she planned to read the notebooks, but because she was curious about what her mother was so determined to throw away but hadn't managed to get rid of.

When Anastasia closed the padlock, she heard a ticking sound. It was a bomb. And then a quick internal smile: this is exactly how contagious madness is, first it infects Mom, and after half an hour in her stinky kitchen, after three sips of her barely drinkable coffee, after a hug where you deliberately breathe through your mouth, it somehow manages to get inside you, she influences your thoughts, and of course there's no bomb down here.

Anastasia stood completely still, trying to locate the source of the ticking, she opened the door and knelt down. It was closer now, coming from down here, from this unmarked cardboard box. She opened it and found piles of old watches: digital watches, mediocre Rolex imitations, children's watches with Mickey Mouse that didn't look like Mickey Mouse at all. They all had the same logo, and all of them had dead batteries, of course they did, they must have been lying in this box for years, there was no chance that the ticking she had heard could come from . . . and then she saw it: a brown men's watch with golden hands, it was ticking away as if it hadn't realized its batteries should have died years ago. Anastasia placed the watch on her left wrist and fastened the band.

Back in the apartment, she returned the key to the basement and said she had found the passport and some old notebooks (she didn't specify whose they were and didn't mention the watch). Selima suddenly looked scared.

Don't go, she whispered. Please.

Where? Anastasia asked.

To Tunisia.

What are you afraid of?

I have a feeling something bad will happen there. Stay here. Please. I beg you. Don't go. Promise me you won't go. Promise.

Anastasia looked at her mother. I can't promise that, she said.

Something shifted in her mother's internal landscape. She looked at her daughter with a new suspicion, as if she wasn't sure who she was. She reached for the baseball bat.

What animals did the Ivarsson family have in their window on Drakenbergsgatan? she whispered.

Mom, stop, Anastasia said.

What. Animals. Did. The. Ivarssons. Have. In their window on Drakenbergsgatan? she said, brandishing the baseball bat.

Mom, we've already been through this. I have to go now.

Fine, go.

But I'll be back soon.

Just come back if you know what animals the Ivarssons had in their window.

Anastasia backed out and closed the door behind her. She heard Selima lock first the door, then the dead bolt and then the security chain. Then Anastasia heard a strange sound coming from the mailbox, at first she thought it was a scream, then it sounded like a sob, but as she leaned forward and listened, it almost sounded like laughter.

Anastasia went home with the intention of using the passport to apply for the language course in Tunis. Then she put the bag with her mother's notebooks in a closet and forgot about it. One year passed. Two years. Three. When Anastasia finally decided to apply for the language course her mother had passed away.

Chapter Forty-Four

One day, early summer 1997, a few weeks before graduation, Emma asked me if I wanted to join her and some
friends for a coffee at a nearby café called Muggen. I had
never really talked to Emma, even though we had been
in the same class for almost three years, she had freckles and dark un-
washed Helmut Lang jeans with sharp turn-ups, the story that I have
told myself and others since Emma died is that I was fascinated by her
from the first time I saw her, but that's not really true, it's just me trying to improve the story, trying to turn a story into a myth. The true
version is that I found Emma a bit annoying before I got to know her,
she had so much energy, she was so intense, she had so many emotions, so much movement, when she came into the cafeteria everyone noticed it, for her voice was hoarse and she spoke loudly due to
a congenital hearing impairment in one ear. She was part of the cool
crowd, the skipping-gym-class, smoking-in-the-schoolyard crowd,
the dating-older-DJ crowd. I roamed the corridors alone with my
headphones, sometimes I pretended to be so focused on my music
that I didn't need friends, sometimes I pulled out my black pager
and pretended I had received an urgent message, I walked quickly
to the gray old plastic landline phone where students could make
free local calls, I picked up the receiver and dialed a random number,
always with one digit missing, so I could have an imaginary conversation about weekend plans and upcoming music festivals with the
dial tone instead of a real randomly called person. I was constantly in
love, I was in love with the brown-haired girl who looked at me once

after French class, I was in love with the theater girl with Peruvian parents, I was in love with the punk girl in my class who had a nose ring and a short leather jacket, I was in love with the flute girl in music class who wore holey cardigans, I was in love with the Christian girl who danced ballet, I was in love with the dark-haired girl I had seen twice at the Fridhemsplan subway station, I was in love with a girl who attended the music program at Rytmus, I was in love with a girl I had seen in my cousin's school catalog just because she was cute and resembled Evelyn and her name was Jamila, which was my half sister's name, I was in love with that dark-haired girl I saw in a drum-and-bass tent at a music festival, I was in love with the short-haired girl who was dating a drum-and-bass DJ, I was in love with the blond girl in a brown polo shirt that Julius talked to in Berzelii Park at the Water Festival, and I treated all these girls exactly the same way, instead of talking to them, I found elaborate ways to obtain their addresses, I got the address of the girl in the brown polo shirt by going to her high school late one weekday evening, I told the janitor that I was working on a school project in social sciences where I was comparing the clothes students wore in their school photos, and therefore, I needed to look in their school catalog, even though I went to a different school.

Normally we sell these, he said, handing me a copy of the school catalog. But you can have one for free, he added with a knowing smile.

As I left Östra Real with the green school catalog in my backpack, a blue car drove past on Karlavägen, the passenger window was down and the person sitting there shouted, "Fucking svartskalle," and he didn't shout angrily, he didn't exert himself, he just said it in passing and his friends laughed, and I smiled at them because they could say whatever they wanted, I would do exactly what they feared, I would fuck their blond sisters, I would get better grades than their brothers, I would become richer than their fucking parents, I would buy their grandparents' ancestral farm just to tear that shit down, and one day I would sit across from them in a conference room and I would tell them that I'm sorry, we had to let them go, they had until four o'clock to pack up their things and leave the building, because I was the new CEO, and all the way home from Östra Real, I imagined how they would start crying, they would beg on their bare knees, begging for mercy, saying they were young back then, when they drove around in a blue car and shouted insults at strangers, they didn't mean anything by it, and now they really needed this job, their girlfriend was pregnant and she was unemployed, and the money they had inherited they had spent on vacations and unnecessary cars, and please, just give me one more chance, just one more, and I would shrug and say, okay, just to show them how fucking unimportant they were, their salary was so small that it didn't matter to me if they kept working, and they would thank me and apologize again and again, and I imagined elaborate revenge scenarios for everyone who had ever said something racist to me, while I walked back and forth outside the house where the girl I was in love with at the moment lived, back and forth, around the block and back, for hours, until dog owners started greeting me, but Emma wasn't a projection, Emma was real, and she stood there in front of me in the corridor, asking if I wanted to join her for coffee, and my immediate impulse was to say no, of course, because I wasn't sure how to go to a café, did you order at the table or at the counter, should you drink café latte or cappuccino or regular coffee, what the hell was an espresso, and would it be considered cheap not to order something sweet, or would it be more childish to do so, like ordering a cinnamon bun?

Sorry, I can't, I said to Emma. I have to look for some CDs during the break. Okay, she said and smiled. But maybe you can stop by on your way back?

Chapter Forty-Five

Hector woke up early. While Ina was still sleeping, he quietly sneaked into the kitchen, brewed some coffee and opened an old document on his computer from when he worked as a guide at the aquarium. He had been preparing for this day for months. After spending the summer with his family, he had made it clear to Ina: now that she knew his family, it was only fair for him to get to know Ina's sisters. And what better way to get to know each other than by going to the aquarium together? Why not the aquarium where Hector's dad had worked for more than twenty years? Hector had suggested several dates during the fall, but one of Ina's sisters always canceled at the last minute. Evelyn had to work late to finish the annual inventory, Anastasia had to go to Gothenburg to visit a friend, both of them messaged Ina the day before, saying they had completely forgotten about this "aquarium thing" and asked if they could postpone it to another day. Later this fall? October? November? Now it was December 10, 2000, and finally, it was going to happen.

Both Hector and his sister had started working part-time at the aquarium when they turned fifteen. Their father was adamant that they should be treated like any other employees. Esmeralda always arrived late and never bothered to learn her fish facts. Hector was so desperate to earn his father's love and attention that he memorized the entire script for his first guided tour at the aquarium. He insisted on adding things the guide didn't mention, and when a tourist asked a question the guide couldn't answer, Hector raised his hand

and said he might know, a person who studies fish is called an ich-
thyologist and killer whales are actually a type of dolphin, the guide
looked at fifteen-year-old Hector with hatred in his eyes.

When it was Hector's turn to have his own groups, he gave them
an experience they would never forget. He overwhelmed them with
facts, a guided tour that usually took thirty minutes and ended in
the shark room always lasted more than an hour when Hector conducted it, and even though he was eager to share his knowledge, he
started receiving complaints, people said he was a know-it-all, tourists
complained that he had shushed their children with a sharp voice,
a group of visitors revolted when Hector spent more than fifteen
minutes talking about the giant squid (the largest creature without
a backbone, the largest eyes of any animal on Earth). They raised
their hands and asked if he could just finish the tour now so that they
could see the sharks.

I'm here for you, Hector said. And those who want to leave can
leave. And many people left, one by one, until only an elderly couple
from Canada remained, and Hector continued his tour for them.

Now, as an adult, looking through the old document, he remembered all the facts, he remembered how he had grown into his role as
a guide and learned to summarize, learned which pieces of information were worth sharing, he remembered himself as a nineteen-year-
old, in a suddenly too-small purple polo shirt with the aquarium
logo on his chest, standing in front of a large group of visitors with
wild children, he told them that fish have been on Earth much longer than mammals (450 million years vs. 200 million) and that there
are 27,000 identified fish species and 15,000 unidentified ones, he
mentioned that swordfish can swim up to 70 m.p.h., faster than a
speeding car, and that rockfish can live for hundreds of years, and the
African lungfish can survive out of water for two years, hibernating
underground until the water level rises.

Now, let's go into the next room. This is the Tropical Forest. Keep
an eye out for piranhas and butterflies, he said as he opened the door
and let the tourist group walk through the room on their own.

The most common questions revolved around sharks. Was it true that sharks had to swim to stay alive (yes and no, they don't have a swim bladder like other fish, so they need to swim, but if they stop swimming, they won't die, they just sink to the bottom and that's where they sleep), and which sharks attack humans (hardly any, and sharks kill only ten people per year, while elephants kill five hundred and deer kill one hundred).

Now, as he read through the document as an adult, he wondered if all these facts were really true. How is it possible that there are 15,000 unidentified fish species? How can one know they exist if they aren't identified? And wait a minute? How can deer kill a hundred people? He had said these things thousands of times without ever taking the time to question the truthfulness of his words. But now, on this early December morning when he was going to meet Ina's sisters, he looked up the annual death statistics. Okay, so the deer statistics seemed to be accurate, but many deaths were related to car accidents, and it didn't feel quite right to blame deer for getting hit by cars.

What are you doing up so early? Ina said, giving him a hug from behind.

Nothing, Hector said, closing his computer.

They were early and decided to walk down from Karlaplan instead of taking the bus.

They passed the spot where there was a fountain in the summer, now it mostly looked like a large lump of cement.

Look, there's the Tunisian embassy, Ina said, pointing to a red flag hanging on one of the old buildings.

Did you go there with your mom when you were little?

I don't think so, Ina said. But every time we passed this corner, my mom used to point at the flag and say the exact same thing I just said to you.

They continued down Narvavägen, the sidewalk covered in freshly fallen crunchy snow, cold noses, steamy breath, hooked arms. They remained silent for almost a block.

Do you miss her? Hector asked, resisting the impulse to bite his tongue because usually when he asked Ina about her mom, she would become tense or silent, or try to change the subject or pretend she hadn't heard the question. But this time she answered.

I miss who she was when we were little, Ina said. I miss who she was before she turned into who she is now. But sometimes I wonder if I miss a person who never even existed. How is it possible to sacrifice so much to create human life and then just abandon it?

But . . . Hector said but was interrupted.

Can you explain it to me? And what if I become the same? What if you and I have children and then I look them in the eyes and say, "Here's some cash, I'm going to a sales conference in Säffle, see you in a few weeks."

But she took care of you, Hector said. If she hadn't, you wouldn't have survived.

I'll never understand it, Ina said.

Or maybe you'll understand it when you have children, Hector said.

I hope not, Ina said.

How is she doing?

We haven't talked in a while. I needed a break. She can't handle seeing me this happy. They reached the bridge and crossed it. Hector checked his phone.

We're still early, should we take a walk?

Ina nodded. They turned left and followed the gravel path next to the frozen water. Have I told you about Anastasia's new project?

Hector shook his head.

She's trying to get into a language school in Tunis. To learn Arabic. It *really* feels like a logical next step in her career.

Hector looked up at Ina's face. There was something about the sarcasm, the quick-edged comment that made her resemble her mom.

Sorry, Ina said, as if she could read his thoughts. It's my sisters' fault . . . They turn me into this person. I just get so frustrated that they don't . . . do anything with all the time they have. Time just passes, and they seem perfectly fine with it, and I . . . I don't understand it.

Maybe you're jealous?

Jealous of their perception of time?

Jealous that they seem able to let time pass without panicking about it?

Maybe, Ina mumbled.

They continued along the water. Hector talked about when his parents (his dad willingly, his mom reluctantly) spent a month smuggling in two baby sharks, using a rented aquarium and a friend's borrowed boat, and Ina talked about the aquarium Anastasia had when she was little, with swordtails and guppies, and Hector talked about when he drew a jungle on the wall of his childhood room with orange chalk and was rewarded with his first slap, and Ina talked about when Evelyn dated that street artist who had never allowed himself to be photographed and who had spent several years of his life pasting black-and-white drawings of deer faces all over town, on utility boxes, on advertising posters, on subway windows.

Why deer, specifically? Hector said.

I actually asked Evelyn that, Ina said. I expected a long, theoretical explanation, like "it's a commentary on how we deplete the Earth's resources," or "the deer's gaze is a symbol of the fleeting nature of time, because the moment the deer catch sight of us, they dart away." But you know what she said? "He just likes deer."

Who doesn't? Hector said.

As often happens, it soon turned out that they had been so early that they had to run back towards the aquarium to avoid being late.

Some things are so much easier to say in English than in Swedish, Hector said when they stood at a pedestrian crossing, waiting for a traffic light to change, in the gust of wind from passing tourist buses.

Like what?

Like "I love you," Hector said. I mean, I can say "I love you" in English to anyone. To colleagues. To taxi drivers. To flower delivery people. To my accountant. But saying "Jag älskar dig" is something else.

I agree, Ina said.

The light changed, they stepped onto the pedestrian crossing. Hector stopped in the middle of the street.

"Jag älskar dig," he said.

They kissed. Ina leaned forward and whispered something in Hector's ear. Then they ran on towards the aquarium.

Chapter Forty-Six

On my way back from the CD place, I passed the café where Emma and her friends were supposed to be, I looked in through the window, thinking that if I saw Emma, I would go in, and if I didn't see her, it would be fate's way of telling me it wasn't meant to be, but I didn't see her and still I went in. I looked around, and there they were, in the inner corner, probably trying to avoid me, maybe Emma had invited me as a joke, to tease me, to ask me for help with some homework, but no, she looked genuinely happy when she saw me and waved, and I waved back. I saw that there was a line at the counter, so I understood that I had to wait in line and not order at the table, and soon I was sitting there with my coffee.

Emma and her friends, a tall girl with a Latin American appearance, another girl with an ironic yellow T-shirt and a red henna-dyed bob, a blond girl whose dad was an architect—everyone knew that these girls dated guys who were five or six years older, guys who were rappers or DJs or worked in sneaker stores, they met at places like East and G-club, mysterious places I had never been to, the guys took them to brunch at a café called Saturnus in Vasastan, and I hadn't been there either, the whole concept of brunch was new to me—breakfast combined with lunch, what a damn thing, I was just happy to be sitting here with these girls, imagine if someone saw us—someone might think we were friends, that I was one of them, that I wasn't myself.

During the first hour, I didn't say much, I just smiled and nodded as they talked about nights out, taxi rides, house parties and film premieres, then Emma started talking about music, and I had something to say, then Emma made a joke, and I joked back, and the whole table laughed, I have no idea what I said, and then I said something else, and they laughed again, even louder, and it was like a drug, I couldn't stop, I said something that got a little less laughter, and then I told a rather long story that no one listened to except Emma, and then someone had to go to class, and someone had to go home, and suddenly it was just Emma and me left, and we started talking, and three hours later we were still talking, the light outside was gone, the café owner cleared our cups, he came over twice and asked if we wanted anything else, but we didn't want anything else, we had everything we needed, we talked about our dreams for the future, she wanted to do something creative, maybe in fashion, she and her friend had started sewing denim skirts with red seams, and every time they wore the skirts to the G-club, people came up and asked where they had bought them, they actually toyed with the idea of starting a company and selling the skirts, and I heard myself say: Ah, the G-club, as if it were the name of an old friend I hadn't seen in years, even though I had never been there, of course not, to get into the G-club, you had to be a member and have a G-card, and to get a G-card, you had to be one of the coolest people in Stockholm—a successful model, a famous art director, a TV personality on Z-TV—or you had to get to know the two bouncers who were in charge of the list, Per and . . . something else, I forgot his name, no, it's coming now, Per and Ove, that's right. Per was tall and red-haired, and Ove was short and round, and even though I had never been to the club, I had heard about Per and Ove, and here Emma sat, eighteen years old, casually mentioning that she had been to the G-club and that people there wanted to buy her homemade skirts, and if it sounds like she was bragging, she wasn't at all, she just had a way of talking about the world as if anything was possible, after school, she would maybe start her own fashion company or go to Paris to study French or study film theory because she really liked Buñuel and Godard and then she asked me what I was going to do after graduation.

I got into Stockholm School of Economics, I said.

She looked at me with those green-brown eyes, her freckles danc-ing as she raised one eyebrow and lowered the other.

Economics? she said.

Yes, I said and started explaining that getting into this school was extremely difficult, and I had the grades that made it possible, and I definitely wouldn't be one of those idiots wasting my time, I'll keep studying until I have my degree when I'm twenty-three. Emma looked at me and said the same thing again, with a slightly different tone.

Economics?

This time she squinted and looked like someone was pushing toothpicks under her nails.

What? I said.

I don't know, she said. I just can't imagine you as an economist. You're way too funny to become an accountant. You know way too much about Tupac to devote your life to Excel.

What's Excel? I asked.

It's a program accountants use, she said.

How do you know that?

My dad is always feeding numbers into Excel, she said.

I tried to explain to her that this education is more like a driver's license, it allows you to do anything afterwards, to get politically in-volved or become a journalist or work at the UN, and Emma nodded.

I know, she said. My dad studied economics, hoping not to be-come an economist.

And what does he do now?

Economist, Emma said, which was kind of true, but she didn't mention that he was a board member in various real estate compa-nies, and it wasn't until later that I would understand that her fa-ther was one of the wealthiest people on Södermalm and when the newspapers printed the names of people with the highest salaries, his name was on the list, and Emma was always embarrassed about it, she didn't want anyone to know that she came from money, just like I didn't want anyone to know that I hadn't heard from my dad in years. But when Emma asked about him, I said he was missing, he had left us and nobody knew where he was, she was the first person I confessed everything to, it just came out, all those things I hadn't told anyone in all these years, I said that Dad had fought his whole life to be the opposite of a stereotype, he had taken paternity leave, he had helped with cleaning and laundry at home, and then, a few years ago, he changed, something happened, maybe it was diabetes, maybe it was depression, maybe it was that Mom wanted a divorce, maybe it was his daughter in the other country who fell to pieces after he left her, maybe it was the house in Tunisia that never got finished, maybe it was just the realization that life would never be as he had imagined it, maybe it was just time that destroyed him.

Do you mean his time here in Sweden? Emma asked.

No, just time in general, I said.

Emma looked at me and touched my hand, I didn't know that a touch could feel so powerful. I had the impulse to withdraw my hand because, on some level, I knew this was too risky, she wasn't one of the girls I had observed from a distance, she wasn't a one-dimensional projection created in my mind, she was a real person, sitting across from me at the café table, with her green-brown eyes and freckled nose and warm hands, and even though I wanted to retract my hand, get up, and run into the twilight, away from her, away from everything I had said, away from myself, I stayed put.

When the café closed, we walked towards the nearest subway station, but when we reached Slussen, we still had so much to say that we continued to Medborgarplatsen, and the same thing happened there, so in the end, we walked all the way to Skanstull, and then Emma said she might as well walk home, and I followed her to her building's entrance, not because she couldn't handle it herself, but so that we could finish talking about whatever it was we were talking about, and of all the words we shared during that long walk, I only remember one thing we talked about, and it was that it's fun when two people are walking to the same place without knowing how to get there, and both of them are waiting for the other to show the way, when we reached the building where she lived with her parents and sister we still had things to talk about, so she turned around and walked back with me to the nearest bus station, where we talked until my bus arrived, and then we said goodbye, and I got on the bus and sat down and looked out the window, and there she stood, with her backpack and her homemade denim skirt and her ponytail and her white sneakers, and I smiled, and she smiled, and I came home and hugged my mom, and she looked at me with a smile and asked if anything special happened at school today, as if she could sense a new energy in my hug, as if she suspected that I had met someone who liked me for who I was.

Chapter Forty-Seven

na and Hector positioned themselves to the left of the aquarium entrance, just in front of a poster that said: "Do you dare to crawl through the shark tunnel?" Hector was silent, and so was Ina.

She wondered why he suddenly felt so nervous, maybe he regretted saying those words to her, maybe he just wanted to make a linguistic observation about the differences between Swedish and English, and she had pressured him into saying that he loved her? He checked the time on his phone and kept going inside to make sure Evelyn and Anastasia weren't waiting for them in there because of the cold.

This is perfectly normal, Ina said. Don't worry. They will come, but they won't be here until twenty past.

Are they always this late?

Not always. Only when they're meeting me. If they were meeting a friend or going on a date, they would have been here fifteen minutes ago.

Ina had initially suggested meeting at 10 a.m. to "beat the crowds." Anastasia suggested noon, and Evelyn negotiated 11 as a compromise. But now, it was half past, and Hector and Ina were still standing alone outside the aquarium. Tourists approached them and asked if they were in line. They shook their heads. Tourists asked them for directions to Skansen, and they pointed the way. After five more minutes in the bitter cold, Hector suggested they wait inside, but now it was Ina who refused. She wanted to stay outside in the cold until her sisters arrived.

When they finally arrived, they came in a taxi. Anastasia was in the front seat and managed to leave the cab without paying, while Evelyn flirted with the cab driver from the back seat.

So sorry we're late, Anastasia said before Ina had a chance to say anything.

What happened? Ina asked.

We were having breakfast, Evelyn said. And lost track of time. Have you been waiting long?

No worries, Hector said, smiling. Let's go inside.

They put their coats in a small square locker, Hector handed out coins for the lockers, and Ina smiled when she realized he must have planned ahead, he knew that the lockers only accepted coins, so he had saved four coins to ensure a smooth entry to the aquarium. For some people, love needed to be proven with diamond rings or sur- prise weekends in Paris, but for Ina, love meant the ability to plan ahead and seeing Hector hand out those coins to her sisters made her realize that he loved her.

Hector gently guided the three sisters past the counter, past the queue, waving and smiling at the elderly lady behind the counter.

Hi, Monica, he said. How are *you*?

The emphasis was on "you," as if he had been going around town asking everyone the same question, but the only person he truly cared about was Monica.

And where do *you* think you're going? Monica said.

Oh, they're with me, Monica, Hector said, repeating her name to show that he remembered her.

And who are you?

Stop it, Hector said. It's me!

But the elderly lady seemed uninterested in stopping anything. Instead, she turned to the next people in line. Hector leaned forward as if the distance was the reason she didn't recognize him.

Hector, he said. Enzo's son! Enzo no longer works here. I know, but . . .

He backed out just when we needed him the most. Now we'll probably have to close. I've been working here for fifteen years, and now: Goodbye.

It's not true, Dad was forced out, he . . .

That's not what I've heard.

Come on, Monica.

You have to pay, just like everyone else. Hector reached for his wallet.

Get in line, please.

They went to the back of the line. When they reached Monica again, Hector had his credit card ready, he paid the entrance fee for four adults to an aquarium that had been like a second home to him as a child, an aquarium full of swordfish and manta rays that his dad and mom had imported through various unofficial means.

Receipt? Monica asked.

Yes, please, Hector said, only because he knew it would annoy Monica to have to reach down to her left, grab the receipt and give it to him.

Did she say the aquarium will close soon? Evelyn asked. What will happen to all the fish?

Do you know what happens to all the animal babies that Skansen doesn't have room for? Anastasia said. All the little kittens and mini rabbits and piglets? Anastasia ran her finger across her throat.

Behave yourselves, Ina said.

Now let's turn this around, Hector said, leading them away from the counter and into the first exhibition room.

Chapter Forty-Eight

want to remember the summer of 1997 as amazing, I want to say that we were in love the way only eighteen-year-olds can be, I want to claim that we were happy nonstop and that for the first time in my life, through Emma, I felt connected to the world, that I was part of something other than myself, my thoughts, my books, and all of that's true, but it only took a few weeks for me to start finding faults in Emma, she was too Swedish, her dad was too rich, they were wealthy but not in the right way, they didn't have an expensive summerhouse, just a normal house, sure it was located in the Swedish archipelago, on the luxurious island of Sandhamn, and yes, their house was close to the water, but they didn't have an outdoor pool and there were some trees that obstructed the sea view, and she was probably too short for me, she had too-cool friends and sometimes it felt like her friends were more important than me and once I noticed that one of the turn-ups on her Helmut Lang jeans had torn at the bottom, and now, twenty-five years later, I guess I had to find faults in her in order to survive if she left me because I had already been abandoned once, and I refused to let it happen again, so carefully and deliberately, I destroyed her, I mentioned that if she wanted fewer freckles, she could use more sunscreen, and she looked at me and said she liked her freckles, when she said she hated the photos from our graduation because it looked like she had a double chin in some of them, I responded that it was an unfortunate angle and that she rarely looked like that in real life, when she asked if I thought she was fat,

I stayed silent for just the right amount of seconds before saying no, to show her that, yes or no, she wasn't fat, but she had gained a small belly, and maybe it was time to reduce her calories and start jogging. And at the same time, in the midst of the storm of criticism I lived in and tried to spare her from, we were connected, we couldn't stop being with each other, every moment felt unreal if I didn't share it with her.

Later that summer, she was going to France with two friends, they were taking the bus from Cityterminalen, I was there to wave goodbye, I had made a special mixtape for Emma to listen to while the bus took them to the continent, when we kissed goodbye I stood in the street and she stood on the sidewalk to shorten the distance between our lips, she started crying and I turned away, then she got on the bus, and I walked up from the street to the sidewalk, we waved goodbye as the bus slowly drove away and I turned so she wouldn't see my tears, and then I cried all the way to the subway, I made strange sounds, it felt like I was going to vomit, it felt like my life was over, like I wouldn't survive the four weeks until they came back. I was alone in Stockholm. I worked as a mail carrier near Mariatorget during the day, and as soon as Emma disappeared, the evil voices returned, they woke me up at night, they forced me to stop eating, in the evenings I was back in Vasastan, I wandered around the same neighborhood as before Emma, but now I had no ambition to meet anyone, the only person I hoped to run into was Evelyn, no one had said she lived in Vasastan, I just had a feeling that she belonged there, somewhere near Odenplan, there were times when I thought I saw her, someone with black curly hair on a sidewalk near a bus stop, someone else with an upper lip larger than the lower one, someone with a birthmark on the cheek, but it was always someone else, and if it had been Evelyn, I don't know if I would have had the courage to approach her, I wasn't in love with Evelyn, I just wanted to run into her, give her a quick hug, ask how she was doing, maybe have coffee, maybe mention to her that my girlfriend was in Paris, maybe tell my girlfriend that I "ran into an old friend last night."

Oh, what's his name? Emma would say, and I would stay silent for a few seconds before saying:

It's a she. Her name is Evelyn, Evelyn Mikkola.

Maybe I would even take a photo of us, develop it, and send it to Emma, just to show her that I didn't need her, that I didn't need anyone, that I was perfectly fine on my own.

I did my best to block out the evil voices with my headphones, but just to be safe, I brought my fortified silver airsoft gun, I had it tucked into my waistband, sometimes I stood on subway platforms, and when the doors closed and the train started moving, I lifted my shirt and showed someone in the train that I had a pistol, I don't know why I did it, maybe I wanted to see their reaction, maybe I wanted someone to notice me and remember me, once when I did it at Zinkensdamm subway station, someone called the police, when I reached the street, there was a police van with flashing lights waiting for me, an officer sat behind the wheel, and two others jumped out of the side door, they stopped me and asked me how things were going, good, I said, they looked at each other, glanced down towards the turnstiles, and asked if I had seen anyone down there with a gun, I nodded and said there was a really sketchy guy down on the platform, walking around, waving his arms and shouting that he had a pistol, but I don't know if he's telling the truth, I said, the police officers ran down the stairs, I walked towards Hornsgatan, the officer behind the wheel followed me with his gaze, I tried my best not to start running, not until I reached the corner, and then I ran, I ran up the hill towards Hornstull so fast that I dropped the pistol, it fell down into my right pant leg, and I had to stop and bend over to wiggle it out through the bottom, I threw it into a bush and continued strolling down Hornsgatan, I looked in the dark shop windows as if considering buying something, I used the reflection to see if the police were following me, I was almost home when the police van caught up with me, they drove up onto the sidewalk and told me to put my hands against the wall, they went through my pockets, and one of the officers ran back to check the bushes, he came back with a dirty airsoft gun.

Recognize this? he said. I shook my head.

Do you understand how dangerous it is to walk around with something like this?

It only shoots plastic bullets, I mumbled.

Yes, but this one doesn't shoot plastic bullets, one of the officers said, drawing his black service pistol.

It's not mine, I said.

The police officers shook their heads and let me go, I went home, I didn't tell anyone what had happened, I had no one to tell anyway, the only person I had was Emma, and she wasn't there.

Four weeks later, Emma and her friends returned from France, and something had shifted between us, I felt it inside me, I couldn't open up like I used to, she had left me once and could do it again, if I became weak or sick she would take advantage of me and replace me, I knew it, and when she told me later in the fall that she planned to go to Paris for six long months to study French at the Sorbonne, I nodded and said: Sure, do what you want, it's not like I care, I have my life here, I have my friends, I've gotten to know some bouncers, who knows, maybe if you leave, I'll still manage to get into the G-club without your help.

In the fall, I was supposed to start studying at the Stockholm School of Economics, but two days before I was supposed to officially become a "småtting" (as the first-year students were called by the rest of the students), I decided to follow Emma's advice, I went to the administration office and talked to a surprisingly sympathetic older lady about the possibility of starting next year instead. I thought she would try to convince me to start right away. I was prepared for a lecture on the transience of time and the inevitable approach of death.

You have nothing to lose by starting now, she would say. And what will you do instead, take drugs and be happy?

But instead, she looked at me with kind eyes behind a pair of glasses as big as a book and said: That sounds wise.

Wise?

To take a gap year. We have so many students who come directly from high school, and I think many of them, not all, but many, would benefit more from their education if they took a break before starting. Enjoy the year. Explore everything out there.

I thanked her, and she thanked me, and I left her office with a dizzying sense of freedom.

I had lived for eighteen years, and this was the first time I felt that everything was up to me. The only thing I knew was that I had to transfer the rent for my room and food costs to my mom's account every month. Other than that, I was free to do whatever I wanted. As I walked down the stairs and passed the janitors' office, I saw a handwritten note on the door. It said, "It was better before." And underneath, someone with different handwriting had written, "The sooner, the better." I saw it as a sign that I had made the right choice in taking a gap year.

Two years later, when I started studying at the Stockholm School of Economics, the note was still there, and at that point, I saw it as a sign that I should have started earlier. Once I went into the janitors' office and asked about the note. Who wrote it? What does it mean? One guy said he didn't know, and the other guy said it had to do with some sort of conflict between their union and the school administration, it had something to do with working hours, but it had been resolved several years ago, and now the note had been there for so long that he had stopped noticing it, and before I could stop him, he reached for the note, turned it into a little paper ball, and shot it in an arc towards the wastebasket.

Chapter Forty-Nine

As soon as they entered the humid air of the aquarium, Hector began his lecture, there was a shift in his tone of voice, he went from socially awkward Hector to middle-aged politician visiting a middle school Hector. Wasn't the whole point of meeting to get to know each other? But instead of talking to Evelyn and Anastasia, instead of asking about their autumn, how Evelyn's inventory had gone, and what Anastasia had been up to in Gothenburg, Hector started reciting facts about sharks and lungfish and dragonhead fish with a metallic voice, as if he were reading from an invisible teleprompter. Anastasia looked at Evelyn with wide eyes and a peculiar expression that made them both laugh. Hector cleared his throat.

What's so funny? Ina asked.

Oh, nothing, Evelyn said.

I just laughed because she laughed, Anastasia said.

Hector continued to speak, and Evelyn tried to focus her gaze on the aquarium tanks, on the other visitors, on the giant collection of delicately floating pink jellyfish to avoid another laughing fit when she saw Anastasia nod and take out an invisible notepad, making a note as soon as Hector turned his back. For some reason, this seemed to be Hector's way of getting to know people, spending an hour filling their heads with fish facts, and as he spoke, Evelyn wondered whose idea this had been, his or Ina's, because it was so typical of Ina, another way for her to control her younger sisters, just like she had tried to control their lives when they were little, when their mother was absent, when their mother was unpredictable, and every time Ina was reminded that she couldn't control her sisters like little marionettes, she looked as if she had been stabbed in the back. In an attempt to avoid a fight, Evelyn tried to listen to Hector, to look impressed by his fish knowledge, to not laugh at Ina's leading questions or Anastasia's vacant stare. Evelyn did her best to free herself, she strolled to the next fish tank to create some distance, but somehow they always ended up close to each other again, with Hector pointing at a fish that looked depressed and reciting facts about its mating habits, while Ina nodded and Anastasia yawned.

They left the rainforest room and descended a few stairs. Hector pointed to an aquarium with squid and said that the giant squid was the largest organism on Earth without a backbone, and Anastasia coughed and took out her phone, seconds later Evelyn received a text message that read:

"Even bigger than Hectore?"

And Evelyn couldn't stop laughing, maybe because Anastasia had added that extra "e" in his name, maybe because Hector had never looked more spineless than when he tried his best to guide them through the aquarium he hadn't visited in years, maybe because Ina got that annoyed wrinkle around her mouth that made her look like their mother, while continuing to nod her head with a furious intensity, to show that at least *she* was listening to all these fascinating facts, and the more irritated Ina became, the more impossible it was for Evelyn to suppress the laughter that was building up inside her, and eventually she had to excuse herself and go to the bathroom just to let it all out. When she returned, Hector and her sisters were standing at the entrance to the shark room.

Are you ready for this? Hector said. These are the aquarium's crown jewels.

They entered the dark room together, a gigantic water tank wider than a bus, taller than a flagpole, three, four, five, six dark gray sharks gliding back and forth on the other side of the glass.

Over there is the shark tunnel, Hector said. Are you brave enough to try it?

Isn't it more of a kid thing? Evelyn said.

No, it works for all ages, Hector said, sounding slightly offended. It's fantastic. You have to try it. But before you get in line, I can tell you some interesting facts about sharks . . .

Evelyn gradually distanced herself from Hector and Ina and stood in line for the shark tunnel. The tank was full of fish, three majestic stingrays slowly gliding back and forth, there were seahorses and sea dragons, flatfish and fat fish, a neon-yellow fish and a green fish with a perpetually surprised face.

A father with curly hair stood in front of her in line. When he turned around, she noticed that his pants were dirty. At first, Evelyn thought it was stains from baby food, then she realized it was probably paint stains. He was here with two children, and while most parents at least pretended to enjoy their time at the aquarium, he did the opposite. The children jumped up and down, they tapped on the window to get a reaction from the fish, they asked him again and again why there were no penguins here.

Because the sharks would eat the penguins, he said.

Why don't the sharks eat the other fish? the children asked. Because they're friends with the fish, he said.

But the penguins, we want to see the penguins, you said there would be penguins, where are the penguins?

The father noticed Evelyn and whispered something in her ear.

Excuse me? she said.

Kill me, he whispered. Please, just kill me.

Here?

Outside. Not in front of the kids. Or the sharks.

And how would you like to die?

What's on the menu?

Well, drowning is popular, Evelyn said. They say it's quite painless.

Yeah, that's good, there's water right outside, he said. But no, it's frozen now, isn't it?

Damn, I forgot, Evelyn said. I knew I should have brought a weapon.

Why didn't you bring one?

I didn't know I was going to a place where a weapon would be needed.

So you're a person who goes unarmed to a fish museum, interesting.

His children grew calmer as they approached the entrance of the shark tunnel.

I guess I could freeze you to death, Evelyn said, just to keep the conversation going.

Takes too long, he said. Electricity?

Maybe I can suffocate you? Evelyn said.

Now we're talking, the father said, just as the children climbed up on his legs and screamed for penguins and ice cream. The boy needed to pee, the girl didn't want to go into the shark tunnel alone.

I can go in with you, Evelyn said to the girl. She went from screaming to shy in a fraction of a second.

Would that be okay? the man said. I'll just run to the bathroom with this crazy crab. I'll be back in four hours.

He ran towards the bathroom with the boy before Evelyn could respond.

Look, it's almost our turn now, Evelyn said. And your dad will be back soon.

He's not my dad, the girl said.

Who?

Simon, the girl said. He's my uncle. Uncle means Mom's brother. Evelyn wasn't sure why this information made her happy.

I understand, Evelyn said. And what's your name?

I'm not allowed to tell my name to people I don't know, the girl said.

That sounds like a good rule, Evelyn said.

Maja, the girl said. Maja Krusmynta Elfriede.

You have many names, Evelyn said. I'm Evelyn. Just Evelyn.

My brother only has one name, the girl said. I have three. One normal name and two extra names.

Lucky you, Evelyn said.

Chapter Fifty

n the spring of 1998, Emma moved to Paris with some friends, we didn't break up, but I knew she would meet someone new in Paris, Paris is full of French people, and everyone knows how the French are, I knew exactly how they were, even though I had never been to Paris, I had never even been to France, I worked at a clothing store in Stockholm, I saved money, I wrote letters to Emma, instead of writing about how much I missed her and how empty my life was without her, I wrote about the latest weekend at the G-club, I wrote about who had been there, I wrote about how cool it felt that I could get Martin, Pontus and Lukas in (even though he was nearly too drunk to get in, and the bouncer even pulled him aside and told him to "take it easy in there"), when she wrote that she missed me, I wrote about sneaking into Bindefeld parties and stealing bottles and getting free headphones at a Sony party and free cigarettes at a Blend party and when she wrote that my letters felt emotionally distant, I wrote that I was thinking of using my saved money to go to New York. Why? Well, because I had always dreamed of seeing New York and had listened to hip-hop my whole life, and I wanted to see all the landmarks, I would visit Wu's Staten Island and Nas's Queens and Jay Z's Marcy Projects and Emma wrote back, asking if I wouldn't stop by Paris on my way to New York, there are trips with a layover here, and then you can continue, and it sounded like a perfect idea, I went to a travel agency on Sveavägen and found a flight with an open return to New York, with a few days' stop in Paris, I bought a *Rough Guide New York* at Akademibokhandeln, I bought traveler's checks, I boarded the flight to Paris, I landed and took a bus to the city center, my French was patchy, I hated everything related to France, not for colonial reasons (which would have been more logical), no, I hated everything French because they spoke so fast, because they didn't understand me, because they thought they were so special, because they had taken Emma away from me.

She lived in a chambre de bonne on Rue Cassette in Saint-Germain, I got off the bus, looked at the map, and started walking, I walked and walked until I reached the Seine, I crossed the bridge, and continued to her building with a blue door, I sat there and waited for her to come home, for some reason, I hadn't told her I was coming, on some level I wanted to be like my father, he never told my mom when he came to Sweden, he just showed up and when I heard that story, about how mom came home and found a note from him, it sounded so romantic, it wasn't until I stood outside Emma's door in Paris that I realized what a power move it was to be here, to be able to surprise her, to see her for a few seconds before she saw me. But what if she comes home with another man, or rather, with a man? Because I still had a strong feeling that I was a boy, I was nineteen and about to turn twenty, I had less facial hair than many of my aunts, my forearms looked like I shaved them, I was a boy standing outside a woman's door, a woman who had recently mentioned a man in our conversations, his name was Rafik, I hated that he was both French and Arab, that he was five years older, that he had connections to the French fashion industry, or so he claimed, he had a shop that sold Japanese T-shirts, he claimed it was the "urban version of Colette," and he hated Colette, Colette was fake, it was Prada and Gucci, luxury of the old times, but still he went there often, to meet the managers, to talk to the employees, Rafik had told Emma that if she just sewed more denim skirts, he could sell them in his shop. Sure, I thought when Emma told me that with her hoarse happy voice, he just wants to sell your skirts to get to what's under the skirts, I thought, he just wants to exploit you, he can't be as nice as you describe him, because people aren't nice, people are just out to harm you and deceive you, but since I knew this wasn't what I should say, I didn't say it, instead,

I congratulated Emma and said it was incredible because she always had that magical ability to attract the right people, and now she was studying French during the day and sewing denim skirts for Rafik in the evenings, and gradually, slowly but surely, she was falling in love with Rafik, he was just like me, only better, an upgraded version, they're probably up in her room fucking right now, I thought when no one answered the intercom, I waited outside the door, I went to the bakery on the corner and bought a baguette, I ate the baguette and waited for her, if this were a romantic comedy, they would cut out this part, these three hours of pre-mobile-phone waiting, when I wondered if I had made a mistake coming here, or a mistake not telling Emma that I was coming, wouldn't it have been easier and more comfortable to just say it? But at the same time, it would have been less like the myth I wanted to construct, and especially if Emma and I were to have children and a family in the future I wanted this to be part of the story, your dad came down to Paris and surprised me, yes, he was so romantic, he just booked a trip and came down, but I wasn't romantic at all, this was the opposite of romance, I had planned the surprise visit for months, I lied to Emma so she wouldn't suspect anything, I visited her, but I was also looking forward to telling her and especially Rafik that I was just passing through, I would continue to New York, this wasn't my final destination, I had places to visit, people to meet, start spreading the news, I was on my way to bigger things, and on some level, I was so hurt that she left me in Stockholm that I looked forward to hurting her in the same way in Paris, but none of this would happen if she never came home.

At 6 p.m., she still hadn't arrived, and the people working at the bakery started giving me strange looks, I had been there again and bought a second baguette, I had finished my Camus book, I wondered if Emma could have moved without telling me, maybe she was living with Rafik, when would she tell me? She's probably there now . . . and then I saw her. She was walking down the street with her quick steps, some people might interpret her body language as stressed, but she wasn't stressed, she just looked like a person who was really looking forward to whatever was happening on the other side of the street corner, she looked like a person with an excess of energy that had to come out somewhere, and right now it was coming out through her feet, her posture was that of a gymnast, back straight, ponytail bouncing, headphones on her ears, I stood on the other side of the street, she didn't see me, she still hadn't seen me, it wasn't too late for me to run away, the house behind her was dark gray, I shouted her name, Emma, she didn't hear me because of the headphones, I shouted again, louder this time, Emma, she still didn't hear me, my voice didn't sound like mine, it sounded terrified, she turned sideways, she took out one of the earphones, she looked across the street, she saw me, and it took several years before I realized that I hadn't come to Paris to construct a myth or for Emma to tell her friends that I was romantic, no, the real reason was that I wanted to see her naked confused face, I wanted to know if I could trust her, and the only way I could do that was to surprise her and try to make her show me how she would react to my presence, in those microseconds before she realized who I was, before her brain kicked in and she screamed my name and started crying, before we started kissing, she on her tiptoes, me with my legs wide apart to minimize the height difference, before we ran up to her chambre de bonne, before we spent those sometimes wonderful, sometimes quite strange days together in Paris, when she introduced me to Rafik and all the other French men she had managed to meet in the few months she had been living here, and I told everyone I met that I was on my way to New York, and before Emma showed me her favorite restaurants and I compared them to the restaurants I read about in my New York guidebook, and we went to Colette, and I talked about the Prada store on Fifth Avenue, and Emma showed me the Palais de Tokyo, and I talked about MoMA, and she said I seemed distant, and I said she was the one who had left, so how the hell could I be distant, before we had that awful night at that club, when I got so drunk that Rafik had to carry me out onto the sidewalk, before I contemplated starting a fight with Rafik, before he helped me when I threw up and all I could think about was that he only helped me so he could tell Emma what a great guy he was, before I realized he never told

Emma that I had thrown up, before Emma and I had broken up and
gotten back together so many times that when it happened again,
both her friends and mine pretended to yawn and said, "Why don't
you just get married?" Before I met Diane, before Emma died, before I became a father, before everything that happened afterwards
happened, we saw each other on Rue Cassette in Paris, and when
she saw me, she didn't look disappointed, she didn't look like she
hated me but was trying to hide it, no, she just looked very, very, very
happy.

Chapter Fifty-One

They arrived at the entrance of the shark tunnel, the sign indicated that they had to take off their shoes, and Maja extended her feet towards Evelyn, who helped her take off her glittering sneakers. Then she took off her own shoes and prepared herself to climb into the transparent glass corridor that led straight into the aquarium and out the other side. Maja crawled in first, completely forgetting that she had been scared to go in just a few minutes ago, Evelyn followed her, having to crawl on her belly to fit, and once she was inside the tunnel, surrounded on all sides by fish, water, sharks and stingrays, she felt the need to focus on her breathing, she had never been claustrophobic before, and she wasn't now either, but there was something about the transparent glass, the water, and the distance to the seabed that made her want to go back out.

Are you okay? Maja asked.

I'm fine, Evelyn said. And you?

Look at Simon! Haha, look at his face!

Her uncle was back, he was in line for the shark tunnel, it must have been his reflection in the glass that made him look strange to Maja because when Evelyn looked at him, he looked just as beautiful, broken, fascinating and alive as he had when he rushed off to the toilets. He waved through the blueness of the water, on the other side of the jellyfish, and Evelyn had a sudden thought that she had to be on guard, that he couldn't be trusted, that she really had to be careful with this man because if she let him in, he could hurt her as no one else had before.

How was it? Simon said when they came out of the tunnel, a smile so wide that his gold tooth showed.

I want to go in again! Maja said.

It was actually pretty cool, Evelyn said.

I want to try, Simon said.

I don't think the glass can hold you, Maja said.

What are you talking about? Of course it can, Simon said and took off his shoes. Look, it holds that giant there.

Evelyn looked towards the exit and saw that Hector was struggling to get out of the shark tunnel. And it was true, the glass held for Simon as well, and when he was deep inside the tunnel, the boy took Evelyn's hand. When Simon emerged from the tunnel, a fire burned in his eyes.

You have to try, he said to the boy.

I don't want to, the boy said, gripping Evelyn's hand tighter.

You have to.

But I don't want to.

But you have to.

You're not my dad.

I know, and that's why I can do this.

The boy resisted, at first reluctantly, then laughing, while Simon took off his nephew's shoes and pushed him into the shark tunnel. It only took a few seconds for him to calm down, he realized the glass held, he reached out his hand towards the sharks, the people behind him cleared their throats and patted him on the back to encourage him to continue forward.

Thanks for not killing me, Simon said.

No problem. You can always reach out to me if you need my services.

Perfect. Do you have a business card or something? A website?

I perform the majority of my murders at . . . Evelyn hesitated before giving him the address of the store where she worked. She would think about that pause in the future, how her life would have turned out if she hadn't given him the address or had given him a different one. But she gave him the correct address.

Interesting, he said. I'll remember it.

They were interrupted by an annoyed voice. What are you doing?

Evelyn sighed.

Where's Anastasia? Where have you been? Who's this?

Evelyn turned slowly. There stood Hector and Ina, looking like two worried parents who had lost their children in a park full of pedophiles.

I can't bring you anywhere, Ina said.

Please, just stop, Evelyn whispered.

Who's this? Hector said.

Who's this?! Simon said.

What's your problem? Hector said.

What's your problem? Simon said, as if talking to a baby.

Are you mocking me? Hector asked.

Are you mocking me? Simon said, with a Norwegian accent.

Who's this clown? Hector asked.

Well, I like clowns. Clowns are funny, so I wouldn't really describe you as a clown, Simon said.

This is my sister, Evelyn said. And this is her Hector.

This is just so embarrassing, Ina said.

You think everything is embarrassing, Evelyn said.

We're going to move on to the frog exhibition now, Ina said. Are you coming?

It was a question that wasn't really a question, but for some reason, Evelyn found herself nodding and followed them towards the frog section.

Give me a sign if you need me, Simon whispered as she walked away, and Evelyn smiled as he put two fingers in his open mouth and blew his brain out in slow motion.

Who's that madman? Ina said. Did you see what he did to his son? He just shoved him into the tunnel.

He's not his son, Evelyn said.

Well, that makes it even worse, Ina said.

Maybe he needed it, Evelyn said. He was too scared to go in by himself, so . . .

That's child abuse, Ina said. Now let's find Anastasia and look at some frogs.

They walked through the gift shop, passed the café and followed the signs to the frog section.

She must be here somewhere, Ina said.

But Anastasia was missing. She wasn't in the bathrooms, not in the café, not in the shark tunnel and not even in the temporary frog exhibition.

But where is she? Ina repeated over and over. How can she just disappear?

Chapter Fifty-Two

was nineteen, on my way home from New York, my planned two weeks had turned into three months, my tourist visa was about to expire, and I was so broke when I left that I bought a subway token with my last dollars and gave the rest of my change to a homeless person, not because I wanted to be kind, but because I wanted to construct my own myth, even then, I was in the process of designing my life to function as a story. It was my first time in New York, my first time in the USA, I had read an article before where the journalist said there are three things that never leave one's memory: the first kiss, the first child, and the first time on a plane descending through the clouds towards New York, and three months earlier, I had done just that, I wondered in real time if I would remember that moment forever, I was already a little tipsy, there was complimentary ice-cold red wine in the middle of the plane, and when I discovered it, I drank with that special focus that comes from having both thrifty and alcoholic genes, when the pilot's voice on the loudspeaker announced that we would be landing soon, I was so drunk that I had trouble filling out the customs form, I looked out the window, I knew the city would soon reveal itself on my right side, I had done my research, I knew that flights landing at JFK from Europe almost always had Manhattan on the right side, so I had wedged my long legs into a window seat and refused to switch, despite the person in the middle seat realizing how thirsty I was and how often I would need to go to the bathroom to stock up on mini bottles of wine, but now as we descended, my knees no longer hurt and I didn't feel as drunk anymore, I just looked out through the round vibrating window, my breath steaming up the plastic, soon I would see the Empire State Building, the World Trade Center, maybe even the Statue of Liberty, even though my guidebooks said she was much smaller than people think, when the plane broke through the clouds, I heard oohs and aahs from the other side of the plane, even the people in the aisle seats were twisted towards the window, I never saw what they saw, and when we landed at JFK, my thoughts told me that I had ruined it, one of my three potential strongest memories in life, I could have had it because my original seat had been by a window on the left side, that's where fate had placed me, but because I had done my re-search, I switched to the right side, and now I was convinced that this was a sign that the journey would continue like this, the city would be a disappointment, it wouldn't live up to its reputation, my flight back to Stockholm was in two weeks, and I would probably need to reschedule my return because this wasn't my city, I already felt it, even though I hadn't yet left the airplane.

I picked up my suitcase, one of the plastic wheels had broken, I dragged it towards the subway to go to Midtown, the sun was shining, the subway voice was speaking, the same subway voice I had heard in numerous hip-hop songs, I got off at Fifth Avenue, walked out onto the street, saw the tall buildings, but I didn't think about the Mikkola sisters, and I walked down the avenue and realized that no one saw me, no one noticed me, it was incredible, I had only been in New York for a few hours, and already it felt like I never wanted to leave, this was my place on earth, I saw Rockefeller Center, I saw the Empire State Building disappear into the clouds, I didn't look up too much at famous buildings because I didn't want to seem like a tourist, I was a future New Yorker, one day this would be my home, I didn't know how or when yet, but that didn't matter, right now I was staying at the Gershwin Hostel in Midtown, I had booked a shared room, two bunk beds in each room, in one bed, a girl from Canada who introduced herself as an exotic dancer, in the other two beds, two constantly drunk Australian guys, when I opened the curtains I discovered that the view was a red brick wall, and I smiled because everything was exactly how it should be, I hadn't eaten in hours, but I didn't need food, I was high on New York air, high on the time difference, high on the wine from the plane, on the first evening I continued down Fifth Avenue, and I couldn't stop smiling, I bought a sandwich at a deli, I crossed a street, I called my mom from a phone booth on a street corner just to tell her that I was here, I was actually standing in Manhattan right now, when we hung up, I heard someone scream, "Motherfucker, I'm gonna kill you," and it turned out to be a homeless man talking to the voices in his head, when I realized that I wasn't about to be killed on my first night in New York, my smile returned, the following days, I walked in patterns on avenues to see everything, I went down to the World Trade Center, took the Staten Island Ferry, hung out in Central Park, visited MoMA, I kept thinking that there must be a way for me to stay here, this is my place, I had no friends, I didn't talk to anyone, and yet I was happier than I had ever been.

After a week, I saw a note on the bulletin board at the Gershwin Hostel, a guy named Steve was looking for someone to help out at his hostel a few blocks south and east, I took down the note from the bulletin board to avoid competition, the next day, I went over to Steve's hostel, but I couldn't find it, I asked people on the street, they shook their heads and shrugged, the name was something in Japanese, maybe I pronounced it wrong, or maybe he had written the wrong address in the ad, then I found it, the hostel turned out to be Steve's apartment, he had filled it with bunk beds and rented out sleeping spaces to Japanese students, Steve wasn't Japanese, he was as American as can be, but at some point he had a Japanese girlfriend who broke his heart, he told me that Japanese women are the best, Filipinas are almost as good, but they're not as good as the Japanese, not at all, he showed me the apartment, to the left was a combined TV room and sleeping area, and to the right was our room, the bed we would share, or no, that was a joke, he would sleep on the bed, and I would sleep on a mattress on the floor, on the door to our room was a piece of paper with the handwritten word "Management." My job, if I accepted, would be to answer the wireless phone and be ready to let in any guests who came from Japan to stay here, Steve had a lot to do during the day, so he needed someone to be present during the daytime, to stay on top of things, as he said, this was my chance to stay longer in the USA, so I called the airline, postponed my trip and moved my things from the Gershwin to Steve's apartment later that day.

Chapter Fifty-Three

Anastasia had snuck out to smoke a quick cigarette, but not because she smoked, she had quit a long time ago in fact. She only smoked one or maybe two cigarettes a day, never more than four or maybe five on weekends, but she was no longer a smoker. When she finished her cigarette and was about to go back into the aquarium, the woman behind the counter demanded to see her ticket.

Anastasia explained that Hector had paid for her and he had her ticket.

Unfortunately, I can't let you in without a ticket, the woman said with a sly smile.

But Monica, that's your name, right? I understand if you're bitter about closing soon. And I get that it's difficult to find a new job at your age. But you just saw me go out, didn't you?

You need to show me a ticket if you want to come back in, the woman said, relishing every second of this revenge.

Anastasia sighed and returned to the lockers, took out her coat, and left the aquarium. On her way out, she realized that the lady behind the counter had done her a favor by not letting her back in. She was halfway across the bridge towards the city when Ina called, she was crying, she said something had happened at the frog exhibition, she and Evelyn had gotten into a fight, Ina had just tried to give Evelyn some life advice, she had recommended that she try to meet someone who wasn't a mentally unstable, sloppily dressed child abuser, Ina kindly asked if it was possible for Evelyn to go anywhere without trying to find someone to fuck, and suddenly Evelyn started screaming, really screaming, like a madwoman, people were looking, someone had called security.

Wait a minute, slow down, Anastasia said. It was just ten minutes ago that we . . .

She attacked me, Ina said. I was just trying to give her some advice, and suddenly she started screaming and lunging at me, she tried to slam my head against a frog tank, I promise she went crazy, she she she became like Mom.

Calm down, Anastasia said. Breathe. Is Hector still there?

I was just trying to help, Ina said. She started screaming that I never loved her and was always jealous of her, and then she grabbed me and tried to smash my head into one of the aquariums, Ina said.

Is Hector there?

Yes. He was the one who stopped her.

And where is Evelyn?

She just stormed out.

Okay, Anastasia said.

I was just trying to help.

It's okay, sis.

I just wanted us to have some time together.

It's okay, sis.

I just I just I just . . .

It's okay, sis, Anastasia said. Listen to me, it will be okay. Don't cry, Ina. Don't cry. I promise you. It will be okay. In three years, we will laugh about this, I promise. It will be like that time when Dad was drunk at that baptism. It felt terrible at the time, but soon after, we joked about it. No one will remember this in three years, okay? Ina? Can you hear me?

Ina was there, Anastasia could hear her breathing, but Ina didn't say anything. She couldn't speak because she knew that if she did, she would break, and everyone, including herself, knew that she wasn't a person who broke.

Chapter Fifty-Four

t quickly became apparent that Steve didn't have much to do during the days, he mostly sat at home, fixated on the big-screen TV displaying the latest stock market developments, he constantly invested, on a good day he made $5,000 by lunchtime, on a bad day he was down $10,000 when the markets closed, the strange thing was that his mood had an inverse relationship with the market's movements, when he made money, he seemed sad and locked himself in his room, not to be seen for the rest of the afternoon, if his stocks collapsed, he would rise from the black leather sofa and stand behind his keyboard, singing '80s ballads with a melodramatic voice, as if he was almost relieved that the money was gone.

This is just my side hustle, he used to say.

In reality, he was more of an actor, he had a large box of casting photos, and he gave me one, I still have it somewhere, it was black and white, and he had no beard in the picture, he looked really handsome, I couldn't believe it was the same person who spent his life in front of the TV and invested in stocks he knew nothing about.

One day, our street was closed for a film shoot, and Steve spent the whole day watching the movie set through the window with binoculars, he commented on their equipment and ran down to the street, with the hopes of being asked to join as an extra. Another day, one of the Japanese students returned to the hostel with gray streaks on his face, Steve started talking to him in Japanese, but the guy barely understood what Steve was saying, they switched to English, and it turned out the guy had been robbed.

Where? I asked.

At Union Square, he said.

In the park? I said.

At Barnes and Noble, he replied.

That's impossible, Steve said. You can't get robbed in a damn bookstore.

The guy didn't respond, he went back to Japan, and another Japanese student took his place, I stayed, I never wanted to go home, during the day I was Steve's audience and kept him company, in the evenings I left the apartment and explored New York, I smoked clove cigarettes in empty bars on the Lower East Side, played basketball in the West Village, I put on my only suit and took the elevator up to the Greatest Bar on Earth, at the top of the World Trade Center, despite (or maybe because of) wearing a shirt and tie, they asked me for my ID, and luckily I had brought my Tunisian passport, it was dark green and had handwritten letters, making it easy to forge my birth year, I added another layer of plastic, applied watercolor, added another layer of plastic, and filled in that I was born in 1976 instead of 1978, which meant American bartenders could see that I was over twenty-one. Once, when I took a bus uptown, a lady noticed me and commented on my height, and instead of shrinking and making myself smaller, as I had done all my life, I said, Yes, I'm tall. I'm really tall. I'm actually six-five or six-six, and she smiled and said, Good for you. I was slowly becoming a person I had never been before, and I didn't understand where this person had been all my life.

I never wanted to leave, but I knew time was running out, soon I would have to go home, I had a long list of things I wanted to do before I left, I worked at a homeless shelter on East First Street, just to be able to say that I had worked at a shelter, I went down to Chinatown and bought one-dollar noodles just because I was short on money, I saw Busta Rhymes outside a clothing store on Broadway, I attended a reading with Paul Auster in Brooklyn and didn't dare tell him how much I loved the New York Trilogy, but at least I dared to borrow his lighter, I went up to Top of the Rock and wondered if the Mikkola sisters had been there, I spent hours at the Strand, reading two pages from every newly published American novel and hating them with a frenzy that surprised even myself, I hated their names, their affected tones, their attempts to create contrived narratives, their perfectly polished sentences, their tiresome efforts to shape their dramatic curves, their beautiful author photos, but most of all, I hated the authors who, in their confident bios, declared that they live in New York (or even worse: in Brooklyn).

Then the day came when I had to leave, my tourist visa expired, I said goodbye to Steve, packed my bag, bought my token, took the subway to JFK and flew home, when the plane landed at Arlanda, I couldn't stop crying, I knew this wasn't home, Emma had moved back from Paris, she surprised me at the airport, and I tried to hide my sadness, but she sensed it anyway, Mom invited us for Sunday dinner, I sat there in the kitchen where I grew up, convincing myself that I had missed them, Mom and Emma, my brothers and my friends, that I was happy to be back, that it felt wonderful to be sitting on Drakenbergsgatan again, on the same black IKEA chairs Mom bought when she left home, to have dinner with the same silverware I used as a child, at the same table, by the same window, with the same topics of conversation, I really tried, I tried to convince myself that I was happy, but it didn't work, and a few weeks later, Emma and I broke up.

Chapter Fifty-Five

As the year 2000 came to an end, Ina celebrated Christmas and New Year's Eve with Hector's family on the west coast, Anastasia went to Gothenburg to be with Fabricia, Evelyn signed up for all the shifts she could get at the store, there was 100 percent overtime pay on weekends and holidays, but since Christmas Eve fell on a Sunday, without any additional compensation, no one wanted to work then. Evelyn signed up. She was there on time. She mopped the floor. She dusted the mirrors and rolled up the electric steel shutters a few minutes before opening. She was supposed to work with Anders, but it was incredibly calm, only six customers before lunch, and after lunch, Evelyn told Anders that he could leave early if he wanted, he had covered for her so many times, and now she was happy to cover for him.

Are you sure? Anders said. My family would be thrilled.

Evelyn nodded and told him to leave, there were no customers anyway, and of course she wouldn't say anything to the managers. Anders gave her a quick thank-you hug, wished her a Merry Christmas and went to the storeroom to get his coat and bags of wrapped presents.

Give your sisters a hug from me, he said as he left the store. She hadn't told him that she would celebrate with her sisters, he had just assumed it, and she didn't feel like correcting him, she had no desire to tell him that her Christmas plan was to close the store at three and then take the subway to Ina's apartment to open the only present she had received this year (from their bosses, all employees got the same thing—last year it was kitchen towels, and the year before that, scented candles). Anders didn't need to know that Ina had been living with Hector since that little dispute at the frog exhibition. Evelyn wanted to say that she missed her sister, but right now, on Christmas Eve in 2000, she wasn't sure if she really did.

As soon as Anders left, she could relax, there was something about being around other people that created a pressure inside her, she needed to be prepared, ready to crack a joke, tell a story, be liked, and when people appreciated her, she despised them for being so easy to manipulate, and if people didn't like her, she despised herself for being so acutely aware of others' disapproval. It was only when she was alone that she could be herself, whatever that was.

She dimmed the lights in the store and turned off the Christmas music, during the next ten minutes, she stood in the corner of the store, looking out at the falling snow, the well-dressed people passing by on the street, everyone with last-minute gifts in bags, everyone on their way somewhere. She thought about Simon. After their meeting at the aquarium, she had expected him to stop by the store on Monday morning and ask her out for lunch. Because she couldn't have been the only one who felt the energy between them, could she? When he hadn't come by on Monday afternoon, she thought he was playing hard to get and would come on Tuesday. When he hadn't come by on Thursday, Evelyn thought he must be married. When the weekend passed without him showing up, Evelyn convinced herself that he was an idiot who had missed the chance of his life. She went out, met someone, spent the night, and came home with a stolen Japanese coaster.

The following week, when he still hadn't shown up, she started to worry that something had happened to him. He wasn't dead, was he? The week before Christmas was hectic, long queues, desperate last-minute shoppers, hundreds of sweaters and shirts and belts and blouses that needed to be wrapped, Evelyn worked at the cash register, and sometimes she saw Simon entering the store, someone of the same height or someone with the same hair color, and even though

Evelyn knew it wasn't him, she felt a surge of joy that reminded her to be cautious if he ever stopped by.

Now she had accepted that Simon wouldn't come, and she knew for certain that he wouldn't come today because everyone was with their families on Christmas Eve. She hadn't had a single customer since Anders left. One of the security guards patrolling the street passed by, wearing his usual uniform but with a Santa hat that looked too small for his large head, he waved to Evelyn and mouthed "Merry Christmas," then he disappeared, and Evelyn got ready to close up. She had already balanced the cash register, counted the bills and reconciled the card payments. Now it was five minutes to three. She took out the key to the rolling shutter from the cash register and stood by the entrance. Normally, she never hesitated to close the store a few minutes early, especially if she knew their bosses were in Milan to view the autumn collections. But for some reason, she waited until three o'clock today. Soon she would lower the shutter, turn off the lights, hide the cash in the storeroom and leave the store.

At 2:58, she saw him, he stood farther down the street, near the entrance to the parking garage, he was carrying a large plastic bag, but it didn't seem to contain square presents; rather, it looked like . . . fabric? Dirty laundry? Towels?

He waved at her and smiled, she knew it wasn't him, it couldn't be, she ignored the wave, she checked the time, 2:59, still she turned the key, and the burglar-proof shutter descended over the shop window and the door, like a slow-motion waterfall. In the corner of her eye, she saw that he had started running towards her, but it was too late, the shutter was already halfway down when he reached the store's entrance.

It's me, he said.

Unfortunately, we're closed, she replied.

I need to talk to you, he said.

He had dropped the bag on the ground and had his fingers under the steel grille to prevent it from moving downwards. The grille stopped window breakers, but it was perforated, and it didn't stop his gaze. Evelyn looked away.

I would have come earlier, his voice said. But I couldn't.

Why?

I couldn't, he said.

Evelyn noticed that, for some reason, she had released the key to the shutter. She reached for it again and turned it, and the shutter continued its descent.

No, wait, wait, wait, he said. Wait. I'm sorry. I've come to cancel our contract.

Meaning?

That I don't want you to kill me anymore, it was just something I said, I was so tired when we met, I had been with my sister's kids for five days, they drove me crazy, I hadn't slept, I was . . .

So now you don't want to die anymore?

Absolutely not.

And may I ask why?

Well . . . I've met someone, he said.

Good for you, Evelyn said and turned the key so that the shutter hit the ground.

No, wait, he said, and now his voice sounded closer as if he was leaning forward to say something important. She heard the raspy sound of his thin beard against the shutter. Evelyn turned around, closed the door and locked it with force so that he would hear that she was no longer there on the other side. Then she stood still in the entrance and listened to the sound of the empty store, the ticking of the spotlights, the hissing in the pipes. After Christmas, they would prepare the store for the sale, and now she just needed to hide the cash in the storeroom and let herself out through the back door. Why had he come, and why didn't he leave? She stood completely still for three minutes. The silhouette of his body was still out there. She opened the door to the store without raising the shutter.

Are you still here? she said.

Here, he said.

Through the small holes in the grille, she saw that the snow had intensified. Actual snowflakes were on his eyelashes, which irritated Evelyn because it was just too much, he can't have those eyes and that mouth and those teeth and that nose and that voice and then walk around in the world with snowflakes on his eyelashes, it's just not possible.

And this person, Evelyn said, whom you've met. Is she, or he, interested in you?

I don't know, he said. That's the craziest thing, that we don't know each other, and yet . . .

Yet?

It feels like we belong together, he said. Not just now. But later too.

Later?

As long as it lasts.

Much later, when Simon and Evelyn had been together for several years, and their first and second meeting had become one of the many stories Evelyn told to give meaning to her life (according to herself) or to gain other people's appreciation (according to Ina), Evelyn described the feeling at that moment as a perfect mix of joy and envy. Even though she understood that Simon was talking about her, she felt strangely envious of the person he was talking about, perhaps because, on some level, she knew that she could never be the person he imagined her to be. Evelyn inserted the key and opened the steel shutter. Never before had a steel shutter moved so slowly. Evelyn turned the key with maximum force as if it would increase the speed. Simon pulled up the shutter with his fingers as if it would make time pass faster. Finally, they could see each other without bars. They approached each other and kissed.

Two weeks later, Evelyn moved out of Ina's apartment.

Six months later their mother was dead.

Chapter Fifty-Six

n December 1999, Emma told me that her friend Hella was having a big New Year's party at a freelance office space, Emma wanted to go, but the guest list was full and it seemed impossible to get in. During the last couple of years, Emma and I had gotten back together, broken up, gotten back together again, but now we had just broken up, when she said she wasn't going to Hella's party. I decided to go, I had started hanging out with some friends from Södra Ängby, one of them I had known since I was a child, and the other was a newer friend, both of them grew up in houses with cars, and they had a different way of talking to each other, they were less afraid to talk about emotions and didn't talk as much about weed and gun replicas, I convinced them that we should go together to Hella's party.

Will we get in? Martin said.

Of course, I said.

But wasn't the guest list full? Pontus said.

It will work out, I said. I know people who are going, and we can mention their names at the door.

But what if they check our IDs? Martin said.

What if the real people have already gone in? Pontus said.

Both of them were right, but I convinced Martin to come along, and then Pontus joined as well, first we drank sparkling wine at Pontus's place on Observatoriegatan, we brought our suits with us, changed and listened to Nas, we smoked indoors and helped each other with our ties, then we went to Hella's party, we arrived early, but when we got there, it was obvious that it wouldn't work, the line was too long and the bouncers shouted that the entrance was closed, still people stayed, hoping for a miracle, they were already here, and soon it would be a new millennium, and no one wanted to celebrate the stroke of midnight waiting for a subway or in the phone queue for a taxi.

While we debated whether to stay or leave, I saw three women pass by the line and go in. From behind, they reminded me of the Mikkola sisters, but I wasn't sure because I had heard that Ina was studying economics in Malmö and Anastasia was in some kind of treatment facility.

I persuaded my friends to follow me around the block, on the back side of the building there were a bunch of strange birds in a tree, we looked up and realized they were people, they had climbed up using a bike rack and were now balancing on a branch to jump in through a third-floor window, the window was closed, and they knocked and knocked until someone inside opened it. I saw the quick hand gestures of someone waving them in, and seconds later, they were gone.

No chance, Martin said.

You're joking, Pontus said.

It's the only way, I said.

I had already started climbing, I was drunk, I was desperate, I had a feeling that the opportunity wouldn't last long, and if I just started climbing, my friends would follow me, when I was high up in the tree, I looked down and saw my friends on the sidewalk, I understood why they had hesitated, it was higher up than I had expected, Pontus tilted his head back so far that he opened his mouth, Martin had one hand on his forehead as if he needed to shield his eyes from the sun, even though it was December and almost midnight. The window was still open.

Come on, I said.

Not in a hundred years, Martin said.

I'm staying here, Pontus said.

Just then, one of the bouncers came running, and my friends, who hadn't done anything, started running, and I balanced on the tree branch and jumped into what I thought was the party, but it turned out to be an empty office landscape. I kept walking towards the bass sound, and after a few minutes of opening doors and exploring corridors, I found the staircase and the party, I stood in the middle of the dance floor, knowing that no one would find me here, I stayed in the safety of the crowd, assuming that I would meet someone I knew, someone I could toast with, maybe someone I had been friends with when I was little, and sure enough, there were a few people I recognized, I nodded and raised my glass, and they did the same, we kept moving, there was no one here that I knew well enough to talk to, no one that I could toast with at midnight, I looked for Evelyn, Ina and Anastasia, but couldn't find them until it was too late, with a few minutes left until midnight, I was back on the main dance floor, I tried to position myself in the middle so that no one would notice I was there without friends, I convinced myself that I didn't feel guilty about leaving my friends, they could have been here too if they wanted, but they chose to stay outside, and that was their loss, not mine, then I saw them, not my friends, but the Mikkola sisters, it was them, I was sure, Ina tallest on the dance floor, in a discreet black top, Anastasia had short hair and nose piercings, she stood on something, maybe a chair or a windowsill, trying to open a bottle, in front of her, I saw Evelyn, wearing a turquoise sequin dress, she was strangely overdressed, as if she had been to a ball before coming here, the material reflected the light from the dance floor, she must have been twenty-one, and I remember thinking that she had aged, which was strange because she must have looked magnificent, no lump on her neck, no gray hair, their mother still alive. They stood there, no more than ten meters away, and yet they didn't seem to notice me. I couldn't stop staring.

Do you need a wingman?

I looked to my left. A big guy with a red beard smiled and nodded towards Evelyn.

I'm not a good skater, he said. A terrible singer. But I'm a fan-fucking-tastic wingman.

Thanks, but no thanks, I said. They're old friends.

Who?

All three. They're sisters.

No way.

Of course they are.

Honestly? I'm not convinced.

I looked towards the Mikkola sisters and saw what he saw. Three women, of different heights, with different skin tones, with differently textured hair, different everything. And for the first time, I wondered to myself why they didn't look more like sisters and less like three dark-haired friends standing on a dance floor, filling their glasses with bubbly from the same bottle.

Well, if you need me, you know where to find me, the guy with the red beard said and disappeared forever.

I gathered my courage and approached. I fought my way through the crowd and tapped Evelyn on the shoulder, she met my gaze.

Hey, I said.

Huh?

It's me, I said, trying to make myself heard over the music. Jonas! From Drakenberg?

Evelyn raised her index finger and shook it in front of me like a metronome. I still don't know what she thought I said. Did she think I was asking for her number? Asking if I could taste from their bottle? Asking for a kiss? Wouldn't it be more logical to first ask for her name? Did she respond to everyone who asked what her name was with a shaking index finger? Or was she trying to tell me that I wasn't who I was because I was an older version of myself? Or maybe she was just drunk and didn't hear what I said. I don't know, and I will never know, because I hesitated and backed away, I observed the sisters from a distance, Anastasia was dancing, Ina was talking to a freckled man, Evelyn had already forgotten about me, as I walked towards the door, everyone started counting down. Ten, nine, eight, and I continued towards the exit, I didn't look back, I couldn't bear to see everyone so happy, so united, so free from pain, so free from their past, when everyone shouted Happy New Year, the dance floor was drowned in confetti, and I opened the door to the stairwell, I turned around to catch one last glimpse of them, but I only saw

Anastasia, she was still up there, on the chair or windowsill or table, for a second, it looked like she was looking straight at me, then I saw her wave to someone else, and then she lost her balance and fell from whatever it was she was standing on, but she didn't need to be afraid because she knew there was a dense sea of people down there, and Evelyn and Ina were there.

On my way down the stairwell, I realized that the bouncer who saw me jump in through the window might be waiting at the entrance. So I turned around and made my way back to the office landscape where I entered, as I approached the window, I heard a new countdown echoing from the party, seven, six, five, I never heard the end of the countdown, it was drowned out by frantic knocking on the window, someone was banging on the glass, it was a guy with a wild look and a shaved head, when I opened the window, he jumped in, claiming that he "knew Anastasia," he had a backpack and chemical breath, before I could respond, he disappeared, he ran towards the music, and I climbed out into the winter air, I balanced back on the tree branch and headed towards the subway. I tried to call my friends to tell them I was sorry for leaving them, that we should have stuck together, that this wasn't how I wanted to start the new millennium.

They never answered.

BOOK 2

2003 (Six Months)

Part I

Chapter Fifty-Seven

The first flight was just a normal flight, nothing special, just normal Swedes and Germans and some Arabs boarding a metal bus with wings, then somehow through the magic of fossilized solar energy and jet engines the metal bus managed to reach enough speed to challenge gravity, this gigantic thing weighing hundreds of tons left the ground and disappeared up through the clouds. Anastasia leaned her head against the vibrating round plastic windows. The pilot turned off the seat belt signs and the flight attendants started their tour of the cabin, their carts always blocking at least one or two people from reaching the bathrooms, and the trapped person had no option but to just stand there, in full view of everyone, counting down the minutes.

The flight took two hours and when Anastasia left the airplane she knew that she wouldn't remember anything from this flight, not the man who snored in the seat next to her, not the takeoff or the landing or the toilet at Frankfurt Airport, not the staircases, the escalators, the shiny floor, the endless corridors, the forgotten soda machines, the screens showing the gates, the cafés with their overpriced coffee, the gates looking just like the gates of every airport that she had ever visited. She passed a police control that marked the frontier between the EU and the rest of the world. At the gate for her second flight she saw her cousins. They were sitting with one Gameboy each, totally engrossed in whatever they were playing. Her aunts had bought fashion magazines and were talking about something in German. There were at least five men who could have been her uncles, one had that black mark on his forehead that showed that he was a devout Muslim, and she still didn't know if that was a thing that the devout Muslims tattooed there, or if it was an actual mark from praying five times a day, with a certain focus. Another of her uncles was talking to someone on his cell phone, he spoke Arabic, so she only understood three or four words, *chamsa* ("five"), *mie* ("thousand"), *brebbi* ("please"), *fehemt* ("understood"). And of course her grandmother was there as well, even though Anastasia had only seen photos of her, she was sitting next to the gate in a wheelchair, driven by someone who worked for Frankfurt Airport, the same hijab, the same henna tattoos, the same cane carved out of the same ancient tree.

Anastasia sat down and waited, surrounded by relatives speaking a language that was hers, that she didn't understand. It was the summer of 2003, and Anastasia was finally on her way. Even though there were times when she had doubted, like when she was at the embassy picking up the forms and the woman at the reception asked her to show her Tunisian passport again because she couldn't believe that someone who looked like Anastasia could actually be Tunisian, or when Ina and Evelyn tried to persuade her to postpone the trip, Evelyn worried that something might happen, Ina wanting to hang on to her belief that Anastasia never succeeded in finishing what she started. But now, as Anastasia sat there in Frankfurt, surrounded by her sleeping grandmother, her angry uncle, her Gameboy-playing cousins, her gossiping aunts, she knew that she had done the right thing.

Chapter Fifty-Eight

The organizers of the event looked baffled when they peeked out the door of the lecture hall and saw the growing crowds. Twenty minutes ago everything had been fine, the people who had gathered in the corridor looked like the typical ABF visitors, a gang of old ladies with canes, curious the way only old ladies are, they had their pens, they had their pads, they had their short hairdos and their pediatric shoes, their foldable umbrellas and their thermoses, they would be here no matter the topic, they were married to husbands whose brains were deteriorating in front of never-ending soccer games, their men had lost their ability to speak, think and listen a long time ago, and these ladies never wanted to become them, so they kept doing their weekly crossword puzzles, they went over to their sister's place to play bridge, and whenever there were free lectures at ABF, they came early to reserve a seat in the front. Normally it was never full, there was always room for the senior citizens and the occasional crazy person who snuck into the lecture hall only to raise his hand to take the opportunity to present his personal take on the South African cover-up of the Olof Palme assassination.

But today the old ladies and the occasional crazy person were joined by a new type of listener, they were young, they had brown skin, they carried books by Fanon, they wore oversized Talib Kweli T-shirts, they had to ask in the reception for the Edward Said lecture, and since this was the ABF, aka the Workers' Educational Association, there was no reception, just an increasingly irritated caretaker who finally wrote a sign with the word LECTURE and an arrow, pointing upwards, so that the crowds of people could stop interrupting him from whatever he was doing. The organizers realized that they had a problem. The young people kept pouring out of the elevators, and the people who had gotten tired of waiting for the elevators simply took the broad stairs up, and now, with twenty minutes to go, the corridors were jam-packed, and there wasn't even any capitalism to keep the waiting crowds happy, nobody sold coffee (the café on the second floor was closed on weekends), nobody was selling books (the association had its own local bookstore, but unfortunately it hadn't been able to secure books in time for the event), so the crowds just stood there, growing more and more frustrated as they realized that there was no way all of them would fit.

When Ina and Hector arrived it was obvious that they wouldn't be able to secure seats. The small venue was already packed and the corridor outside was full.

Let's leave, Ina said, in a quiet voice, trying to hide her disappointment.

No, Hector said, even though he hadn't been even remotely as hyped up about this talk as she was. Sure they had both read Said, Hector had read *Orientalism*, mainly because it was an important point of reference at the university, while Ina had read everything Said had ever written, *Orientalism*, yes, of course, his essays about Palestine, check, even that recent letter exchange with Michael Walzer.

So wait, let me get this straight, Hector had said when he heard this. My future wife actually pleasure-reads Said. That's hot.

Ina had leaned forward to kiss him on his ear so that he wouldn't see how happy she was to be called his future wife. She didn't tell him that one of the pleasures of reading Said was that he was an Arab intellectual. It would sound weird to say, maybe even a bit racist, because really, Ina wasn't Arab enough to claim any affiliation with other Arabs, she didn't speak Arabic, she had only been to her mother's home country three or four times and what did she remember from those visits, they had gone somewhere by bus, they had stayed in an apartment with white walls, there was a turquoise door downstairs, with light flowing in on all sides of it as if the door was too small for the opening, or as if the light outside was too bright to be held back by the walls. She didn't remember the names of her mom's relatives, she didn't remember their faces, she only remembered that they butchered a lamb and one of the relatives dipped her hand in the blood and put a red handprint on the wall of the courtyard and the same relative kept referring to Evelyn as "fellous" which possibly meant little yellow chicken, or maybe meant small bird, or maybe just meant young Swedish baby with incredibly long eyelashes. One night the adults had been arguing about something, loud voices, doors slamming, and the morning after they had moved to another place, with a door that wasn't turquoise. That's all she remembered. Still Said's words did something to her, he was the dad she never had, or rather: the dad who would have fit her better, there was something about his perspective, his tone, his author photo, his last name, something about the knowledge that he too had been displaced, he too had started in one country, and lost another country, or rather: he too had a country of his dreams that he on some level knew he would never be able to revisit because it only existed in the past (or maybe not even in the past).

Chapter Fifty-Nine

The second landing was nothing like the first one, instead of gray chimneys and green fields, Anastasia saw white square buildings and green palm trees, descending through the clouds, Tunis looked like a field of sugar cubes, the palm trees looked like pine needles, when the doors opened the heat struck her like a slap in the face, it wasn't hot, the sun wasn't shining, this was another planet, this sun must be a different star, she stood at the top of the staircase, took a deep breath of warm air and felt her body relax. It was her first time here, and she already felt at home.

Two buses stood ready to drive them to the arrival hall, but only one of them worked, so everyone had to squeeze into one bus. Anastasia expected the men to leave room for families, but they didn't, so she didn't either, she squeezed her way onto the bus and tried to stand still as the bus swayed towards the sliding glass doors that welcomed them into the AC coldness of the passport line.

Another airplane with tourists had just arrived, and Anastasia took a form and waited for her turn, it wasn't until she reached the officer that she realized that she was in the wrong queue, she had traveled here on her Tunisian passport, and the man in the blue uniform smiled and guided her to the front of the right line, while people in the back grumbled and shook their heads. A few stamps and then she was through, she was home, whatever *home* meant, she walked through the airport, it looked just like Frankfurt Airport, even though the shops offered more shisha tobacco and less liquor, she walked towards the exit, looking for a sign, looking for someone who looked like they were looking for her.

She had contacted a cousin before leaving, the cousin said that they lived far from Tunis, but had arranged for her to be picked up, the cousin had spoken with an uncle who had spoken with a friend and everything was planned, they would help her, even though they didn't live in Tunis, even though they had never met, they were still family.

But the driver wasn't there, she walked back and forth until the police officers started noticing her, nobody had come, nobody called her name, nobody reached out their arms and hugged her and said welcome, she tried not to feel disappointed, okay, maybe there had been some kind of misunderstanding, maybe she was supposed to take a cab herself, she knew the address and had been alone in foreign countries before, she was twenty-three years old and knew her way around, she asked a smoking man for the tourist information booth, he shook his head, she asked for a taxi, he pointed towards the exit, she walked towards the exit where there should be taxis, there were no taxis, just a mustached man who offered to drive her to Sousse, for a very cheap price.

I just need to go to Avenue de la Liberté, Anastasia said, and as she said it, she saw him. He was sitting on a bench next to the sliding doors, she recognized him, he had lost some of his hair and gained some weight, but it was him, it was the man that their mother had known before she met their father. They had lived in the same area for a few years. Last time Anastasia saw him he worked as a subway driver in Stockholm, last time she saw him he was raising three sons, what was he doing here, at the Tunis airport, looking like he didn't want to be seen? She approached him and asked in Swedish if he remembered her.

Of course, he said.

Are you here to . . . She stopped herself. Of course he wasn't here to pick her up, why would he, and if he would have been here for her, he should have been standing by the ropes holding a sign with her name, he would have reached out and hugged her, not hidden himself by the entrance.

I'm here to pick you up, he said and motioned for her to follow him. He didn't take her bag, he kept walking five steps ahead of her, as if he was afraid of getting too close to her. They exited the building, once again, the heat, it felt like the air was vibrating, he opened the trunk of the black car, his eyes overlooking the parking.

I will drive you to the flat, he said.

Are you . . . have my family . . . , she said. He nodded.

They told me that you were coming and since they live a long way from Tunis I offered to pick you up and let you live in my apartment, he said.

My place is your place, he said.

You can stay there rent-free, he said.

You don't need to pay anything, he said, as they drove out from the parking place, following a perfectly straight road towards the city center. The posters all showed the same thing: the president, gently smiling, looking like a king. The roundabouts had cactuses and palm trees in the middle and after ten minutes of silence, the AC started to blow cool air. She put her overheated hands to the fans, she was here, she was finally here. He looked at her and smiled.

Tomorrow it will be hot, he said.

Hotter than this? she said.

This is nothing, he said. Today is cold compared to what will happen tomorrow.

I'm not used to this, she said. My dad's Swedish genes you know, she added, as a joke, but he didn't smile, he just looked straight ahead.

I live in Jendouba, he said. It's a three-hour drive from here, so you don't have to worry about me, I won't disturb you, just give me a call if you need anything, he said and parked the car in front of a TV store.

Before entering the building he gave her the key, just one single key, small and silvery, looking more like the key to a padlock than the key to a flat.

And the front door? she said, just to say something.

It's always open, he said. And if it's closed, it is easy to open.

He put his hand through the hole that lacked a window and showed how she could open the front door from the outside.

It's on the fifth floor, he said, and looked like he wanted to leave.

Can you show me? she said.

He nodded. They entered the building. He had to stop three times and breathe for air before they reached the right floor. She wondered what had happened to his body, when did it start breaking down, how could he have aged this much in less than ten years.

This is it, he said, and let her open the door.

He stayed outside.

I left some food in the fridge, he said. And water. Don't drink the tap water. There's a washer in the bathroom, but it hasn't been connected yet.

She thanked him before he turned around and walked back down the stairs.

He looked at her and said: I was really sorry to hear what happened to your mom.

She nodded.

You look just like her, he said, and even though Anastasia knew that it was a lie, the compliment worked. She never looked like her mother, Evelyn had their mother's looks, Ina had their mother's planning skills, and the only similarity between Anastasia and her mother was their uncontrollable rage that bubbled up when things didn't go their way.

Remember to always lock the door, he said. These people are crazy.

He said goodbye and walked down the stairs. He didn't tell her not to bring visitors, he didn't say where to find linens for the bed, he just left her his apartment, and now Anastasia stood there in the dark hallway, in a city she had never been to, about to start a course in a language she didn't speak, and she wasn't really sure why she felt so incredibly happy.

Chapter Sixty

And now Edward Said was here, in Stockholm, to give a lecture. When Hector informed her that he was coming, and that Lagerhjelm, one of his professors from the university, had been instrumental in getting him to accept the invitation, Ina jumped from her seat. She had looked forward to this for weeks, and still they hadn't been here early enough to get seats. She had told Hector that they needed to go, and then he had started stroking her breasts and gently put his finger outside and then inside and now we really have to go and Hector guaranteed that it would be fine, Lagerhjelm would be able to get them in, even if it was full, then he kissed her neck and pulled her back to bed, and now this was their punishment, with ten minutes to go all seats were taken.

Look, there's Evelyn, Hector said and pointed.

Hector was right, there she sat on the third row in the packed lecture hall, next to the strange guy she had picked up at the aquarium last autumn.

What is *she* doing here? Ina said. She has never read Said.

At least she got a seat, Hector said.

The contact between Ina and Evelyn had been sporadic during the spring. After the incident at the aquarium, Evelyn had moved out, and they hadn't spoken to each other for several months.

We should leave, Ina said.

Wait, maybe Lagerhjelm can get us in, Hector said.

Hector bulldozed his way through the corridor and managed to get into the lecture hall.

He came back astonished.

I'm so sorry, he said. Not even Lagerhjelm can get us in. I saw his wife waiting in line. All the seats are taken. No one expected this. I'm sorry, Ina, all of this is my fault. Should we leave?

Ina looked at him.

No, let's stay, she said. Let's wait and see.

It might work? Hector asked with a smile.

It might work, Ina said.

There was something strange about this man who always seemed to believe that things were possible, regardless of the situation, and now, it was starting to rub off on her. Pre-Hector Ina would have seen the crowded corridor and turned back on the stairwell. She might not even have entered the building. But now, in the spring of 2001, Ina stayed, she waited, she repeated "it might work" to herself.

Love without a new vocabulary is not love. The expression was born after their first official dinner as a couple, they had been in a suburb south of Stockholm on the green line, visiting some of his friends and after dinner, wine, dessert and dessert wine, they said goodbye and walked back to the subway station, it was late, the trains ran every twenty minutes, as they descended the hill towards the station, they saw a train emerging from around a curve, there was no chance in the world that they could run faster than the train, rush up the stairs, and reach the platform on time, even if they had wings, but Hector saw the train, looked at Ina, and shouted:

It might work!

So they ran, they ran, despite both knowing it was impossible, they ran down the hill, across the street, past the closed locksmith, past the closed pizzeria, across another street, up the stairs and when they reached the platform, the subway was still there, the driver was returning to the front of the train, one of the doors in the middle of the train had gotten stuck, but he fixed it, the other passengers seemed annoyed by the delay, they just wanted to get home, seemingly unaware that the world had just produced a miracle. Ina and Hector sat down on two empty seats, sweaty and out of breath. The doors closed.

Hector leaned forward and whispered: It worked!

But this time, it would be harder. The lecture was supposed to have started a few minutes ago, and now the doors were closing. Even worse than missing the lecture was the realization that Evelyn and Simon were inside.

She's doing it on purpose, Ina mumbled.

Doing what on purpose? Hector asked.

Evelyn, Ina said.

She didn't specify exactly what it was that Evelyn was doing, simply because she wasn't sure what to call it, but she knew that Anastasia would never have done something like this to her, never, ever.

Chapter Sixty-One

Since the apartment was located on the fifth floor, Anastasia had developed a strategy to avoid being sick from the smell of cat pee and rotting garbage. She simply exited the apartment holding her breath, then ran down the stairs and out to the already warm pavement of Avenue de la Liberté. It was eight thirty in the morning and the stray dogs were already panting for air, the mustached men at the nearby café were already fanning themselves with the plastic menu, the thermometer in the nearby TV shop projected that it would be even hotter today than yesterday, and Anastasia wondered how that was physically possible because yesterday it was so hot that the windows of the classroom seemed to buckle, the single fan seemed to be sweating.

During the morning break, when their teacher thought that nobody was looking she took the cloth she used to wipe her face and squeezed it in a corner of the classroom. At lunchtime the puddle had evaporated. Everyone hated the heat, everyone avoided the burning sunshine, walking and waiting in the corridors, to avoid getting their feet burned, everyone except Anastasia. During the morning break, she was the only student out of two hundred who willingly went down to the square open courtyard and smoked a cigarette in the sunshine. The French Tunisians looked at her and said she was folle, the American Tunisians said she was cray cray, the Spanish Tunisians called her loca, but Anastasia didn't care, she had been starving for this sunshine all year, or rather all her life.

For the last couple of years, Anastasia had had the feeling that she was growing lighter each winter. While Ina was getting darker and Evelyn was getting curlier, Anastasia had noticed that she looked more and more European every year. When she was a teenager, people always asked where she was from, if she was half or whole, if she spoke Arabic, if she was Muslim, if her dad would allow her to go on a date and watch a Steven Seagal movie at Filmstaden, but now people rarely asked about her heritage, and as much as Anastasia had hated the questions back then, she missed them now. She wanted people to know that she was not like them, that her family had not been afraid of crossing borders, that she and her sisters had the whole world in their genes and that's why she was the only Tunisian standing face up in the sun of the courtyard during the morning breaks, not caring about the snickering from other girls who seemed to think that she stood there with her cigarette to make sure that everyone saw her.

Once a French girl called Latifah walked out in the courtyard with a metal chair, similar to the one that Anastasia was sitting on, she walked like someone trying to imitate a model, she took out her pack of Mars Légères and lit a cigarette, she smoked it incredibly slowly, with pouting lips, blowing smoke from her nose, and everyone in the shadows watched and laughed, waiting to see what Anastasia's response would be. Anastasia just looked at her, took a deep drag from her cigarette and, with a kind smile, blew smoke in Latifah's eyes. Latifah got up and yelled something in French, but before she had time to raise her fists, Anastasia, in one quick perfectly coordinated move, had flicked away her cigarette, got up from her chair, grabbed the backrest and lifted the chair high over her right shoulder, now it hung there like an axe, ready to land on Latifah's spine. The strange thing was that Anastasia didn't look the least bit angry, instead, it seemed as if she was asking Latifah if she wanted to dance, the metal chair had been waiting its whole life to end up right there, above Anastasia's right shoulder, and as Latifah backed away, spitting insults, Anastasia's lips turned into a smile, as if she enjoyed being mocked, and in a way she did, because it was good to know where her enemies were, it made her feel even more at home than if everyone had been kind and talked to her, this was how it was supposed to be, how it always was—whispering, giggling, pointing, gossiping girls keeping their distance, claiming that Anastasia only sat in the sun in the courtyard to make the boys like her.

Latifah returned to the shadows and her group of fast-talking French-Tunisian friends, and Anastasia returned to her chair, lit another cigarette and turned her head up towards the sunshine, trying to hide the adrenaline flowing in her veins. They were right, she was crazy, and she needed the sun to recharge her energy, and if they thought they could mock her into becoming one of them, they were wrong, now she would sit in the sunlight during every break, with or without sunglasses, with or without cigarettes, they would know where to find her, and if they wanted a fight, she would crush them, she wasn't the Crow anymore, she was ready to kick Latifah in the face if needed, she could bring a sharpened screwdriver from her apartment, if Latifah and her gang wanted war, then they would get war. Anastasia had been at war her entire life, and this school was no different from Hovsjöskolan in Södertälje or Ringtorpsskolan in Helsingborg or Kvarnbäcksskolan in Haninge, sure the students here were older, aged eighteen to twenty-five, but people were the same everywhere and if they thought Anastasia was someone who would back down, they were mistaken.

Chapter Sixty-Two

The lecture was about to start.

Maybe we should go? Hector said. This is all my fault.

No, it's not, Ina said, even though it clearly was his fault.

I think Lagerhjelm could have gotten you in, he mumbled. If we would have been here ten minutes earlier.

But you said his wife was in line, Ina said.

Yes, but Lagerhjelm has a thing for young beautiful women, Hector said.

Ina looked at him, he wasn't looking at her for a reaction, he wasn't cracking up, he didn't look like he had just told a joke, he actually seemed to think that she was beautiful and Ina stood there in the sultry corridor and thought to herself that she didn't care about this lecture.

Just then three women close to the entrance of the lecture hall started chanting something, Ina couldn't see them, their voices sounded like teenagers', they had been so close to getting a seat and now they turned their frustration into a melody, at first it sounded as if they were joking, their voices weren't committed, it sounded more like a desperate last attempt, but then the rest of the waiting crowd heard what they were saying and joined in, the random voices grew into a choir of people screaming BYT LOKAL BYT LOKAL BYT LOKAL, and inside the venue Edward Said must have heard the voices and asked the organizers what was going on, are these militant Mossad supporters or what?

No, Professor Said, maybe Lagerhjelm or someone else said,

these are your fans, they have read your groundbreaking work, they are just frustrated that the lecture hall is full.

And what are they saying?

"Byt lokal."

Which means?

Change the venue.

And is there another venue available?

No, unfortunately not.

So this is the biggest lecture hall you have?

No, but the big lecture hall is booked.

And we can't have their venue?

Well, the organizers said. Well . . .

After two minutes of chanting, a handsome man in his mid-fifties emerged into the corridor, raising his arms in the air until the crowd fell silent. There was something about his eyes that made the upper part of his face look youthful, even though he had that type of grown-out hairstyle that older men who have received compliments for their hair in their youth often have, his age showed in the lower part of his face, the wrinkles around his mouth, the creases on his neck.

Is that Lagerhjelm? Ina whispered.

Sure is, Hector said. Look at him. He loves this.

He didn't say it with contempt, but with a tone of admiration. It took a few moments for the crowd to quiet down.

Thank you all for coming to this event, Lagerhjelm said, looking as if he believed they were all there for his sake. We, who have organized today's lecture by the distinguished Professor Said, are so happy about this turnout.

The audience cheered as Lagerhjelm mentioned Said's name, as if they wanted to remind him that they were actually there for Said and not for him.

We have done our best to find a larger venue, Lagerhjelm continued, but unfortunately, all the other . . .

The rest of Lagerhjelm's words were drowned out by boos and whistles. But Lagerhjelm kept smiling. He raised his arms again and waited for silence.

But now we have found a solution. The organization that booked the Z-hall has agreed to move their event to a smaller room, so . . . if we could . . . in an orderly and calm manner . . .

The doors swung open to the gigantic Z-hall, and the crowds rushed down the sloping aisles to get seats at the front. The ladies, Evelyn and Simon, who had arrived early in the other room, ended up at the back, while Ina and Hector secured two seats in the middle of the fifth row.

It worked! Ina said, leaning over to kiss Hector on the ear.

Said walked onstage. He looked pale and frail, but as he took out his papers and began to speak about the intellectual's role in society, he seemed to grow. Ina understood perhaps half of what he was saying, not because the language was difficult, but because he spoke with such a death-defying speed, and because it was hard to take it all in, to realize that Edward Said, the man she considered her intellectual father figure, was physically present, and his voice echoed in the hall, filling her with pride, without her fully understanding why.

When it was over, Lagerhjelm came up onstage and thanked Professor Said, asking if it would be all right to take questions from the audience, and Said, who was sweating and looking pale again, said that he would save the questions for "next time."

The audience applauded and left the room. Ina looked at their faces, they seemed, not disappointed, but rather confused, as if they had just woken up from a dream they did not quite understand the meaning of, they had fought so hard to attend this lecture, and now that they had gotten what they wanted, they looked as if they were not sure what it was they had obtained or why they had fought so hard for it.

When the lecture was over Hector took Ina's hand and moved towards the stage. Said put his papers back into a red paper folder. Lagerhjelm saw Hector and waved to him. Hector introduced Ina, Ina said hi to Lagerhjelm, they shook hands.

What a lecture, Lagerhjelm said.

Ina and Hector agreed, but no one said anything more, all three of them were acutely aware of every movement Edward Said made, he was still on the stage, someone had come up to him from the other side, handing him a package and a book, he took off his glasses and thanked her, Hector, Ina and Lagerhjelm stood silently, waiting, Hector seemed to wait for Lagerhjelm to introduce them to Said, while Lagerhjelm seemed to wait for them to leave, waiting for them to understand that Said was tired and jet-lagged and not feeling well, and not someone to be introduced to random PhDs and their way-too-tall girlfriends.

I guess we should start moving, Hector said.

See you on Monday, Lagerhjelm said, looking relieved.

Hector and Ina headed towards the exit.

Sorry about that, he said when they reached the sunny Sveavägen.

Sorry about what? Ina said. Without you, I would have left.

He was talking incredibly fast, Hector said.

I zoned out after ten minutes, Ina said. But I'm so glad we stayed.

Outside they bumped into Evelyn and Simon. Simon had just lit a cigarette, and now he waved to them with the cigarette, as if trying to send a smoke signal.

Wow, wasn't it incredible? Evelyn said when they awkwardly hugged and went through their "Oh, I didn't know you were here" routine.

It really was, Hector said.

What did you like about it? Ina asked.

Well . . . Everything! Evelyn said. His presence. His message. His political perspective on how the intellectual can contribute to the world. His nuanced questioning of apolitical art.

Ina tried not to look surprised. Could it be possible that Evelyn had understood more of Said's message than she had?

I agree, Simon said. So inspiring. It actually made me want to go back to university.

Simon said this with a surprised expression, as if going back to university was the equivalent of going back to a war zone.

What did you study? Ina asked, trying her best not to sound condescending or mocking.

She expected him to say ceramics or astronomy. Maybe some scattered courses in guitar.

Some philosophy, Simon replied.

Didn't you study philosophy for two and a half years? Evelyn asked.

Yes, but that was a long time ago. Before I studied law. When I was young and foolish.

He smiled, Evelyn smiled, and Ina smiled too, although she wasn't sure if she was smiling because he implied he was old now or if it was a joke, since he looked quite young, or maybe it was not a joke at all, perhaps it was just one of those things people said when everyone was quiet.

Law? Ina said. Are you . . . a lawyer?

He nodded.

Graduated last year. Now I'm a judicial clerk.

In Stockholm? Hector asked.

Simon nodded.

Don't you need incredibly good grades to be a judicial clerk in Stockholm? Ina said.

Simon shrugged and blew out smoke.

Lawyer, huh? Ina said, just to say something.

Is it hard to believe? Evelyn said.

Not at all, Ina said.

It wasn't hard to believe. It was impossible to believe. He had the hair and beard of a caveman, his pants were dirty, his sneakers had holes.

These are my work clothes, he said, and again everyone smiled, so Ina tried to smile too. She didn't know why the thought of Evelyn being with a lawyer, a future attorney, future judge, future politician, future prime minister, future TV celebrity, future millionaire, future architect-designed summerhouse with a pool, future perfectly happy family with a son and a daughter, irritated her. After a few more throat clearings and comments about the weather and the lecture, Hector suggested they should "do this again sometime," and every-one agreed, parting with faces full of relief.

Chapter Sixty-Three

A few days later Anastasia came out on the courtyard after a morning session of practicing the pronunciation of *fellah* and *mohandisah*, and someone else was sitting in her spot in the courtyard. He wasn't smoking, he wasn't talking to anyone, he just sat there in the scorching sun, reading a book, and Anastasia almost laughed at how silly he looked, he really looked like he wanted everyone to see him with that book, he looked like he was on a brightly lit stage. He was deeply immersed in whatever he was reading, and Anastasia couldn't shake the feeling that he was putting on a performance, and the next second, she wondered if that was what the other students had seen in her.

Anastasia approached him and asked him for a light. He looked up, squinting against the sun. He responded something in Arabic.

Sorry, my Arabic bad, Anastasia tried to say in Arabic. The guy looked over her shoulder, almost as if he wanted to make sure that she wasn't out to make fun of him, and then he answered in English.

Sorry, I don't smoke.

His voice, it sounded nothing like him, he spoke English with a German accent, but his lips were Moroccan and his nose was Egyptian and his eyes were Nubian and his skin was Jordanian and his cheeks were Filipino and his underarms were Finnish and it wasn't until he introduced himself as Daniela that Anastasia realized that he was a she.

Anastasia borrowed a lighter from two other girls who were standing in the shadows. Anastasia could have gone up to Daniela and told her that she was sitting in her chair, which would have been weird, because the whole school was full of chairs, for some reason every corridor was overflowing with metal chairs that nobody used. She could have said that this courtyard was not big enough for two, which would have been even weirder, since it was huge and empty. Instead she returned to the sunny square, feeling the scorching warmth of the stones through her thin sandals.

What are you reading? she asked Daniela in English.

Daniela held up the cover. Anastasia had actually read another book by the same author, which was strange, because Anastasia didn't read, at least she didn't read in the same way that Ina read, and Anastasia knew that Ina hated this particular author, his book had topped bestseller lists worldwide, and Ina would regularly claim this book to be the worst book ever written (Ina had a long list of those kinds of books, and they were especially awful if they managed to sell a lot of copies and had an uplifting ending and a strong female heroine and had been made into a movie starring an actress who was even more beautiful than the character in the book, and sometimes Anastasia wondered how Ina could even keep track of all the awful books out there, did she read them when nobody was watching, or was there something in their success that made them automatically terrible?).

My sister hates that book, Anastasia said.

Why? Daniela said.

She doesn't understand why it has sold so many copies.

It's easy to hate things you don't understand.

Do you like it?

I enjoy being in it. I don't care if it's good or bad, but it affects me in a way I like.

How does it affect you?

It opens me up, Daniela said. It allows me to take a break from myself.

When the break ended Anastasia and Daniela walked up the stairs together. When Anastasia came out of class, Daniela was waiting on the staircase. She was in intermediate Arabic, Anastasia in beginner,

Daniela studied classical Arabic, Anastasia had chosen the Tunisian dialect. On the way home, Daniela said she lived in Düsseldorf, she studied engineering, she had two older siblings and four older half siblings, she seemed completely unconcerned about the sweat stains on her dark pink tank top, and she used a yellow pencil to put up her hair, seemingly forgetting it up there. When they said goodbye, Anastasia made sure to stop way ahead of her foul-smelling stairwell so that Daniela wouldn't suspect for a second that the smell of cat urine and garbage came from Anastasia.

Later that afternoon Anastasia called Evelyn and Ina from a cubicle at a nearby Web café, the connection was shaky, their images froze every five seconds, their voices echoed, after a few restarts Anastasia was finally able to hear her sisters' voices, they said that Simon and Hector had been "out with the boat" (which boat, Anastasia wondered). Ina mentioned that Evelyn had been offered a job as a hair model and turned it down.

Evelyn said, "Aren't you going to tell her?" and Anastasia said, "What?"

Ina said, "I'll tell you when you get home."

Is it something bad? Anastasia said, thinking about the curse and their mother's death. No, nothing bad, Ina said, smiling, while Evelyn pointed to her belly with wide eyes. What about you? Ina said. How are you doing?

Anastasia told her sisters about the arrival at the airport, the landlord who had three sons and used to live in Drakenberg, this new friend of hers called Daniela, and after having gotten to her feet and made a quick scan of the Web café, to make sure that nobody from the school was here, Anastasia leaned towards the computer and cupped her hand around the microphone of the headset and listed all of Daniela's potential nationalities, claiming that her hair was French and her back was Portuguese and her underarms Finnish.

What does that even mean? Ina said.

Wait, did she say Finnish underarms? Evelyn said.

No hair, Anastasia said, as if it was the most normal thing in the world.

And an Egyptian nose? Broken like the sphinx?

Hell no, Anastasia said, laughing. Of course not. An incredibly royal, fantastically long Cleopatrian nose, and her eyes are brown with a circle of blue around the pupil, which can only be seen from certain angles.

Someone's in love, Evelyn said.

Of course not, Anastasia said. We just met.

They spent the next week walking to and from school together. When Anastasia came out of her building, Daniela was there, during breaks they met up at their spot in the sunny square, after school they met up outside the big entrance, on the boulevard, where the French girls were smoking and the French guys were yelling and the American guys were strangely quiet. The language course was four weeks and every evening they had homework. At the end of the second week, Anastasia and Daniela walked back towards Anastasia's flat, they talked about the strange mixture of people in their respective classes, half the students were like them, Tunisians who had grown up abroad, with one or two Tunisian parents, there were Canadian Tunisians and Belgian Tunisians, UK Tunisians and even one very lonely Polish Tunisian, they were all similar but so different, some defended the current political rule, some hated it here and couldn't wait to go back, some were devout Muslims and studied Arabic to get closer to Allah, some were here to get the free food and the free airplane ticket and couldn't wait for the weekend to go party it up at La Marsa. The other half of the class consisted of people from all over the world who had come here voluntarily to learn Arabic. There were people from Latin America, from South Africa, even a couple of Japanese students, who were studying like crazy, always handing in their homework, always raising their hands to answer grammatical questions, struggling with their pronunciation.

At first I hated it here, Daniela said. I came here to get away from my family. To take a break from it all. To try and find a direction in life.

Me too, Anastasia said, even though it wasn't entirely true. Then I met you and I started liking it a bit more.

They had stopped in front of Anastasia's building. Daniela leaned in for a double cheek kiss, and then she gave a third cheek kiss, and then she kissed Anastasia on the forehead, and then they just stood close to each other and breathed for a few seconds, cheek to cheek. Then they kissed, and Anastasia realized that she had never kissed lips before, not lips like these, all other lips had been lifeless worms, all other lips had been stiff rubber, and as they kissed, first one car honked, and then another. Anastasia didn't understand at first why, they were just kissing, hadn't they seen a couple kiss before?

People normally don't kiss in the street here, Daniela said. Especially people like us.

Anastasia took a moment to look at their reflection in the TV store's display window, she had never seen a more beautiful couple, Anastasia with her short hair and darker than usual complexion, Daniela with her long curly hair and hairless arms.

I think they honked because they were jealous, Anastasia said.

Very possible, Daniela said, and kissed her again. I would be if I saw us.

Anastasia didn't feel like inviting Daniela to her filthy apartment, and Daniela lived in a shared dormitory where visitors were strictly forbidden. So instead of spending nights together, they met up after school and went to the nearby Bellevue Park. They sat in the shade with their watermelons and casse-croutes, "blesh arisah" for Daniela and with arisah for Anastasia, because it was the only thing that made Anastasia feel at home here, that she could eat spicy food without getting teary-eyed, while Daniela, who had grown up in Germany but had visited Tunisia every summer since she was little, and spoke a softly flowing Arabic that made glibet vendors smile and ask if she was Saudi, still couldn't eat sandwiches with arisah without breaking a sweat and needing something sweet to alleviate the pain in her mouth. Every time they grazed each other's hands, cars honked, and once when they kissed in the park, Anastasia asked why it was so empty here, and Daniela said that nobody was crazy enough to come here when it was 55 degrees Celsius in the shade.

That's why we have the park all to ourselves.

One afternoon, as they lay down and kissed, Anastasia noticed a moving bush, first she thought it was an animal, then she realized it was a person, she screamed and felt silly for having screamed, so in an attempt to hide it, she jumped up and started walking, then running towards the moving bush, she yelled in Swedish that the damn pervert should go to fucking hell and the man tried to escape, but in order to do that he had to pull up his pants, and Anastasia picked up a stick and chased him away, while Daniela yelled things in Arabic that Anastasia didn't understand. After that, the empty park felt less safe, and they started meeting at Anastasia's place instead. The first time, she instructed Daniela to hold her breath in the stairwell and get ready for the worst, but if Daniela was shocked by the apartment, she managed to hide it. Daniela didn't seem to notice the anthills and cockroach colony in the kitchen, and she just laughed when she saw the broken bed and the Tunisian-made fridge that could only be closed with a rubber band, and the power sockets surrounded by brown burn marks on the walls.

They made love in the broken bed, in the dirty bathtub, in the bed again, and somehow, Daniela's presence purified the apartment for Anastasia. The second time Daniela visited, Anastasia showed her the roof. It was just one flight of stairs up from the apartment, not even behind a door, just an opening in the wall, and two steps out, they were on a white, flat roof. The dark red sun was slowly setting over the white and turquoise city. Clotheslines with bedsheets gently swayed in the breeze. Anastasia stood there on the roof, looking at Daniela's silhouette, wondering if this was the most beautiful view she had ever seen. She wanted to tell her about her sisters, about the curse, but not here, not on the roof, it was too risky. Back in the apartment, lying next to each other, on each other, in each other, afterwards, Daniela's fingers played with Anastasia's necklace, the one she had had since she was a child, with Fatima's hand and the red crystal and

Anastasia decided to tell her, she had never told anyone before, not Fabricia, not Mathias, but she wanted to tell Daniela, she said that when she grew up in Stockholm with her two sisters, their mother claimed they had to be extra careful because someone in their family had placed a curse on them, someone had seen them when they were young and become jealous of their beauty and privileges, and the curse stated that everything they loved and valued would eventually be taken away from them. Anastasia expected Daniela to laugh, to say something engineery and scientific about how curses weren't real and that Anastasia and her sisters were being childish still thinking about things that happened in their childhood. But instead, Daniela remained silent and continued to breathe warm air into Anastasia's scalp and when Daniela didn't say anything or laugh, Anastasia kept talking, she told Daniela about her mother's episodes, how she could be exuberantly happy on Tuesday and barely talkative on Thursday, how she would plan vacations one week and her funeral the next, she told Daniela about her mother's secret notebooks, which Anastasia had found in the basement but still hadn't read, she described how happy her mother had been when Ina shared that she had received a scholarship to study and play basketball in the USA, how proud she had been that Ina was so good at English, how joyful she had been when they waved goodbye to Ina at the airport and how deeply she had sunk as soon as Ina had left, especially when Ina started talking about staying longer than half a year, that's when it all went downhill, that's when we couldn't keep her anymore. That's when she jumped.

Jumped? Daniela said.

She went out onto the balcony, climbed over the railing, and jumped, Anastasia said, closing her eyes to be able to continue telling the story.

She survived, she broke her leg, her fall was softened by a bush, she jumped even though Ina had come home earlier than expected, even though she interrupted everything to take care of Mom, to take care of us, and I don't think Ina has ever forgiven us, and she has never forgiven Mom, then things got better, or maybe not better, but as long as Ina was there, everything was more stable, Mom moved to a new city, took her medication, claimed to be happy, I was there, I visited to check on her, to get my Tunisian passport, then she felt worse, but I wasn't worried about her, she had been through rougher times, we stayed in touch, in the summer of 2001, a doctor called Ina in the middle of the night and informed her that Mom had been involved in an accident, she was trying to merge onto a highway, waiting for a truck to pass, but then drove straight into the path of the next truck, the driver tried to brake and swerve, so her car was only partially crushed, the doctor asked us to come as quickly as possible, suspecting she had had "another stroke" and lost control of the car, we didn't even know she had had a first stroke, Ina and Evelyn borrowed Simon's car and drove all the way to the hospital, they couldn't get ahold of me, it was the middle of the night, I was out, I was dancing, I saw their calls, one missed call from Evelyn, one from Ina, another from Evelyn, another from Ina, I assumed that they were fighting and wanted me to mediate, I ignored their calls, I didn't read their messages, I had been drinking, I had popped a couple of pills, I stood on a dance floor and felt exceptionally happy, I didn't want to be pulled into their conflicts: "Ina did this," "Evelyn said that," "Ina never respects my boundaries," "Evelyn keeps refusing to invest in the cheap index funds I recommended," "Ina always finds fault in everything I do," "Evelyn can't plan for the future," "Ina thinks she's our mother," "Evelyn just assumes everyone will take care of her," "Ina is not our mom," "Evelyn was always spoiled by Mom." And then both of them: "I've done everything I can, but now I can't do it anymore"—I didn't check my messages until four in the morning, and by then it was too late, the taxi driver had to check with his boss if he could accept such a long ride, he looked at me through the rearview mirror, he asked if there was anything he could do, he had a water bottle in the front seat, he handed me tissues, he opened the windows and closed them when he realized that it didn't seem to work, I just asked him to go as fast as possible, I sat there in the back seat, trying to figure out if this was real or not, if my shaking hands were mine or someone else's, please just go fast, fast, faster, even faster, the cab driver nodded, sped onto the highway, he left the city, he crossed the bridge at Södertälje at 140, the sun was rising, the radio played a cheerful Elton John song, the highway was empty, Mom is dying and the radio plays Elton John, Mom is dying and the sun is waking up, Mom is dying and the trees are still here, the taxi is still here, the road signs, the white lines, the exits are still here. He dropped me off at the main entrance, I had already swiped my card, good luck, he said, though I hadn't told him what happened, somehow I knew that if I had said the words, Mom is injured, Mom is dying, I wouldn't have been able to get from the taxi to the room where they were waiting for me, they had sent me the room number, Ina had texted instructions, which elevator, which floor, but I still needed to ask someone, just to be sure, the girl at the reception looked oddly rested, she pointed to the right elevator and then ran out of her booth to help me press the button, she also said good luck, as if everyone I met could sense that I really needed it, the elevator stopped on the wrong floor and then the right one, and when I finally managed to step out and turn right, I realized that it was too late, Ina and Evelyn were waiting for me in the corridor, stretching out their arms, running towards me, hugging me and lifting me up from the floor when I couldn't stand, they half carried me to the empty room where Mom had been lying, but now she was gone, I walked into the room, unable to look at what was now on the bed, I saw that the sun was still rising out there, the bed was metal, the sheets were white, Mom was not Mom anymore, she was just a shell, her face and arms were yellow, her mouth was open, I saw her fillings, her lips, there were just a few bruises on her face, all the other injuries were internal, I forced myself to take her cold hand, strangely enough, it felt good to be there because it was so evident that this was not Mom, not our real Mom, this was what she left behind, this was nowhere near who she was, this wasn't the sound of her high heels echoing through the courtyard when she returned from a sales trip, having bombarded three nearby cities with carpets, this wasn't her outstretched arms or her voice calling out, "Where are my girls?!" This wasn't her fingers reaching for the stereo and turning up the volume on Cyndi Lauper on Saturdays, challenging us to clean the entire apartment in under half an hour, this wasn't the person who stayed home when I was sick, taking out the crayons, saying, "I don't care if you're sick or not, sometimes you just need a break," that person wasn't here, she was far away, over the next hour, we took turns breaking down, every time one of us collapsed and sobbed, the other two were there to pick her up, to hug her back into her body, to whisper gently that it would be okay, everything would be fine, but no, it won't be fine, it will never be okay, but no matter what happens, we're here, we're here for each other, first it was Evelyn who broke down, then me, then Evelyn again, and then me again, finally, when Ina had gone out to refill the water pitcher, when Ina had asked the kind nurse if there was anything practical we could do, like filling out some forms, when Ina had fetched a new box of tissues, opened the window and said something about the blue sky as she went to fluff up the pillows under our dead mother's head, Ina finally broke down, she fell to the floor and made a sound that I can still hear in my nightmares, it wasn't a human sound, it was the sound of a drowning animal, it was years and years of filling out forms, opening windows and refilling water pitchers, it was the sound of the realization that no matter how many forms and windows and water pitchers there were in the world, everything was meaningless, and it would all end like this, in a metal hospital bed, while the sun rose outside, and Evelyn and I tried to hold Ina up when her legs gave way, and we tried to restrain her when she attempted to strike the lifeless body, she screamed insults at our dead mother, calling her a failure, a damn weakling, a betrayer, for they had a pact, they promised each other, and this idiot broke the pact, she she she, and then Ina cried and cried and cried, and as we struggled to calm Ina, a male nurse entered the room, I remember his expression, he looked at Ina, then at Evelyn and me, and instead of offering to help or asking if our sister needed assistance, he just stood there, as if hypnotized by our struggle, and then he lowered his gaze and left the room, there was something about the nurse and his strange reaction that brought Ina back to reality.

Look, Ina, you even scare the male nurses, Evelyn said, and Ina calmed down, she took a few deep breaths, her muscles relaxed, and we let go of her, Ina sank down onto a chair in the corner of the room, reaching for the water pitcher, I was sure she would throw it against the wall and start fighting again, but instead, she raised it to her mouth and started drinking large gulps, with water running down her neck, and then we just sat there, panting, watching the sun rise.

Part II

Chapter Sixty-Four

n the spring of 2003, I had an exchange semester in Paris, and in June I returned home to be in Stockholm for the release of my first novel. I organized my own book launch at Galeasen Theater, the publisher covered the cost of hummus and tzatziki, which we bought in two white buckets from the owner of Café Vurma, I managed to get a sponsorship discount on Castillo de Gredos, Systembolaget's cheapest wine, priced at 54 kronor per liter in a Tetra Pak.

My brother was graduating from high school, and I was at my mom's place in Hornstull, then I took the subway into the city, it was June 6, Sweden's National Day, at Zinkensdamm station there was shouting, and fifteen young skinheads filled the car, it was too much, too symbolic, I remember thinking I'd never be able to write about this because it was just so typical, one of the guys was shirtless and had the Swedish flag draped around him like a cape, they were yelling and drinking beer, moving around the car, burping, at Mariatorget station people changed cars, but I stayed, an older man also remained, he looked like my dad, the skinheads approached him, pretending to do wrestling moves near his face, they never hit him, but they swung their elbows close to his nose, mimicking hammer blows that stopped just above his neck, they lifted their boots and aimed a kick so close to his mouth that he could smell the leather, what made me react was that the man surrounded by skins smiled, he tried to laugh as if to show them that he found this whole situation amusing. I got up and approached them, I couldn't fight, I had no weapons, I was alone and there were fifteen of them, I had no clue what I was doing, instead of kicking and fighting and pushing and yelling, I went close to one of the guys and hooked his foot, I extended my foot to make him lose balance, the subway stopped at Slussen station, the skins were getting off, me too, they stumbled out through one set of doors, I exited through another, we stood there on the platform, staring at each other, a woman farther away shouted:

Just go!

At first, I was convinced she was talking to them, but then I realized she was addressing me.

I'm alone here, I said. I'm alone here.

They stared at me, the subway doors closed, the train started moving, then I heard footsteps behind me, at first I thought it might be someone coming to help, maybe the older man from the subway, perhaps some old basketball friends, anyone from my past who saw that I needed help, maybe Ina, Evelyn or Anastasia, then I realized it was one of the skins, the shirtless one with the flag cape, he must have been behind me, which explained why they didn't attack earlier, he had a knife, a glass bottle, a baseball bat—now everything was over, but it turned out he only had his bare hands, he gave me a push, and I spun back towards the subway that was already moving, I did a pirouette but managed to stay on my feet, the skins laughed and went down towards the buses heading to Nacka, while I took the stairs up to Slussen.

In the summer of 2004, I needed to get away to clear my thoughts, I was afraid that I would never be able to write a second book, the advance I received for my first book had run out, and my mom reminded me about the possibility of going to Tunisia to study Arabic at the Bourguiba Institute, there was a special scholarship for Tunisians living abroad, and apparently, my dad had mentioned it to her, he said I could come and visit if I wanted to, he had a large apartment in Tunis that I could borrow, and I wouldn't even have to pay rent, he had told my mom, I assumed it was a joke, but I wasn't entirely sure.

We hadn't spoken to each other for five or six years, the last time

I saw him was when he passed by NK, where I worked part-time at a clothing store, the first time he just looked at me, shook his head and walked away, the next time he approached me, and I thought he might apologize for disappearing, I was ready to maybe accept his apology, but instead, he told me he was ashamed of me, it was embarrassing that I hadn't achieved more in life, had I worked so hard to get good grades just to end up working in a clothing store? The third time I saw him, I was prepared, before he could say anything that would drill itself into my brain I shouted at him to leave me alone, that he had no right to disappear and then come here making demands, then I quickly went into the lunchroom so no one could see my tears.

My father picked me up at the airport in Tunis and we went straight to the flat, I was afraid of looking at him, I kept looking at him in the mirror of the window of the car, he looked kind of the same, he had some new dark spots on his cheeks, and his eyes, there was something different about his eyes, but I couldn't make out what it was, he hid his eyes behind his dark brown Ray-Bans, he had grown out his hair, he had a small ponytail, it almost covered up the bald spot, the shirt was new, when we hugged at the airport I expected him to smell of Paco Rabanne, but he smelled of another aftershave, I couldn't place it.

As we approached the center of Tunis, we remained silent, we hadn't spoken in so many years, and still here we were, in a car, with nothing to say to each other, I asked him about the family, he said they were good, he asked about my brothers, I said they were good, then we were quiet again. As we approached the gas station we saw two cars that had collided, I saw something poking out of one of the cars, it was a foot, it looked like a periscope, a brown foot, at a weird angle, crying women in hijab. Dad accelerated past the accident and shook his head.

Idiots, he said. These idiots can't drive, they can't organize their society, they can't do anything right.

We spoke French with each other, but for some reason he said this in Swedish, and I remember thinking to myself that this was his inner voice, and I wondered why it was speaking to him in Swedish, when Swedish wasn't his mother tongue. It was dark when we arrived at the flat, the lights in the stairwell didn't work, but there were no clouds in the sky and the light from the stars and the moon were enough for us to make it up to the fifth floor without a problem. Dad opened the door, he walked in with me to show me the rooms, bedroom, living room, kitchen and bathroom.

That's a brand-new washing machine, he said, pointing to a large square covered in blocks of Styrofoam.

But don't try to use it, he added. It's not installed yet. And be careful when using the power outlets. And don't tamper with the meter.

Why would I tamper with the . . . ?

I had a girl living here last year and her stupid German friend did something with the electric meter, my dad said.

Okay, I said, I won't touch the meter.

I was just trying to be nice, my dad said. I let her stay here for free, just because I knew their mother, it was one of the Mikkola sisters, you remember them, right?

I wondered why he had chosen to stay in touch with the Mikkola sisters and not with his real sons.

Never try to be nice, he said. Never invite people into your life and try to be kind. The only thing that happens is that they will do their best to fuck you, to betray you, to sue you.

Was she okay? I said, trying to steer him away from the negative spiral that I knew would just end us up in no-man's-land.

Who?

The German friend?

Of course, Dad said. She was just faking it, she probably had a huge check from her insurance company waiting when she got back home.

Stupid Germans, I said, smiling sideways to see if he remembered.

Almost as stupid as the French, Dad said with a smile.

And don't get me started on the Belgians, I said.

They are only lucky that they are not Danish, Dad said.

Europe as a continent is fucked, I said.

Only the Middle East is worse. And don't get me started on the Americas, Dad said.

North or South? I said.

North *and* South, Dad said, they are almost as stupid as the Asians, and on we went, condemning the world for its stupidity while we drank a glass of Safia in the kitchen. My dad would sleep in the apartment for one night and then go down to Jendouba the next day.

You want to come? he said.

Do you want me to come? I said.

You choose yourself, Dad said.

I would be happy to come if you wanted me to come, I said. But I only want to come if you want me to come.

We were quiet for a while, then at exactly the same time he said: I think it's best if you stay here, and I said:

I would be happy to come.

Great, then that's decided, Dad said and we went to bed, neither of us knowing if this meant that I would ride with him to Jendouba or not the next morning.

Chapter Sixty-Five

Anastasia woke up with Daniela next to her, lying completely still to make these dawn minutes last forever. The curse whispered: Wake her up. Kick her out. Insult her. But Anastasia didn't move, and Daniela woke up when the mosque called for morning prayer, she stretched out her catlike arms and yawned. Anastasia knew she would remember this morning, just as she would remember last night—the train ride to La Marsa when she had to resist leaning forward to kiss Daniela, the beach, the outdoor café in the sunset, Daniela's serious gaze when she asked about their mom's funeral, but instead of asking about her emotions, Daniela asked about facts, she asked if they had cremated the body, she asked where the church was located, how had they picked out a tombstone, gray or black, what kind of material, shiny or matte, and somehow these questions made it easier for Anastasia, people were always afraid to talk about the things that hurt, as if they believed their questions would resurrect forgotten pain, as if they failed to grasp that the pain was constant, and there wasn't a single second when Anastasia forgot that her mother was dead, but talking to Daniela was different, and Anastasia didn't quite understand why it felt so soothing to talk about it, she told her that the small church was located south of Stockholm, she wasn't sure when it was built, but it was old and gray and made of stone, and there is a railway track nearby, so you can hear the trains passing, which we liked because our mother was always calmed by the idea that she could leave, Anastasia's body was present at the funeral, but her mind was elsewhere, her ears heard the sound of passing trains, her eyes saw guests arriving, her mouth said something to the first guest, she said what Ina had said on repeat, that it was fitting that their mother would be laid to rest here, next to a railway track, since she was always on the move, always heading fast in one direction, and then in another, and the person who she said this to nodded and agreed, and it wasn't until the person had excused himself and left that Anastasia realized that he was part of the catering crew, and had never met her mom.

The guests kept coming, they left their coats in the unattended wardrobe, they adjusted their necklaces, they checked their makeup in the mirror, they corrected the makeup, they brushed off white dandruff flakes from shoulders, the flakes seemed to dance with joy in the sunlight that came pouring in through the church windows, Ina had arranged everything, but now she seemed to have lost her ability to speak, instead it was Evelyn who welcomed the guests, Evelyn who informed them about the practicalities, we will wait here and then go out and say our goodbyes and return here to have coffee and restrooms are in there, Ina stood next to her and nodded, Evelyn kept talking about their mother, it didn't matter if it was an old colleague or an old friend, she spoke about their mother's high heels, her hoarse laughter, her cigarettes, her perfectly arranged color-coordinated folders filled with sales statistics, her random collection of talismans, her theories about feng shui and energies and crystals, and her thoughts on the sun and the stars and tectonic movements that had created everything we loved and valued on Earth, regular people only cared about diamonds and considered crystals to be trash, but they didn't understand that it's the same material, sure, diamonds were a bit harder and rarer, but they were all made of the same carbon atoms, some forms of carbon were delicate with enough space between the atoms to be used for pencils, while other carbon atoms clung so tightly together that they formed diamonds, and these crystals are something in between, Anastasia looked up at Evelyn and saw their mother in her, they were the same person, it was their mother's soul that had seeped into Evelyn, when she displayed the gemstones around her neck, this is an obsidian that protects against negativity, and this is a citrine that brings joy and energy, this one is called tiger's eye and is great for motivation, and while Anastasia watched Evelyn imitating their mother, more and more people filled the waiting room, and someone from the church came out and politely asked them to lower their voices not to disturb the ongoing ceremony.

Is it another funeral? Evelyn said, but the person from the church didn't hear her or chose to ignore the question. Everyone tried to speak softly and sob without making sounds. Their mother's friends had come, and her former boss mentioned that she still held the sales record for a vacuum cleaner called the Hoover Dimension Supreme, even some of their mom's customers had shown up, mostly older people from small towns who somehow found one another, they formed small circles, talking about their mother's incredible warmth and energy, they agreed that her carpets were expensive but well worth the investment, comparing knots per square meter and joking about that promised certificate of authenticity that everyone had been promised but only a few had received.

A farmer named Bengt told Anastasia that he had bought a cream-white Persian Nain rug with a green dome pattern, and it was so beautiful that he bought another one in red for his daughter, he shared how Anastasia's mother had spent an entire afternoon in his living room, teaching him how to position the rug's pile away from the light to achieve the right shine, his rug had 300,000 knots per square meter, and it was not just a rug but an illustration of the passage of time, it was made of corkwool, which was the wool from the neck, chest and shoulders of young lambs, only six months old.

Do you know why they take the wool from there?

Anastasia shook her head.

It's the wool that hasn't been damaged by the sun, Bengt said, his eyes welling up with tears.

The only ones who didn't attend the funeral were her Tunisian family, Ina had reached out to them, but they wanted her to be buried there, Ina refused and reminded them that she had left the country for a reason, but they were welcome to come to the funeral, no one came, a few distant cousins from Brussels RSVP'd, claiming they would come with two children, but they never showed up.

The sisters had requested a priest who was not too "priestly," since their mother hadn't been particularly "religious," as Ina explained, she believed in many "strange things" but never went so far as to believe in God, at least not in a "biblical sense." The mouth of the representative from the church turned into a straight line. Evelyn tried to salvage the situation by saying that their mother was indeed faithful, she truly was, she had always been a member of the Swedish Church and willingly paid taxes to support churches, she just wasn't very enthusiastic about the whole "Father, Son and Holy Spirit thing," and the church representative looked even more annoyed.

It was Anastasia's turn to speak, she shared that their mother was born as a Muslim, tried to live as a Buddhist, and eventually became a Christian, she explained how their mother had been forced to flee her Muslim homeland and found freedom here, this made the church representative more empathetic, promising to find a priest who would be suitable for "guests not accustomed to church visits."

They met with the priest before the funeral, he asked about what their mother enjoyed most in life (coffee, tea, foot baths, a successful sale, Chinese proverbs, crystals, gemstones and tarot cards), he inquired about any challenging phases in her life and what she had struggled against (instability, anger, depression, unfaithful men, estranged family), he asked if she had any nicknames (not really) and how she had died (they said stroke instead of a car accident).

The priest appeared calm during their pre-meeting, but on the actual funeral day, he seemed nervous, perhaps it was due to the large number of people who had shown up, or the fact that they were so different from one another, it was challenging to find a common denominator, when everyone had entered the church, and the priest had cleared his throat and tested the microphone, he said that he hadn't had the privilege of personally knowing their mother, however, he considered himself lucky to have spoken with many people who did know her, and he expressed awe at what an amazing person she must have been, he praised her as a kind and wonderful mother, continuing with clichéd platitudes that could have been just as fitting for Fabricia's mother. The priest kept talking, but their mother was not there in his words, and Anastasia comforted herself by thinking that she would say a few words at the funeral reception and then everything would be set right, she would share her perspective on who their mother really was, she would not let this priestly, false image of their mother win, she would speak up and say that their mother had never been religious, at least not in the traditional sense, and if it had been possible, we would have buried her at a nuclear power plant because that's what she was—true energy, or we would have buried her on a beach, because she was constant waves, back and forth, in eternal motion, she was the person who saved us from the world, she grew up in a household that hated women, with parents who hated women, in a religion, country, world that hated women, and somehow, she broke free, she left her home, she left her city and made it all the way here, and made us, and if someone here thinks she's weak you can all go to fucking hell. Anastasia would keep screaming until Ina came up and gently took the microphone from her.

But after the ceremony, when everyone gathered at the reception in the nearby parish hall, Ina raised the microphone and thanked everyone for coming, and then she handed the microphone to Anastasia, and everyone turned their heads to her like a tennis audience and weirdly enough she couldn't speak, she had swallowed her tongue, she had lost her breath, she just stood there with the microphone close to her lips, it smelled burned and dusty, it smelled like a youth center, the black cord dangled limply towards the ground, after what felt like hours, she felt a soft hand on her shoulder, it wasn't Ina, it was Evelyn, Evelyn took the microphone from Anastasia and said that what my sister is trying to tell you is this, and then she started speaking, she talked about their mom, she said that she was a very special woman who believed more in people than in God, more in energies than in dogmas or boundaries or rules, she trusted that her energy would guide her to do the right thing, and that's how she met our father, before him, she had been with a man surrounded by dark, heavy, sad energy, but then she met Raimo, our dear father, whose energy was different, a light energy, an everything-is-possible energy, and yes, our dad was *not* the hardest-working man in show business (smiles from the audience) and Lord knows that I have inherited his procrastination skills (laughter from the audience), but Mom was different, she was the opposite, I never remember her doing nothing, she was always in motion, always heading somewhere, a new project, a new activity, a new hobby, our mom wasn't religious, not in a classical sense, but she believed in miracles, and she believed in destiny, and she believed in energies, and if she were here today, she would have reminded us that there is no reason to be sad, no point in crying, no use in feeling lost, I know she would have said that thing she told me and my sisters when we worried about death, that the most important law of thermodynamics states that energy can't be destroyed, it can only change form, and thus death does not mean death, it just means that the building blocks we consist of, the atoms that have been here since the big bang, have changed form, our bodies may enter a phase of decay, but our energy will never die, it will vibrate forever, just like our mom's energy will survive, since all of her energy, every single vibration, lives on in our memories, in our eyes, in our bodies, she will continue to exist, she's here right now, nothing has disappeared, she has just changed form, she's just even less orderly than she was before.

After a few seconds of silence, the guests caught their breath and wiped their cheeks with their already wet tissues, then thunderous applause, they raised their glasses in honor of their mother, even if there were no glasses, so people lifted their coffee cups, thanking Evelyn for the incredible speech, Evelyn smiled and passed the microphone to Anastasia, who held it for a moment before passing it on to Ina. Ina was about to say something, but then she just listened to the applause and put the microphone back in its holder. She leaned forward and whispered something in Evelyn's ear, making Evelyn smile.

Later, after the guests had left, and the catering guy poured the leftover coffee down the sink, Anastasia asked Evelyn how long it had taken her to write that incredible speech.

I just improvised, Evelyn said. I spoke from my heart.

And Anastasia wanted to believe her, or perhaps she desperately wanted to believe her, but she still searched through Evelyn's handbag, looking for notes for the speech, while trying to convince herself that their mother had indeed said those things about thermodynamics when they were little, and Anastasia had just forgotten.

Two years later, when Anastasia had been accepted into the language course in Tunis, Ina sent her a link to an American radio program. The host jokingly recommended inviting a physicist to one's funeral, and Anastasia understood what Ina was trying to prove—that Evelyn's speech was inspired by that same radio program. Anastasia didn't want to be convinced and tried to tell herself that Evelyn might not have heard it or had forgotten about it, since Evelyn was just as excellent at telling stories as she was useless at remembering where her stories came from.

Chapter Sixty-Six

We are in Dad's black Passat heading west on the road that leads from Tunis to Jendouba, we pass goats, motorcycles carrying whole families, only one person with a helmet, lorries full of green watermelons. We left early and have driven for half an hour in silence, Dad has a bunch of old cassettes in the car, and I pop one of them in the tape deck, expecting some Oum Kalthoum or possibly some Jacques Brel, but instead I hear the soothing voice of Peter LeMarc, a Swedish soul singer who I know my dad idolized when he lived in Stockholm, and as the black Passat slowly descends towards the inland of Tunisia, leaving the water and the capital behind in a cloud of gravel dust, Peter LeMarc sings a song about being at home by the sea, here nobody can hurt us, because we are at home by the sea.

Hemma vid ett hav, Dad said. That's real poetry.

We listen to the full album, twice, we don't speak about his absence, we don't speak about why he never called on our birthdays or why he never paid child support, we don't speak about the forbidden thought that I had a strange feeling of relief when he left, as if on some level I knew that his influence was so strong that I could never have developed into myself if he had stayed. At the same time, I'm sitting there in the passenger seat, as a twenty-five-year-old, doing my best to make him love me. I tell him about the positive review of my first novel, I talk about the courses I have taken in international economics while taking literature studies and I got an A on both statistics courses, it was the best result out of four hundred students.

Nobody was better in statistics, I tell him in French to get a reaction. He corrects my grammar.

La statistique, he says. Not *le* statistique.

We stop for gas, we stop for water, Peter LeMarc sings, the scenery goes from red and occasionally green to only red, even the palm trees look tired here, the AC is on max, but there is something wrong with the AC, it is only blowing warm air.

This car is made in the same factory as a Mercedes, Dad says. It's a Volkswagen, but it's better quality than a Mercedes. German quality. It's a top-of-the-line Volkswagen. I had a friend who had a Mercedes, I lent him my car, he told me that this car was so much better than his Mercedes.

Is it okay if I open the window? I say.

The AC is on, Dad says.

But the AC doesn't work, I say.

It will work, Dad says. It just takes a bit of time for it to start working.

We drive through small villages, white houses, a shop that sells plastic bags, a Cola-Cola stand. We pass a few kids without shoes, the AC still doesn't work.

Can I open the window now? I say.

I will do it, he says.

He opens the window on his side. I try to open the window on my side, but it doesn't move.

There's something wrong with the windows, he says. It's an electrical issue. I don't understand why they have to put electricity everywhere. What's wrong with manual cranks?

We get stuck behind a truck, it's so full of hay that it looks like it will fall sideways, Dad tries to pass the truck, he honks, he wants the driver of the truck to slow down, to let him pass, to drive to the side, to just take his stack of hay and evaporate, but the driver of the truck honks back, and this goes on for another ten minutes. Dad tries to pass him, he honks, the other driver honks back.

We are not in a rush, are we, I say.

I hate this fucking country, Dad says, and then he finally manages to squeeze past the truck, a car going in the opposite direction honks and flashes its headlights, Dad honks, the driver of the truck honks, and for a few seconds I close my eyes thinking that it will all end here because we are going at full speed in the opposite direction of a car heading towards us, but somehow the other car manages to brake and we slide past and afterwards Dad seems really happy, he starts humming along to the Peter LeMarc song, he asks me if I remember when we cleaned Tre Backar together.

Of course, I say.

Peter LeMarc played there once. In the basement. It was the best concert I have ever seen. Women cried. Men cried. Even the owner cried.

Impossible, I said, because I remember the owner, he paid his employees under the table, wore a leather jacket and lived on a houseboat. He had been a taxi driver for ten years before moving abroad and returning with money that needed to be "invested." I couldn't imagine him with tears in his eyes.

He tried to hide it, of course, Dad said. But he cried. Everyone cried.

Did you cry?

Almost everyone cried, Dad said. I had to keep an eye on the bar. I didn't have time for tears.

He smiles. That smile, those white teeth, never a cavity despite hardly brushing them, those eyes, for a few seconds, I see the man Mom fell in love with, the man who had so many girls when they met that he was called "the Jailer from Jendouba" just because he had a huge bunch of keys to girls who hoped he would come back soon. He taps the steering wheel to the rhythm of the music, he has managed to pass the idiotic truck driver, and he was almost hit by another stupid driver coming from the opposite direction, sure, the solid line in the middle indicates that passing is forbidden right there, but those lines are just recommendations, no one cares about the rules here, especially not my dad. The next time we stop, he celebrates life and

the successful overtaking and his recently bought Passat by going
into a bar with white plastic chairs and ordering two bottles of Celtia.

Isn't that beer? I say.

Yeah, but it's a small beer, Dad says.

But you're driving?

A small beer is okay to drink.

I take a sip, mostly to prevent Dad from having two beers.

Evelyn said her dad played keyboard with Peter LeMarc, I say.

Dad nods.

Was he there when they played at Tre Backar?

Dad shrugs.

Don't you remember?

Yeah, he was there.

Did you talk to each other?

We talked.

What did you talk about?

Things.

What kind of things?

Different things.

Do you know what happened to our clock collection when you
moved?

I gave it all away.

To whom?

A friend.

Which friend?

Are you working for the secret police? Are you employed by
Mossad?

Dad finishes his beer and orders another one.

We are back on the country road, heading towards Jendouba. The
signs indicate that we are getting closer. I want to ask him why he
lives here when all his children are in other countries. I want to ask
him why he created four children and left them all. I want to ask him
if he ever thinks about us. I want to describe how it felt to have him
in our lives and then lose him. I want to ask if he misses us, and if he
does, then what the hell is he doing here? Why is he driving back

and forth between Jendouba and Tunis, back and forth, in a Passat that works perfectly, a Passat that is better than a Mercedes, except for the AC and the windows? If this were a book, I would definitely ask him now. It's the perfect situation, a chance to have an honest conversation, to confront him, to argue and come out on the other side better, stronger, smarter, more forgiving. But because this isn't a book, it's just a random memory, we sit there next to each other for hours, listening to Peter LeMarc, he who performed on TV with eyeliner, hat and umbrella, he who often hid half of his face on his album covers, he whose music I always secretly liked.

Ten minutes later, we approach a truck full of hay.

For fuck's sake, Dad says. Don't tell me it's him.

But it's not, this is an exactly identical truck and this guy is kind enough to use his blinkers to signal when Dad can pass, and Dad accelerates, flashing the hazard lights for a few seconds to show his gratitude. At two in the afternoon, we roll into the dusty university town of Jendouba.

Damn, I hate this place, Dad mumbles.

Chapter Sixty-Seven

During their last week together the power in Anastasia's flat came and went and then came back on, and then disappeared. She asked Daniela about it, Daniela suggested that she could call her landlord, Anastasia explained that he lived in another city, three hours away, she didn't want him to drive all the way here for something that could be easily fixed. She also didn't want him to come to this apartment that she had hated at first, but that she now considered her home, she didn't want to have more contact with him than necessary, there was something about his heavy body and sad eyes that made her think of her mom.

On Tuesday, Daniela came over after school to have a look, she turned on all the lights and then turned them off, she got a chair from the kitchen and climbed up to check the fuse box.

Be careful, Anastasia said.

Daniela moved the chair to check the meter.

Here's the problem, she said, holding up a small rubber thing, it looked like a guitar pick. This was blocking the meter.

What is it?

I think your landlord is trying to save money on electricity, Daniela said. Can you try to turn on the light in the kitchen now?

The fluorescent light in the kitchen turned on at the first attempt.

Thank you, Anastasia said.

No worries, Daniela said.

They sat down in the kitchen to eat the food that Daniela had brought. Was it Anastasia's imagination or had the silences between them become longer this week? Was it because they knew that they would need to say goodbye soon? Was it because neither of them had dared to talk about the future? Was it because Anastasia made the mistake of telling Daniela about the curse?

I'm just grateful that it wasn't my fault, Anastasia said.

How could it be your fault that the electricity doesn't work? Daniela said.

Did she sound a bit irritated?

When we were kids our mom used to tell us that we were special because we were high-energy people, Anastasia said. We have a thing with electricity. A few years ago, when all three of us were living together in Ina's apartment in Stockholm, the lightbulbs burned out much faster than normal.

Well, lightbulbs only have a certain life span, Daniela said. It's perfectly normal.

I know but we had to replace the lightbulbs really often, Anastasia said. Then when Evelyn moved out, the lightbulbs started lasting much longer.

Daniela nodded and Anastasia wondered if the small smile she saw on Daniela's face was imagined or real. She kept talking in the hope that more words would make her feel less silly.

Even Ina noticed it, and Ina is like you, she doesn't believe in anything that she can't measure, she even contacted the neighbors to ask if they had had any problems with the electricity and they said no, and, I'm not saying that it was our fault, I'm just saying that . . .

Anastasia became quiet because, in reality, she was not sure what she was saying, but it felt like she was talking about lightbulbs when she should be talking about how they could stay in touch in the fall, would they see each other again, would Daniela return to her engineering school in Düsseldorf, would she get back together with the guy she had been seeing this spring, or would she leave the engineering and the guy behind to move to Stockholm to be with Anastasia?

There were other strange things as well, Anastasia said. When we lived together our plants grew much quicker. And Ina's microwave oven started behaving weirdly. It started turning on by itself and once, when I tried to make popcorn, there was a loud bang and the popcorn came out all burned.

Daniela looked at her, Anastasia tried to get her mouth to stop speaking or at least speak about other things, but her mouth wouldn't listen, it kept chatting away, in a desperate attempt to avoid saying what she needed to say.

Weird coincidences happen, Daniela said. And every generation before us has been convinced that they knew everything about the world and they have all been wrong, so there's a good chance that we are wrong as well.

But you don't believe in energies? Anastasia said. Or curses?

Not for a second, Daniela said, and touched her arms without touching them. Anastasia looked down, there were a few centimeters of air between her arms and Daniela's fingertips, still she could feel the tips of her fingers. Daniela carried Anastasia to the bedroom, and later that evening, after they had taken a cold shower together, after they had opened the windows and the turquoise wooden blinds on both sides of the apartment in hopes of creating a cross-breeze, after Anastasia had held Daniela tight and whispered that she would never let her go, Daniela whispered that she had read somewhere that the human body produces 100 watts just through existing but that she was sure that them being together generated much more.

How much more, Anastasia whispered.

At least 102, 103, Daniela said with a smile.

That's the most romantic thing a German-Tunisian engineering student has ever said to me, Anastasia said. No, but seriously, how much more?

Infinitely more, Daniela said with a straight face.

Anastasia had never talked about these things with anyone before, and found it hard to stop now, but after fifteen minutes Daniela started yawning and said that she needed some sleep, and when Anastasia kept waking her up with questions about different energies, Daniela said in a condescending tone that in all seriousness, no human being can generate more energy than any other, and Anastasia felt offended that Daniela made fun of her and Daniela felt offended that

Anastasia was saying that she and her sisters were special, implying that Daniela was not. Anastasia became irritated that Daniela didn't understand how special Anastasia was, Daniela became irritated that Anastasia spoke more about her special abilities than of Daniela's, hadn't she managed to fix her electricity, hadn't she just given her three orgasms in one evening, Anastasia became angry when Daniela was speaking to her as if she was a child, Daniela became angry when Anastasia was behaving like a child, Anastasia became furious when Daniela kept yawning, Daniela became furious when she realized that she would only get four hours of sleep and tomorrow she had a grammar test and instead of sleeping she lay here beside a strange, hyper Swedish girl who insisted on claiming that she and her two sisters could absolutely generate more than three times 20 watts together.

Okay, I respect that feeling, Daniela said. But just like your sister said at your mom's funeral, the first thermodynamic law states that energy can't be created, just change form . . .

So, if we hadn't met, Anastasia said, if we hadn't spent this month together, if we hadn't made love just now, would the total energy in the world have remained the same?

Absolutely, Daniela said. The first law of thermodynamics . . .

I don't care about thermodynamic laws! Anastasia screamed, not really sure why she was shouting. I just know what I know! And I know that I refuse to live in a world where this kind of encounter results in an energy status quo.

I think we are just talking about different kinds of energies, Daniela said, in an attempt to make peace. And I really need to sleep now. We have our first grammar exam tomorrow, and . . .

But you just said that there are mysteries out there that we can't explain! Anastasia screamed.

Calm down, Daniela said.

You calm down, Anastasia said, turning away. Then they were silent, they turned off the lights and pretended to fall asleep without saying good night. Daniela lay in bed, tossing and turning. In the middle of the night, she sneaked out of bed and started getting dressed.

Anastasia heard Daniela going to the bathroom. She heard her walking towards the hallway. She heard her in the kitchen, cutting a piece of baguette, eating it standing up, testing the lamp switch, on and off, on and off. Anastasia was certain, she heard the sound of the lamp switch, the echoing plastic sound, the sound of the fridge opening and closing, a few seconds of silence, then Daniela picked up a chair and carried it into the hallway, Anastasia heard the legs of the plastic chair squeaking when Daniela climbed up on it, then a few more seconds of silence, Anastasia wondered what she was doing, was she putting back the thing that blocked the electricity or was she just checking the meter or did she want to get a second look at the fuse box, and why was she doing this at 3:30 a.m.? Anastasia wasn't sure and she didn't care, her eyes were still closed when her ears heard a buzzing sound, and then the sound of what could only be a body falling from a chair, landing on the floor.

Chapter Sixty-Eight

We arrived in Jendouba, we passed the old cinema and the dusty railway tracks where there's an outdoor market, we stopped in front of an abandoned building with an empty lot on one side and a gas station on the other. Two large ditches were in front of the house, but no workers were present.

What are we doing here? I asked.

Wait in the car, Dad said.

He went out and talked to the guy who had a small shop on the ground floor, there was space for three shops, but only one was rented. The man who owned the shop was sitting on a stool when we arrived, looking as though he had been sitting there for years, he got up and shook his head when he saw Dad, and then they raised their voices, shouting at each other for a few minutes. Eventually, they fell silent, and the man went into his shop and brought out a bag of glibets, warm because the sunflower seeds had just been roasted, or warm due to the heat in his shop, he handed the sunflower seeds to me, and I thanked him in Arabic, Dad and the man continued talking, but with calmer voices, I did my best to eat and spit out the sunflower seeds in a way that wouldn't reveal that I was European.

Finally, the man went inside and brought some money, he handed it over to Dad without looking him in the eyes, Dad slid back into the driver's seat and reversed out of the property.

Whatever you do, never build a house, he said.

Is this your house? I said.

Our house.

We continued towards the center of Jendouba. I thought about that movie with Denzel Washington that I accidentally watched after giving a reading in some Swedish city (perhaps it was Borås, Växjö or maybe Skogås?). I turned on the TV and flicked through the channels, stopping when I saw Denzel's face. He had a thin mustache, playing some kind of military man who took care of a young man who had lost his family. Perhaps he had been adopted as a child, or maybe his parents had died from an overdose. In the film's ending, the young man opens the door to a house, and there they all are, the family he has longed for all his life, we see the house from his perspective as he enters the hall and is welcomed by children, cousins, aunts and grandparents, he continues through the house, passing through the kitchen, the living room, upstairs, and wherever he goes, he is hugged and kissed and welcomed by people he has never met, yet everyone seems so sure that he is a part of their family, as if they have been waiting for him since the beginning of time, and now the family is finally complete. The scene ends with him opening a final door, and there he finds his oldest relatives, they can barely see, their skin is wrinkled, they have canes and hearing aids, but they look up at him as he enters, and they smile, I couldn't stop crying when I saw that scene in that hotel room in that small town (Linköping? Norrköping? Köping?), even though I hadn't seen the beginning of the movie, as if that was what I had dreamed of my whole life without knowing it—a house full of relatives who looked like me, where it was evident to everyone that I was a part of them, now when we drove into Jendouba, I wondered if I had vague memories of something similar when I was here as a child. Mom, my brother and I were welcomed by Dad's family, by our family, by Dad's eight siblings, by Grandfather, who was still alive, by the kind sister who would soon die from ALS, by the joking sister who always bit our noses when we leaned in for a cheek kiss, but now when we arrived in Jendouba, everything was different, no one cared that we were here, and if they did, they concealed it well.

The first afternoon, I walked around the city with Dad. I was too tall, too Swedish, too French-speaking, too European, too feminine, my T-shirts were too tight, my hair was too long. I was introduced to relatives, or random people that Dad knew or was friends with, or maybe disliked, as "oueldi kabir" (the eldest son), and everyone asked me, "Tetekelem arabi?" (Do you speak Arabic?). I replied, "Shwaya shwaya" (a little bit), and they started speaking Arabic, and I barely understood a word. I tried to explain that my French was better. One of my uncles told Dad that I shouldn't say that I speak "shwaya" Arabic when I clearly don't speak Arabic at all, so I began answering "la" (no) when people asked if I spoke Arabic, but that answer always led to the question "woalesh" (why?), and neither Dad nor I had a good answer for that.

In the evening, we went to the local bar and had beer. Dad introduced me to everyone as his son, the eldest son. Then we went to Grandma's house. She wasn't home, so we waited in the courtyard with the birds, dogs and chickens. When she arrived, we hugged each other, and Dad sneaked some money into my hand to give her. I didn't want to start by giving her money, I wanted to show her that our relationship was free from money, that we were family and money wasn't needed. But I was also jealous of the sum, it seemed unreasonably large, and I wondered why he could give so much to his own mother while fighting so hard to avoid paying child support to our mother.

Grandma was the only one in the family with whom I couldn't communicate in French.

She said she understood French, but her French was as bad as my Arabic, and we ended up miming that it had been a long time and that it was nice to see each other. She said something to Dad and gestured with ten henna-colored fingers towards the sky.

What is she saying? I said.

She says that if you come back here and speak Arabic, she'll give you material for ten books, Dad said.

She smiled and signaled ten again.

I tried to ask questions about our family's history.

I read somewhere that our surname has a connection to the

mountain range, but it also has Berber roots and possibly Jewish origins?

Dad translated my questions into Arabic. Grandma nodded and answered in Arabic. Dad translated back into French. Grandma's responses were three minutes long, while Dad's answers were often just one or two syllables.

It's not true. It's not true at all. It's just rumors. You must learn Arabic, Grandma said.

That's why I'm here, I said.

Later that evening, we passed Dad's uncle's house. He was the wealthiest in the family and owned a travel agency. They took out soft drinks from the fridge, and we drank them while Dad's uncle talked about politics. Then we passed by Dad's sister's apartment. They took out soft drinks from the fridge, and we drank them while Dad's sister's husband talked about politics. The TV was constantly on, showing clips from Palestine, soldiers shooting into demonstration crowds, funeral processions attacked with tear gas. After finishing our drinks, we left and returned to Dad's apartment.

Wasn't there a big apartment at the top of the new building where you were supposed to live? I asked.

I didn't like it there, Dad said. It was too big. I rented it out instead.

We had barely eaten anything all day, just sunflower seeds and beer, sunflower seeds and soft drinks. I thought I would be welcomed with homemade feasts, chakchouka and brik, but no, instead, Dad and I ordered pizza and ate it in front of the TV. Then we went to bed. I slept on the mattress in the hall, and he slept on the living room sofa. No one slept in the bedroom. The TV was on all night for Dad to sleep. We woke up to a loudly ringing cell phone, and Dad answered it. He sat up, and his face turned gray.

What happened? I said.

Radhi is dead, Dad said.

I didn't understand why his hands were shaking. Radhi was married to one of my aunts and nobody liked him. He used to beat his children and never smiled or danced or told jokes.

Get dressed, Dad said.

Where are we going? I asked.

We need to pick up Grandma, Dad said.

Now? I said.

Yes, now! Didn't you hear what I said? Radhi is dead!

 I didn't understand anything, but I did as I was told. Ten minutes later, we were parked in front of Grandma's house. She came out, her veil flowing in the wind. She hadn't taken the time to put it on properly. She looked even more shaken up than Dad. I didn't understand why they were so upset. I had heard them speak ill of Radhi since the day Dad's sister married him.

Get in the back, Dad said, and I moved to the back seat.

Dad closed the door on Grandma's side, and then we drove off into the night. It was pitch-black, except for the stars and the moon. I wondered if the beer Dad had earlier that evening had left his system. I told myself that everything would be fine and that if I stayed awake all the way to Tunis, we wouldn't crash into a truck and die like Radhi. Grandma and Dad talked in the front seat, but even if I could understand Arabic, I wouldn't have heard what they were saying. Dad was speaking quietly as if he was trying to keep something from Grandma. I fell asleep in the back seat. When I woke up, we were in Tunis. Dad had parked in front of the house where Radhi and his family lived, with a supermarket on the corner. The supermarket was closed, and I wondered if I had ever seen it closed before. Dad opened the door for his mother, and we helped her up the stairs. It felt great to do it, for about three minutes, I knew exactly what I was doing and why. I was helping my elderly grandmother up the stairs to the apartment where her dead son-in-law lay. But as soon as she went into the apartment, my usual insecurity and feeling of being in the way returned. Dad came out and stayed with me in the stairwell.

What are we doing here? I whispered in Swedish.

Radhi is dead, Dad said impatiently.

I know, but why are we here?

We need to transport him to Jendouba, Dad said.

I looked at him.

Why?

Because if the government finds out that he died here, it will be very complicated to get him down to Jendouba, Dad said.

He was silent, I was silent, the sun was rising, soon the mosques would be calling for prayer.

Is your sister in there? I asked.

Yes.

And Radhi too?

Yes. Do you want to see him?

We went inside the apartment. Grandma took care of her daughter. My aunt wasn't crying, just sitting there on a sofa, looking down at her hands, in shock, her husband lay on another sofa, there he was, his skin looked even more yellow than usual, his mustache was even thinner than I remembered, his eyes were open. Grandma talked, Dad talked, Radhi's teenage children talked, and I heard the Arabic word for "ambulance." Then Dad stood up and left the apartment, and I followed him to the stairwell.

Is the plan to transport him to Jendouba in the trunk? I said.

Dad looked at me as if I was crazy.

Of course not, he said. That would be bizarre.

What's the plan, then? I said, making one last attempt to understand what was going on.

We'll try to get an ambulance to transport him to Jendouba, Dad said.

But he's dead? I said.

Yes, but if the police stop the car, the ambulance personnel can say that he just died. We just need to bribe them.

We stood outside the building when the ambulance crew arrived, two young guys, one of them finishing a tuna sandwich. They took out their stretcher and went upstairs at a leisurely pace. They came out with Radhi, his face was not covered with a cloth, they talked while they loaded the stretcher into the ambulance, I don't know if they were pretending to talk to Radhi or if they were talking to each other. Dad gave them money, and one of the guys wanted more. Dad handed him another banknote. The ambulance started its siren and drove away. Grandma came down to the street; she had managed the stairs on her own. She looked strangely young, she had survived three bouts with cancer, she had survived her husband, she had survived colonial powers and fundamentalists and revolutions, and now she had survived her son-in-law. She looked at Dad and asked if he needed to sleep. He shook his head. We returned to the car, and Dad bought some coffee at a café, black coffee in a white, thin plastic cup, one of those cups they give you water in at hospitals. He drank the coffee as we drove out of Tunis, accompanied by crowing roosters and echoing calls to prayer.

First, we caught up with the ambulance, and Dad complained that they were driving like "fucking queers." But he said it in Swedish, so Grandma wouldn't understand. When we left Tunis, the ambulance sped up, and we watched the flashing lights disappear behind a bend. Dad complained that they were driving like "fucking maniacs," but this he said in French, then he looked over his shoulder to see if his mother had heard him swear, and when he saw that she was sleeping, he reached over and patted her cheek gently with the back of his right hand.

Chapter Sixty-Nine

Anastasia walked in circles in the apartment trying to remind herself that Daniela is okay, Daniela is fine, it wasn't anything really, just some electricity, it was Daniela's own fault, Anastasia only asked her to have a look, she never told her to climb up on a chair and stick her fingers into the meter, Daniela should have known better, she is studying to be an engineer, how could she be so stupid that she, it didn't make sense, unless she had done it on purpose, to punish Anastasia, no, why would she, Anastasia had left first one and then another note at Daniela's dorm room, she would call soon, any minute now, she was not about to leave Tunis without saying goodbye, she knew that this wasn't Anastasia's fault, she didn't blame her for anything, she knew there was no such thing as curses, so why wasn't Daniela calling, Anastasia wasn't sure, she knew that Daniela was back from the hospital, she knew that Daniela would be okay, she has to be okay, and Anastasia kept walking from room to room in the apartment, she tried to gather her thoughts, on Monday she would return to Sweden, if she could she would leave now, just get up and go to the airport, for a moment she wondered if that was a possibility, but no, she had no money to rebook her ticket and she was stuck here for another seventy-two hours, she stood in the living room, she looked at the dark brown wall-to-wall carpet, she checked the landline, it worked, she sat down on the dark brown couch with holes from cigarette burns, the white padding of the couch spilled out from its inside, she put her feet on the glass table that had breadcrumbs stuck between the glass and the metal rim, there were two speakers, not connected to anything, a TV not connected to anything, an old metal VCR, all buttons worked except REW, she got up from the couch and checked the bookshelf, she found a couple of old Swedish newspapers, one *Expressen* and one *Aftonbladet* from the same date, twelve years ago, a half-written postcard with the motif of the Prophet Mosque in Al-Madinah al-Munawwarah, an illustrated sticker from a cereal box, an empty brown paper bag, a bunch of old boarding passes, a time-table from Swissair, she read it in an attempt to keep her thoughts stable, *be at the right place at the right time, Flugplan, Horaire, Time-table, 31 Oct 1999–25 Mars 2000,* she found a ticket cover from Tunis-air, with its slogan *Je préfère Tunisair,* six smiling people underneath the orange and pink text, a photograph of a black shoe, an empty postcard with the stamp *Retour á l'envoyeur* written in capital letters and in Arabic, an informational brochure about different laboratory machines, a postcard from someone called Gunilla—two illustrated birds happily toasting with champagne, *2000* spelled out in big large numbers—Gunilla wrote in French, and ended the postcard with *Je te souhaite une bonne 2000! Stor kram, Gunilla. PS: Tes fils te passent le bonjour,* Anastasia found handwritten receipts, empty boxes of medicine, empty cassette boxes, instructions for medicines, she read them through, she had no idea what they were, Eferalgan, Antacide, Glucophage 850 (metformine), Alphachymotrypsine Choay Pommade, Lysanxia, Calcibronat, another empty postcard, this time from the Gefion Fountain, Gefion Springbrünnen Copenhagen Denmark, a fountain, oxen that looked to be dragging a wagon, a Danish flag in the middle and *København* written in red. A brochure from Arlanda tax-free shopping, she read the brochure, *To travel is to be reborn. New experiences, new encounters, and new acquaintances. Traveling is also coming home. To loved ones, family who have missed you. Friends who are waiting. Have you remembered to buy something nice or fun for your close ones?*

She found a box full of electrical cords, batteries, screws and nuts, a box for cleaning shoes, a dried-up tube with black shoe polish, a once yellow but now black toothbrush. She found an empty tube of Vaseline, a book called *Horoscope 2000* by Frédéric Maison, *Vos Prévisions, mois par mois, ascendant par ascendant*, in the corner of the room, one card of the game UNO, a yellow 7, why isn't she calling? The curse answered: Guess.

Chapter Seventy

Radhi's funeral was scheduled for the next day, the body was lying in my grandmother's living room, someone came to prepare the body, then covered it with a green fabric, there were women in the room crying, I didn't recognize them, Dad said that they were hired mourners, but I wasn't sure if he was joking or not, I mostly stood outside the house, not knowing what to do, waiting for something, for the funeral to begin, I guess, I didn't know what to do with my arms, my dad came out from time to time to check on me, he said that we would soon take the body to the cemetery, soon, first we had to fix some things, then he came out of the house and asked me to follow him, we walked to a house a few streets away, Dad knocked on the door, a woman answered the door, Dad talked to her, she looked at him, she said something really short, it sounded as if she just told him yes or no, but I heard clearly that the word she used was something other than yes or no, and my father sighed and nodded. Then he looked at me and said, "Oueldi hathi," and I smiled, and she smiled, and then she closed the door, and we walked back towards my grandmother's house.

Who was that? I said.

Radhi's family, he said. They won't come to the funeral.

Why not?

Dad was silent.

What did he do to them? I said.

Dad was silent.

They can't even leave their house and walk a few blocks? I said as if their absence from the funeral was due to logistics. Dad just walked beside me, he asked if I was thirsty, he asked if I was hungry, we stood outside the house for half an hour waiting for the funeral to begin.

Are you hungry? he said for the third time.

Not really, I said.

Let's eat, he said. This will take forever.

We went to a nearby restaurant and ordered a sandwich, Dad took his insulin. When we came back we had missed the body, we had to run towards the cemetery to catch up with the procession, there it was, we saw it at a distance, we ran past a small corner store, we crossed the railway tracks where there was a market and all the vendors moved their fruit stands when a rare freight train passed, we caught up with the body at the market, it was lying on a wooden stretcher, under a cloth, people were carrying it, random people ran up to the stretcher and carried it for a few blocks, then they let go and let someone else take over.

Who are these people? I said.

Just people, Dad said.

Were they friends of his?

No, Dad said, sounding as if he doubted my intelligence for even asking such foolish questions.

Of course not, he added, with a gentler tone. Some might have known him, but most of them just want to show their respect.

We didn't carry the stretcher, we just walked alongside it to the cemetery, where the crowd of carriers dispersed, the body was placed in a hole, Radhi's eldest son made a wailing sound, they put the body in the ground with the green cloth that had covered it, but when the body landed in the hole I saw part of Radhi's foot, then he was covered with earth and the family lined up to say goodbye to the visitors, the line of family members mostly consisted of people from our family, and we almost outnumbered the people who had come to pay their last respects, I didn't know where to place myself, in the line with the family or in the line with the visitors, I decided to stand next to my father, but slightly behind him, so when people came up to offer their condolences they looked at my father and then at me, and there was a few seconds of uncertainty, is this person family or not, is he a mourner or a caretaker, is he a Khemiri or just a random passerby who has ended up at this cemetery in Jendouba by chance, is he a participant or a voyeur, is he alive or is he just here to gather material for a future book? My dad looked at me and said "Oueldi hathi" and the mourners looked at my father as if they felt sorry for him because I was his son.

My Arabic course started in Tunis the next day, so after the funeral, we got into the Passat and made the same journey back to Tunis for the fourth time in thirty-six hours. Dad drove, and when he had dropped me off, he would turn back and drive to Jendouba, then he would come back to Tunis to drive me to the airport. This could be the last real chance I had to speak to him. I cleared my throat. I didn't ask where he had been all these years. I didn't question why he had submitted all those letters and forms, trying to avoid paying child support to my mom, appeal after appeal, with a determination that he had never shown for anything else. I didn't tell him about Mom's stomach cramps, her going in and out of the hospital without doctors finding anything, and that it was somehow connected to his disappearance and him stopping child support.

Instead, I asked him about the girl who had lived in his apartment last year. Which Mikkola sister was it? The tall one or the short-haired one, or could it be Evelyn, perhaps?

The crazy one, my father said.

Who's the crazy one?

The youngest.

Anastasia?

Yes.

Why do you call her the crazy one?

Because she's crazy! Just like her mother. When I picked her up to drive her to the airport, her things were scattered all over the apartment.

Really? I said, making a mental note not to scatter my things in the apartment.

She was high on something and kept saying she wanted to come with me to Jendouba to break a curse.

A curse?

A *curse*!

He said the word with the same disdain he would say the name of an Israeli prime minister.

I tried to calm her down, he said. I tried to explain to her that there are no curses, not in reality, but she wouldn't listen. She kept talking about her German friend who almost died and another friend who moved to Gothenburg and a boyfriend who destroyed himself with drugs. While she spoke, I packed most of her things, but she still didn't want to leave. She kept asking me for help, and I told her that my mother's aunt used to say that the only defense against the evil eye was to wear blue clothes, and the only way to break a curse was to ask for forgiveness. But now we really have to go because otherwise, you'll miss your flight. And you know what she said then?

Tell me.

"I refuse to leave." Okay, I said. But you can't stay here. Do you have any money? Do you have a plan? Then she broke down and started crying.

Anastasia? Crying? You're making this up.

I promise, my father said. She cried like a little girl, this crazy woman, and I comforted her, telling her everything would be okay, and I managed to get her into the car. She reeked of alcohol, and I wondered if they would even let her through security. I drove her to the airport. She kept saying she wouldn't go home, she wanted to stay here. Stay where? I asked. Here, she said. In my car? She smiled. No, in Tunisia, she said. I have to find the person who cursed us. Listen, I said. You're going home. And I'm going to Jendouba. And I'm going to find the person who cursed you. And I'm going to make them take back the curse. Okay? Do you promise? she said. I promise, I said. That was the only way I could get her out of my car. We said goodbye, and I drove back to the apartment to find someone to clean up after her.

And did you find the person?

What? Someone to clean up? Yes, it was difficult, but I managed it in the end.

No, I mean, did you find the person who cursed them?

Yes.

Who was it?

My father didn't answer.

Who was it? I said again, feeling that it was important, even though I didn't understand why.

It's complicated, my father said.

Why?

It just is, my father said.

What happened?

My father didn't answer.

Is it someone I know?

My father ignored me.

Give me a clue, is it a woman or a man? Is it the guy who sells fish? The butcher? Dalanda? The guy who owns the bar?

I spent five minutes listing all the people I had met in Jendouba. My father remained silent, never nodding, never shaking his head. He just pretended I wasn't there.

Look, we're approaching a village, he said. There used to be a pharmacy here.

Isn't it there anymore? I said.

I'm not sure, my father said.

We drove through the village in silence, my father steering, I riding shotgun, Peter LeMarc singing. We reached Tunis at dusk.

Chapter Seventy-One

The next time they met was at school, Anastasia was waiting outside Daniela's classroom, but Daniela didn't want to talk about it, on their way down the stairs she said it was her own fault, she had been foolish, she just didn't want the landlord to discover that she had removed the thing blocking the electricity meter and blame Anastasia, so Daniela decided to put it back before she left (but why was she leaving, and where was she going?), and then she received a shock.

It wasn't strange, it wasn't magic, it wasn't connected to any curse, I was just tired and dumb, Daniela said.

But when Anastasia asked if she wanted to come over after the last day of school, Daniela said she was tired and needed rest.

On Saturday, one of the American Tunisians at school had arranged a farewell party. He lived in the Medina. Anastasia hadn't planned to go, but since Daniela refused to call back, Anastasia had to do something to keep from going crazy, so she went to the old town alone, ignoring the whistles from men on mopeds and not responding when carpet sellers thought she was a tourist and offered her tea, she arrived and rang the bell, and the door opened to a house that looked like a movie set.

There was a seating area on the ground floor, with shishas and sofas, red ornamented cushions on the floor and a pool shaped like an old-fashioned keyhole with an actual indoor fountain. She continued up the stairs to find disco lights and a dance floor. Then a few bedrooms, and then the roof, where most people hung out, the sky, the stars, the small alleyways of the Medina and the host of the party, who explained that he had hired two "local guys" to work the bar, sure they weren't professionals, they were just two "great guys" whom he had gotten to know here, and he figured that he might as well pay them for taking care of his guests, it was his way to "give back to the community."

Anastasia looked at the guys behind the homemade bar, both were nicely dressed, both interacted with the guests, both refilled glasses, and cut lemon slices, and fetched ice, and offered weed, and cleared empty glasses from the edge of the roof, but one of them was drinking and the other was not, and the one who was drinking became drunk really fast and starting questioning why the American Tunisian had turned him and his friend into employees, "I thought we were friends," he said again and again, while the American Tunisian tried to change the subject, but the drunk bartender persisted, addressing him as "sir" and asking him if he wanted more ice in his drink, and when the American Tunisian said, "Yes, I actually would love some ice," the drunk guy told him to get his own fucking ice.

Anastasia stayed on the roof, someone had a joint, Anastasia hadn't taken drugs for years, the last time must have been with Mathias on New Year's Eve 2000, and she wasn't about to start now, she settled for first a beer and then some wine, but then someone started passing around a second joint, and a third, and Anastasia came to the conclusion that weed can't be called drugs, it was natural, it was medicinal and calming, she took two puffs, and then two more, then she got up and danced around the circle of friends, so that she would be invited to take two more puffs when the joint reached the other side, then two more before she handed the joint to the next person, then some drinks and some more drinks and it felt right, she was back to being herself, finally, after all these years, this is what it was supposed to be like to be her, in the corner of her eye she saw Daniela, what was she doing here, and why hadn't she called, ah who cares, Daniela walked with a limp and held her glass with her left hand, since the right one was covered with a bandage, they nodded to each other, they didn't kiss, they didn't hold hands, they didn't say a word to each other, at some point later in the evening Daniela came up to Anastasia and tried to say something, she tried to pull her away from the dance floor, she tried to convince her to leave the party, but Anastasia resisted, she had done enough, she yanked herself free, she wasn't leaving, not now, not ever, she had just arrived, she had all this life and all this energy in her, and this was her song and these were her people, Daniela disappeared and Anastasia didn't care, instead she climbed the stairs back to the roof, there were speakers here as well, and even more people, she had nothing to go home to, no apartment, no partner, no friends, no job, at least not a real job, she stood there looking out over the old city, the bats, the stars, the street below, one of the guys in her class, a Portuguese Tunisian or possibly Spanish Tunisian, approached her and asked if she was okay, of course she was okay, couldn't he see with his own eyes how happy she was, he told her to climb down from the ledge, she realized that she had climbed up on the barricade that some people were sitting on, she didn't climb down, instead she looked towards the street, she was only three flights up, she wouldn't die from here, he reached out and grabbed her wrist, she could still break free if she wanted to, there was nothing holding her, but he pulled her down when she wasn't expecting it, and they went to the bar, he didn't let go of her wrist, Daniela had left, of course she had left, this party was too much fun for her, too many happy faces, the music was too loud, she was more of an Excel kind of girl, she was probably at home calculating equations right now, fuck her, fuck her engineering school, fuck her German accent and potential boyfriend, fuck her care for Arabic grammar, fuck her ability to draw secrets out of Anastasia, fuck her adorable nose and soft tongue, Anastasia kissed the guy who pulled her down from the roof, then she made out with the Japanese guy in her class, then she saw Daniela, she had come up from the lower floor, she had waited down by the fountain, hoping that Anastasia would change her mind, Anastasia looked away, it was the last time they saw each other, it was early morning when Anastasia headed home, the sun was out, the last guests had left, first she puked in the corner of the souk, then she puked outside a bookstore, some guys on a moped offered her a ride and took her to Avenue de la Liberté, they helped her inside the building, they didn't follow her up, they just looked at each other and shook their heads.

Chapter Seventy-Two

spent a month at Bourguiba School in Tunis, just like Anastasia had done the year before. I tried to learn Arabic, just like her. I smoked Mars Légères, just like her. I lived on Avenue de la Liberté, just like she did. I ate casse-croutes, just like her, and drank coffee in plastic cups and became friends with a bunch of people whom I promised to stay in touch with but I haven't seen or heard from since then, just like her.

After a few weeks I started dating a French-Tunisian girl with a nose ring named Fazila, in France everyone knew her as Lili, but here she preferred to be called Fazila, which was also the name of her guardian angel. I thought she was joking when she told me this on our third or fourth date, but no, she was serious, she had a very strong sense of being guided and protected by an angel named Fazila. Fazila was with her whenever she was in trouble. In Fazila's (the human's) extremely heavy backpack were things that belonged to Fazila (the angel), desert sand in a glass jar, drawings, sacred stones, more drawings, it sounds insane that I took this seriously now that I'm writing this in October 2021, at a library in New York, but back then, in the summer of 2004, when I was staying in my dad's apartment where the toilet was broken and could only be flushed with a green bucket, I actually believed her. She was so convincing when she spoke of the apparitions of this angel, how she had appeared and saved her that time outside Lyon when she was volunteering in a disadvantaged area and almost got raped by one of the organizers, and that time when a drunk friend of hers was about to drive her home, and Fazila appeared and told her not to get in the car, and the friend had driven off the road and died.

One evening, after we had eaten and were sitting next to each other on the cigarette-burned sofa in the living room, I told her about the Mikkola sisters.

When I was growing up in Stockholm, I had some friends who were convinced that they were cursed, I said, perhaps to show her that I wasn't as boring as I felt.

That's terrible, Fazila said.

They were also half-Tunisian, I added, maybe to show her that we weren't as alone as we thought we were (or maybe to see if she would get jealous).

Do you know what kind of curse it was? she said.

Are there different kinds?

Hundreds, Fazila said.

I have no idea, I said. This was many years ago. It had something to do with the evil eye.

Fazila nodded.

And something about them losing all their loved ones.

Do you know who put the curse on them?

I shook my head. I haven't seen them for years. I was closest with the middle sister. Then I played basketball with the youngest sister. First their dad died, then their mom.

Fazila's eyes widened.

You have to help them, she said.

How?

You have to find the person who cursed them and convince her to take it back, she said.

How do you know it's a woman?

Men don't have the same powers as women. Especially if it's an intergenerational curse.

That doesn't sound very feminist, I said.

Sometimes you are so extremely Swedish, she said.

I shook my head and felt slightly offended, without really knowing why.

I don't even believe in curses, I said.

Of course you do.

No, I don't.

On some level, everyone does.

Not me.

So why do you knock on wood and touch your earlobe and kiss your knuckle every time you mention your second book?

It's not the same thing, I said. That's just a habit. I believe in science. And science says men and women are more alike than different and there are no curses, no such thing as destiny or bad luck and no . . .

I wasn't sure why I sounded so upset. Fazila looked up at the ceiling and shrugged her shoulders as if to say "Well, I tried" to her invisible angel, and that made me more irritated.

Curses are about as real as angels, I said, and Fazila looked like I had slapped her.

So you wouldn't mind if I put a curse on you now? she said.

Go ahead.

I mean it, if you don't believe in them, I could put one on you right here and now?

Be my guest.

She lit a candle and took out a small notebook from her backpack.

I don't want it to be too harsh though, she said.

Use the strongest one you've got, I'm not afraid.

What if I told you that one of your close friends would become ill?

Thank God for hospitals.

Or I could put a curse saying that someone in your family will lose all of his or her belongings in a flood.

I sure hope they have good home insurance.

What if I put a curse on you saying that you will never be able to write another book?

Stop it. That's not even funny.

Okay. Now I know. How about a curse that makes it impossible to get close to anyone?

Do it, I said.

Sure?

I. Don't. Believe. In. Curses, I said.

But you will, she said with a sad smile.

She closed her eyes, muttered a few sentences, and blew out the candle in front of her.

Is that all? I said.

That's all, she said.

A quick curse, I said.

I'm a pro, she said.

Chapter Seventy-Three

Many years later, when Anastasia was one of the most sought-after advertising executives in Stockholm, when the agency she worked for had offered her a partnership so she wouldn't quit and start her own business, when Åhdal threatened to take their daughter, Nina, to the small town where he grew up because he was tired of raising their daughter alone, when Anastasia worked eighty-hour weeks and still came home angry because she never had enough time to work, when she crashed and had to take a break from work because she couldn't sleep anymore, couldn't think, couldn't put two sentences together, when she called in sick and started going into churches just to sit completely still in silence and watch the sunlight as it moved from one window to another, the shadows slowly shifting, reflections swirling up dust and illuminating the altar and the empty pews and worn hymnals, that split second when the church went dark because a bird flew past the window, when Anastasia sat there and listened to the sound of nothing, she remembered one of the last days with Daniela, when they sat at the café in Sidi Bou Saïd, each with a mint tea with cacahuètes, it was just as quiet as it was now, the crickets had stopped singing, the wind had calmed, the waves of the sea held their breath, and Daniela leaned forward and said: I love you, and Anastasia couldn't answer, not because she didn't know what she felt, but because she was terrified of saying it and facing the consequences, so instead, she smiled and gently touched Daniela's cheek and looked

out over the sea and now it had been seventeen years since that summer, and Anastasia still wondered what would have happened if she
had answered what she felt.

Chapter Seventy-Four

After I had spent a month at Bourguiba School, my dad came up from Jendouba to drive me to the airport. He was strangely happy, he sang along to the song playing from the stereo, he waved to some girls at a bus stop. I had been in his country for thirty days, we had spent maybe forty hours together, a majority of those hours had been spent in silence in his car, or in silence waiting for someone, or in silence in front of the TV, and now he seemed relieved that I was finally going back to Sweden. As we were approaching the airport, I didn't ask him if he had any plans to move back to Sweden, I didn't tell him that I had missed him, I didn't say that I sometimes wondered if we were more alike than he understood, because I also had an uncanny ability to abandon people and not feel anything other than relief. Instead I asked him if he ever found the person who had put a curse on the Mikkola sisters.

Of course, he said.

Who was it?

I told you who it was.

No, you didn't.

I did. You have a very bad memory. You must practice it. Play more chess. Try sudoku.

You didn't tell me. Who was it?

Their mother's sister, Dad said. Selima.

Wait, wasn't their mother called Selima?

Well, Dad said. She wasn't called Selima until she stole her sister's passport and used it to flee to Europe.

Oh, I said.

We drove past the gas station where there had been a crash when I first arrived, it was only a month ago, it felt like a year. Fazila had cried when we said goodbye. I looked at her tears and thought to myself that she was even uglier when she cried, how could I have been attracted to this person just a few weeks ago, a person who believed in angels and curses, what the fuck was I thinking.

And is this Selima, the sister, still alive?

Yes, of course, Dad said, sounding as if I had questioned the existence of oxygen in air. What do you think? She is young, Selima, not older than me, and I will never die.

He smiled, and somehow I knew he was right.

Her relatives are still in the same house, Dad said. You know the cinema? Across the street from the railway tracks? They live there in an old house with a tin roof. I went to talk to them. They told me that Selima, the real Selima, was supposed to go to Europe, she had good grades, she was responsible, then her younger, more beautiful sister stole her passport and went to Europe instead of her, which made the parents stop Selima from going. For many years she had to wait here, until her dad died, then a man came from Canada, he looked for a wife, he had imported one wife before, she had left him, bad sign. He was bald but had golden rings and had an embassy connection that could help Selima to get a new passport and finally she left.

Where is she now?

According to her relatives, she is in New York, Dad said. But everyone who goes to North America says they live in either New York or Los Angeles. In reality, she is sitting on a farm in Wyoming and longing to go home.

Why Wyoming? I said.

She could be anywhere.

We arrived at the airport, he parked the car and even walked with me to the check-in desk, despite the extra parking fee. I took out my special folder with the letter stamped by the university to show the police officers that I'm a student at home, which should exempt me from being forced to do military service here, even though I have my Tunisian passport.

You know their mother? Dad said.

Selima?

Her name isn't Selima, Dad said. She was a fantastic woman.

Is it true that you two were . . .

He smiled.

Lovers?

I have never been in love, Dad said. I don't fall in love. Love is for weaklings. I have only been in love once and that was with your mother. Look, do you think I do this for every woman I meet?

He pulled up his shirtsleeve to show me the initials of my mom's four names on his underarm. G for Gunilla, M for Matilda, E for Erika and B for Bergman. A tattoo he made himself with ink, a needle, and a candle, a few weeks after he had met my mom, when they were young and happy and everything was possible.

And what about this one? I said and pointed to the other tattoo, higher up on his arm, two letters that were not my mother's initials.

Dad smiled.

So many women, so little time, he said.

Are those her initials? I said.

You have to go now, Dad said.

And I went, we said goodbye, we did the three bises, we promised to stay in touch, I told him that I would text him as soon as I had made it to the gate, so that he didn't have to worry that I was in a cell somewhere, waiting to be transported to an army base for obligatory military service.

Just tell them that you're a student, he said, and I nodded and walked towards security.

They didn't even look at the letter, they just let me pass, it was as obvious to them as it was to me that I didn't belong in their military. I texted my dad at the gate. I boarded the plane. I kept checking my phone to see if he would respond until the flight attendant told me to turn off my phone.

Part III

Chapter Seventy-Five

The first official meeting of Hector's still-unnamed publishing house took place outdoors. In August 2003, Hector invited his friends Kim and Åhdal to Gamla Stan, they met up by the docks, Åhdal brought coffee in a metal thermos, milk in a separate bottle, disposable plastic cups, he even had three copies of the free newspaper *Metro* for them to sit on.

You're on another level, Kim said. Don't tell me you have cigarettes too?

This was a joke, of course, because everyone knew that Åhdal didn't have cigarettes, he had lighters, notepads, pens and printed information about how to start a publishing house, but no cigarettes. He had smoked for years, but he had a principle of not buying cigarettes, simply because he wanted to avoid becoming addicted, he wasn't addicted, he just smoked whenever his friends smoked, and luckily his friends smoked a lot, at least Kim smoked and Hector smoked when he was with Kim. They poured themselves a cup of coffee from Åhdal's thermos, Åhdal lit one of Kim's cigarettes, inhaled and blew smoke out of his nostrils, with such a joyful sound that Hector couldn't help but smile.

If this is not happiness, I don't know what is, Åhdal said in English.

Hemingway? Kim said.

Åhdal shook his head.

Fitzgerald? Hector said.

Roth?

Didion?

Vonnegut, Åhdal said and inhaled again.

Hector cleared his throat and started the meeting. He wanted to talk about the Edward Said lecture at ABF, the Workers' Educational Association, that Ina had taken him to, but as soon as he mentioned ABF, Åhdal interrupted, explaining that ABF is an embarrassing relic, a symbol of a labor movement that has lost its focus, a tired left that hasn't managed to update its worldview since 1966, and Kim quickly jumped in to defend ABF, reminding everyone of their important grassroots work, their now-closed publishing house and their affordable courses in computer skills and languages. Hector tried to steer the discussion back to Edward Said, but Åhdal informed his friends and some passing tourists that Said's *Orientalism* is a seminal work that will outlive us all, while Kim proclaimed to his friends, the passing subway train, and a few startled seagulls that Said was an intellectual fraud who had stolen everything from Foucault.

Anyway, Hector said. Said's lecture convinced me that we should do this. We have a responsibility to do this, and if we don't do it now, we'll regret it for the rest of our lives.

And by "this," his friends knew exactly what he meant. They had been talking about starting a publishing house for five years, ever since Kim discovered that there was no Swedish translation of Apollinaire's *The Amorous Adventures of Prince Mony Vibescu*. Their plans didn't change when Åhdal found out that there actually was a translation published in 1966 by the pornographic publisher Termac. Instead, they decided to start a publishing house that could reissue the first translation. Hector would investigate how much it cost to buy a printing press, he had heard of a socialist association in Axelsberg that might be interested in selling theirs, Kim, who spoke (kind of) fluent French, had promised to go through the translation, and Åhdal was just happy to be part of the process, in all honesty, he had never read Apollinaire or Bataille, and in fact, he hadn't read most of those obscure authors that Kim and Hector seemed to worship, every time he tried, he was strangely affected by the rapes and sadistic scenes with lit candles and mutilation of schoolgirls, the forced sex scenes between young boys and horses. When he was alone in his dorm room, he mostly read old-school American authors like Vonnegut and Steinbeck, Huxley and Heller, still he had said yes when Hector suggested they start a publishing house, he loved the idea of being part of a group, of creating something, that three friends who had met studying Literature A would be meeting regularly to discuss titles, plan their spring releases, smoke cigarettes. But most of all, he liked the thought of presenting himself as Åhdal, the publisher. Currently, he was studying economics at the university, but only during the day. At night, he would transform into an underground book publisher, with the mission of destroying big publishing houses like Bonniers and Norstedts because they were not worthy of calling themselves real publishers, especially after rejecting four (FOUR!) of his secretly written manuscripts just because they were written in classic third-person past tense, with white male protagonists, and not tiresome contemporary language experiments written by posers like Khemiri, who had just released his debut novel. Kim was pretty much done with his review of the Apollinaire translation ("it works fine—we can publish it as it is"), and now they just needed to agree on a name for the publishing house to take the next step.

Are you ready? Hector asked.

His friends nodded.

But why now? Åhdal inquired.

It's now or never, Hector replied with a secret smile.

He didn't mention that Evelyn's boyfriend, Simon, had just started his own law firm, and that there was something about the effortless way he had created a website, ordered business cards and acquired his first clients that filled Hector with a mix of inspiration and jealousy. He didn't mention that Ina's period was late.

Have you started thinking about names yet? Kim said.

For what? Hector said and looked guilty.

For the publishing house, Åhdal said.

Oh, right. How about . . . Substance, Hector said.

The brief silence spoke volumes about their enthusiasm.

Tell us more, Åhdal said.

Well, since the common thread for the books we'll publish is that they have substance?

Kim and Åhdal didn't look convinced, but being Kim and Åhdal, they shot down the suggestion for different reasons, Kim found it too commercial, while Åhdal thought it was too cryptic. Not even Hector felt convinced, it had felt right when he wrote it in his notepad but felt wrong when he said it out loud to his friends.

What about Assfuck Editions? Kim said.

A bit long.

Just Assfuck?

A little vulgar.

How about Publishing House Samurai Number Eight? As a tribute to Mishima?

Too obvious, Hector said.

Substance Publishing House sounds like a course at ABF, Kim said.

I thought you loved ABF? Åhdal said.

Sacrilege Publishing?

Too religious.

Word Publishing?

Not specific enough.

Fanta Zesty Berry Publishing?

Too specific.

Surrealist Publishing?

Already taken.

Flying Start?

Sounds like a tire company.

Flying Start Publishing?

Just forget it.

Wu-Tang Clan Ain't Nuthin to Fuck With?

Probably copyrighted, Kim said.

And it will create a lot of problems when our books are published in the USA, Åhdal said without a smile.

Hector shivered.

What about Slakthuset, Åhdal said. "Slaughterhouse Books." A few seconds of silence, but this silence was different.

Slakthuset, said Hector.

Have you heard about the new publishing house? Kim said.

No, what's it called? Hector said.

Slakthuset, Åhdal said. They publish some seriously twisted stuff. Texts that no other publishing house dares to touch with a ten-foot pole.

I like it.

Me too.

We have a winner.

It sounds hardcore.

It sounds underground.

It sounds authentic.

Who's going to be slaughtered? Hector said.

Everyone will be slaughtered, Kim said.

The big publishing houses will be slaughtered, Åhdal said.

Cowardly editors will be slaughtered, Hector said.

Timid critics will be slaughtered, Kim said.

Contemporary society will be slaughtered!

Everyone who hasn't read Ariosto's *Orlando Furioso* should be slaughtered!

Boring American authors who write in the third-person past tense should be slaughtered! Hector exclaimed.

Åhdal cleared his throat.

Jonathan Franzen should be slaughtered! Kim shouted.

Five hundred kronor says you haven't read Franzen, Åhdal said.

Hemingway should be slaughtered! Hector yelled.

Enough now, Åhdal said.

Orwell should be slaughtered! Kim screamed.

He's not even American, Åhdal hissed.

The three friends spent the rest of the meeting making plans for the future. They wrote lists of potential titles to be translated or retranslated, wrote down the names of potential acquaintances who could design a logo for free or help with distribution contacts or knew someone who knew someone who owned a café where they could have their first book-release party.

We need business cards, Hector said. Åhdal agreed. And so, Slakt-huset was born during an outdoor meeting with thermos coffee in Stockholm, just a few weeks before Edward Said took his last breath in a hospital in New York.

Chapter Seventy-Six

Anastasia walked from the subway to the address her friend Fabricia had given her, with a cell phone number and clear instructions: Do *not* use the intercom, instead, send a text to this number when you are standing outside.

Okay, Anastasia had said to Fabricia. But won't this so-called medium be able to sense my presence with her remarkable powers of intuition?

I'm doing you a favor here, Fabricia said. The waiting time is normally several weeks. But I told her about you and she agreed to squeeze you in.

Thank you, Anastasia said, and meant it. Because she didn't know where else to turn. The first thing she did when she came back from the language course in Tunisia was to go to the library, she asked the librarians for books about curses.

Do you mean fantasy books? one librarian said.

Why don't you try this one? another librarian said, handing her a red book called *Benedictine Maledictions*, full of Christian curses ("May the sky above them be brass and the earth they walk on iron. May the Lord toss their bodies as bait to the birds of the sky and the beasts of the land. May the Lord strike them from the bottoms of their feet to the tops of their heads"), but Anastasia couldn't find any clues about how to break a curse.

I'm sure she will be able to help you, Fabricia said. You remember my friend Jeanette? She couldn't get pregnant. She went three times and then she became pregnant. She calls it a life-changing experience. And she's a chemist!

Fabricia wasn't a chemist, she was still doing art, and now she had a gallery in Stockholm and was working to finish her first solo show, but she had been interested in horoscopes and tarot cards since she was a teenager. A few years ago, before she moved to Gothenburg, Fabricia had invited Anastasia to an open seance with another medium, the event was in a conference room rented by the hour, close to Fridhemsplan, it had a whiteboard up front displaying partially deleted numbers and graphs from a previous sales meeting. Anastasia paid 150 kronor at the door, and then someone turned off the lights and a middle-aged man entered the room with a candle, he closed his eyes, communicated with the spirits and asked an old lady if she had recently lost her husband.

No, my husband is at Ica, buying tomatoes, she answered. When the snickering died down, the medium asked an older man if he had recently suffered the loss of a relative or a pet. He shook his head. Or a job? Well, my mom died, he said. But that was over twenty years ago.

I sense her presence here, the medium said, and she wants you to know that she really really loved you.

Okay, the man said. Can I ask her a few questions? If she really loved me, then why did she marry a man who repeatedly abused both me and my sisters to the point of . . .

I'm sorry, she's gone, the medium said.

That sounds just like her, the man said, and Anastasia wondered if there was any way of getting her money back.

This lady is different, Fabricia promised her. She's amazing. She has a true gift. She got so many things right the first time I met her, it was uncanny.

The front door looked like any other door, and the building just like any other building in this southern suburb, a small apartment complex of three floors, probably built in the 1920s.

Anastasia looked down at the watch she had found in her mom's basement. It had stopped working when she was in Tunisia, and at first she thought the heat had damaged its inner mechanism, but when she returned home, she went to a watchmaker who replaced the battery, and now it kept time perfectly. It showed that she was five minutes early. She positioned herself near the front door, trying to appear as though she were just a person waiting for a friend rather than someone crazy enough to believe in mediums. She took out her phone but barely had time to check it before the door opened on its own. For a moment, Anastasia was ready to let go of all her doubts. This woman had powers. She was in contact with the spirit world, she had magic in her fingers. Then she realized that an old woman with a walker had pressed the door's opening button. She walked out with a small dog, the size of a squirrel, on a leash. She looked at Anastasia and smiled.

Do you want to come in?

No, thank you, Anastasia said and smiled back. She was not here to see a medium, she was just standing here, on a random street twenty minutes south of the city, looking at her phone.

The woman wandered away, and Anastasia observed her frail trembling body, her small steps and her peculiar smile—as if she knew that something significant was about to happen. When the clock struck the hour, Anastasia texted the medium, thinking to herself that Ina would have been proud (and surprised) by her punctuality. The medium responded with "on my way" and came down to let her in. She looked completely ordinary—no blue hair, no snakes around her neck, no pipe, no tattoos, no crystal ball in hand. She wore a beige crewneck sweater and a brown skirt with white sandals that resembled Birkenstocks, but Anastasia noticed they were actually knockoffs, she wasn't sure how she could tell with such certainty, she had never owned a pair of Birkenstocks, but her mother used to tease women who wore them, in what felt like a different time and a different life. As she followed the medium, who looked more like an accountant or a therapist, up the stairs, she hoped this would be over quickly.

Is it your first time? the medium said when they sat down in the kitchen. Apples in the fruit bowl and half a loaf of bread on the counter.

Anastasia nodded.

You're not alone, the medium said with a smile, as if Anastasia had said something different. People come here thinking that I live in a tent, that my kitchen will be filled with crystal balls and incense. But I'm just an ordinary person.

Anastasia glanced at the children's drawings on the fridge.

The only thing special about me is that I have an enhanced sensitivity, the woman said. Would you like something to drink? Water? Herbal tea? A gin and tonic?

Anastasia smiled and asked for water. The woman poured glasses from a carafe on the kitchen table.

May I see your hands? she asked, and Anastasia extended her hands.

Turn them the other way, the medium said, palms facing upwards.

Anastasia turned her hands. The medium held her hands over Anastasia's and closed her eyes. There was a distance of at least five centimeters between them, still Anastasia could feel the warmth from the medium's palms.

She's here, the woman said in a strangely neutral voice.

Who's here?

Now she's laughing, the medium said, still with her eyes closed.

Who's laughing?

She says you know better than to question who she is.

Anastasia nodded.

She says she's sorry for how everything turned out. She says she only wanted to keep you and your sisters safe.

Anastasia shuddered.

She says you must find your own place to live.

It's temporary, Anastasia whispered.

The medium fell silent for a moment, and Anastasia thought she had lost contact with her mother. But then she started speaking again, faster than before, as if her mother were slipping away and needed to say as many words as possible before the farewell.

She says you must find your own path instead of following someone else's. She says she loves you and your sisters very much. She says she's sorry, it wasn't intentional. She says she misses you. She says she's always here, even when you can't see her. She says you should eat more meat. She says if she could go back in time, she would do things differently.

What things? Anastasia whispered.

All things, the medium said. She says there's a person who can break the curse.

Anastasia chuckled and tried to pull her hands back. She couldn't, someone or something was keeping them fixed to the table.

It's a strong curse, the woman said. Someone put it on your mother, and now it has been inherited by all of you, and if you don't break it, it will continue to shape the lives of your children and your grandchildren . . .

We don't have any children, Anastasia said, trying to sound relieved.

Of course, you don't have any children, the woman replied. Not yet. But you will. Your eldest sister first, then you.

Anastasia attempted to laugh to show the woman that she was immune to this kind of nonsense, and if anyone would have children first, it would be Evelyn, but her laughter didn't sound right when it came out. She felt strange, and for a brief moment she wondered if the woman had put something in her water, but Anastasia hadn't even tasted it, she wanted to pull back her hands, stand up and leave, but she remained seated.

She says you are the only ones who can break it, the medium said. You and your siblings.

Sisters.

Siblings.

I only have two sisters, Anastasia said.

She says "siblings." And if you and your siblings aren't able to . . .

The medium fell silent. Anastasia's mouth turned dry, the room had darkened somehow.

The medium looked as if she were listening to a long tirade of words in a language she didn't quite understand.

If not what, then? Anastasia said. What will happen?

The medium opened her eyes, there were tiny beads of sweat on her upper lip. She's gone.

What did she say?

I'm not sure.

It seemed like you were listening.

She disappeared, the medium said.

Can you help me? Anastasia whispered.

With what?

To break the curse?

Unfortunately not.

Why?

I don't have that kind of power. I'm just a fifty-eight-year-old woman who sometimes hears voices from the other side. Maybe your siblings can help?

I don't think so. We are very different.

There might be strength in your differences, the medium said. Have you talked to your brother about this?

Finally, the enchantment was broken. Anastasia woke up from what felt like a dream and saw herself from the outside, sitting in a random kitchen south of Stockholm with an old, eccentric lady.

What did you say? Anastasia said triumphantly. My brother? I don't have a brother.

My mistake, the medium said with a smile.

She pulled back her hands to take a sip of water. The spell was broken, and Anastasia's hands felt numb and sweaty, as if she had first cooled them in ice and then held them over an open fire.

Anastasia paid in cash, exact change, as per Fabricia's instructions. The woman didn't ask if she wanted a receipt, nor did she inquire if Anastasia wanted to book another session in the future, as if she had just enough supernatural powers to understand that Anastasia would never come back here.

That night, Anastasia had trouble sleeping, and after tossing and turning for a few hours, she turned on the lamp and opened the bag with her mother's old notebooks.

Chapter Seventy-Seven

To celebrate the birth of Slakthuset, the three friends decided to switch from coffee to beer. They got up and poured the cold coffee into the water, picked up their cigarette butts and threw them into a trash bin before leaving Gamla Stan and starting to walk uphill towards Södermalm. They only made it halfway because the sidewalk was blocked by metal fences.

Police cars patrolled the empty street.

Crowds with cameras stood waiting for something to begin. Was it a marathon? A political demonstration? Before they could ask, they heard the gut-wrenching sound of roaring motorcycles, here they came, around thirty bikers, wearing black leather caps, dark aviator sunglasses, heavy boots and silver-studded belts, adorned with tattoos and leather pants, none of them wearing helmets but proudly displaying numerous rainbow flags.

Hector, Kim and Åhdal stopped. After Dykes on Bikes the samba trucks arrived, with male dancers in tights tossing confetti, shaven-headed girls holding hands, labor unions with rainbow flags, military personnel with rainbow flags, all the political parties except the Sweden Democrats with rainbow flags. Then came the techno trucks, the Brazilian samba trucks, and the somewhat quieter queer party truck.

Hector looked at his friends. Åhdal smiled. Kim looked disgusted.

This is incredible, Åhdal said.

It's capitalism at its worst, Kim said.

You're just jealous, Åhdal said.

Jealous? Of what? Jealous of idiots who willingly turn themselves into a corporate spectacle?

Jealous that they have a parade, and you don't.

I'll organize my own parade, Kim said. Only queers who have read Foucault's complete works will be allowed to join.

It will be a short parade, Åhdal said.

True, Kim said.

Relax, Åhdal said.

I'll be at the front, Kim said. With a sign that says truth is the only aesthetically measurable category.

Hector turned his gaze back to the parade. Kim said that this so-called movement was a step backward, hijacked by commercial forces, Åhdal argued that visibility is always a step forward.

Not if it reinforces every existing stereotype, Kim said.

Hector noticed the crowd reacting to Kim and Åhdal's disagreement, a sense of unease emerged, people moved away, not wanting to be near this kind of friction. For Hector, this was normal, he knew that if Åhdal had said something cynical about the parade, Kim would have jumped in to defend it, if Åhdal defended abortions, Kim turned Catholic, when Åhdal spoke about the long-term Darwinian value of religious moral codes, Kim turned into a fundamentalist atheist, when Kim talked about the importance of high taxes and a broad social safety net, Åhdal transformed into a free-market neoliberal defending the market's free will. They were not disagreeing for the sake of it, they were disagreeing to sharpen their arguments, to understand what they truly believed, and the only time when Hector had been forced to step in and separate them was when Kim had spent fifteen minutes savaging marketing, calling it the opium of the people, saying that to give out prizes to the best ads was like giving out prizes to the best cover-ups or the best conspiracy theories, and Åhdal, who had just chosen marketing as his specialization at the university, defended his choice of degree with an anger that had surprised all of them, including himself.

Let's go, Kim said.

Just then, Hector spotted Klara in the parade. There was

something about her clothes and camera that made her stand out. Not because her clothes were spectacular in any way, quite the opposite, in a parade where everyone was trying to stand out (they had just seen the second person dressed as a golden Statue of Liberty), Klara stood out with her regular short haircut, black jeans and worn white T-shirt. The only sign that she was part of the parade was the rainbow flags she had drawn on her cheeks, just above her clearly marked mustache. She walked close to the metal fences, with a camera constantly flashing, which was odd because it was sunny and there was no need for a flash. Every time someone in the audience took a photo of someone in the parade, Klara took a photo of that person. It happened again and again, a person took a picture, and Klara was there with her camera. Some people in the audience tried to hide their faces, others smiled and waved. Hector had a strange impulse to run alongside the parade and talk to Klara, even though he didn't know her, even though he didn't know her name was Klara. He wanted to ask if she wanted to join them for a beer to celebrate their new publishing house and the fact that he was going to be a father—not because he was interested in her, it was obvious she would never be interested in him. No, he felt like she was one of them, part of a small and steadily shrinking tribe. He knew she read Arthur Schnitzler and Alfred de Musset, he knew that she preferred the early Mishima, but instead of waving to her and trying to convince her to leave the parade, Hector simply stood there and watched her back disappear towards Slussen.

Chapter Seventy-Eight

In September 2003, Anastasia had gone through her mother's thirteen notebooks. The text was written in a mix of Swedish, French and English, with occasional words in Arabic, mostly written in the margins near crossed-out words. One page could be a long list of things she was grateful for (her daughters, the years with Raimo, her job, her driver's license, her importers in Hamburg, her Toyota Celica, her legs, the relief from her wisdom toothache), while the next page could be a rather convincing enumeration of reasons to end your life prematurely. But the strangest thing was that her mother had written poetry. Here and there, Anastasia found unfinished or fully completed poems that could only have been written by her mother. One poem was about a customer who tried to haggle over a carpet, then attempted to buy it on installments and finally, when she had the carpet, she set it on fire. Another poem portrayed two sisters attempting to embrace each other, but inadvertently strangling each other, their arms shaped like a "sideways eight," they died and were reborn, again and again.

Sometimes, the handwriting was hard to decipher, and maybe that was why Anastasia began to borrow Ina's computer to transcribe it, not because she wanted to show it to anyone, but rather to get closer to her mother, to understand what drove her to write all these words.

Some entries were dated, while others were lists of things that needed to be done, Christmas presents in 1995, a packing list from 1997, customer invoices to send and quotes to offer. Other pages were addressed to a person her mother called "S," and Anastasia wondered if it was her mother's attempt to write to herself, but why would she ask herself for forgiveness?

Over time, the entries became more fragmented, her mother wrote that she didn't want to feel this way, that she should seek help, that she wanted to handle things herself, that she absolutely refused to take medication, that a number of famous historic events were linked to curses. Towards the end, there was a several-pages-long poem about ethnicity and procreation, her mother claimed that children from mixed ethnic backgrounds were "genetically superior" and then she dedicated three pages to defending an authoritarian approach to parenting, writing that she found herself in a country where "children ruled" and adults had "abdicated," she claimed that the only way to make children take responsibility was to teach them that they are children and don't need to take responsibility too early. The more Anastasia read, the more she wondered if her mother wrote down what she was least capable of achieving in her own life.

After spending a night with her mother's notebooks, Anastasia started to realize that there was something seriously wrong with the parents who sent their children to Gullvivan Preschool. One father rushed from his car in the drizzle to drop off his twin boys, and the twins demanded he go back to get a stuffed animal from the car. One daughter insisted that her mother play with her in the sandbox before leaving, and an adult mother in a green suit, with her work ID around her neck, sat down next to her daughter in the sandbox, playing with a bucket and shovel before hurriedly heading towards the subway. Parents waved and blew kisses, mouthed "darling" and "I love you," and shaped their hands into little hearts, and Anastasia observed their behavior and wondered what they were trying to hide. Perhaps they genuinely hated spending time with their children and loved their jobs, and compensated for it by acting so strangely.

And the children, of course, sensed it too, they realized they could treat their parents poorly and continued to do so, Wilma threw a tantrum because her father had brought the red helmet when she had said the purple one was her favorite, Helge, a super-cute five-year-old, transformed when his mother appeared, demanding fruit but refusing bananas, and his mother complied without hesitation. Anastasia couldn't believe her eyes. True, she had already gained a reputation for being a bit tough on the children, but they seemed to like it. She had clear rules, and if she told a child to put on their socks, they did it without discussion. At one point, Kerstin called her into her office to inform her that some colleagues had expressed concern about her "authoritarian style," and Anastasia asked if she had received any complaints from the parents. When Kerstin shook her head, Anastasia calmly explained that she wasn't the least bit authoritarian, she just refused to accept certain behaviors.

But you have to remember that they are children, Kerstin said.

Exactly, Anastasia said. They are children. Not adults. And they need to learn to respect adults, or they'll grow up to be little monsters.

Kerstin didn't argue with her but asked her to tone it down a bit, and Anastasia promised to try. Later that afternoon, she saw Felicia's mother crouch down and ask five-year-old Felicia what she wanted for dinner, and Anastasia had to bite her lip to keep from shouting, "She's five fucking years old, she doesn't have the right to make decisions like this. You're her parent, please act like one!"

On her way home from work, she heard footsteps behind her. Dino tapped her on the shoulder and asked how the meeting with Kerstin had gone. As they walked towards the subway, they discussed the differences between the children's parents and their own. Dino agreed that these parents were crazy.

My dad was a real asshole, Dino said. But at least he taught me that there were certain rules that you have to respect.

What kind of rules?

Never get high on your own supply, Dino said with a crooked smile.

They had stopped outside the subway station. Dino looked around before saying that he had been clean for several years, and he only smoked from time to time and on special occasions, and if she wanted to join, he had some brown in his backpack.

What's the special occasion? Anastasia said with a smile.

Well, we survived another workday at Gullvivan, Dino said.

And it's almost fall, Anastasia said.

Exactly, Dino said. And while the sun may not be shining, at least it's not raining.

Great minds think alike.

Instead of saying goodbye at the turnstiles, they headed towards the water.

And look! The supermarket has avocados on sale.

Three for thirty-five, what a bargain. Let's celebrate, Dino said.

They passed the school and followed the path towards the wooded area. However, there were too many dog owners by the water, so they climbed a nearby hill and sat at the very top, with a dizzying view of the water and the empty docks, lighting up a joint that quickly burned in the wind. Anastasia took a deep breath and leaned back, her back against a rock. Dino smoked with his eyes half-closed.

Now, that's more like it, he said.

Then they fell silent. Anastasia watched the screaming seagulls hover in the wind without moving their wings.

Chapter Seventy-Nine

When the fall term began, Hector lifted his gaze from the desk to give the new students his usual welcome speech and discovered Klara in the classroom. It must be her, he recognized her from the Pride parade—the same short hair, curious face, the faint shadow on her upper lip and a mouth that always seemed on the verge of forming a smile, even though it only surfaced when her classmates said something particularly idiotic during their introductions (the guy who wrote poetry "inspired by Bukowski," the girl who chose to study intellectual history because she was interested in "social anthropology").

After the second seminar, Klara had already started to attract envy from the rest of the class, especially the girls, simply because Klara was brilliant, somehow she had already read all the required and additional literature and didn't seem to realize that she needed to hide her knowledge a bit to avoid being seen as a threat.

After the third lesson, where they discussed Habermas and Hegel, Klara stayed behind in the classroom, and Hector took the opportunity to ask if he remembered correctly that he had seen her at the Pride parade over the summer. Yes, it was her. She had taken an old camera without film and pretended to photograph everyone in the crowd, just so they could experience what it felt like to be photographed by a stranger. She had passed by the protest gathering at Slottsbacken, where a hundred clean-shaven men with boots and placards that read CRUSH THE GAY LOBBY and LOCK UP PEDOPHILES had assembled, just minutes before they attacked the Pride parade with bottles and fists. One of Klara's friends was still in the hospital with a skull fracture.

Sometimes I regret not having had film in the camera, Klara said. Why?

It would have made it easier to catch those pigs, Klara said.

Before the fifth lesson, Ina asked Hector why he always wore cologne on Wednesdays.

Hector looked surprised and asked what she meant. Ina explained that she might be extra-sensitive to smells now that she was pregnant, but she had noticed that he always wore cologne on Wednesdays, always putting on one of his favorite shirts and was there a particular student in his class that he liked? Is it a guy or a girl? How long had this been going on?

Hector immediately told her about Klara, explaining that he had seen her in the Pride parade to reassure Ina that Klara wasn't a threat, he mentioned that Klara was older than the other students to make sure Ina didn't get any ideas that he was interested in a young student, which he wasn't, they were just friends, they shared similar tastes in literature, he just enjoyed talking to her and he liked the person he became when she was around, but he never forgot for a second that they both had girlfriends.

In October, Klara asked if she could stop by his office later in the afternoon, maybe around two, to talk about something "unrelated to the class."

Sure, Hector said and went straight to his messy office, he opened the window to let some fresh air in, hiding book titles that were a bit too popular, not because he cared about her opinion of his taste, but because he still, after a few weeks of friendship, wanted to impress her without quite knowing why.

Hector suspected that Klara wanted to discuss her essay on Husserl (even though Lagerhjelm was supposed to supervise and grade it). Or perhaps she would come to the office and confess her love for him? Would she tell him that she had seen him there, next to the Pride parade, and thought about him all autumn? That she had also felt a flutter of something, without quite knowing why?

He checked the time. A quarter past. She's not coming. Hector felt oddly relieved, she must have forgotten about him, and if she forgets about him, she can't be in love with him, and then he can't be in love with her. Fifteen minutes later, there was a soft knock on the door. He got up a little too quickly and opened it. Klara came in and sat at the edge of the chair. She didn't look at him. She didn't apologize for being late. She took a deep breath and told him what Lagerhjelm had done to Frida Olofsdottir.

Hector nodded. He had to admit that he had heard similar rumors before.

These aren't just rumors, Klara said.

Lagerhjelm has always been something of a . . . Casanova, Hector said.

Did you just call him a "Casanova"? Klara said. Didn't you hear what he did to her?

Okay, Hector said, unsure why he felt attacked. Lagerhjelm is married, and Frida is an adult, and what they do as private individuals is not . . .

He abused his position of power, Klara said.

Hector cleared his throat.

Who are we to moralize about others' sexual preferences? Hector said. What moral authority . . .

She's not alone, Klara said.

Klara had collected testimonies from at least five other students with similar stories. She told Hector what Lagerhjelm had done to Jeanette Graflund, to Maria Hellström, to three other girls who wanted to remain anonymous because they were afraid of the consequences.

Klara didn't cry. She didn't scream. She just reported what had happened. The pattern was the same; Lagerhjelm asked them to stay after the seminar, complimented them on their intellectual sharpness, invited them to dinner at a French place in Kungsholmen or another French place in Vasastan, claiming he knew the owners and that there would be several others from the department. When they arrived, it was just him and a bottle of wine. He said the others had canceled at the last minute, he talked about his meetings with the intellectual left, about meeting Habermas backstage at a Foucault conference, visiting Žižek's humble home in Ljubljana, having lunch with Said, exchanging texts with Chomsky. Towards the end of the evening, Lagerhjelm always found a way to lure the students to what he called his "hideout," his apartment where he worked, filled with books, a miniature kitchen containing only wineglasses and an old espresso machine. There, on the double bed, he seduced his students, according to Hector, or he raped them, according to Klara.

How do you know this is true? Hector said.

Because he tried it with me, Klara said.

Hector got up from his office chair and just stood there, with a dry mouth and a pounding heart, in his way-too-small office, not knowing what to do with his arms. Klara looked up at him.

I just thought it would be good for you to know what kind of person you're sucking up to, Klara said and got up to leave.

Chapter Eighty

Anastasia had been to this warehouse before, but never this early, it was just after midnight, DJ Terminology aka Dino aka her colleague, who had spent the afternoon changing diapers and trying to find a compromise in a complicated conflict related to a big red-colored *T. rex*, was a few minutes away from doing his first-ever DJ set.

But of course I've DJ'd before, Dino said, when they were up on their regular mountaintop, smoking their regular lunch joint, looking out over the harbor, the forest, the partly frozen water. But this is the first time I get paid to DJ.

How much do you get for one set? Anastasia asked, between puffs.

Well, they are not actually paying me in money, Dino explained, they are paying me in drinks. But still, it's a start.

Anastasia walked past the illuminated, abandoned postal terminal, she passed a car tire place, then another car tire rack, she hadn't seen anyone for ten minutes, but she wasn't afraid, she was just too broke to take a taxi, she could hear the bass as she approached, she knew that in a few hours the industrial area would be full of regular taxis and black taxis, people waiting to get in, people wanting to leave, people looking to score, people wanting to sell, people needing a lighter, people searching for a calm quiet dark corner to pee, shoot up, make out, people looking for that special someone who had been to a similar party like this one, but out on the blue line, three years ago, maybe even Mathias would be there somewhere, looking for a taxi, trying to buy or sell, trying to wave to someone at the front of the line who could help him bypass the queue.

But when Anastasia arrived there was no queue, it was so early that the bouncers hadn't even started their shift. Anastasia opened the metal door and walked up the stairs, nobody charged her an entry fee, nobody asked her if she was a member (which was a standard question they always asked, not because this was a real membership club, but because that was the only way they could serve alcohol, if they claimed to the government that this was a party for a "closed circle," so if you weren't a member, you could become a member on the spot, simply by saying, yes, sure, I'm a member).

She entered the club. The bartenders looked up at her, surprised as if they had been caught doing something they were not supposed to be doing, but the only thing Anastasia saw them doing was cutting limes and carrying ice, getting ready for the crowds of people who would be arriving in a few hours. She passed the bar and entered the main dance floor. It was completely deserted. She had never noticed that the floor was full of black marks from the soles of shoes, or that there were multiple inflatable palm trees in the corner of the room, or that the party organizers had taken the time to cover the large sloping windows with black plastic, it looked like they had used garbage bags. As she walked towards the DJ booth she had the feeling of being a jet plane, coming in for landing, at the least secure airport in the world, all those lights, twisting and turning, the stroboscope blinking, the smoke machine puffing out new layers of mist. Behind the decks she saw him, Dino, in deep concentration, his left shoulder drawn up to his ear, the next song in his headphones, focused on getting the rhythms synced, he still hadn't seen her, even though she was the only person on this dance floor, his head started nodding, he leaned forward and adjusted something on the mixer board, now he had it, she saw that he was in sync, he had that interior smile that new DJs always try to hide when they know that their next mix will create havoc on the dance floor, and Dino had it, despite playing for an empty dance floor, he gently pushed the crossfader sideways and she heard the new song, it was flowing into the old song, and she had never heard anything like it, the melody was, it doesn't make any sense to try to describe it, but still, let's try, there was a melody, but the melody was moving on its own, it was going up and down and around, sometimes it was in sync with the beat and sometimes out of sync, and then the bass hit, and those thumpy snare drums, and what sounded like a reversed sample of a gospel choir, Anastasia looked down at her feet, they were moving, almost against her will, then her legs joined in, at first they weren't convinced, then they heard the progression of the melody and the strange raising of the tempo and the legs couldn't deny that the feet had been right all along, her hips started bending, her butt touched the floor, she raised her arms to the ceiling, she never made a conscious decision to start dancing, her body parts decided for themselves, she had been going to clubs since she was fifteen, she had seen British drum-and-bass DJs crush the opposition at music festivals, she had seen American house pioneers explode dance floors in the city, but nothing came close to what she experienced by herself, on that empty dance floor, on that early Thursday night in that industrial area in the south of Stockholm.

When the song reached its inevitable climax Anastasia screamed and Dino looked up and saw her, he smiled, but it was a kind of sad smile, as if he thought she was making fun of him, teasing him about the empty dance floor, then he seemed to realize that she actually was lost in the music, and then he became convinced that she had taken something, that she was high out of her head, and that's why she reacted like this.

When he was done and unplugged his sweaty headphones, and left the booth to the second of five DJs to play that night, he descended the stairs and made his way through the dance floor, it was still kind of empty, only small groups of people standing around in circles, some of them talking, one or two of them trying to get the dance floor going, despite their friends' unwillingness, Anastasia came running and pressed her sweaty body to his and asked him about the song.

Which song? he said.

That song, she said, with eyes so big that Dino for a moment thought that if she made them any bigger the top half of her head would crack open.

The one with the melody, she said, and she tried to hum it.

You liked it? Dino said.

I never heard anything like it, Anastasia said. Who is it?

It's me, Dino said. I made it. It's mine.

He said it three times, as if he had to convince himself that it was true.

The DJ after Dino played one banger after another, the dance floor filled up quickly, people screamed, the fire alarm was triggered twice because someone insisted on smoking indoors, but the sound from the speakers was so loud that the fire alarm only seemed like a sound effect, Dino and Anastasia danced and drank, but no song moved her like Dino's song.

On her way home, Anastasia tried to re-create it in her head, but she couldn't, she only had small fragments of it, first the melody went up, then down, then around and around, the melody was in search of something, it was continuously looking, and sometimes it thought it had found what it was looking for, then it was actually moving in sync with the rest of the song, but only for a few seconds, then it was released, and it kept searching again, it was searching for something else, Anastasia thought about a bacterium, a virus, an atom, it was always moving, never still.

When she came home Ina and Hector were in the kitchen having breakfast.

Where have you been all night? Ina said.

Anastasia sat down at the table, took a deep breath and tried to explain the brilliance of Dino's song. She tried to hum it, she said that the melody was like a virus, that the song was like a rainforest, that the gospel choir was like a tornado.

Are you working today? Hector said.

I start late.

How late?

Late enough, Anastasia said, irritated that her sister and her boring boyfriend always focused on the wrong things.

What have you been taking? Ina said.

Nothing, Anastasia said. I was sober, this was early, like half past midnight.

Ina laughed, Hector focused on putting butter on his toast.

Early?

Yes, early.

If half past midnight is early, then what is late? Ina said.

You're not listening, Anastasia said. This song. It was not a normal song, it didn't have the same rhythm, or it had the same rhythm, but after a while it sped up, and every time you thought the song was heading in one direction, it turned and did something unexpected, it was impossible to . . . capture.

Sounds like a hit, Hector said.

Ina smiled and shook her head.

It will be, Anastasia said. Mark my words. This song will be massive.

Try to lie down, sis, Ina said.

This song will change the world.

Try to get some sleep.

Remember where you heard it first, Anastasia yelled, as she walked towards the bedroom that she had taken over when Evelyn moved out. This song will change everything.

What's it called? Hector said.

"OAR003-B," Anastasia said and closed the door to avoid Hector and Ina's irritating laughter. She lay down under a blanket, she closed her eyes, she heard the melody, it came closer, it would save her, no matter what happened in the future, the melody would be there to pick her up, to help her make sense of everything that felt empty at that moment. When she woke up, she realized she had missed her entire workday. Instead of contacting Kerstin at Gullvivan Preschool and coming up with an excuse (stomach flu, nervous breakdown, flat tire on the car/bike/sled), she started working on an email that would change both her and Dino's lives.

Chapter Eighty-One

The emergency staff meeting took place in November 2003. When Hector entered the classroom, he had the feeling that they had started without him. Everyone was already seated and Kristersson and Lagerhjelm stood at the front by the whiteboard, speaking in hushed voices.

There you are, Ann said, turning to him with a smile.

We said ten, right? Hector said and looked up at the clock on the wall. He knew he wasn't late, he just wanted everyone else to take note of it too.

Yes, ten, Kristersson said. But now that everyone is here, I suggest we start.

So they began, with Kristersson taking the role of moderator, he first asked Lagerhjelm to give his take on the "recent events" and he did, he did it the Lagerhjelm way, the way only Lagerhjelm could do it. First he took a deep breath, then he looked out over his twelve colleagues as if scanning an audience of thousands, then he smiled and closed his eyes, or rather squinted as if there were a link between his memories and his squinted eyes. He started telling them the story, he reminded them that he had been at this distinguished institution for more than thirty years, thirty-seven to be exact, and he had seen it all, he had seen the ebbs and flows, he had been through the storms and the droughts, he was a student during the occupation back in the late '60s and a teacher during the labor protests in the '80s and now he was standing here, in front of them, as a senior professor, he had been a guest lecturer at Berkeley, he had been invited to speak at both Columbia University and Universidad Nacional de Colombia, Kristersson smiled, Ann smiled, but Hector had heard him use this exact phrasing several times before, and this was the first time he managed to refrain from smiling.

Lagerhjelm continued to talk about his articles, his books, the recent conference where he had a meaningful exchange with Judith Butler. After ten minutes, Kristersson raised a finger and, in a low voice, thanked Lagerhjelm for the overview. He, and everyone else at the institution, was grateful for all he had done for the subject. But could Professor Lagerhjelm talk a bit more about the rather "special events" that had brought them all here today?

Absolutely, Lagerhjelm said, sighing. This is nothing new. It's a wave in the sea, a wind in the desert, rain in the rainforest. It's a long-standing tradition. These situations are as old as the institutions we love and respect. Occasionally, a student, man or woman, but mostly a woman, falls in love with a teacher. And what I've learned over the years is that this infatuation has nothing to do with the individuals involved. A student isn't in love with the professor, he or she, but mostly she, is in love with the institution, the subject, the knowledge. And while it's flattering for me as a professor, we must remember that we are not the institution, we are merely symbols of what the student, man or woman, but mostly woman, has yearned for their whole life. So, our responsibility as teachers and professors is to remember that and honor it and not take adv—

You raped her, Hector said without raising his hand.

Lagerhjelm looked like someone had shoved a lime down his throat. Kristersson's strangely visible Adam's apple went up and down like an elevator.

This student, she was in crisis. She came to you for support, and you took advantage of her and raped her, Hector said, attempting to sound calm.

Let's try not to interrupt each other, Kristersson said.

And she's not the first, Hector said, heart pounding. And she won't be the last.

Rumors, Lagerhjelm said. Just rumors. Show me one man, or a

woman, who has reached any level of success and I will show you ten jealous people doing their best to sabotage that person's success.

They are students, Hector said. They have no interest in bringing you down.

This woman is emotionally unstable, Lagerhjelm said. She can't be trusted. She has been in and out of institutions since she was fifteen.

I trust her more than I trust you, Hector said.

Kristersson cleared his throat. May I ask you, Ann, to weigh in? What are your thoughts?

Ann was one of those people who has an acute allergy to conflict, she spent five minutes talking about the value of Lagerhjelm's research and then three minutes talking about the importance of creating a safe environment for all students, regardless of gender, ethnicity and . . .

Now it was Kristersson's turn to interrupt.

And what's your impression of this specific student?

She's a gold digger, Lagerhjelm said. She fell in love with me, even though I told her I was married, and when I didn't give her what she wanted she made up a story of me attacking her and . . .

She showed me her bruises, Hector said.

She could have gotten them from anywhere! Lagerhjelm screamed. It was the first time anyone had heard him raise his voice. His hands shook, sweat broke out on his temples, he looked ten years older than when the meeting started.

Ultimately this is not our decision, Kristersson said, trying to end the meeting before it got worse. Until the student in question files an official complaint, our hands are . . .

I brought her testimony, Hector said and pulled out a stack of papers from his backpack. I will leave it here for anyone who wants to read what this glorious institution has done to one of its most talented students.

That's classified, Lagerhjelm said.

Eh, no, it's not, Hector said.

I forbid you to read that garbage, Lagerhjelm said and walked up to Hector, took the paper stack from him and walked over to the trash can. But not even Lagerhjelm could resist glancing at the first page, and when he read the first sentences, he realized that the papers belonged in the nearest shredder.

Hector stood up from his chair and uttered a sentence that changed his future:

If you don't get fired for this, I will resign.

He left the room. He walked back to his bike. His heart was still pounding. As he started pedaling away from the gray university building, he felt a jolt of freedom, the kind of freedom that only appears when you know you have done something really really stupid, and it's too late to go back.

Chapter Eighty-Two

n November 2003, Anastasia received a text from Mathias. She hadn't seen him since 2000, the last time he messaged her was in April 2001 at four in the morning, she hadn't responded then and she didn't intend to respond now, despite him saying he missed her and was sorry. Eight days passed, and then she wrote back (Sorry for what?), he immediately replied, sorry for getting you kicked out of your office, sorry for getting you to try drugs, sorry for not being clearer about what I wanted, sorry for vomiting in Ina's handbag, sorry for accidentally kicking your friend's cat, sorry for getting us kicked out of that taxi, sorry for stealing your money, sorry for trying to pawn your necklace, sorry for getting angry with you when she said the crystal was worthless, sorry for calling one of your sisters an arrogant know-it-all, sorry for calling the other sister a fake prima donna, sorry for everything, want to meet up?

Anastasia entered Kafé Valand on Surbrunnsgatan for the first time in years. The owner stood behind the counter, an old German man with three fingers missing on one hand, he served everyone drip coffee, no matter what they ordered, and the regulars who wanted tea knew they could reach behind the counter, pour out the coffee in the sink, refill the cup with hot water and get their own tea bags. When a beginner came in and tried to order an espresso or a latte, the man either served them regular coffee or asked them to leave because this was not an ordinary café, they had coffee and tea, herring sandwiches and gingerbread cookies—nothing else. The interior of the café had not changed since its opening in 1954, the walls were covered with teak wood panels, and the chairs and tables were also made of teak, the lamps had old-style cords, and the toilet in the corner was locked with a key, if someone needed to use it, they had to signal with their hands, otherwise, the owner would think they wanted a refill, which cost five kronor, but the toilet key was free for customers, the restroom had no heating and only cold water, and it was so small that you had to leave your backpack outside, otherwise there wasn't room for you to turn around and wash your hands.

Anastasia had spent much of her youth at this café, and now she was back. She expected the owner to at least remember her, but he just poured her some coffee, took her money and told her that a refill was five extra kronor. She had arrived early in order to get the corner table, where you could sit without being seen from the street. But the table was occupied. Someone was sitting there with a newspaper, and it took her a few seconds to realize that it was Mathias, he had let his hair grow, he had gained weight, there were no unexplained bruises on his arms, he smiled and they hugged, and over the next fifteen minutes, Mathias explained that he was clean, and he had found Jesus, he was at peace, he hadn't taken anything in over nine months, he had stopped painting but started studying to become an art conservator, he was so much happier now than he had been before, and if Anastasia wanted to get clean, he could help her, it was the least he could do after all she had done for him.

I haven't taken anything since we stopped seeing each other, Anastasia said.

Mathias took her hand, looked her deep in her eyes and said: That's not what I've heard.

Who has told you what?

Oh, I hear things, Anastasia.

Have you spoken with Ina? She doesn't know anything.

I want to help you.

Let go of my hand.

I'm here for you.

Stop it.

Is it that painful to need someone?

I mean it, let go of my hand or I'm going to scream.

Jesus is here for you. I'm here for you.

Let go.

Stop resisting the power of Christ.

Anastasia screamed, and it was a scream so loud that even the owner heard it, he came running to the corner table with a rolling pin that looked too heavy for him to carry.

What's going on here? Is he bothering you?

Yes, Anastasia said. He is.

I'm afraid I have to ask you to leave, the old man said.

Mathias smiled, got up and left the café. The owner escorted him to the sidewalk, where they stood talking for a few minutes, Mathias handed over a piece of paper to the owner, it looked like a flyer. The owner tucked the paper into his shirt pocket, and then they said goodbye and the owner returned to his place behind the counter.

Chapter Eighty-Three

Slakthuset's first real office space was a basement storage room not far from where they had their first outdoor meeting. Much later, in a blog post published by Hector a few days after announcing the release of their last book, he referred back to this time as the "basement years" of the publishing house. Many thought it was a nickname for their office or a symbolic reference to a basement, but it wasn't. Hector's aunt had an apartment in Gamla Stan, and it was so spacious that her basement was quite empty, except for a few carpets, some moving boxes and an old globe that had belonged to one of Hector's ancestors. When Hector left the university, he moved his boxes of books, his desk and his lamps to his aunt's basement. Working from home wasn't an option because Ina was pregnant and transforming their spare room into a nursery. Ina's apartment was occupied by Anastasia, and Hector wondered how it made sense that Anastasia, who didn't have her own place, lived with Ina, and Ina lived with Hector and Hector found himself here, in his aunt's damp basement, which he initially considered a temporary storage space because he was certain the university would get in touch and apologize at any moment.

He expected that they would soon realize their mistake, he even imagined they would contact him with an offer he couldn't refuse in exchange for his silence about what had happened, maybe a new title, perhaps a higher salary or even an offer to get Lagerhjelm's old office, hoping that he would forgive them.

But the weeks passed, and no one from the university reached out. Eventually, Hector started leaving his home and used his aunt's basement storage room as his office. The only working power outlets were in one corner of the ceiling, so Hector bought two incredibly long extension cords, which he connected and draped over the gray hissing water pipes so that nobody would notice he was borrowing electricity from the house. As impractical as the basement was (no toilet, no running water, no coffee machine, no fruit bowl), he loved the silence and darkness. Most of all, he enjoyed the symbolic significance of the revolutionary Slakthuset publishing house growing into an unstoppable force deep underground in Gamla Stan, among gurgling sewer pipes and squeaking rats.

Ina told him to call Simon and inquire about the possibility of suing the university, and Hector considered it but never did. Instead, one day Simon called him and said that Ina had reached out, and Simon was willing to help. He had taken the time to review the documents, labor union agreements and previous legal cases.

Unfortunately, I don't think we can do much, Simon said, and Hector noticed how happy he felt that Simon had already included him in this "we."

Technically, they didn't fire you, did they? Simon said.

No, I resigned, Hector said and thanked Simon for the time he had put into this.

Afterwards Hector wondered why he felt so happy. He didn't have a job, which meant no income, which was exceptionally bad timing considering Ina was pregnant. On the other hand, he didn't have any students, which meant no teaching, no grades to give, no essays to correct, and that meant he had received an incredible gift: time that he could finally dedicate to Slakthuset.

And work, he did, with a new kind of frenzy. He worked like someone who knew that when the child was born, he wanted to stand there with something to be proud of.

In December 2003 he called Kim and Åhdal to the basement space, and when they couldn't come as often as he did, he outlined the future of the publishing house on his own, made lists of books they would publish the following year, wrote a manifesto about the importance of publishing uncomfortable books (the same manifesto that became infamous when the guy who attacked five students with a sword in a school in Trollhättan cited one of Slakthuset's titles as inspiration), he contacted authors who struggled to get their books published and asked them to write for him, they wouldn't get paid much, probably they would be writing for free, but in exchange for their time they would be offered something money couldn't buy: freedom. They could use pseudonyms, write texts that were racist, homophobic and pornographic, they could kill infants with harpoons, penetrate anuses with prickly baseball bats, seek revenge on the critic who hated their last book, take out their frustration on their ex-spouse, use real names or fake names.

The most important thing is that Slakthuset is a place where you can be unbounded, he repeated to the authors and himself so many times that he began to believe it himself.

When he discovered an email from Ina's sister Anastasia in his inbox he was convinced it was something practical, maybe she needed a rent extension for Ina's apartment, or perhaps she needed to borrow money, but no, instead she contacted him with a manuscript attached as a PDF, Hector downloaded the file and started reading it the same day.

Two days later he forwarded the manuscript to Kim and Åhdal. Hector had made up his mind but still wanted to hear their opinions about the text. They met in the basement between Christmas and New Year's in 2003, Kim arrived first, snowflakes sparkling on the collar of his gray coat, he wore hat and gloves, probably long johns too. Shortly after, Åhdal appeared with red hands, peeking out from the short sleeves of his leather jacket. No hat, and despite the snowstorm, Åhdal wore sneakers.

Hector was about to comment on this and ask if his friends coordinated such things, making sure not just their opinions but also their clothing choices were as different as possible, when he heard footsteps from a fourth person. His friends froze and Hector quickly closed his laptop and turned off the lamp. He stood up from his chair and bent down over a box, as it was important to show the neighbors that rumors about someone working full-time from their basement were false. He was just here to help his dear aunt find something in this box, and these were his two closest friends, who were here to assist him.

Hector?

He recognized the voice, it was Ina's voice, but huskier and darker. Hector, are you here?

Hector saw the light from a cell phone and two feet descending the stairs and heading towards them in the corridor. He recognized the shoes, sneakers with thick soles and two sparkling laces. He had seen them in Ina's hallway.

He turned on the table lamp and gestured to Anastasia.

In here, he whispered.

Luxurious place, Anastasia said with a smile.

It's all about image, Hector said. We have a certain reputation to maintain.

We? Who's "we"? Are you all involved in this?

Hector introduced Kim and Åhdal, who looked strangely guilty standing in different corners of the basement storage room.

I heard you got fired from the university, Anastasia said.

I resigned. But I had a good reason.

Ina told me. I was impressed when I heard it.

Hector wondered if Anastasia could see that he was blushing in the dim light.

If I'm being honest, this is the best thing that ever happened to me, Hector said.

I know the feeling, Anastasia said. Do you have a minute?

Absolutely.

You've been avoiding my calls?

Not at all.

But you haven't called back?

There's pretty bad reception down here.

So, what do you say?

About what?

About the manuscript?

Well, I'm not sure where to begin. Åhdal? Kim? What do you say?

You've read it, right? Anastasia said.

Hector had read it, and to show that he had, he went to a moving box and pulled out a printed version of the manuscript.

Anastasia, he said. To be completely honest, I'm not sure what to make of this.

I know, it's almost too good, isn't it?

Well, or . . . is this . . . your words?

It's a collaboration.

By whom?

We prefer to remain anonymous.

You can tell me.

My mom and me. It's her work, I just arranged it.

Hector looked at Kim and Åhdal for support.

Okay. I wasn't sure if it was some kind of experimental novel, or an essay, or . . . more of a poetic work?

It is what it is.

Meaning?

A vital work for our time and for the future.

Yes, you used it as a subtitle.

Exactly.

Hmm.

Hmm, what?

I'm just not sure if you were serious about publishing it or if it was another one of your . . . phases.

Phases?

Like when you came home from Tunisia and only wore blue clothes.

I still wear at least one blue thing every day.

Or before that when you wanted to become a performance artist. Or after that, when you decided to become a manager.

Dino will have a contract soon, thanks to me.

That's wonderful, said Hector. Congratulations.

And this text deserves to be published.

I'm not so sure about that.

Anastasia looked confused. Why? Are you worried about the consequences? Is it too much? Too radical?

No, it's just . . . it's . . . what do you say? Kim? Åhdal?

Kim cleared his throat and said that it was a fascinating text, but
that the form was a bit unfocused. Åhdal said that he loved the surprising form, but that there were too many lists in the manuscript,
especially grocery lists.

I really liked the section where a bunch of disasters were explained
by curses, Hector said. I didn't know that Gavrilo Princip was the
victim of a family curse, or that Amelia Earhart had a nemesis. But
is it really true that Nancy Reagan used astrologers to break the
Tippecanoe curse and that's why Reagan survived the assassination
attempt?

Anastasia shrugged.

I liked that part too, Kim said. It really captured a crazy person's
logic.

Anastasia swallowed.

What I struggled with was the ending, Kim continued. Where
your mother . . .

And I, Anastasia said.

Seem to argue that only mixed people should have the right to
procreate.

Anastasia smiled.

Listen, the basic principle is straightforward, Anastasia said. But
most brilliant ideas are simple.

I agree, Åhdal said.

I'm not so sure, Kim said.

Let me summarize it like this, Anastasia said. We all know in-
breeding is bad. Don't marry your sister. Your children will lose
their teeth and become schizophrenic. They'll start doing drugs and
commit suicide. So, if we want to take responsibility for improving
the human race, we have to forbid people from reproducing. Only
people from sufficiently different backgrounds get a so-called . . .
birth card. Like a driver's license but for reproduction.

Hector coughed.

I'll think about it, okay? he said. Let me think it over and get back to you.

If you publish the book, I can help with the marketing, Anastasia said. I'm great at getting things out into the world. It'll be your first bestseller.

Anastasia, Hector lowered his voice but knew Åhdal and Kim could still hear him, have you started using again?

Not at all.

Because if you need help getting out of it, I have contacts who can . . .

I'm clean, see.

Anastasia rolled up her forearms, revealing scars from cutting and cigarette burns, but no signs of needle marks.

If you've started using again, I have to tell Ina.

Tell her whatever you want. I don't care.

Anastasia snatched the bundle of papers and backed away towards the stairs as if the manuscript were a loaded gun. Åhdal followed her with his gaze as she disappeared up the stairs.

Tell Ina I'm moving out. I have my own life, my own dreams. I don't need her! I don't need you!

She turned around and ran up the stairs. Hector turned to his friends.

Okay, Kim said, stretching out the second syllable.

Just a regular morning meeting at Slakthuset, Åhdal said.

It's a crazy text, Kim said.

Crazy but freeing, Åhdal said.

I'd rather publish *Mein Kampf*, Kim said.

Some of the poems were really nice, Åhdal said.

But it was about five hundred percent too long, Kim said.

I liked the title, Åhdal said. I'd love to read a book called *The Ticking Curse: A Carpet Seller's Memoirs*. I'm just not sure if I want to read this book with that title.

It's completely unpublishable, Kim said.

What an incredible presence she has, Åhdal said. Do you know if she's single?

That's Ina's youngest sister, Hector said.

Is she single? Åhdal said again.

She's crazy, Hector said. She just got fired from her preschool job.

But what a presence, Åhdal said.

Hector looked at Kim, expecting him to disagree. Instead he nodded and said: I agree. Incredible presence.

Much later, when Slakthuset Books had been around for ten years and had incurred losses each year, when Hector had sold the apartment in Vasastan, and he, Ina and the children had moved to a town house in the south of the city, when his parents had given him an ultimatum he refused to listen to and decided to stop supporting him financially, when Hector was forced to sell his stocks to avoid bankruptcy, while Anastasia was interviewed in industry magazines as one of the few female partners in the advertising industry, Hector looked back on the meeting in the basement. He wondered what would have happened if he had taken on Anastasia's mother's text, if they had published it, if Anastasia had taken over responsibility for their marketing, and if this was the first in a long series of mistakes.

Chapter Eighty-Four

F or the rest of the year, Stockholm's DJs started to wonder about the girl with piercings on her face who began show-ing up at every damn club where they played, she really was everywhere, in the city (East, Tranan, Gino), outside of town (one-time parties in Årsta, Huvudsta, Rågsved), sometimes she was alone, other times with a shy guy in a cap who never dared to ap-proach the DJ booth, but this girl, she was completely crazy, she had no respect for DJ etiquette, she simply walked up and handed over a shiny, unlabeled CD to the DJ, who was kind in that reserved way guys are when they choose to DJ instead of dancing to the music, they thanked the girl for the CD and promised to listen to it later, but this crazy girl didn't give up, she stood there, waiting for the DJ to listen to it right away, in the middle of their set, then she asked if the DJ could play a song from it, preferably track three, or five, or four, the first few times it was kind of cute, but then it became an-noying, because the girl who introduced herself as Anastasia refused to give up, on the first CD there were eight tracks, and on the second one, there was a long 23-minute song that was impossible to dance to, the tempo increased and decreased, the melody was wild, some-times in sync, sometimes completely out of sync.

Isn't it catchy? she said, and somehow all the Stockholm DJs man-aged to nod and shake their heads at the same time. They thanked her for the CD, explaining that it wasn't really their thing, but they said they would pass it on to some DJ friends who were "more into trance." It should have ended there, but the crazy girl kept showing up. The next time they played somewhere, she was there again, handing over another unlabeled CD before they could say no and remind her that they had spoken last week, she said that this one had a new song, even better than the last one, even catchier, even more danceable, they thanked her and promised to listen to it.

Listen now, she said.

No, I can't, I'm in the middle of a set, they said with a smile that probably looked a bit frustrated. Then they went home and listened to the CD, and after a while, the music started to grow on them, sure, the songs were way too long, the soundscape was noisy, even the handwriting on the CD labels with contact information was messy, but somehow, rumors about Dino's songs began to spread, Stockholm DJs started using them in their sets, at first they played the songs in the beginning as "confusers" to show the dance floor that whatever idea they had of the DJ's taste was simplistic, then they noticed the effect the music had on the audience, so they saved the songs for later in the evening, they used the tracks as "bridges" when transitioning between tempos, as "fire starters" to ignite the dance floor, as "bone crushers" or "mass murderers" or "final detonators" when they wanted to take everything to the next level, they always worked in the beginning but never at the end, the audience became too confused when they heard the sound of a wild oboe followed by a tuba and then a sampling of a Danish lady sounding like she was imitating a baby, it was too much for the polished O-bar crowd to handle, but some kept dancing, and one of those who remained on the dance floor was the crazy girl with piercings, it was her, she was there, jumping up and down, screaming and pointing at someone in the line to the restrooms, it was the shy guy, the one who probably hid behind the English alias written on the CD covers.

Soon, record label representatives started reaching out to the email address on the CDs, they wrote in Swedish and got replies in English, the woman claiming to be DJ Terminology's manager signed the emails as Anastasia Mikkola.

Before long, Dino had a contract with a British underground label, in the spring, he released a vinyl that was praised by *Pitchfork*, six months later, everyone was waiting for Dino to follow up his success with more songs. Three years later, they were still waiting, five years later, they had stopped waiting, no more songs ever came, nobody seemed to know what had happened to Dino, maybe he became a dentist, maybe a city planner, none of the Stockholm DJs knew, but they all remembered the persistent girl who promoted her friend's music in late 2003, and when someone wanted to open a restaurant at Norra Bantorget or try to attract people to a new club under the bridges at Skanstull, the DJs would recommend Anastasia, she was an excellent promoter for anything, if she couldn't get guests to the restaurant or kids to visit your club, then no one could, she wasn't the most innovative promoter, far from the most professional, but she had determination, she was like a werewolf, no, a fox, or no, a badger, an animal that bites and won't let go until it hears the crunch of bone, is that really it, okay, she was like a fucking badger, she refused to let go, soon she was promoting restaurants and clubs, and many years later, when that generation of Stockholm DJs became parents and developed beer bellies, when the invitations to play abroad had dwindled, when they were most often hired for fortieth birthday parties and friends' weddings, they were contacted to do a corporate gig at an advertising agency on Nybrogatan, usually, they declined such gigs, it wasn't good for the soul to play for such stiff people, but the money was good, and they had just gone through a divorce, they needed the money, they went there, set up their equipment, and then they saw her, she had removed her piercings and looked younger than when they first saw her on the dance floor, they couldn't figure out how it had happened, they wondered if she was aging backward or if all the drugs she had in her system as a youth had finally seeped out through her pores, they asked the guy who hired them what she was doing here, they had a feeling she might be working in catering, maybe she was responsible for the snacks, or perhaps she was bartending the event, but he said:

Anastasia? She's the creative director here.

And when the DJs didn't seem to understand what it meant, he said: She's my boss. She's everyone's boss. I can introduce you if you want?

The Stockholm DJs said no, they didn't want her to see them doing corporate gigs, or maybe they didn't want her to see that they were still just DJs and hadn't made any music of their own while she had climbed the career ladder and become a boss, they nodded at each other later that evening, but they never said hello, the DJs got their money and left and it wasn't until later that they realized that if Anastasia was the creative director, she must have been the one deciding who would play the records, and all the way home, they wondered if she had chosen them out of gratitude or to show off the success she had achieved.

BOOK 3

2009 (Three Months)

Chapter Eighty-Five

And then, suddenly, it was 2009, Evelyn wasn't sure how it had happened, of course she remembered things from the years that had passed, the meeting with Simon at the aquarium, the first months of insanity, the weekend in Prague when they barely left the hotel room, the road trip to Copenhagen, their attempts at being the couple that they weren't, the camping trip that ended with them packing up the tent and checking into a Scandic Hotel, the planned hike up a mountain that ended with them staying in the hotel and watching *Friends*, back then, everything had felt magical, even a *Friends* episode they had both seen before, even a slightly too long, slightly too boring lecture by a frail political theorist at ABF had felt life-changing just because Simon and Evelyn had been there together.

Evelyn remembered the exciting arrival of Ina and Hector's first child, Primo, and the somewhat less interesting birth of their second child, Saga, and the more or less routine birth of their third child, Pikko. She remembered when she and Simon had to look after Primo when he was three while Ina and Hector had to go to the hospital with Saga, as the doctors had discovered water in her lungs. Ina had warned her in advance, saying that the preschool staff had described Primo as "high energy," having a "strong will," and that sometimes, or quite often, he ended up in conflict with the other children, Evelyn smiled and said it would surely be fine, after all, she had taken care of Anastasia when they were little. The day after,

Evelyn texted Anastasia and asked her to remind her "never to have children."

Evelyn remembered the surprise party she arranged for Simon when he passed his bar exam after two years of clerkship. He was stressed about having people from different parts of his life in the same room, the friends from the floorball team, the study mates from law school, the colleagues from the firm, his shy family members huddled in a corner acting as if they weren't invited. They came from a small town four hours south of Stockholm, his brother worked in cement, his sister was a train conductor, his mom worked at a dry cleaner, his dad was a middle school teacher, and their three children were adopted from the same country, making them 100 percent siblings despite having different birth parents, Simon's friends gave speeches and raised toasts, Simon's family seemed to long for their hostel, Evelyn couldn't understand where Simon's ability to talk to anyone at any time came from, considering his mom blushed when handed a glass of punch, his brother answered all questions with single-syllable grunts and his sister couldn't utter a sentence without criticizing herself.

Evelyn remembered how proud she had been when Simon was invited to his first TV interview. He was going to comment on the case of an elderly woman who was to be deported to Macedonia. She was ninety years old, had her entire family in Sweden, had heart problems and was suffering from dementia. Simon had worked on the case for months, memorizing the case number, knowing there was a chance to appeal the Migration Agency's decision to the European Court of Human Rights, and now the opportunity was here, it was the country's biggest debate program, aired live, and the studio audience reacted in real time, the Migration Agency's lawyer was present, five days before the show, Simon had asked how many questions he would get and how much time he would have to respond, and even though he knew the case inside out, he spent hours polishing his arguments, he stayed up late at night with an old-fashioned stopwatch, rehearsing his statements repeatedly, calculating the exact number of words he could say to avoid being interrupted by the host, he brought two suits to the TV studio.

Why two? Evelyn said.

So that I can change if the Migration Agency's lawyer wears the same color, Simon said.

As the broadcast approached, Evelyn was nervous, she knew how much was at stake, if public opinion shifted, Simon would have a better chance to bring the case to the European Court of Human Rights, giving the woman a chance to stay in Sweden. When it was Simon's turn, he listened to the host's question as if hearing it for the first time, then thought for a moment and began to speak, the cameramen stayed on his face, they couldn't look away, they noticed that there was something wild in his gaze, something about his unruly hair, well-pressed suit and calm, determined way of explaining why Sweden was violating basic human rights, his ability to make people understand that this wasn't just about some random old lady, it was your grandmother, your aunt, she was sick, she had heart problems, she suffered from dementia, and now she was going to be deported to a place where she had no relatives, Evelyn almost felt sorry for the stuttering lawyer from the Migration Agency, doing his best to explain that there were no legal possibilities for them to . . . the audience shook their heads and sighed. When it was Simon's turn to respond, he nodded and agreed with the lawyer, saying that they were just doing their job and following the rules, but the question is: What rules should we have in this country? The camera cut to a middle-aged man in the audience wiping away a tear.

When the show ended, the participants received flowers and Evelyn noticed that even the hosts wanted to be close to Simon's energy, a blond girl gave him a bouquet and touched his forearm, Simon smiled at her, a few months later, the European Court of Human Rights took up the case and ruled that Sweden had violated the woman's human rights, allowing her to stay, Simon came home from the studio with makeup stains on his collar, and Evelyn was both proud of him and jealous, not because she wanted to be a lawyer, not because she wanted to sit in a TV studio and recite rehearsed arguments to change immigration policy, no, she was jealous because Simon had something in his life that he was so passionate about that he stayed up half the night with a stopwatch to time his answers to the second, because he was moving on to the next big case the day after the TV recording, because he had something to give him meaning, while Evelyn returned to the clothing store where she had worked for more than ten years, attaching anti-theft devices to merino sweaters, making budgets, having increasing purchasing responsibilities, now it was her and Kattis who had been there the longest, while everyone else had moved on, they worked there for a year or two before studying film, learning German in Berlin, enrolling in architecture school for five years and, more recently, starting their own businesses, but Evelyn remained, her life on pause. The strange thing was that the more successful Simon became, the more radio programs he was invited on, the more journalists contacted him for comment on cases he wasn't even involved in, all enchanted by an attorney who looked so bohemian yet was so articulate, the less interested Evelyn became in finding her own career, it became apparent to everyone, including herself, that it was too late, everyone else was already far ahead of her.

There was only one question that Simon refused to answer. He cited legal precedents, commented on current politics and recent judgments, once he even agreed to participate in a taste test of ice cream flavors for a tabloid newspaper, but if a journalist made the mistake of asking Simon about his background, he fell silent. He never answered questions about adoption, he just remained quiet if someone wondered if he dreamed of finding his "real parents," and once, he abruptly ended an interview before it had even begun because the journalist's first question was about whether he had ever been to the Philippines.

A few weeks later, Simon started talking about getting a cat.

Absolutely not, Evelyn said.

Why not? Simon said. Just imagine, a little meowing kitten that cuddles with us in bed when we're sick.

My mom had a cat, Evelyn said.

She thought that would end the discussion. But Simon persisted, and as not giving up was his job, he launched an advanced persuasion campaign, using all sorts of tricks (cat videos, cat pictures, more cat videos), even imitating a purring cat after they had sex, once he "accidentally" arranged to meet Evelyn right around the corner from a pet store, but even after all this, she still refused to give in, and he began to question why.

Is it because you don't want a cat in general, or because you don't want a cat with me? he said.

Cats are hairy, irritating creatures, Evelyn said.

We are all animals.

Have you ever cleaned up cat vomit? Have you cleaned a litter box? It's not very pleasant.

But they are so cute, Simon said. Look! He held up his mobile phone.

Well, yes, but no, they aren't. They are cunning, fake predators that only show affection when they want food. And have you seen an apartment where five cats have lived alone for a week because their owner died?

What about a dog, then?

Forget it.

As is often the case in close relationships, their recurring argument about one thing (cats) quickly turned into arguments about completely different things (cell phones, phone plans, and other unphone-related matters). When they first met, Simon found it charming that Evelyn spent a fortune on makeup and designer clothes that made stylists jealous, but her phone always had a cracked screen and a battery that required her to carry around a charging cable in her handbag. Now, after nearly nine years together, the constantly malfunctioning phone drove him crazy, especially when she blamed missed calls on the phone running out of battery if she didn't answer.

Before her thirty-first birthday, he didn't just buy a new mobile phone for Evelyn, he also started a phone plan in her name, it required him to forge her signature, but he did it to make her happy, to make her life easier, so they could always reach each other. But instead of being happy, she screamed that he wanted to control her, that he treated her like a child. She returned the phone and canceled the phone plan.

But why? Ina asked when the three sisters met at a Chinese restaurant in Liljeholmen to celebrate Evelyn's birthday.

It's about principles, Evelyn said.

What principles? Anastasia said.

I don't know, Evelyn said.

To me he just sounds kind, Ina said.

It's not kindness, Evelyn said. It's something else masked as kindness, something I can't put my finger on. Maybe control. This morning, we had a big fight about pens.

Pens? Anastasia said.

Ah, the pens, Ina said, as if she were talking about an old friend.

Yes, pens, Evelyn said, shaking her head. Simon thinks I am both terrified of commitment and incapable of finishing anything, which in itself is paradoxical, isn't it? If a person can't finish anything, how could they ever end a relationship?

What do pens have to do with all this? Anastasia said.

He believes I never put the caps on pens, Evelyn said.

Did it take him nine years to notice that? Ina muttered in Swedish.

But what does it matter? Evelyn said in English.

It matters because if you don't put the cap on, someone else has to do it, Ina said in Swedish.

Evelyn sighed and turned to Anastasia.

You get it, right? Evelyn said in English (as usual they spoke English with one another when no one else was around, it was their true language, when they spoke it they were their real selves, even though Evelyn had never been to the USA). It's not about pens or caps or phones or cats. It's about how I can spend five hours cleaning our entire bathroom, the mirror, the bathtub, the "fogarna" (this word Evelyn said in Swedish), the shower curtain. And when he comes home, his first comment is that I "haven't put away the sponge."

Pens dry out, and if they're left without caps, there's a risk of staining the sheets, Ina mumbled.

There's something in the way that he treats me, which drives me utterly . . . AAAAHHHH, Evelyn said, clawing her fingers at her cheeks.

Sounds like love, Anastasia said.

The crazy thing is that I love him, I really do, Evelyn said. Truly.

Her sisters stopped eating and looked at her.

Are you serious? Have you told him?

Of course not, Evelyn said, signaling the waitress for another round of beer. Told him? she said, and shook her head as if it was the most unthinkable thing she could imagine.

Bitter about Evelyn's refusal to get a cat and apparent fear of committing to something for longer than a week, Simon decided not to propose to her. Disappointed that Simon never proposed, Evelyn continued to have coffee with guys who weren't Simon, not to go home with them or anything, not at all, the coffees and conversations with strange men were just a reminder of how grateful she was to have Simon, a reminder that she still existed, despite the relationship, despite Simon's successes, despite the sounds he made when he saw strangers' babies on the subway, despite Simon's contemptuous gaze when she carefully pulled out her charging cable and charged her phone for the third time on the same day, which made her want to explode the whole world. More and more, Simon talked about the names he would give his future children. More and more, Simon asked Evelyn about her plans for the future. He said he'd be glad to help if she wanted to quit the store and try something else. At first, Evelyn thought it was caring, then she realized it was shame, it didn't fit with his public image to be with an embarrassing clothing store clerk.

What are you talking about? he said when she brought it up for the fifty-eleventh time. Of course I'm not ashamed of you. I love you. I just want you to venture out into the world before it's too late.

I'll know soon what I'll do, Evelyn said.

When is soon?

Soon is soon.

You've been saying that since we met. And I wouldn't have any problem with your job if it didn't seem like you were ashamed of it. Why don't you introduce yourself as the store manager? Or a buyer?

What would that change?

At least it sounds better than saying you 'work in a store.'

So, you are ashamed of me?

Oh, come on, he said, and the discussion started all over again, it was about cats and cell phones, pens and careers, Simon declared his love, and Evelyn said she'd soon know what she would do with her life, but soon never came, and now it was 2009, she was thirty-one, and it was too late to start something new.

Chapter Eighty-Six

I n 2009 I moved to Berlin for a DAAD fellowship, before I left I organized a party to celebrate turning thirty in the basement of a restaurant called Roxy, walls covered in red velvet fabric, a staircase leading down into the underground, a small black bar counter that reminded me of Tre Backar, where Dad used to work, I invited friends from the past and present, friends who were like sisters and friends I had been in love with, friends I had lost touch with and friends I never really liked from the start, friends whom I had worked with and friends I wanted to work with, friends from when I played basketball and friends from when I studied international economics, my brothers were there, and my uncles and my cousins, and Grandma, even Dad came, he happened to be in Sweden by chance, as always he stayed at my apartment while he was in town, sleeping in my bed while I crashed on a friend's sofa. When I asked if he wanted to come to the party, he wondered if my mom's "new guy" would be there.

They've been together for five years, I said. And yes, he'll be there.

Then I'm not coming, Dad said.

I had to bribe him with a taxi ride and assure him that there would be free drinks and food before he finally agreed to come along, and as we descended the stairs to the party, he turned and said:

I won't hit him.

Who?

Your mom's new guy.

Thanks, I said.

No problem.

I even invited the Mikkola sisters to the party, which was a bit strange, since we hadn't seen each other in so many years. While looking for their contact information, I realized that none of them were on social media, but I found Ina's email address by searching her name. A company near Thorildsplan claimed to have an employee named Ina Mikkola, I wasn't sure if it was an old email address or not, but I sent her an invitation, mentioning that she could bring her sisters and adding that many people from "Draken" would be there. I never received a reply.

Chapter Eighty-Seven

n February 2009, Cecilia and Evelyn arranged to meet for a walk. The trees, the gravel path, the light bright sky, the rhythmic steps of two friends walking in sync. It was Cecilia who suggested they take a Saturday stroll, and there was something about the way she asked and planned it that made Evelyn suspicious. Cecilia hadn't called Evelyn earlier in the day to ask if she wanted to meet after work. No, this walk had been planned for more than a week, and when Evelyn suggested inviting Lugo and Marcus along, as it had been so long since they all hung out together, the Bear Quartet, like in the old days, Cecilia fell silent for a few seconds and then said:

I'd prefer if it's just you and me, if that's okay.

Of course, Evelyn said, and as she walked up the escalator in the subway, a bit too warm in her thick coat and turquoise scarf, she wondered what was going to happen. All of Evelyn's friends had graduated and moved to bigger apartments, they all talked about children, when they would have them, if they would have them, and with whom. The Bear Quartet hadn't hung out together in several months. Lugo had moved to a villa in Årsta with his girlfriend and their newborn baby. Marcus lived in Blackeberg with his girlfriend and two young children. The only one left was Cecilia, she still lived in Gröndal, still single, she had climbed the career ladder in HR at an insurance company, and now it was so well paid that she found it hard to quit. But even wild Cecilia had started talking about having children, which Evelyn thought was insane, Cecilia with a child was like imagining a lion befriending a squirrel, it could never end well.

Either Cecilia would say she was pregnant or she would reveal that she had had a crush on Evelyn for years, it was probably the latter, Evelyn had suspected it since they met in high school, Cecilia rarely went home with guys, and when she did, she invited them in for tea and actually served tea, it's not like she was a virgin, of course not, she had sex with a Greek guy when she was on vacation, and she had a brief fling with a married journalist who lived in Täby, Evelyn could barely remember his face and had forgotten his name, but she remembered he had red eczema all over his hands, it would hardly have been noticeable if he hadn't always tried to hide his hands with gloves in May or with extremely long-sleeved shirts, they had been together for a few weeks until Cecilia asked him to define what they were doing, and he stopped answering her calls and went into stealth mode. Cecilia had returned to being single, which suited her much better than being in a relationship, she was too much of herself to fit with anyone else. Everything about Cecilia was too much, too much makeup, too much perfume, too-full lips, her curves made taxi drivers slow down, when she drank, she drank until the bartender declared they had run out of alcohol, and when she threw up, she didn't do it like a normal person, she never ran towards a bush or the restroom and tried to hide it in shame, no, when Cecilia threw up she did it at parties, behind sofas, in potted plants, once, at a big outdoor party on Stora Essingen, she had vomited on the dance floor, they were all there, the whole Bear Quartet when Cecilia bent sideways, vomited and then came back up, at first Evelyn thought she had just scratched her shin or hidden some pills in her sock, but then she noticed people gliding around the dance floor sideways as if they were wearing roller skates, they looked disgusted when they saw the dance floor, but Cecilia didn't reveal herself, she just kept on dancing, her face a bit paler than usual. When the bouncers came running, trying to find the culprit, Cecilia looked as confused as everyone else, gazing at the vomit on the dance floor with disgust, never giving away that what she was looking at had just been inside her.

Evelyn was ten minutes late, and Cecilia was already waiting by the fountain, her made-up face turned towards the winter sun. She wore double layers of woolen cardigans under her purple coat and smiled behind her oversized black sunglasses. They hugged and began walking towards Gärdet.

Cecilia didn't look pregnant, and she had been out drinking the night before, so Evelyn became curious about what Cecilia wanted to confess. Would she try to kiss her or hold her hand, or . . . They walked along the road, passing stretching joggers, dog owners and a school class that had been to a nearby museum and, for some reason, was walking back towards the city center. Why don't they take the bus? Evelyn wondered to herself. And why are they on an excursion on a Saturday? A few seconds later, she realized they were probably wealthy kids. She noticed their branded backpacks, their fluttering hairstyles, and she heard the teacher talking to them as if they were little adults, knowing she didn't have to watch over them to prevent them from starting a stick war or throwing chestnuts at passing cars. They continued in silence towards the sharp shadow cast by Kaknästornet.

Look, it's open, Cecilia said, nodding towards the tower's antenna-adorned top. Shall we go up?

I've never been up there, said Evelyn.

Me neither.

They headed towards the tower, talking about work, their crazy families. Evelyn said she was incredibly tired of her job and that she really needed to quit, and Cecilia reminded her that she had said the same thing for at least ten years.

What's stopping you from quitting?

I just need . . . a plan, Evelyn said. I have to figure out what to do with my life.

Cecilia looked as if she had a candle burning inside her skull, but she didn't say anything, not yet. As they approached the tower's entrance, a large red bus had just dropped off a group of tourists who were queuing in front of the elevators.

Let's keep walking instead, Cecilia said.

Absolutely, Evelyn said, and they continued walking, back out into the cold winter sun, leaving the gray tower behind. They passed an overgrown football field, a meadow with horses, their breaths and bodies steaming with vapor.

On a small yellow bridge, wide enough for only one car to cross at a time, Cecilia stopped and looked around to make sure no one could hear them.

I need to ask you something, she said.

Here it comes, Evelyn thought.

Don't laugh, Cecilia said.

I promise.

What I'm about to tell you might sound like a joke, but I'm one hundred percent serious, Cecilia said.

I promise, Evelyn said again.

Okay. So, here's the thing, Cecilia said, taking a deep breath. Evelyn braced herself to appear flattered, confused and supportive. I have decided to apply to Nama.

Evelyn's confusion was genuine. Nama?

Yes! Nama! Cecilia said, sounding as if she was in love with the very word.

What's Nama?

You've got to be kidding me, Cecilia said.

No, I'm serious, what is it?

The National Academy of Mime and Acting! Cecilia said, looking a bit disappointed. It's only the most prestigious acting school in Sweden. I can't stop thinking about it, it all makes sense, my grandmother dreamed of being an actress but it was impossible in her country, and my mom talked about being an actress, but never dared to try, and when I saw the application I started to cry because it just felt so . . . right.

You know the feeling, Cecilia said, and Evelyn nodded, not because she knew the feeling but because she knew a nod would keep Cecilia talking so she wouldn't notice the spikes of envy settling in Evelyn's chest.

I've never been this excited about anything, Cecilia said.

Congratulations, Evelyn said. I'm so happy for you.

Can you help me?

Of course, Evelyn said, hugging her friend, not really sure how she could increase Cecilia's chances of getting into a school she had never heard of.

They continued their walk on Djurgården, passing frozen fields and streams. Evelyn talked about Simon's latest legal case, and Cecilia talked about the five monologues she needed to learn by the end of the month. Evelyn talked about Simon's conflict with a colleague, and Cecilia looked at her and said:

You know you talk more about him than yourself. Why is that?

Evelyn shrugged and changed the subject. On their way back towards the city, they made plans to meet up so Evelyn could give Cecilia feedback on the monologues. Evelyn nodded and said she looked forward to helping, and when they said goodbye, she did her best not to reveal to anyone, not to Cecilia, not even to herself, that the sadness she felt was caused by her best friend's happiness.

Chapter Eighty-Eight

A man with a white van picked me up at Tegel Airport and drove me to the apartment the scholarship organization had chosen for me. It was located farther west in Berlin than I had ever been before, on the fifth floor, a family apartment with four or five beds, and more plates in the cupboards than I had ever owned. The apartment was so big that I immediately wanted to return home, but I had said goodbye to and let my brother take over my apartment, it felt embarrassing to turn a year abroad into just a weekend in Berlin, so I stayed, I hardly slept during the first few days, instead, I watched grainy videos of Israeli missiles bombing Palestinian hospitals, Israeli soldiers shooting rubber bullets at stone-throwing children, Israeli bulldozers uprooting Palestinian olive trees.

After three days, I contacted the scholarship organization and told them I had to move, I sent an email to everyone I knew with some connection to Germany, including my German-Tunisian cousins whom I hadn't seen in over ten years, I asked if anyone knew someone who wanted to rent out an apartment in Berlin, a Swedish-German translator put me in touch with a friend who needed a tenant for her apartment in Friedrichshain, I lived there for a month, eating frozen Lidl pizzas, noodles with cabbage and fried eggs, and then I moved to another friend's apartment in Prenzlauer Berg, it had large yellow coal stoves and an Alpine wallpaper in the bathroom, I lived there for more than a year, I furnished the apartment with things I found on the sidewalk, a found desk, a found chair, I was here to write, but I was too stingy to buy a printer, so I just wrote and threw away, wrote and threw away, wrote and deleted, wrote and started over.

Later in the spring, one of my German cousins contacted me and asked if I wanted to come to her wedding in southern Germany. Alma was getting married, I remembered her as a chubby eight-year-old girl, we had spent summers together in Sousse when we were children, she was the daughter of my father's brother Younes, he had two girlfriends at the same time, and had had Alma with his legal wife, who had dark curly hair, and then Younes (my uncle) had Younes (my cousin) and Malika with his mistress, who was tall and blond, and I remember my mom was bothered by this arrangement, that we would vacation with my father's brother, and that his three children would be there all the time, first my uncle's wife would be there, and then his mistress.

The children are friends with one another, Dad said. They know everything. If it's not a problem for them, it shouldn't be a problem for us, right?

We spent a month with them in Sousse, renting a house a quarter of an hour from the sea by car, every morning, we took the white Suzuki jeep that Dad had borrowed from his friend Fathi to go from the house to Port El Kantaoui, every day, we walked along the harbor and watched the sailboats, commenting on their flags, look, that one is from South Africa, and that one is from Argentina, the beach where we laid out our towels and placed our coolers actually belonged to a luxury hotel nearby, but we were allowed to use it because Dad knew the hotel's owner through his friend Fathi, we swam in the sea, snorkeled, buried each other in the sand, which was too hot to walk on without sandals, if there was a guard there who didn't know about our special arrangement, Dad would give him some dinars and tell him to talk to someone, we'd stay there all day, we ate the sandwiches we brought from home with mackerel and eggs, I must have been around twelve, in the fall, I would become friends with Evelyn and tell her about our time here, I was the oldest among the cousins, and I was the only one allowed to go up to the pool area by myself, technically, it was only for hotel guests, but since we knew Fathi and

Fathi knew the owner, it should be okay, Dad still accompanied me the first time, we went together to the pool area, passing a restaurant full of sunburned tourists, their shoulders white with sunscreen, their drunk loud laughter, we passed tennis courts and outdoor showers, then the children's pool and the adult pool, it was the most luxurious pool I had ever seen, complete with an actual bar in the pool, I could barely comprehend the brilliance of it all, take something fantastic, a pool, and add something fantastic, a bar, what else is out there ready to be combined, can you combine ice cream with a flight simulator game, combine Stephen King novels with blow jobs, I thought about it while Dad talked to the guards, explaining that we knew Fathi, who knew, et cetera, et cetera, and then I could jump into the pool.

I spent hours in the artificially blue water, swimming from one end to the other with a snorkel, pretending to be a fighter jet patrolling my airspace, every body I saw underwater was an enemy plane, I used heat-seeking Tomahawk missiles to shoot them down, if I ran out of missiles, I used the machine gun, the first day went fine, the second day too, but the third day was a bit cloudy, and there were fewer people down on the beach, my family stayed behind as I went up to the pool to secure my area with my F-14 Tomcat, I was about to jump in when I noticed one of the lifeguards giving me a suspicious look, he was wearing a white T-shirt and red shorts, I tried to say hello in Arabic, I jumped into the pool to start my top-secret mission, I shot German ladies with heat-seeking missiles, I massacred Japanese families with my machine gun, I grazed the pool bottom with the plane's belly to investigate a suspicious object (it turned out to be a lost Band-Aid). When I resurfaced, I felt someone pushing me back under the water, the lifeguard, who was there to assist tourists and prevent drowning incidents, ripped off my snorkel, I swallowed water, he screamed as if he had been screaming for a long time, but I hadn't heard him, since I was underwater, he continued to scream, he pulled me up out of the water and threw my goggles to the ground, then picked them up again, at first it seemed like he was considering confiscating them, but then he tossed them even farther away, they landed near a bush on the artificial lawn, he continued to scream, I only understood the swear words, I ran down to Dad, trying not to cry as I told him what happened, Dad stood up before I had finished telling the story, he went up to the pool area, as we passed the tennis court, he bent down and picked up a large stick from the ground, signaling the guard over with the stick, the guard responded with a curse, Dad screamed, the guard screamed louder, Dad yelled even louder, waving the stick, I heard many swear words, I heard the word *family* and the name *Fathi* and a word that I think means "embassy" or perhaps "ambassador" or "governor," or possibly "politician." The guard stopped screaming and looked worried. Dad looked at me and said:

Jump in the pool.

I don't want to anymore, I said.

Jump. In. The. Pool, Dad said.

I jumped in, swam around a bit, treading water. Dad looked at the lifeguard, who pretended I was invisible. Dad walked away and brought back my snorkel and goggles, inspecting the glass to make sure it hadn't cracked.

Stay here as long as you want, Dad said, giving me the goggles and snorkel.

Ten minutes later, I left the pool and went down to the beach.

Already done? Dad said.

I nodded.

What happened up there? Mom asked.

Nothing, Dad said. Just a misunderstanding.

Did he think I was Tunisian? I asked.

You are Tunisian, Dad said.

But did he think I was from *here*? I said.

Yes, he thought you were some boy who had snuck in from the street to swim in their pool, Dad said, and I was lying there, in the shade of the beach umbrella with my back on the soft warm sand, unable to stop smiling.

And now my half-Tunisian, half-German cousin Alma was getting married. I hadn't heard from her since we were kids, but I had some contact with her half brother, Younes. I knew he lived in Hamburg.

He had attended a reading I did last year. The Thalia Theater had staged a play of mine and invited me to read short stories and participate in a discussion with the dramaturge. But something went wrong with the marketing, or perhaps they had advertised it but everyone had better things to do. When I stepped onto the stage, there was only one person in the audience, and it was Younes, my cousin. We looked at each other and laughed.

Lucky I was here in time, he said. Let's get drunk.

We left the theater and got drunk. Later that night, we met up with his sister, the real sister, not the half sister who was getting married. We got even drunker and promised to stay in touch, even though we hadn't heard from each other at all until now when they sent me an invitation to the wedding, which would be held in a small town in southern Germany. Before accepting, I checked the cost of train tickets, added the hotel expense and wondered what I should bring, a gift or money, I didn't want to come empty-handed, especially since I would be representing my whole side of the family, my brothers wouldn't be there, and, of course, neither would Dad, or would he? I felt compelled to attend and to be honest I was also curious to go there and see if I could write about it, that's how I justified saying yes, believing it would be worth the expense if it could lead to a future book.

A few months later I took a train down south, I changed trains and took an even smaller train even farther south, the smaller train had a dining car with pink plastic seats, I sat there and drank coffee, and I think I ordered some food as well because I started feeling anxious and nervous, with a headache and a queasy feeling, but I believe it was just nerves because as soon as I got off the train and heard the honking from Younes's rental car and saw his big smile, I knew I was in the right place, finally, after years of searching, I was exactly where I was supposed to be at that moment, in the German countryside, for a wedding between two people I didn't know.

I jumped into the passenger seat, and we exchanged a stiff, awkward front-seat hug.

No, this won't do, Younes said, turning off the engine. We got out and embraced each other properly, a cousins' hug, clenched fists, chest to chest.

I'm so glad you could come, he said. This is going to be epic.

He used the car's GPS to find our way back to the hotel where everyone from our side of the family was staying.

Who's coming? I asked.

Everyone is coming, Younes replied, starting to name all those who had already arrived. Awatef, Dalilah, Dalanda, Achraf, Hammah, Ahlem, Bilal and Casso, you remember Casso, right? Younes said, turning the steering wheel while keeping his eyes on the GPS.

Is my dad coming? I said.

No, your dad isn't coming, Younes said, glancing at me as if he was surprised that I didn't already know this or that I even needed to ask.

The hotel is just five minutes away, he said. Everything is five minutes away in this damn backwater place. Still, he kept his focus on the GPS.

Why are they getting married down here? I asked.

He's from here, or part of his family lives here. And it's much cheaper to get married here.

I nodded, trying to lower my shoulders and relax. I wasn't sure why I was so nervous, it wasn't my half sister getting married, it wasn't my dad, who had a reputation for drinking too much, and it wasn't me driving around in a brand-new, very large rental car in a small German town, with instructions from a GPS that insisted on losing our position. But Younes seemed completely unaffected, he looked happy rather than stressed, even though the car behind us was honking and the wedding ceremony was about to start in less than five hours.

Chapter Eighty-Nine

A few days later, Evelyn went over to Cecilia's apartment in Gröndal. Cecilia closed the balcony door and turned on instrumental music so that the neighbors wouldn't hear her, then she started reading the monologues. First, she was Biff from *Death of a Salesman*, with the script in hand, she looked into Evelyn's eyes and recounted how she had run down eleven floors with a pen and suddenly seen the blue sky, realizing she didn't want to become the person she was. Evelyn couldn't take her eyes off her, even though Cecilia hadn't memorized the lines and needed to start over a few times when she stumbled. Cecilia was enchanting, more like Biff than she had ever been herself, and there was a strange glow about her as she pronounced Miller's words. Evelyn sat there on Cecilia's secondhand sofa, realizing her mouth was open.

What do you think? Cecilia said when she finished and returned to her normal self.

Incredible, Evelyn said.

No notes?

Just keep going.

And Cecilia continued, transforming into Clytemnestra, who had been forced into a marriage and lost her son. Then she became Phebe, who wasn't really in love with the guy who was quite handsome, but not really, and after each short monologue, Cecilia turned to Evelyn for feedback, ideas for improvements, tips on emphasizing certain words, and after a while, it got boring to say everything was fantastic, so Evelyn tried giving suggestions.

What if you put a little more emphasis on this word? Maybe try playing Phebe as if she really hates the person she's talking about? What if Biff is, like, twenty years older than you are?

Cecilia tried the text again and again, and Evelyn saw how her tips changed the performance, how the same syllables forced her friend to open her eyes, stand up straight, lisp, start limping, and suddenly three hours had passed, and the automatic lighting on the balcony turned on.

Thank you, Cecilia said when they were done.

Thank *you*, Evelyn said. You're amazing, you'll get in, there's no doubt about it.

Do you think so? It's incredibly hard, they have thousands of applicants for ten spots.

They will reserve at least one spot for Cecilia Bakic, Evelyn said. I feel it in my bones, and my bones are never wrong.

They had dinner together, and it wasn't until afterwards, while Cecilia was loading the small dishwasher, that Evelyn found another monologue Cecilia hadn't tried.

What about this one?

We only need to memorize three, Cecilia said. And I never really got into that one.

Evelyn looked at the text, someone named Trofimov was talking about love and stars and how their ancestors had owned people, and just for fun, Evelyn stood up and started reading the lines, she just wanted to test it out, see what happened to her body when the old words filled her, her tongue said:

And now, doesn't something human look at you from every cherry in the orchard, every leaf and every stalk? Don't you hear voices . . . ?

And she continued:

For it's so clear that in order to begin to live in the present we must first redeem the past, and that can only be done by suffering, by strenuous, uninterrupted labor, understand that, Anya!

When she finished, she made a little bow and probably expected Cecilia to applaud or at least look at her with the same impressed gaze that Evelyn had given her friend, but Cecilia just stared at her, smiled crookedly and asked if she wanted coffee or tea after dinner.

Chapter Ninety

Younes told me that Alma was going to marry a Kurdish guy. I mean, he is Kurdish in the same way we are Tunisian, Younes said in English because his French was poor, and my German was nonexistent.

I wasn't sure what he meant by "he is Kurdish like we are Tunisian," did it mean he's not Kurdish at all, or somewhat Kurdish, or Kurdish on the outside and German on the inside? When Younes talked about Alma's fiancé and his family, they seemed genuinely religious, at least the fiancé who had recently found Allah, before that, according to Younes, he was "very irreligious," which I interpreted as him being involved in some sort of criminal activity, but it might have just meant that he drank and dated blond women.

We were sitting in the car, the GPS had led us the wrong way, and we were waiting to make a U-turn. I nodded to show that I either understood or wanted to understand. I had played basketball with guys like these, one weekend they were dealing weed, eating hot dogs and asking if anyone wanted to buy a starter pistol that looked "one hundred percent real," two weeks later they showed up at practice wearing kufis, quoting the Quran, and condemning everyone living in sin, or sometimes, which was worse, they looked at us sinners with a kindly condescending smile that said: "Go ahead, eat your pork and drink your beer and enjoy your one-night stands because we both know you're empty inside." And the smile hurt more because, on some level, they were right, they had found peace, they had found something we were all searching for, and I remember there was a strange correlation between how much sin they had lived in and how critical they were of the sins we were living in, as if their condemnation of us was a condemnation of their own past.

Younes made a U-turn and explained that the wedding would be very traditional and solemn. An imam would officiate the ceremony, and there would be no alcohol, only traditional dance and absolutely no drinking, he said again.

So, what does Alma think about all this? I said, since I only remembered her as a kind German girl with black cropped bangs, and I sometimes felt sorry for her because she was an only child, while the mistress's children at least had each other.

It's the craziest thing, Younes said. She seems perfectly fine with all of this. Her ex-boyfriend was a bit out of control, so maybe that's why.

Younes parked the car outside a hotel with a white sign.

I need to run some errands, he said. But if you get ready, we can have a drink before the ceremony?

I got my key from the reception, paid for my room, saved the receipt, thinking it could be considered a business expense if I found something to write about. I went to my room, it was as large as a closet, when I stretched out on the bed, my feet touched the door, and I could touch the ceiling without standing on my toes, it reminded me of the temporary accommodation Dad had after the divorce. I splashed some water on my face, sprayed cologne on my neck, I never used cologne on regular days, it was too much of a luxury just for myself. But when I went out clubbing, I'd spray myself once, and today was Alma's wedding day, and the train journey here had been long, so I indulged in two sprays of cologne. Then I put some wax in my hair to achieve just the right level of messy shine, changed into a suit and tie, and left the hotel room.

Chapter Ninety-One

Evelyn was at work when Cecilia came by and told her that she had received a date for her first audition.

It's next Monday, she said. Please, can you come with me? I'm so nervous, and I need your energy to do it in the best way, please.

Evelyn checked her calendar, even though she knew she had to work.

Unfortunately, I can't, she said. But don't worry, you'll be fantastic, you can do this, I promise.

Please, Cecilia said again. Please. I need you there. I was so much better when you listened to me, you calmed me down, helped me focus on the words, please.

Kattis overheard their conversation.

I can cover for you, Kattis said. How long will you be gone?

It won't take more than an hour, max two, said Cecilia.

Only that? Kattis said with a smile. It's shorter than Evelyn's usual lunch break.

Evelyn thanked Kattis and promised to come, even though she didn't really want to, and she knew that Kattis understood she didn't want to. She wondered if Kattis offered to cover for her as some sort of bizarre punishment, as if Kattis understood that the hardest thing for Evelyn right now was being around other people who were pursuing their dreams. They agreed on where and when to meet next Monday, so Evelyn could be there as a support, a calming presence, as a best friend, and Cecilia left the store, full of gratitude.

A few days before the audition, they had a final rehearsal on the phone, by now Evelyn had heard the lines so many times that she could recite them herself, when Cecilia stumbled and forgot a word, Evelyn could fill in the gaps, and sometimes, when Evelyn was peeling a cucumber in Simon's kitchen, when washing her underarms in Simon's bathroom, when half listening to Simon's frenetic rant about some particularly inept prosecutor, when smiling and nodding to indicate she almost heard what he was saying, when ignoring his sighs over her failure to roll up her yoga mat, when searching the storeroom for a blue medium, when asking a customer if they needed help with something, when Anastasia called to tell her that she and Åhdal had made an offer on an apartment in Södermalm, when Ina called to complain that they never met anymore, when waking up at three in the morning to a scream only she had heard, Chekhov's words echoed within her, and she had to quietly mumble them to herself to get them out of her system.

Chapter Ninety-Two

The entire inner courtyard of the hotel was filled with Khemiris, cousins I barely remembered, several were five or ten years younger than me and already had children, at least the women did, we exchanged cheek kisses, and they rattled off the names of their children, I repeated the names but immediately forgot them, then I heard my name, pronounced in the Arabic way, Younes. At this particular wedding, it could mean a) my uncle, b) his son or c) me, but the way it was said and the voice made me certain it was me. I turned around, and there she was, my grandmother, the powerhouse named Yamina Khemiri, mother of nine now-grown children, she always said my name with the tone of a slightly irritated mother, blaming her children for being two hours late, Younes, as in, "Where have you been?" Younes, as in, "So you finally show up," Younes, as in, "If only you knew how much love I have for you that I cannot express right now, because if I were the kind of person capable of experiencing feelings like that I wouldn't have made it through this life," Younes, as in, "I envy that your own life allows you to be so sensitive," Younes, as in, "But now you're overanalyzing everything again, my dear grandchild, I just said your name to get your attention in a small German town in the summer of 2009, that's all, none of us knew it would be the last time we saw each other, the last time I would say your name in this tone, the last time we would hug as if it were the first time."

I leaned forward for three kisses, her scents, the fabric of her hijab, the henna tattoos, her kitchen in Jendouba, DeLaval cleaning products, after the kisses she gave me a hug, since she was about half my height, her hands rested on my lower back, she wanted someone to take a photo, and those photos must exist somewhere— cheap, lousy early digital pictures documenting a 198-centimeter-tall grandson and a 158-centimeter-tall grandmother, both more affected by the meeting than they realized at the time. Then she commented on the length of my hair ("Aren't there any hairdressers in Sweden?"), asked why I hadn't married yet ("I know some nice girls in Jendouba") and why I didn't visit more often, and just like last time she said that if I really wanted something to write about, I had to learn Arabic, she could give me material for ten books, her fingers, dark red with henna, extended to show me that she meant what she always said—ten books, TEN!

I smiled and said I was working on a new book, which wasn't true, as I had spent the last few years writing about a thousand worthless pages that I had thrown away, but I didn't tell Grandma that, instead, I just stood there not knowing what to do, family members hugged each other and spoke Arabic, I smiled as if I understood what they were saying, then my cousin Younes came back, now in a suit, asking if I could help him with something, and I said yes a little too quickly, we left the hotel area on foot, heading to a nearby bar where we ordered beers and talked about the wedding, his girlfriend, his dreams of becoming a film director. He mentioned his concern for his father, who had started forgetting things, simple things, like the names of his colleagues at the used-car dealership where he worked as a mechanic.

The strange thing is, he's still the best mechanic there, Younes said. It's as if his brain doesn't have room for everything it needs to hold on to, but instead of forgetting how to fix a cracked fuel filter on a Škoda combi, he forgets his sisters' names.

That's the Khemiri curse, I said.

What do you mean? he said.

I wasn't quite sure what I meant, and I can't remember if I tried to explain myself or change the subject, he paid for the first round, and I wanted to pay for the second, he ordered beer, so I did too,

I hadn't eaten anything since the train, so I felt quite tipsy when we got up from the bar stools to head to the ceremony. As we walked towards the street, I heard a voice say: Freeze, hands up! It was Younes, my uncle, he was sitting in the corner of the same bar with a man I didn't recognize, for a brief second I wondered if he was the groom's father, but then I remembered they were deeply religious, so he must have been someone else. Their table had four glasses, and my uncle smiled, his gold tooth sparkling. Younes, my cousin, said something in German, and his father's smile disappeared immediately—the sun didn't go behind a cloud, it was shot down by a missile. His father said something in German that sounded like an insult, and my cousin looked down and fell silent, looking like a little boy. We left the bar.

Is everything okay? I said.

Yes, he said. Of course.

We walked back to the hotel in silence. When we arrived, we stumbled into a photo shoot, the bride and groom were there, she wore an off-white sequined dress with a matching white handbag, and he looked like a stylish soccer player in a black shiny suit, white tie, white waistcoat and white shirt, all decorations perfectly matching Alma's dress, both looked equally stunning and terrified, the sleeves of his shirt were too long, and he kept tucking them into his jacket, Alma smiled and waved, always with her hand adorned with the new ring, both her arms were covered with henna in circular patterns, just like the women I had seen at weddings in Tunisia, but Alma was born and raised in Germany, and standing there in the inner courtyard of a hotel in a small German town, I noticed that she had very few German friends at the wedding, her mother was there, of course, and Younes and Malika's mother, the father's mistress, but not many of Alma's friends. I remember asking Younes about it, but I did so in a way that wouldn't be seen as criticism, I asked something like: Are Alma's friends coming straight to the ceremony? And Younes, my cousin, said that Alma's friends didn't get along with the groom, and although he said it as if the friends didn't like the man, I had a feeling it was more that the man didn't like Alma's friends.

We posed for photos, Alma noticed me and hugged me, making

sure there was enough space between my face and hers not to ruin her makeup. She had sparkling earrings and a matching tiara, and her hair was sprinkled with blue glitter.

We posed for more photos, there was an official wedding photographer and an unofficial one who seemed to be a family friend who had brought his expensive camera equipment, he always wanted to capture the exact same shots taken by the official photographer. I kept track of the time, feeling more and more stressed as the ceremony was about to begin, yet we were still here, posing for photos.

Then we got into cars, but instead of heading towards the ceremony, we went to a park where more photos were taken. Alma and her future husband stood under a tree, walked over a small bridge, and then another photo with our grandmother, followed by one with all the cousins and another with all the guests. I kept checking the time, didn't they realize that the ceremony should have started already? Finally, the official wedding photographer was satisfied, and he packed up his equipment. The unofficial photographer wanted one more shot, but people didn't pay as much attention to him. He took one final picture and said: That's a wrap.

Everyone went back to the cars, the ceremony was supposed to start half an hour ago, but we were still there, in an abandoned city park in the German countryside, debating who should ride in which car. My uncle had driven his mother to the park, but now she objected to going to the ceremony in a Škoda. Younes, her son, said that he had worked for Škoda for many years, and they built fantastic cars. His mother said: But it's not a Mercedes, and Younes replied: No, it's better than a Mercedes, then Yamina said something in Arabic that I didn't understand, and then I heard the word *Kurds*. After that, Younes allowed her to ride in another car, on the condition that he would drive her back because he didn't trust anyone else to take his mother to the hotel.

Finally, the caravan started moving towards the reception hall, and someone began honking, and the rest of the cars joined in.

Chapter Ninety-Three

On a crisp afternoon in March, Cecilia and Evelyn took the subway to Stadion, despite Karlaplan being technically closer. Cecilia was too nervous to wait there and preferred to walk a little farther. Despite this, they arrived twenty minutes early. Evelyn came directly from work, dressed in her expensive work clothes, while Cecilia wore comfortable jeans and a worn-out lucky T-shirt. The school yard was filled with anxious people, a big guy in a corner was singing arias to warm up his voice. Evelyn looked at him and wondered if he had positioned himself there to create a perfect echo and intimidate the other applicants. Evelyn and Cecilia went inside to find the registration area, on the stairs they saw a young white girl with dreadlocks giving a massage to another girl in sweatpants, breathing exercises that sounded like childbirth classes could be heard from all directions, and Evelyn felt sorry for Cecilia, who would have to spend four years with people like this. She turned to Cecilia.

Are you sure about this?

I've never been more sure about anything in my life, Cecilia said as she approached the registration table. Evelyn went out to the yard to escape the sound of the breathing exercises. She stood there in the cool spring sun, wondering why she was there. An older lady with purple hair smiled at her, and Evelyn smiled back.

Which monologue are you auditioning with? the woman asked, gesturing towards Evelyn with her cigarette.

Oh no, I'm not here to audition, Evelyn said. I'm just here to support a friend.

You should audition, the woman said, flicking her still-glowing cigarette away. Then she entered the building and disappeared upstairs with surprisingly youthful agility. Cecilia came out to the yard with her time slot.

Do you know who's on the jury? she said.

Evelyn shook her head. She knew she wouldn't recognize the name anyway, sure enough, Cecilia mentioned the name, apparently she was very well known in the Swedish cultural scene. She had done movies, worked at the Royal Dramatic Theatre and directed in Germany, and . . .

Evelyn shrugged to show that she hadn't heard of either the movies or the plays Cecilia listed. This wasn't her world, and it would never be. Anastasia would feel at home here, and Evelyn could see Cecilia fitting in too, but for the first time since she started, Evelyn longed to be back at work.

When it was Cecilia's turn, she stood up and swallowed nervously.

Go get 'em, Evelyn whispered and gave Cecilia one last hug. Remember, I'm there with you, all the time.

Thank you, Cecilia said and disappeared up the stairs towards the audition room. Ten minutes later, she was back, paradoxically pale and blushing at the same time.

I just got feedback from my idol, she said.

How did it go?

It was a little strange. But a good kind of strange, Cecilia said. She gave me completely contradictory notes. She asked me to perform the monologue "as if I had forgotten the words," and then she asked me to do it as if I really hated the text.

And could you do it?

I think so. But sometimes it was hard not to burst out laughing. She's around sixty years old with purple hair, and she kept interrupting the other jury members all the time.

I saw her, said Evelyn. She was out here smoking. She thought *I* should audition.

Evelyn emphasized the "I" to signal that it was the craziest idea ever suggested. Cecilia was silent for a few seconds.

You should do it, she said.

Of course not.

Can you imagine? We could be in the same class.

Stop, Evelyn said with a smile.

Yes, you're probably right, said Cecilia. It might be weird.

They walked back towards the subway, but when they reached Valhallavägen, Evelyn turned around.

Are you considering doing it? Cecilia suddenly looked terrified.

Why not?

Do you want me to come with you for support?

No, it's fine, Evelyn said, as she didn't need any support, she was strongest when she was alone. She hugged Cecilia goodbye and headed back up to the school to inform the guy behind the registration table that she was here for an audition.

Unfortunately, you need to preregister, he said.

I did register, but I never got any confirmation, Evelyn said without blinking, switching from polite to ready to sue the school in a matter of seconds.

Right at that moment, the woman with purple hair returned from yet another smoke break. She leaned over the table, placed her hand on the guy's shoulder and told him that it should be okay, they could sort out the practicalities later, right?

She smiled, but her voice sounded as if she had just made a bomb threat. The guy blinked and nodded.

Yes, of course.

Thank you.

She turned to Evelyn:

Ready?

Evelyn followed her up the stairs, then left into a corridor and left again into a gigantic room. Long curtains tried and failed to block the sunlight from the courtyard. The wooden floor was full of scratches. Five people sat behind a wide table, and there was a piano in the corner, covered with black cloth. A middle-aged man with a strange hairstyle or an obvious toupee asked for her name, and she told him. They asked which monologue she had chosen, and she said Chekhov, and a bearded man in a turtleneck corrected her pronunciation.

You mean Che*khov*, he said.

Just let it go, said the woman with purple hair.

What? In Russian, they stress the second syllable, he said.

He's been saying the same thing all day, the woman whispered to Evelyn, and when the rest of the jury smiled, she added: And it's not even true.

Evelyn mirrored their smiles, even though she wasn't sure if the woman was referring to the comment about pronunciation or the fact that he had been doing it all day.

We're ready when you are, said the man with the artificial hairstyle.

Evelyn took a deep breath, closed her eyes, and leaned into the words—there was no better way to describe it, she wasn't sure if she was making eye contact or not, had no idea where to place the emphasis in different words, she just stood there in front of the evidently well-known theater people and let her body become a tool, the words came alive inside her, they danced on her tongue, they emptied her mind, focused her movements, and for a few minutes, she stopped being herself, there was no self-hatred, no inner voice telling her she was deeply broken, worthless, that there was something wrong with her heart because she hated the whole world, something wrong with her memory because no impressions stuck, something wrong with every cell in her body because she never managed to connect with something greater, during the minutes she spoke, everything ceased, and when she finished, she was met with silence.

Evelyn could hear the bearded man's breath. The woman with purple hair looked at her and smiled.

Thank you, she said. That's all.

Do you not want me to . . . ? Evelyn said.

No, that's all we need to see. Thank you very much, and Evelyn left the room with the feeling that the woman had tricked her into thinking that she was something she was not, and she hated her for it.

She went back to work and spent the afternoon listening to Kattis complaining about how difficult it had been to be alone in the store for four hours and what would have happened if their bosses had shown up and Kattis had to lock the store to go pee, and this was the last time she would do Evelyn a favor, and Evelyn nodded and agreed.

Sorry, she said. Everything took longer than expected. It won't happen again, she told herself, because she would be here until she died.

Three weeks later, both Cecilia and Evelyn received a letter informing them that they had made it to the second round of auditions. This time, Cecilia didn't ask Evelyn to come along for support.

Chapter Ninety-Four

We arrived at a large open parking lot, and the event venue looked like a school closed for the summer, the groom's family was already there, they looked so serious, so well-dressed, so extremely pious and calm compared to our rowdy family, who arrived forty-five minutes late due to a car breakdown. Someone had to go back to the hotel to retrieve something important, and someone else forced our section of the caravan to take a detour through town, honking all the way to make sure everyone heard us. While the children in their family sat quietly on plastic chairs, waiting for the ceremony to begin, the children in our family rushed straight in and attacked the dance floor, even though no music was playing, the men in their family wore well-fitted suits, and the women wore high-quality hijabs, I could feel their eyes on us, and I started to see us through their eyes, one of my uncles had a black jacket with the white label still on the sleeve, he seemed eager to show off the Italian brand, which I had never heard of, the jacket almost but not quite matched the black pants he was wearing, another uncle wore just a T-shirt and a sweater, I wore a suit but had black Converse shoes instead of leather shoes, it took some time before everyone found their places, and we needed more tables and chairs, they brought in white plastic outdoor furniture, my grandmother wasn't happy with the table she was seated at, so we got another table for her to sit at, closer to the stage, I was at her table, I heard her muttering something, she didn't say anything about the fact that the marriage was taking place in a gymnasium, she didn't say anything about the purple cloth that was too see-through to cover up the basketball hoops, she didn't mention the fact that the dance floor was covered in court lines and that the walls were lined with parallel bars, she didn't care that we were being served juice and sodas in white paper cups, no, she was muttering about something else, it was the nuts, she thought the nuts that they had put out on the tables were of bad quality, and she leaned over to me and said that these Kurdish people are poor peasants who should be happy that we are allowing them into our family because we are Arabs and they are Kurds, and we all know that there is a big difference, it's not even comparable, it's like comparing a Mercedes with a Škoda, and I nodded, trying to look like I knew what the hell she was talking about.

But don't we have some Jewish background too? I asked, with a glimmer of hope in my voice.

Grandma shook her head, and I wasn't sure if she shook it because she didn't understand my broken Arabic, disagreed with me or didn't hear me over the music that started blaring from the oversized speakers.

We sat there waiting, eating nuts, drinking warm soda, wondering why it was taking so long. Then suddenly, at a quarter to six, two hours and fifteen minutes after the official start time of the wedding, the couple arrived. Everyone rushed out to greet them as they made their way up the hill in a shining white limousine.

Is that a Škoda? someone in our family said, and Younes, my uncle, pretended not to hear.

The couple emerged from the back seat, first Alma, then her husband with his soccer haircut, Alma's face was covered with a red cloth, the wedding photographer asked them to get back into the car and come out again so he could capture everything with his video camera, they got back into the car and came out again, waving and smiling, this time the band was ready, a guy had a metal flute, the other guy had a drum, both had silver bells and short-sleeved blue shirts, they played like their lives depended on it, and the Kurds began stuffing money into the drummer's mouth—fifty euros, twenty euros, another fifty, my family looked at them as if they were crazy.

Show-offs, we muttered to each other. Or maybe it was just me muttering that to myself.

Alma and her husband entered the main hall, her face still covered with the red fabric, I let everyone else go first because I didn't want my tall frame to be in the way of the photographers, I didn't want to be too visible in the pictures, I was still unsure of what I was doing there, in an abandoned school in the German countryside, with a bunch of people I barely knew (my family) and a bunch of people I would never meet again (the Kurdish family), I remember standing outside the building, looking down at the limo, I saw the driver, he stood next to the back doors, wearing a black suit, white shirt, gray tie and dusty black leather shoes.

He had driven the couple here, left his driver's seat to open the door for them and now he just stood there, looking like he didn't know what to do next. He seemed too old to drive a limo, the little hair he had left was gray, he went back to the driver's seat and drove down to the parking lot in that unparkable car.

Alma and her husband had started dancing on the dance floor, and her face was no longer covered, the red cloth now lay on top of her head like an extra veil, she danced with one arm around her husband, holding a bouquet of purple and white flowers adorned with what looked like spiderwebs, aunts were crying, even her father, Younes, took out a dazzling white handkerchief and held it to his eyes, the musicians took a break, and the music now came from the large speakers on either side of the stage, a man was singing up there, he had a fantastic voice, despite the feedback, the official wedding photographer moved in and out with his video camera, assisted by someone handling the cords and a light screen, they were closely followed by the unofficial wedding photographer, walking beside them and trying to take pictures of what they were filming. At first I thought I had missed the ceremony and come all this way for nothing, but Younes said the actual ceremony took place somewhere else. This was just the party, and the paperwork had been taken care of with the imam at another location.

At the mosque? I said, but Younes didn't hear me, he was too busy taking pictures of the dancing couple, his eyes were red, his face beaming with excitement, he wore a dark gray pinstriped suit, then everyone started dancing, my aunts, my cousins, even my old grandmother, who suffered from rheumatism and shouldn't have been able to dance, stood in front of the stage and moved her compact body to the rhythm, and I joined in, not knowing what I was doing, the band played only Kurdish music, but I gave it my best shot for ten minutes, trying not to care if people were watching or if kids made fun of my dance moves, then everyone sat down, so I sat too, the bride and groom were led to the stage to take their seats behind a table covered with the same purple fabric as the basketball hoops and handball goals, large silver candelabras on the table, with candles that were not lit, and even the chairs were covered in white and purple fabric, behind the couple stood two giant plastic marble columns, obviously made of plastic, as one toppled when the couple went up onstage and a relative of the groom rushed forward to prop the column up again without effort, as if he were helping a toddler back on its feet, and now the column stood there again, adorned with plastic flowers, ready to be preserved for posterity.

Guests started lining up to have their picture taken with the bride and groom, I remember the wedding as being enormous, but looking at the arranged pictures from that day, it doesn't seem like there were more than maybe seventy people there, the same kids in the same shirts keep appearing in the pictures, how the photo session could take so many hours remains a mystery, maybe the wedding photographer wanted to capture all possible combinations, the couple with just the Kurdish family, with Kurdish cousins, with Arab and Kurdish aunts and uncles, with parents, with parents and siblings, with that weird guy from Sweden that no one seemed to know, no one seemed to recognize, not even himself.

It was getting late, and there was still no sign of food. I was still waiting for the wedding to start, but then I realized that this was the wedding, this was it, dancing, nuts, soda and a photo session. I noticed that the men in our family went out to check on their cars fairly often, they left the building, walked down to the parking lot and returned happier, more emotional, more prone to let loose on the dance floor.

When I had gotten my photo taken in four or five different combinations (always feeling like they were taking the pictures to get rid of me, as if I were photobombing the pictures, and that they would remove the ones with me in the final selection for the family album, as no one would know who I was or why I was there), my cousin signaled for me to follow him outside.

We went towards the rental car, he opened the trunk, he had red wine and champagne, Campari and orange juice, whiskey and vodka, beer in a cooler bag, plastic glasses and cigarettes, he even had extra-strong mints so that we wouldn't smell of alcohol when we went back in. We smoked and drank until a voice shouted:

FREEZE.

Younes flicked away his cigarette and closed the trunk, I poured out the contents of my plastic cup and dropped it on the ground. We turned around, it was Younes, my uncle, approaching us with a threatening grin. He made Younes open the trunk of the car.

What's this? he said in German.

It's nothing, his son replied in German, looking down.

My uncle searched through his son's selection of alcohol, shook his head, and said: No white wine?

He started laughing, and I laughed too, but it was a hollow laugh, as I was still unsure if my uncle was angry or not. My uncle poured a glass of whiskey and asked for a cigarette, then turned to me and started speaking in English.

Your brothers okay?

I answered him in French, telling him that my brothers were doing great—one was studying to become an actor, and the other was studying to become a doctor. My uncle nodded.

Doctor is good. Actor is . . . less good, he said with a smile. And your mother? Gonilla! She good?

I continued answering him in French, telling him that my mother was doing great, she had taken a break from physical therapy and was now training to become a qigong instructor.

Chi-what? my uncle said.

Qigong, I said. It's a bit like tai chi.

My uncle nodded.

I always say to your father: You make a big mistake leaving your Gonilla.

Well, it wasn't really he who . . .

Your father. Very kind man. Too kind.

Okay.

When we are young. Always he is too kind to women. They crush his heart. One girl. She has very very very very bad what's it called . . .

Breath? Younes my cousin said in an attempt to make a joke.

Shut up, you idiot, Younes my uncle said. Don't you see grown folks are talking? Then you are silent.

He turned to me.

Comment on dit *reputation* en anglais?

"Reputation," I said in English.

Yes . . . this girl has very bad "reputation," my uncle said with French pronunciation. This girl. She lie. She cheat. She steal. She fuck. You understand me? She fuck fuck fuck many many peoples.

I nodded and looked over my shoulder to make sure that the groom's family didn't hear my uncle.

She fuck one man. Then fuck another man. Then fuck his brother. Then fuck his uncle. Every man she fuck fuck fuck.

I get it, I said.

No good girl. Very poor. Very stupid. Very very beautiful. And I tell your father: watch out. This girl will destroy your life. Don't give money for ticket to Europe. Don't write her invitation letter so she can come to Sweden. Don't believe when she says they beat her and lock her in the house. Of course they beat her and lock her in the house! She's crazy! But did your father listen? Nooo. Your father is too kind. He help everyone. He help this girl. He help Mahmoud with cheese factory, he help Khamis with new taxi, he help Fathi with hotel business and soon this girl come to Sweden and your father help her with contacts for carpets and then she meet man and man is not man enough to make babies so this girl ask your dad for help and I say for the last time. Say *no*. Say no! You will regret it! But he say yes. Stupid man. But kind.

My uncle raised his glass for a toast, signifying that his speech was over. My cousin was quiet.

Wait, I said. You're telling me that my father gave his . . . "sperms" to this crazy girl? (I didn't know the French word for "sperm" and hoped it would be "sperms" with a French accent.)

You didn't know? my uncle said with a big smile. Ask him! But he was always very "fidèle" to your mother. He simply can't say no, your dad. He's so kind.

He has said no to us the last fifteen years, I said.

That's different, said Younes. You're his sons.

I nodded to show that I understood, even though I didn't. We stood there, three men with the same name in a car park outside a school closed for summer in the German countryside. We had four potential languages, but none of them seemed to work well enough. I looked at my cousin. He hadn't said a word since his father told him to be quiet. Younes my uncle looked up at the dark sky and the stars. Someone familiar with constellations would have seen patterns, but I saw only a random collection of white dots like pins on a bulletin board. Suddenly, a light appeared from the limousine as the driver opened the door and left the car. At first, I thought he would come up to us and ask for a glass, inquire if it was okay for him to come in and have some food, maybe share his views on my father's alleged kindness, but the driver didn't leave his car, he just stood near the driver's door, smoking a cigarette, the light inside the car turned off, the glow of the cigarette danced up and down in the dark, turning red every time the driver inhaled. We went back inside.

Chapter Ninety-Five

During the last week of April, both Evelyn and Cecilia were called to the mythical fourth and final audition. Thousands of applicants had now been reduced to twenty-four, who met up over three full days to do theater exercises with the actual teachers from the school. Before they started, Evelyn spotted Cecilia in the school café, she raised her hand and smiled, Cecilia nodded and left.

Ever since Evelyn made it past the second round of auditions, things had been awkward between them, and they hadn't even spoken to each other after the third round. Evelyn sometimes considered dropping out and returning to her job at the clothing store. She felt much older than the other applicants, and she questioned whether risking her friendship with Cecilia was worth pursuing something she wasn't even sure was her dream. But she reminded herself that she had just as much right to be there as Cecilia did and nothing in her thirty-one years had been as fulfilling as doing theater exercises.

People always had plans for what Evelyn should become, strangely enough they never gave career advice to Ina or Anastasia, but they always looked at Evelyn and wanted to decide her future, when she was little, model scouts tried to convince her mom that Evelyn should become a child model, in her teenage years, her philosophy teacher tried to persuade her to study political science, one ex thought she should become a chef, another ex suggested she become a "secret agent" simply because it was difficult to get to know her, since she was always holding something back, always aware that if she let someone in fully, they would turn around and run away screaming, not because her interior was dark or evil, but because it was empty and emotionally dead, inhuman, a shell.

Her mom always declined the modeling offers, saying it was impossible, it would attract too much attention and envy, she had experienced the consequences of drawing envy from others, it led to a curse being placed on her, causing her to lose contact with her family, and Evelyn didn't question that version of the truth until now, during the final audition at the drama school, when she entered the room among the twenty-four selected individuals, she could feel their energy, their nervousness, their focus, and time flew by as they did improvisations ("Get up and scream your absolute biggest abyss-like YES!!!"), stood in a circle and sent messages through telepathy, rolled on the floor pretending not to have a spine, learned about Stanislavski, attempted to speak without consonants, spoke in verse, performed scenes from contemporary plays. Some students who didn't smoke began smoking, and those in relationships fell in love with other students or teachers. During a restroom break, Cecilia finally spoke to Evelyn.

Why are you doing this? Cecilia said.

Because I want to, Evelyn said.

No, you're only doing it because I want to, Cecilia said.

That's not true, Evelyn said. And you know it.

Cecilia lowered her voice so that not even potential eavesdroppers in the corridor could hear.

The only reason you've come this far is that all the teachers want to fuck you, Cecilia hissed.

Evelyn had hundreds of clever and witty comebacks, but unfortunately, she didn't think of them until hours later.

As a warm-up on their last day, the teacher instructed them to awaken their creativity by wandering around the room, pointing at things and calling them anything other than what they were. Evelyn was already standing up, walking in circles. She pointed at a chair and yelled FROG, she pointed at a wall and yelled MAP, she pointed at herself and yelled TABLE, she pointed at a lamp and yelled TIGER.

Then she heard Cecilia's voice. Cecilia was right behind Evelyn. She pointed at Evelyn and said FRIEND, then she pointed to the floor and shouted TRAITOR, then back at Evelyn, saying FRIEND again, then she pointed at the piano in the corner and said REVENGE and Evelyn just stopped and looked at Cecilia, considering her options, she could scratch her eyes out, kick her in the face, grab Cecilia's blond hair and drag her out to the school yard, but no, that's what Anastasia would have done, and instead of doing anything, Evelyn smiled and decided that the best revenge would be to make it into this school that she wasn't even sure she wanted to attend.

Chapter Ninety-Six

When we came back inside, the photo shoot was still going on, we went back outside, we drank and smoked some more, then we went back inside, still the photo shoot, back outside, on our fourth exit we were caught, the husband's brother came out to the parking lot with his cell phone as a flashlight and said something angrily in German to Younes, my cousin. My cousin answered something angrily back in German. For a few seconds, I thought they would start throwing punches, then my cousin offered him a plastic cup, and the husband's brother scanned the dark parking lot before taking the cup and pouring himself some beer, they toasted to something in German, I didn't know what the word meant, but I repeated it, to the best of my ability.

Then we went back inside, they had brought out the cake, it was also purple and white, with four tiers, on top was a sculpture of Mickey and Minnie Mouse getting married.

Kurdish men lined up in front of the cake.

What are they up to now? my grandmother said. These peasants and their weird traditions.

The Kurdish men approached the man with the microphone, they handed him something and the man with the microphone announced that this family had just donated five hundred euros to the newlyweds, and everyone cheered. My grandmother looked stunned.

Did he say five hundred euros?

Everyone nodded, the next man approached, he handed the man with the microphone something, there was a brief pause, then the man screamed that this family had donated a thousand euros and everyone cheered even louder. My grandmother looked pale, I had a strange metallic taste in my mouth, I knew that I should have come prepared, I had, like, thirty euros in cash, who else had cash, we started to scramble around the table while the Kurdish uncles and cousins gave unimaginable sums to the newlywed couple.

Finally it was time for someone from our side of the family to approach the man with the microphone, nobody wanted to do it, not Younes my cousin or Younes my uncle, so finally I agreed to do it, I imagined that if I did it, they would forgive us, they would say that the tall Swede gave way too little money, but still he gave something, he wasn't from around here, he didn't know the traditions, he's not from around here, he wasn't aware that you should bring your life savings in cash to a wedding.

I got up and approached the man with the microphone, I handed him the cash I'd collected, it was 320 euros, I expected the crowd to boo, I prepared for the Kurdish side of the family to start throwing chairs, but the man was silent for a few seconds and then he announced that the Khemiri family had given 3,200 euros to the newlywed couple, and everyone applauded and my grandmother looked proud and calm, and as I sat down I wasn't sure if he had made a mistake or was just trying to help us save face.

The next time we went outside to the parking lot, we were joined by the groom's brother and a few of his friends, I asked them about it in English, they had a hard time understanding, so Younes, my cousin, translated, they smiled and said that this is how it is done, it's a tradition in their family, you just add a zero, and we raised our glasses to celebrate their tradition.

When we went back inside, it was time for dancing, but not like before, no, now the groom's family wanted to show us their dance, and it was all about ring formations, everyone had to hold hands and dance in a circle, no one was allowed to dance alone, and then there were smaller circles within the bigger ones, and even smaller circles within those, whenever someone wanted to break free and dance on their own, their family found a way to form a circle around them, we danced in circles until midnight, when the music stopped abruptly and the fluorescent lights came on, the official wedding photographer packed up his equipment, and the unofficial photographer stood beside him, seemingly commenting on their collaboration, the unofficial photographer even handed over his business card, in case the official photographer ever needed help documenting a really big wedding, the official photographer tossed the card into his camera bag, so focused on leaving that he almost forgot to capture the newlyweds' final farewell, with a sigh, he pulled out his video camera again and filmed the couple rising from the table on the stage and heading out towards the parking lot, in the background, people started removing the fabric from the basketball hoops and deflating the marble pillars.

The white limousine was ready, and Alma and her husband waved as they climbed into the back seat, the driver slowly drove away into the darkness, and the guests stood waiting, children ran alongside the car, the red taillights disappeared, my cousin looked at me and said:

Now let's get drunk, as if we weren't already drunk, and so we got even drunker, we drove back to the hotel, carrying his alcohol to the room, we were joined by his sister and their mother, and we talked about the grumpy wedding photographer, the groom's friends, and played music from a tinny Bluetooth speaker.

Someone knocked on the door, we lowered our voices and hid the alcohol for what felt like the tenth time today. My cousin put on his jacket and opened the door, but it wasn't someone from the reception complaining about our loud voices, it was Younes, my uncle, and his wife, the bride's mother, they sat down on the floor, Younes loosened his tie, his wife asked for whiskey without ice, we turned up the volume on the speaker again and talked about the Kurds and their crazy traditions, especially their bizarre obsession with ring dancing, we decided that their favorite breakfast was probably Froot Loops, and their favorite sport might be hula hooping and their favorite song was probably "Ring the Alarm" or "Ring of Fire" or "Ring Ring Ring" with De La Soul or maybe "Single Ladies (Put a Ring on It)" and we spent well over fifteen minutes doing ring-related jokes, and since we were drunk and no longer nervous, we couldn't stop laughing.

Then Younes, my cousin, said:

I bet their favorite movie is *Lord of the Rings*, and everyone burst into laughter except Younes, my uncle, who looked at him and said:

Enough. They are family now.

The laughter stopped, and Younes, my cousin, looked as if he had been slapped.

I returned to my room and fell asleep with my shoes on. I woke up with stomach cramps, convincing myself they were from the laughing fits yesterday, but they might also have been due to drinking alcohol for six hours and eating only a few nuts and a slice of purple-and-white cake.

Chapter Ninety-Seven

The day was cloudy, harsh winds made it hard for newspaper sellers to change their displays, nobody was playing basketball in the park and despite the sudden cold, Evelyn decided to walk to the school from Östermalmstorg, just to avoid accidentally running into Cecilia. There were only two ways to get the results from the final audition, either you went to the school and looked at the fabled paper that they taped inside the glass door at ten in the morning, or you called a phone number and heard a neutral voice reading the names of the ten people accepted to Sweden's most prestigious theater school.

Do they read the names in alphabetical order? Ina asked.

I have no idea, Evelyn said. I'm going there in person.

Don't you have to work? Ina said.

This is more important than work, Evelyn said and didn't even bother to call Kattis and Anders to tell them that she would be late.

As she approached the school she saw two people who had been part of the final selection, Peter and Franka. They were crying in each other's arms and Evelyn wasn't sure if they were tears of joy or not, had one of them been accepted, or both, or neither? Evelyn continued towards the entrance, expecting the list to be gigantic, a neon-colored sheet with blinking names, but no, it was just regular A4 with holes, and the names of the ten students who had been accepted, produced by a printer running low on ink. Evelyn took a deep breath. She approached. The ten names were listed in alphabetical order. Evelyn saw her name. She searched in vain for Cecilia's.

Evelyn left the school yard and walked towards Valhallavägen. She turned right and passed the video store, the Persian restaurant, the tobacco shop and the ice cream place with pastel-colored walls. She didn't know where she was going, she just walked, down Sturegatan, through Humlegården, for what felt like an eternity she sat and watched the statue of Linnaeus, he stood high on a pedestal, his vest giving him something resembling a six-pack, his shoulders covered in bird droppings, his gaze fixed on the horizon, she tried to explain to Linnaeus that what had happened wasn't intentional, it just happened, like everything else in her life, she had applied to see if she would get in, and now she had, but did that really mean she should . . . ? Linnaeus turned his head towards her and started speaking with the voice of the curse:

Of course you shouldn't go there. You'll attract jealous looks, something very bad will happen to your sisters if you pursue what you truly want. Give your place to someone else, someone who really wants this, someone like . . . Cecilia.

Evelyn nodded and stood up. When she arrived at work, she had decided to decline the spot at the theater school and continue working in the store. It was safer. It was best not to tempt fate. Kattis looked at her and said: You. Me. Back there. Now.

Evelyn followed her to the storage room. Before Kattis could start yelling, Evelyn said: I'm quitting.

Excuse me?

Kattis's anger turned into concern. Are you sure? she said. Has something happened? Are you okay?

Evelyn nodded. I'm great.

And there was something about the joy in Evelyn's voice that brought back Kattis's anger, and she told her that if she really wanted to quit, then she could quit.

But don't come back asking for a job when what you are planning doesn't work out.

I won't, Evelyn said with a smile. I promise. I'm done here.

Chapter Ninety-Eight

When I returned to Berlin, I convinced myself that I should reach out to the Mikkola sisters, I should write an email to the address I used when inviting them to my thirtieth birthday party, I should give Anastasia a call, I found her number online, she seemed to be working for some kind of event company. But I never reached out to them, I just continued living in Berlin. I found a worn-out black Dutch ladies' bike that I rode until the frame broke. I biked back and forth to the Potsdam library. I dreamed of meeting someone but couldn't because I hated myself too much to interact with the real world. Every time I met someone, I tore her to shreds within a few days. She was too tall, too fair, too dark, too average, too something, too educated, too uneducated, too smart, too foolish, too different from me, too similar to me. Every short relationship ended with me sitting alone at home, thinking that I was too broken to be with anyone else and that I would die alone and isolated, just like my father.

In the autumn of 2009, Mohamed visited me in Berlin. On the third evening, we biked to a basketball court and played one-on-one. Soon we were challenged to play two-on-two, and the game grew to three-on-three and four-on-three, and soon we were playing full-court five-on-five. We were just taking the lead when I went up for a simple layup and got a push in the air, landing on my right little finger. At first, I thought it was just a regular sprain, but the pain persisted, and I couldn't straighten my finger.

In December 2009, I went up to Stockholm to have it checked at

Södersjukhuset. While I was in town, I accepted the invitation to my uncle's traditional Lucia gathering, where they would serve mulled wine and gingerbread, saffron buns and more mulled wine. I arrived with my grandmother, planning to stay for just half an hour. In the kitchen, I started talking to someone, she had curly hair, cheekbones like an Egyptian queen and unrealistically beautiful eyes, we talked about sports injuries and which body parts have the most nerve endings, we talked about how strange it is that more TV shows don't take place in hospitals, she told me about the animals in Australia, where she had lived for many years, the most dangerous-looking spiders were often harmless, but there was one spider in Sydney that could bite through fingernails and kill a person in fifteen minutes.

What are you talking about?

Her tall boyfriend came up and put his arm around her.

Spiders, I said, downing my glass of mulled wine. We said goodbye, and I went into the living room and sat next to my grandmother, not because I wanted to talk to her but because I wanted the girl to see that I was the kind of person who cared about grandmothers.

Back in Berlin, I realized my scholarship was about to end, a whole year had passed and instead of working on my novel, I wanted to get in touch with the girl I had met at the Lucia party at my uncle's house. But she had a boyfriend and I couldn't even remember her name, just that it started with a D.

On a hungover Tuesday, I decided to skip the library and biked to a café near Helmholtzplatz. I ordered a coffee and found a cozy corner where no one could see what I was writing. I opened my computer and started writing a letter to the Mikkola sisters, but in reality, I sat there for half an hour writing a sentence and deleting it again and again, Hey, it's me, what's up, sisters, so what's happening, WZAP, howdy-doody, but I couldn't find the words, what was I supposed to say? That we may be related just because my drunk gold-toothed uncle seemed to think so, and that could explain the strong connection I felt to you when we met a hundred years ago? Is that the reason I can't stop thinking about you? But before I contacted them, I should at least talk to my father, and since we didn't talk to each other, except when he needed help with something practical, I never wrote that letter to my potential sisters. When the coffee was gone, I checked social media and saw that the boyfriend from the Lucia party had added me as a friend. I accepted and went through his friend list, he had many friends, but there she was, the one whose name started with a D. I sent her a message. She replied. I sent another one. She replied. I suggested we meet. She said it couldn't happen.

When the scholarship was over, I was supposed to go back to Stockholm, but I had nothing to return to, so I stayed in Berlin.

One weekend, Nico came to visit. He had grown huge shoulders and started working as a firefighter. I convinced him to rent a bike, and even though he hadn't ridden a bike in years and didn't feel comfortable cycling in traffic, we started exploring the city using bike lanes. While we were taking a break in a park, Nico did fifteen pull-ups just for fun, he could climb a rope without using his feet, but he was terrible at cycling, and I got a strange kick out of watching him wobble around on the sidewalks, wearing that rental helmet he refused to take off.

He was newly in love and happy, and when we parked the bikes and had coffee in Kreuzberg, he asked if I had met someone. I told him about the woman I had been emailing with, the one I had met at the Lucia celebration and with whom I had kept in touch, despite her having a boyfriend and that nothing ever would come of it.

What's her name? he said.

Diane, I said.

Say her name without smiling.

She has a boyfriend.

You glow when you talk about her, he said.

As we biked towards Alexanderplatz, I asked if he had heard anything about the Mikkola sisters. Nico said that Evelyn was dating some well-known lawyer, he had seen them both at the Socialist Forum a few months ago.

What were you doing there?

I was just there, he said. To listen. He gave a fiery speech about immigration law.

Who did?

Simon. Her boyfriend. Evelyn was in the audience.

He mentioned their names as if they were both old acquaintances of his. It seemed like they had had a fight, he added.

Why? I said, wondering why that made me happy.

I just had that feeling, Nico said.

He told me his sister had been at a record release at Lydmar, and when she got past the bouncers, she realized it was Anastasia organizing the party. She smiled and hooked his sister up with some extra drink tickets, and apparently, she looked "super fresh despite the tattoos." Tattoos? I thought. What tattoos?

And Ina? I said.

He shrugged. He hadn't seen her in years. The last time was on Vasagatan, she was walking with a stroller full of groceries, one child in her hand, and another child in a baby carrier.

What did she look like? I asked.

Like she was walking on clouds, he said.

BOOK 4

2013 (One Month)

Chapter Ninety-Nine

na hadn't been to the theater since she was little, a friend's mom had taken her to see a play, the room looked like a storefront, and everyone had to take off their shoes and sit on the floor, then a lone actor came out on what wasn't really a stage, just some planks stacked on top of blue milk crates, she didn't remember much of the performance, except that at some point, the girl who had welcomed them at the door, the one who checked their tickets and told them to take off their shoes, the one in charge of the lights and sound, pulled some strings and a blue sheet fluttered over the stage, the actor didn't say he was on a boat or at sea, but Ina understood that the sheet represented the sea, and in a strange way, it felt more like the sea than if they had used real water and sprayed it on the audience.

On their way out of the theater, Ina's friend and her older sister were bored. They thought the play they had seen the week before was much better, they found the story boring and "full of holes." Ina nodded and agreed, and when she got home, her mom asked how it had been. Ina repeated what her friend's older sister had said, still unsure of how a story could contain "holes."

Now, thirty-three years later, Ina, a mother of three children, the head of the tax team at a publicly traded company, owner of a slow cooker, a juice machine, an air fryer and an ice cream maker (still in its original packaging), a member of a local gym she continued to pay for even though she hadn't been there in six months, holding on to hope that one day she'd have time to go, was on her way to the city to witness the first and last presentation of what Evelyn referred to as the "Chekhov block."

But please don't think of it as a performance, Evelyn had told Ina a few days before. It's more of a . . . "redovisning." (For some reason she said this particular word in Swedish, and Ina wondered if she used it because it could mean both "presentation" and "accounting").

The performance that wasn't a performance would take place in a building near the school. People were already waiting outside, and Ina looked for Anastasia but couldn't see her. To avoid the risk of accidentally bumping into any of Evelyn's many friends and not recognizing them, and then spending ten minutes awkwardly talking about Chekhov, Ina took a book from her ergonomic backpack and sat on a bench in the school yard, waiting for the doors to open.

Some kids were skateboarding in the yard, two were doing tricks, and the third was acting as a judge, awarding points and commenting on the style of the tricks.

Oh, that's a crushing ollie, will he try to do a double spin, he does, oh, and he comes up short, too bad, five, no, six point five points.

When the doors opened, Ina stood up and joined the not-so-structured line. Evelyn had said many of her friends would be there, but Ina didn't recognize anyone, and Cecilia, Simon and Anastasia were not there. There were no tickets, you just had to be on a list to get in, but everyone not on the list still got in. Ina was surprised to see that the gray, shack-like building with a metal staircase beside the school actually had what appeared to be a real theater inside. There were proper seats, real speakers, real lighting rigs, a real technician in headset and work clothes.

The seats filled up quickly, and if Anastasia didn't come soon, she would miss the first performance that Evelyn, after three and a half years, had agreed to let her sisters come and see.

The technician closed the doors. Then the doors opened again, and a breathless Anastasia stumbled into the auditorium, she waved to Ina and signaled that she would sit over there instead of struggling to get to the seat Ina had saved for her. Probably that's why she had chosen to come late, to sit undisturbed, to avoid being associated with her boring older sister. When Anastasia took off her jacket and sweater, Ina noticed that she had lost weight, her shoulders looked sharp, her hands seemed strangely large compared to her wrists, she appeared to have a new tattoo on her left shoulder.

The lights went out, and a guy with a big beard came out and started acting. A woman joined him and also started to act. Their voices moved in a prearranged pattern, they looked at each other and then gazed off at an invisible horizon. They sighed and talked about going to Moscow, and time stood still, no, time moved backward, Ina thought about the invoices she needed to pay for Saga's preschool, and tomorrow there's a parent meeting for Pikko, and they need to order a few more presents for Primo, who turns nine next week, nine, she could hardly believe it, just a few seconds ago, she held him in her arms, trying to comfort him when he woke up with night terrors, now he collected Pokémon cards and made his own playlists with favorite songs, just a few seconds ago she was worried about his tantrums and his struggle with the letter "r," then she was worried he seemed to stutter when he got too excited, then she worried that he would start school and not make any friends, and then she worried that he started school and immediately got the wrong kind of friends, he was unable to hang out with the nice boys in glasses, instead he was fascinated by the older boys, the ones with dads with neck tattoos, boys whose moms wore too much makeup and let their sons have unlimited screen time on their phones, and when Primo became fascinated with something, a new game, a new friend, he devoted his entire life to it, just like Hector with his publishing house, Ina thought, while the play continued with more actors, more gestures, more empty words.

Then, in the background, Ina heard the skateboarders, they were just outside the building, she heard their voices, the commentator-slash-judge giving scores, the other boys questioning his judgment, the sound of skateboards echoed against the asphalt, the actors kept acting, but the audience began to giggle, after a few minutes, the technician ran out to make the boys shut up, and they fell silent, staying that way for at least five minutes.

A new scene started, two new actors came out and acted, ancient dusty words flowed from their lips. And then, in a pause, in what was probably meant to be a charged interaction, the skateboarders began to roar, Who let the dogs out? Who, who, who, who, who? Who let the dogs out? The technician rushed out to chase them away, and the audience felt sorry for the poor actors who had still not come out onstage. How could they turn this around? They couldn't, it was hopeless.

After a short break, the performance that was not a performance resumed and there she was, in the background, her younger sister Evelyn. She still hadn't said anything, she just listened and watched. But still, Ina could feel it, Evelyn was different, she had something that made it impossible not to look at her, was it her energy, her eyes, the fact that she was dressed in an old-fashioned pink dress with long sleeves and a giant hat, was it because everyone else in her class was younger, was it because everyone else seemed to be waiting for her to say something, and then she spoke, and when she spoke, she didn't sound like an actress, and she didn't sound like herself, she sounded like the person she was always meant to become, her voice was deeper than usual, her voice seemed utterly uninterested in the audience's approval, her voice sounded like it had all the time in the world, and Ina couldn't look away.

Afterwards, Ina couldn't speak. Anastasia climbed over the backs of the chairs and sat beside her.

I actually liked this, Anastasia said.

Ina nodded.

Anastasia asked about Ina's children and told her about some prize she had won for an advertising campaign, and she was actually nominated for another, even bigger prize. But Ina didn't hear her, she was just thinking about Evelyn, her little sister who was still running around in diapers, she had been Ina's responsibility when their mom couldn't be there, Evelyn, who had cried when she saw a dead seagull at the age of seven, who rebelled against everyone at thirteen, who had worked in a clothing store for God knows how many years, and now, here she was, with her head filled with Russian words translated into Swedish, and somehow she had managed to say the old words with a confidence that made Ina want to see the whole play again, right now, or tomorrow if possible.

They waited for her outside but soon noticed that most of the audience was waiting inside. So they went back in. The actors jumped down from the stage, still in their theater makeup and ancient clothes, but now the enchantment was broken, Evelyn was her usual self, thanking them for coming and saying that there was a bar downstairs if they wanted a drink. Ina just looked at her and said:

That. Was. Incredible.

Really? Evelyn said.

It was great, Anastasia said. You were all amazing.

How did you do that? asked Ina.

Evelyn shrugged and smiled.

I just went out there and said what I was supposed to say.

But Ina knew it wasn't true, and she knew that Evelyn knew it wasn't true, because when they met downstairs over beer in a place that wasn't really a bar, but more like a spot where the former technician sold warm bottled beer from a red crate, and Anastasia surprised everyone, including herself, by ordering a Diet Coke, there were five or six guys lining up to express their appreciation for Evelyn's performance, and Ina noticed that Evelyn looked strangely sad. Sure, she smiled her professional smile and hugged friends of friends and accepted a business card from an overweight guy in a flannel suit who claimed to be an agent, she placed her hand over her heart, as she always did, to express how incredibly grateful she was for their compliments. But Ina sensed that there was something else going on, Evelyn wasn't quite here, her body longed to return to the stage, to the world where things had meaning, back into the world where time stood still and she didn't have to be herself.

Anastasia ordered a second and then a third Coke, before Ina had finished half of her beer bottle.

Are you okay? Ina said.

Absolutely. I just . . . I quit drinking, Anastasia said.

Good for you, Ina said.

Yeah, it's great, Anastasia said. Such a relief. I also quit smoking at the same time.

Wow, that's awesome, Ina said. Congratulations.

Thank you, Anastasia said. It feels amazing. Truly.

Ina noticed that Anastasia's hands were constantly in motion, first turning a paper napkin into a ball, then turning the ball into a roll, then turning the roll into thirty very tiny balls, and then Anastasia started arranging the miniature paper balls in different patterns, first a triangle, then a square.

Is everything okay? Ina said. You look like you've lost weight.

Me? I haven't noticed, Anastasia said. I think I'm just a bit stressed, I have a lot of work deadlines coming up.

She started talking about an upcoming advertising campaign for an Italian coffee company. Ina listened and nodded, or nodded without really listening. On the other side of the room, Ina saw Evelyn stand on tiptoe and hug a tall bearded man with black hair tied up in a samurai bun on the top of his head. She brushed against his forearm.

Is that him? asked a voice she didn't recognize.

Anastasia stopped mid-sentence. Simon was standing slightly behind them, he must have come directly from work, navy-blue suit, shiny brown shoes, a black briefcase with a gold buckle.

Did you come just now? Ina said.

Is that him? Simon repeated with tension in his voice.

Him who? Anastasia said.

The one she's fucking now? Simon said.

What are you talking about? Ina said.

Simon laughed.

Can't you take a joke?

He stayed there, slightly behind them, as if trying to make himself invisible using their bodies.

Is everything okay? Anastasia said.

Evelyn and the samurai guy were saying goodbye, but it was a goodbye that dragged on. They had already exchanged cheek kisses, but now they were going to hug too, and maybe he'd try to get a high five, just to stay close to her a little longer, just to delay the inevitable farewell. They were still standing there, and finally Simon had had enough, he walked up and interrupted them, tapping Evelyn on the shoulder. She flinched when she saw him. He reached out his arms like he was proud of teleporting himself there, and she took a step back before kissing him.

Ina and Anastasia were too far away to hear what they were saying, but they saw Simon put his arm around Evelyn, saw him smile at the samurai guy, saw him extend his right hand and hold the guy's hand for what felt like thirty seconds, he wouldn't let go, he held on and smiled and held on and smiled, and when the samurai guy finally got his right hand back, he flexed his fingers a few times, as if trying to regain feeling in them.

Chapter One Hundred

n the spring of 2011, I moved back to Sweden, I returned to the cafés where I used to sit before moving to Berlin, Citykyrkan, Valand on Surbrunnsgatan, Ritorno on Odengatan. Diane and I had sporadic contact, I wanted to share everything with her, and I saw her everywhere, on a subway between Slussen and Gamla Stan, on the other side of Liljeholmsbron on a bike, and every time I saw her I emailed to ask if it was her, it turned out not to be her, and it was strange that I kept seeing her because I had never seen anyone who looked like her.

Periodically I would suggest that we should meet, and she said it was impossible and then we ran into each other, one of those coincidences that could never work in a novel, I was working at a corner table at Ritorno when she entered with her flowing hair and radiant eyes and sharp cheekbones, her body always seeming like it was about to break into a dance to a rhythm only she could hear. My coffee cup almost tipped over when I stood up, we hugged, she was studying with a friend on the outdoor terrace and had come inside just to use the restroom. I returned to my corner table, a few minutes later, I went out to smoke and chat, then Diane and her friend came in and sat at my corner table. Her friend left, and Diane and I talked until the café closed. I followed her to the bus stop, we hugged goodbye, and now the impossible had to be possible, we had to be able to see each other. I promised myself to be patient, to wait a bit before emailing, to play it cool. But a few hours later, I couldn't resist and emailed her asking if she wanted to meet. Diane replied that it wasn't possible.

I promised myself never to contact her again, but for weeks, I sat at Ritorno like a lunatic, I hated her for filling me with these emotions I didn't know existed, and I loved her because she made me feel connected to the world, after thirty-two years of waiting, I had finally met a person who made me feel normal, it had never happened before, and I still don't know what it was that made it so, yes, she was beautiful, but many people are beautiful, yes, she was funny, but many people are funny, yes, she was smart and quick-witted, and had those lips and that nose and that voice and that figure and she wrote fantastic emails and had a fascinating family history from Martinique that on the surface resembled mine. Yet I still don't understand how I knew, I just knew

She never returned to Ritorno, and eventually, I convinced myself that the only thing to do was to be honest. I went back to Ritorno one last time, and wrote her an email describing my feelings, how I imagined our future together, trying to make her understand that this was different from anything I had experienced before. It felt life-threatening to press send, but eventually I did and left the café, the streets vibrated, facades crumbled, I walked home over a bridge, checking my email three times a minute, no reply the next day, still no reply the day after that. Three days later, I received a response. She wrote that she wanted to meet.

That night, I woke up three or four times, my body produced a kind of energy I had never felt before, I took a picture of myself with my phone each time I woke up as if to document and try to understand that something extraordinary was happening.

We decided to meet on a blanket on Skeppsholmen in the summer of 2011. We were supposed to meet at two o'clock. I arrived early, the lawn behind the colorful sculptures was empty, and then she came walking, she was wearing a striped dress, blue shoes, carrying a tote bag from the Strand, and her hair filtered the sunlight.

What are you doing here? she said when she saw me.

This happened almost twelve years ago, and since then, we have had two children, gone mad from sleep deprivation, argued about time, gone to bed angry, discussed whether to break up, yelled at each other, stormed out of the apartment (me), only to realize too late that we forgot the keys (me again), furiously knocking on the door because somehow even the forgetting of the keys was the other person's fault (definitely me). Despite all that, I smile when I think of that first meeting when Diane pretended it was a coincidence to run into each other on Skeppsholmen.

She sat down on the blanket, and ten minutes later, it had been six hours. Suddenly, it was eight in the evening, and all we had done was talk, talk and drink cold coffee from the thermos, talk and laugh and take short breaks for restroom visits at the Moderna Museet, talk and cry and eat the sweets Diane had brought.

The shadows of the trees grew longer, it became cold, my legs trembled as I stood up from the blanket. We were supposed to say goodbye, but we couldn't say goodbye. Instead, we walked up to the church, stopping at the church steps. It was completely quiet, no tourists, no Italian school classes, no priests. On a sign, it said the church was no longer a church but could be rented for private events. She looked at me with eyes that had been green when we sat on the blanket but were now blue. She closed her eyes, and we kissed. I touched her hair, her cheekbones, her neck.

We walked to the viewpoint. It was so cold that I turned the blanket into a mantle. We ate peaches or maybe nectarines. We decided she would leave first. We were still worried about someone seeing us, it was over with her boyfriend, but we were both paranoid enough to understand that it was best to avoid prying eyes. She went first, and I stood at the viewpoint watching her blue shoes, her striped dress and her curly hair disappear over the bridge.

My whole life, I had been told that there was something seriously wrong with me, ex-girlfriends, friends, family members were all in agreement, you will never meet someone, your standards are too high, the perfect person doesn't exist, love is about revising your dreams downwards and settling. As I stood there at the viewpoint, watching Diane vanish, I wanted to scream to the whole world that there was nothing wrong with me, the problem was with you, you were the damn fools who settled, who lowered your standards, who went on your first dates, who said yes to engagements, who walked down the aisle, who signed the house deed, who wrote your wills, who planned your retirements, and all along deluding yourselves into thinking you were happy even though you never were because deep down, you knew this wasn't the right person, there was someone else out there who could complete you, and it was your life's mission to find that person.

I had never been as happy as I was that first autumn with Diane, and for the first time in my life, I allowed myself to be happy, I didn't sabotage my happiness, I embraced it, I allowed it to exist, I opened up to the possibility that life could be different, and in reality, we didn't do much, we mostly stayed at my one-bedroom apartment on Kungsholmen and talked, we planned to go to a concert in Vitabergsparken but decided to stay at home, we borrowed my grandmother's car and drove to a lake called Glömskan, I introduced her to my friends, she introduced me to hers, but mostly we talked, we talked more than we slept, more than we had sex, more than anything else, and somehow we never ran out of words.

After a month of being together, we sat in my courtyard when Diane asked me something; I can't remember what it was, but I replied:

Why would I do that? I love you!

I hadn't planned to say it, it was just obvious to me, and I said it, not even thinking it could be awkward if Diane didn't say the same thing back.

I love you, Diane said.

Chapter One Hundred One

Anastasia sat in a taxi on her way home from Evelyn's performance, trying to understand why she felt so empty and tired after meeting her sisters. Had it always been like this, or had it gotten worse lately? When did it start? When Anastasia started earning more money than them? When Ina had her third child? When Evelyn started attending acting school and suddenly began wearing thrift-store sweaters instead of fashion ones? When Anastasia and Åhdal bought an apartment that was larger than the town house where Ina and Hector lived with their three kids?

Tonight, Evelyn had been onstage, but it was Anastasia who felt drained after a long performance. Anastasia's jaws were tired from forced smiles, her brain exhausted from trying to create conversation with the unusually silent Ina.

In the taxi on the way home, Anastasia promised herself that she would take a break from hanging out with her sisters, and she tried not to think about how many times she had made that promise to herself before. The taxi driver was a non-talker, which suited Anastasia perfectly, she would give him a good tip when they arrived. Anastasia had offered Ina a ride, saying she could order a car on the company account without any problem.

No, it's fine, said Ina. I'll take the subway.

And it was just a short sentence, a few words, "I'll take the subway," so why did it feel like Ina was criticizing her as if those few words contained a whole world of guilt and suppressed anger? She said, "I'll take the subway," but Anastasia heard, "I'm not wasting my undeserved money like Queen Marketing here, I care about the environment, I'm practical, I make my own bone broth, I dye my own roots, I haven't been to a concert since 2002 because I never understood the point of them, the sound is better when you listen from home and you don't have to be in a crowded room dealing with people complaining about your height. My husband works as a publisher, and his attempts to publish books that no one wants to read have ruined our family, but I don't complain, no no, I just take the subway, hashtag nomartyr."

The taxi drove along the Central Bridge towards Södermalm, the dark silhouette of Gamla Stan to the left, City Hall to the right. Soon she would be home in the apartment she shared with Åhdal. When they bought it, it cost 1.4, a staggering amount, today it was probably worth five, if not six million, she still couldn't believe she lived there, bay windows and three-meter-high ceilings, original oak floors and custom-built bookshelves that made Ina sweat with envy when she saw them. It was the first and last time Ina had come over, since then, she had declined all invitations, and tonight it became apparent to Anastasia that her sisters didn't understand her. Sure, they had grown up together, and they had been there for one another when they were young, and they lived together as adults, and when someone needed something, the others tried to help. But now something had come between them, and it wasn't that they had changed, it was that her sisters somehow made Anastasia behave strangely.

Like that thing with drinking. Anastasia hadn't stopped drinking at all. Not really. She had considered taking a month off and then decided to start that tonight. So why did she tell Ina that she had stopped drinking? And why did she tell Ina about all her career successes? And why did she drink all those Cokes without going to the bathroom before getting into the taxi? And why did it hurt so much to see how touched Ina was by Evelyn's performance?

During the show, Anastasia had looked over at Ina, and Ina had looked at Evelyn with so much love and pride that Anastasia had to remind Ina that Evelyn wasn't the only successful sister. But the more she talked about her career successes, the more bored Ina seemed to become. She just nodded and waved her away as if she were an annoying fly, to return to talking about Chekhov with Evelyn.

I don't understand, Ina said. How did you *do* that?

How hard can it be? Anastasia thought to herself. You memorize the words. You say the words. Anastasia's job was so much more creative than Evelyn's. Global companies paid her five-figure amounts for a slogan, four-figure amounts for a free-flowing brainstorming session.

She never prepared anything, she just showed up at the meeting and asked the nervous suits what they wanted, then did the exact opposite, if they dreamed of radio commercials, she suggested using hot-air balloons, if they wanted to reach a young audience, she proposed advertising in retirement homes, she was a disrupter, someone who got paid for thinking differently, and Ina would always hate that about her, and Evelyn would always be jealous of it, because as charming and intelligent and beautiful as Evelyn was, she didn't have the ability to come up with something original. It became painfully clear to everyone towards the end of the evening when Simon had shown up, and Evelyn started talking about her personal project.

Each student has to create their own monologue, she said. And most of them are already done.

And you?

I have nothing, Evelyn said with a sigh. Nothing! And if I don't do it, I won't be able to graduate, and then these three and a half years will be wasted. First, I lost more than ten years in the clothing store, and now four years here.

Why don't you write something about Mom? Ina said.

Because that's exactly what they want me to do, Evelyn said. They would love it if I went onstage and talked about Mom, if I imitated her accent when she sold her carpets, if I made fun of how she hit us with her rubber slippers, if I sang her songs and talked about her dreams and dramatized her death and showed how much we miss her, and . . .

And? Ina said. What's wrong with being honest?

It's just so . . .

Predictable, Anastasia said.

Exactly, Evelyn said.

So, what are you going to do?

No idea, Evelyn said, looking at Anastasia. Can you help me?

I'm happy to help, Ina said before Anastasia could respond.

I have a budget for research, Evelyn said, still facing Anastasia.

I have some ideas, Ina said.

Don't listen to her, Anastasia said. Then it'll end up being a musical. I'll send you some ideas tonight.

Thanks! Evelyn said, giving Anastasia a spontaneous hug. As soon as the hug ended, Simon reached for Evelyn's hand, or no, her wrist; he was actually holding her wrist.

Are you ready? Simon said.

And my ideas? Ina said.

You can help with proofreading, Evelyn said, and Anastasia thought Ina would take offense, but she actually looked strangely proud, as if being a proofreader for her middle sister's future monologue was more important than coming up with ideas for its content.

Anastasia didn't have time for this, she was in a taxi, it was late, she had client meetings tomorrow, a work thing tomorrow night, on Thursday she and Åhdal had planned to have sex, they had been trying to get pregnant for over a year. At first, they relied on chance, and when it didn't work, Anastasia started counting days and planning sex in a shared electronic calendar.

She took vitamins and underwent acupuncture, ate healthy food and cut back on exercise, she needed sleep to be sufficiently rested to start a life inside her, but she also knew that if she didn't get this done tonight, it would stick with her and itch, so she got home, decided to postpone her dry month, poured a glass of white wine, sat down at the kitchen table with her laptop and quickly came up with a proposal for Evelyn's monologue. She decided to call it *Sisters Raised to the Power of Three*, and instead of being about their origins and their mother, it would be about the other version of their story, revolving around skyscrapers and wide avenues, what Evelyn and Anastasia needed to do was to go to New York for a long weekend, as soon as possible, to find their roots, to see Rockefeller Center, to make peace with their past. The trip could then become the backbone of Evelyn's future monologue. Anastasia sent the email to Evelyn at 3:23 a.m., and when she woke up at eight, Evelyn had already replied: Yes, YES, YES!!! When are we going?

She had added Ina as a recipient.

Chapter One Hundred Two

Emma and I were still friends, but not like we used to be, we contacted each other less frequently, we texted and scheduled a coffee that one of us canceled the day before, we promised to catch up the following week, but then we didn't. One evening in the spring of 2012, we arranged to meet at Babylon near Medborgarplatsen, Emma arrived with Fijona, who had been my friend originally, they told me that Emma would produce Fijona's upcoming short film, they spent the evening discussing the requirements for the summer shoot, extras and actors, applications for financial support from the Swedish Film Institute and the challenge of finding talented scriptwriters. I sat beside them, nodding, asking follow-up questions and laughing at their inside jokes. I went home to Diane, with a strange feeling in my body, Diane said she felt the same way, we went to town and bought three different pregnancy tests at the late-night pharmacy on Klarabergsgatan.

The last time we met was at a hotel bar near Norra Bantorget, Emma was wearing a fluffy blue wool sweater, and so was I, we laughed at the coincidence and joked with the bartender about coordinating our outfits, the bartender looked at us as if he didn't speak the same language. After getting our drinks and finding a quiet corner, I was about to tell Emma that Diane was pregnant, but before I could, Emma said she was disappointed in me.

Me? Why?

Because you haven't been there for me lately, she said. And I've really been struggling. She described the recent turbulence, it seemed to be cyclical, summers were the worst, when approaching her birthday, she crashed, it wasn't depression, it was something else, something worse, she described it as like riding a wave, when she was at the top of the wave, she had rocket power in her heels, speeding through life, everything she did worked, the plays she produced were praised, the burlesque club nights she organized were epic, but then, when the wave leveled out, she sank, not underwater, but all the way to the bottom, everything just disappeared, she couldn't think, read or listen to music, her thoughts just raced, and she couldn't handle life.

It sounds terrible, I said. Why didn't you tell me about this before?

Because you are so judgmental of anyone who is weak, Emma said.

Am not, I said.

Yes, you are, even now, sitting here, I feel that you judge me. That you disdain me because I don't have a proper reason to feel this way.

Not at all, I said, wondering if it was true.

Stop lying, Jonas, please.

I looked at her. We had aged, we were eighteen when we got together, and now we were thirty-three, I had my first gray hairs, she had small wrinkles at the corners of her eyes.

So what do you want from me? What can I do to make you feel better?

You don't need to do anything. I just need to know that you are there for me.

But how?

Call me more often. Text me. Come over.

It's been difficult lately.

Why?

I've met someone.

I know, she said.

She's not like the others, I said.

I know, she said again.

I've never felt this way before.

Emma looked at me. We said goodbye without me telling her that Diane was pregnant. I didn't want to make things worse than they already were. Instead, I texted Emma on my way home, I wrote that I was sorry for not being there for her, promised to get in touch more often, and of course, she was right, even though she had many friends, it wouldn't hurt to have more friends. She replied with a heart.

Chapter One Hundred Three

n April 2013, a plane took off from Arlanda Airport heading towards JFK with three sisters on board, none of them had been to New York before, Ina had played basketball outside Austin, Anastasia had been to San Diego for a few days to film a car commercial, but for Evelyn, this was her first time setting foot on American soil.

While waiting for takeoff, Evelyn thought about her great-grandfather who had come from a small village near Falkenberg and risked everything to make the journey across the ocean, he had mortgaged his farm, left his wife and probably twelve children to take the boat from Gothenburg, four months of seasickness, barely edible food, sleeping on thin flea-infested mattresses, huddling close to other passengers just to stay warm, the fear of getting measles, waking up to rats nibbling at his toes or something like that, in all honesty, Evelyn had no idea how long it took for her great-grandfather to cross the ocean, she only knew that she and her sisters were flying over the same ocean in nine hours, Ina kept saying that they should have taken the flight with a layover in Frankfurt, since it was much cheaper, and Anastasia reminded them that she had paid for all three tickets with her frequent flyer miles and Evelyn reminded them both that the research funds for her monologue would cover the trip, or at least part of it.

But it wouldn't have worked without Fabricia, Anastasia said. I can't wait to see her.

She looked out the window. The airplane had passed Iceland

and begun its descent towards New York, the dark gray clouds were moving upwards.

How long has she been there? Evelyn said.

A few months, Anastasia said. She has some sort of scholarship that includes a studio. She's already talking about staying longer.

Do you miss her?

Strangely enough, I missed her more when she moved to Gothenburg, Anastasia said. Leaving me for Gothenburg felt like an insult. But leaving me for New York feels . . . okay.

The plane broke through the clouds, the seat belt sign turned on and everyone with a window seat craned their necks to catch a glimpse of what they hoped would be a view of Manhattan, the sparkling skyscrapers, the long straight avenues, the dark rectangle of Central Park.

Is that the Empire State Building? Ina said, who had chosen the window seat to avoid getting bruises from the flight attendants' carts.

She leaned back so that Anastasia and Evelyn could also look out the window.

Maybe, Anastasia said.

It's so far away, Evelyn said.

That's New Jersey, someone from the row in front of them said.

On the other side of the plane, people pointed and gasped, and Evelyn heard a father say: Look! It's the Statue of Liberty. Can you see her? She's right there! Wow.

The plane landed, and everyone stood up, but they had to wait for the first-class passengers to disembark first, then the business-class passengers, and finally, it was their turn.

Welcome to America, Ina said sarcastically.

What are you talking about? First class always gets off first, Anastasia said.

They walked through the airport corridors, and Evelyn could hardly believe she was in America, it had to be America because the guards standing at every corner spoke American, and their uniforms were marked with the American flag, and they all carried guns, and the vending machines had candy she had only seen in movies, like

Skittles, and the electrical outlets in the endlessly long corridors were different from home, the European outlets looked like outlets, while the American ones resembled a sad face with two squinting eyes above and a surprised, disappointed mouth below, so this must be America. But why was everything so dirty and poorly lit, and where did that weird smell come from?

They got in line for passport control, and Ina suggested they spread out, each taking a separate line, so the others could join the person whose line moved fastest, but before she could convince her sisters of the brilliance of her strategy, a stern guard told them to stand in a specific line, and she had a police badge and a uniform and small splinters of what was probably once a toothpick in the corner of her mouth, so they all got in the same line and waited to be called forward.

How long are you here for? the man behind the glass asked.

Five days, the sisters said.

What's the purpose of your trip?

Well, actually, it's quite a funny story, Evelyn said. We are sisters, and we are here because our great-grandfather was American, and we want to find some research material for a monologue that I will be doing as part of a very prestigious acting school in Sweden called . . .

The guard looked at her with a dead expression. Business or pleasure? he said.

Pleasure! Ina and Anastasia said so loudly that Evelyn jumped. As they walked towards the baggage claim, they explained to Evelyn that if you say business, they send you back, no discussion, they just take you to the side and force you back to your home country.

So I guess we are tourists? Evelyn said.

We sure are, Anastasia said.

Chapter One Hundred Four

n the summer of 2012, Mohamed called at dawn and said that Emma was dead.

Chapter One Hundred Five

The taxi drove over potholes on a road so uneven that Anastasia had to look to make sure they were driving on asphalt. She leaned forward to the driver and double-checked that he was taking them to Bushwick in Brooklyn, since there was no other Bushwick, right? Not in Queens or Long Island?

The driver assured her that he knew exactly where he was going, and Anastasia leaned back and tried to relax.

When did you last meet? Ina said.

Not too long ago, Anastasia said, thinking back to that strange evening in Stockholm when Fabricia exhibited two works in a group exhibition at Galleri Index on Kungsholmen. Anastasia had brought flowers, congratulating her friend, but from Fabricia's face, she could tell that if anyone deserved congratulations, it was the gallery's director, who had the honor of showcasing Fabricia's works and basking in her presence on the opening night.

I'm only here for you, Fabricia said, but it hardly seemed true, because as soon as she had been introduced to Åhdal, she was whisked away to talk to a curator from the Moderna Museet, leaving Anastasia to hand over the flowers to Åhdal, who thanked her and selected three works, pretending they were his creations.

Åhdal was always by her side, never abandoning her, he wasn't the most handsome man she had been with, but he didn't try to hide his thinning hair, he wasn't the smartest, but he didn't pretend to be buying books he never read, he wasn't the tallest, the most exciting, or the best-dressed guy, but he was undoubtedly the funniest person

she had been with. He had a magical ability to turn a stiff opening at a small gallery in Stockholm into a party just by being present
and quick-witted, soon he had gathered a small audience by talking
about the thoughts and theories behind these three artworks, for
which he claimed to have gotten the original idea in the spring of
'93 when he was at his aunt's lumberyard, drinking homemade wine
and eating chestnuts, suddenly, he had a vision, an epiphany, he saw
the light, four significant theorists inspired him: Baudrillard, Bour-
dieu, Blanchot and Bourgogne, he instantly knew that he wanted to
create something revolving around the body and hearing, decay and
degeneration, the ravages of time and the basilisk of memory and the
illusion of freedom and the grimace of history and the underside of
the welfare society, and if Anastasia hadn't burst into laughter, Åhdal
could have gone on for another ten minutes, because once he got
going, it was hard to turn him off, it didn't matter that the real artist
behind the three works was probably there because none of those
who were part of the art world were looking at the artworks, they
were busy refilling their plastic glasses with free wine, talking about
their CVs, planning studio visits, exchanging business cards, artists
trying to talk to curators, and curators trying to show how tiring it
was to get attention from artists.

Åhdal and Anastasia brought some plastic glasses and a bottle
of wine down to the water, sitting on a bench, Anastasia told the
story of that peculiar night in Gothenburg when she and Fabricia
had become really close, it felt like it had just happened, but it had
been thirteen years. Anastasia heard herself claiming that the night
in Gothenburg led her to go to Tunisia, which led her to meet Daniela, which led to her what? Changing her life? No, realizing the
curse was true? No, changing direction, maybe, and meeting Åhdal?
Perhaps. But deep down, she wondered if anything had changed in
Gothenburg, if anything had changed in Tunis, if anything would
change in New York. If everything were a book, things could have
been more logical. The language course in Tunis would have led to
something concrete, something more than a broken heart and some
quickly forgotten verb conjugations, something more than a visit to

a medium she never returned to. But Anastasia's life was not a book, far from it, her life was just a series of randomly assembled scenes, and sometimes, on very rare occasions, she had felt that everything had meaning, that her life had a place in a larger narrative, that she was connected to the past and the inevitable future. But as soon as the drugs left her system, she was back in her own body and the randomness of everything.

The taxi passed tall brick houses and eventually stopped outside a white square building, across from a bodega. Fabricia was waiting for them outside. She looked unchanged, just as many necklaces, the same radiating warmth, but she had gained some weight, and Anastasia wondered if it was because of New York or if she was pregnant. They all hugged, even Ina, who usually reserved physical contact for her immediate family, if even that.

Let me give you the tour, Fabricia said and opened the door to the white staircase.

This used to be a sewing machine factory, Fabricia said as they climbed the stairs. Now it's all artist studios.

Are we really allowed to stay here? Ina said.

Just say you're here to visit me, Fabricia replied.

Who's going to ask? Ina said. Are there guards who are . . .

Nobody's going to ask, Fabricia said and turned right into a corridor. The walls were as white as the ceiling, the doors, the windowsills and the mailboxes.

Here it is. Welcome.

She opened the door to a gigantic white room with white walls and a church-like high ceiling.

I borrowed some mattresses, Fabricia said. And there's an inflatable one too.

This is perfect, Evelyn said.

Thank you so much, Ina said.

No problem, Fabricia said. To be honest, I mostly work from home anyway.

Fabricia left for a work meeting, Anastasia took out her laptop to check her work email, Ina unpacked her belongings, but when she realized there were no wardrobes to put things in, she packed them up again. There was a dresser with a few drawers, but they were full of unused brushes, fabrics and, unexpectedly, an iron lying in a box that seemed to have never been used.

Evelyn just stood in the large white room, breathing in the air of New York. She tried to comprehend that she was finally here, in her great-grandfather's city.

Are you ready to go? Evelyn asked.

Give me a minute, Anastasia said.

The windows were placed so high that she had to climb up on a chair to see anything other than the sky. And there it was, a real New York street, with real streetlamps, real people, a real bodega on a real street corner. The storefront was covered with advertisements, a white cartoon dog offered Slush Puppies, a green poster advertised Newports, a yellow sign with a red stop sign said: "Stop bedbugs now, don't be an innocent victim, board-certified specialists," and below it was a gigantic photo of a bedbug with smaller text stating that the specialists spoke both Spanish and Russian.

I'm ready, Ina said.

Just one more minute, Anastasia said.

She typed emails with a speed Evelyn had never seen before, attacking the keyboard as if it had insulted their deceased mother, she used shortcuts to send the emails, and every twenty seconds, there was a swoosh sound indicating she had sent another one.

Let's take the L to Union Square, Ina said.

Look at you, trying to sound like a local, Evelyn said.

Just trying to fit in, Ina said with a smile.

Aren't you tired? Anastasia said.

We only have five days, Evelyn said. Let's make the most of them.

Anastasia nodded and closed her laptop. Despite the six-hour time difference and jet lag, the three sisters left their luggage in Fabricia's studio and took the subway into Manhattan.

I'm actually here now, Evelyn repeated to herself. My feet are crossing this New York street, my hands are holding this railing, my fingers are swiping this MTA card. My fingers are swiping this MTA card again and again. My legs are passing through the turnstile. My body is approaching the building my great-grandfather risked his life to construct. When the train stopped at Bedford Avenue, a man dressed as a pirate entered their car. He had a black triangular hat with a gold emblem, a black patch over his eye and a gold telescope around his neck. It took a few stops for Evelyn to realize that the red parrot perched on his shoulder was real. It didn't speak, but it turned its head and looked at fellow passengers, one eye at a time. Not a single person in the car raised an eyebrow. Anastasia tapped Evelyn on the shoulder.

You can use this, Anastasia whispered and nodded towards the pirate.

Evelyn gazed at her sister, trying to understand what she meant. Use the pirate? For her monologue? She tried it in her head. "Hi, and welcome to my monologue, jealous classmates, potential agents, horny theater directors, I am so thrilled to be here. Let me start by telling you about a guy I saw a few weeks ago in New York. He was dressed as a pirate and had a real parrot on his . . ." She fell silent and shook her head. She needed something else—an opening, a theme, a story, a narrative that began in the past and took the audience into the future, a beginning and an end, not just a random sequence of scenes. It couldn't start with a damn pirate on the L train with a somewhat worn-out parrot on his shoulder, or maybe it could, Anastasia knew more about this stuff than she did, and perhaps it was a sign that she could never create something valuable on her own, without someone else's help.

The subway stopped at Union Square and half of the people in the car disembarked. The pirate and his parrot remained, and the three sisters followed the crowd up the stairs, out through the turnstiles, and into the light.

Chapter One Hundred Six

Emma is dead, Mohamed said. We were in the countryside, Diane was pregnant, it was five in the morning, the day after Midsummer. I tiptoed up and answered the call on the old gray sofa someone bought at a flea market so long ago that no one remembers who bought it. On the walls hung drawings that my brothers, cousins and I made as children: sunsets, Pokémons, Transformers, and underwater worlds with made-up fish. In the corner, on a rickety brown table, there was a black Bakelite phone that no one used. On the wall-mounted bookshelf were vacation books that people had read and left behind.

Emma is dead, Mohamed said with a hoarse voice. I read the book titles on the shelf. Are you still there?

What do you mean dead? I said.

She's dead, he said.

The world swayed, and I looked out towards the lawn. Everything was still there: the edge of the forest, the pine cones, the bluish-green water pump that hadn't been used in more than twenty years, the pine tree we had debated whether to cut down for five years, the water pistols and buckets from yesterday's water fight.

How did she die? I asked.

She took her own life, Mohamed said.

Diane must have woken up from the sounds I made, she came out and wrapped her arms around me, my brothers are there, my grandmother too, I tell them what happened, I say I have to borrow Grandma's car and drive back to Stockholm, it's a six-hour drive,

Diane says it's not a good idea, my brothers agree, I think about how I filled up the gas tank yesterday, it cost over five hundred, there must be something seriously wrong with me to be thinking about the price of gas when my friend is dead, I grab the car key, but my brothers hold me back and force me to stay, Grandma comes out from the house, she's old and forgetful but still understands what has happened, in the end, we book train tickets to Stockholm, before we board the train I call Mohamed and ask how she did it, how she took her life, I need to know, I need concrete details to try to comprehend that it has actually happened, that it's not some bizarre misunderstanding.

Mohamed tells me how she did it. He describes it in detail. Then we fall silent. I regret that I asked.

Chapter One Hundred Seven

People's gazes were different here, Evelyn felt it as soon as they stepped onto the sidewalk at Union Square, throughout her life, she had always needed to explain herself, in every room she entered (classrooms, conference rooms, guest rooms), to every person she met for the first time (dentists, friends' parents, part-timers in the store), there had been something about Evelyn that needed a background story, something about her appearance, behavior, smell, hair, eyes, her entire existence that required a table of contents, there was an unspoken question in the minds of everyone she met, and despite spending her whole life trying to avoid it, she still didn't know how to answer it. Ina had her standard responses, Anastasia made up something on the spot, Evelyn answered like a therapist, by deflecting the question or throwing it back to the person who asked, to avoid being held accountable for her own history, avoiding the category they were trying to place her in, seeking a small piece of freedom and sometimes, after yet another cat-baby-phone fight with Simon, she wondered if the strongest bond between them was their constant attempts to escape their pasts.

But now, as Evelyn stood in the bustle of Union Square with her sisters, amid skaters and street artists, shopaholics and tourists, nannies with strollers, bankers with expensive perfectly worn-out briefcases, homeless people with shopping carts, she noticed that the scrutinizing gaze was absent, these people weren't looking at her, searching for an explanation, they didn't even see her, they were preoccupied with their own lives, even if someone glanced at her, wondering if she were a washed-up age-old supermodel, just emerged from the L train, newly arrived from Sweden, it wasn't remarkable, old supermodels emerged from the L train in droves every day, and when Ina suggested they start walking up Broadway, Evelyn nodded, she was ready to go anywhere to explore whether the sense of freedom existed beyond this place.

They walked north on Broadway and reached a large bookstore with a red sign. Ina convinced them to go in, just for a quick look. They spent an hour wandering the shelves, with Ina picking up so many books that her sisters had to help her decide which ones she could carry for the rest of the day. Then they continued north, only realizing when they reached Eighth Street that they had been walking south. They turned around and headed back up towards Union Square.

On the other side of the square, Ina spotted a giant Barnes & Noble and began gravitating towards it, her sisters took her hand and led her back towards Broadway, back to their planned route, back north.

Do you know why all real New Yorkers say "uptown" instead of "north"? Ina said. Because Manhattan is slanted like this, and it feels like we're going north, but we're actually going . . . slanted north.

They passed a narrow triangular building that only Ina knew the name of (but she wasn't sure if it was pronounced Flat-Iron or Flat-ee-ron Building), they passed the Empire State Building, which Ina said was constructed in record time, taking only twenty months, they passed the famous library with the lion statues, and Ina waved to them, calling them Patience and Fortitude.

Someone has studied the guidebook, Anastasia said with a smile.

Evelyn tried not to look up at the sky, not wanting to be like the other tourists, she wasn't like them, she was part of the city, even though she had never been here before and had arrived less than six hours ago, even if she had no idea how they ended up on Fifth Avenue while following Broadway north.

It should be on the left side, Ina said.

Ahead, Evelyn saw an old church, reminiscent of the sandcastles Ina used to make on the beach when they were kids, taking wet sand

and letting it slowly drip from the right height to create a pile that turned into a hill that turned into a steadily growing tower, and one day it became a church in Manhattan.

That's Saint Patrick's Cathedral, Ina said.

The church looked like an old relative in a family photo, all her family members had been dead for years, but she was still here, hanging on, with her ancient spires, outdated shapes, impractical windows, surrounded by the youthful polished glass facades of her grandchildren.

There it is, Anastasia said and pointed to the other side of the street.

Sure enough, there it was: Rockefeller Center, a beige ruler stretching high into the sky, straight lines, hundreds, maybe thousands of identical windows.

Are you sure? Evelyn asked, a hint of disappointment in her voice.

Hundred percent, Ina said.

They crossed the street, and as they got closer, it became increasingly evident that it wasn't a ruler but an ancient beige spaceship, built in the 1930s and far too heavy ever to reach orbit.

Unbelievable, Anastasia said. This. Building. Is. Insane.

They stood silently for a moment. A tourist group passed on their left side, the guide had a microphone, he pointed at a bronze relief and explained that the barefoot mother and the naked screaming child were works by Manzù, a tribute to immigrants fleeing poverty to find a new life.

I think it's going to rain, Ina said, looking at the sky.

Evelyn began walking towards the entrance.

Shouldn't we wait for a day with fewer clouds? Ina said.

Evelyn didn't stop, and neither did Anastasia.

Hey, I think it costs, like, thirty dollars per person, and it might be smarter to go up on a day with a bluer sky, Ina said.

Evelyn didn't listen, she was already in line, Anastasia too, Ina stood a little way behind them, still gazing at the sky, saying it might be better to visit another day when the view would be more optimal.

Stay down here if you want, Evelyn said. But I'm going up there.

She placed her hand against the facade, feeling her own pulse. She leaned her head back, struggling not to take a step back.

Me too, Anastasia said.

Ina nodded. I'll come along.

Anastasia leaned in towards Evelyn and whispered: You can use this.

Evelyn looked at Ina, Ina shrugged. They were allowed into the golden revolving doors and passed through a security check like at an airport. In the next room, several posters recounted the history of Rockefeller Center, Evelyn lingered in front of a placard describing how the parking attendants in the old Rockefeller garage had red fire poles to quickly retrieve visitors' cars. A special wall was dedicated to *Lunch atop a Skyscraper*, with other black-and-white photos taken on the same day, showing photographers, men in white tank tops, men working to complete the building on time. In the middle of the room there was the actual photo, but in a larger format. Evelyn had seen it so many times that she had become immune to it, but now, seeing it at this gigantic size, in the place where it belonged, it moved her.

That's so tasteless, Anastasia said.

Evelyn looked up to see what Anastasia was nodding towards. There was a fake steel beam set up in front of a green screen. Tourists were queuing up to take pictures, sitting on the beam that appeared to be suspended high in the air. They kissed, gave thumbs-up, stood on the edge looking scared of falling.

Two women with tired voices repeated the same instructions over and over.

Hands out like you're falling.

NEXT.

Hands out like you're falling.

NEXT.

Let's do it, Ina said.

You're kidding, Anastasia replied.

I'm in, Evelyn said, with a surprised voice, as if she was just as astonished as her sisters.

Ina and Evelyn stood in line while Anastasia moved as far away from them as possible.

In the first three pictures, only Ina and Evelyn appear, sitting on the beam and smiling, hands stretched out as if they are afraid of falling. Ina is pretending to read an invisible newspaper, while Evelyn holds an invisible bottle, in the fourth picture, a black-clad projectile enters the frame, and in the fifth picture, Anastasia joins them, pretending to eat lunch with invisible cutlery, in the sixth picture, all three sisters are there, three smiling sisters with sharp outlines sitting on the obviously fake beam against a green screen that will soon transform into Manhattan, in the last picture, Ina and Evelyn are seated while Anastasia stands behind them, as if her feet are held up by clouds, she embraces her sisters with a proud smile.

The elevator ride up to the sixty-seventh floor was supposed to take forty-two seconds, and it did, but it didn't because Evelyn couldn't grasp how long it actually took, they moved at lightning speed, but it seemed to last forever, there were even light projections on the ceiling to make the elevator ride more exciting, yet they still hadn't reached the top, they kept going and going, and they were still on their way up. Evelyn thought about how many buildings she had been in during her lifetime—let's say a thousand, ten thousand—and she had never taken the time to think about the person who had soldered the elevator buttons, the person who installed the light fixtures, the person who hurt their back to pour the cement needed to lay the foundation for a building that stretched 260 meters above sea level.

When they finally stepped out of the elevator, Evelyn realized that Ina had been right, they were so high up that the view was limited, and southern Manhattan was covered in clouds. Strangely enough, it only made the experience better because they could focus on what was closer, there were the dirty rooftops with their spinning fans, the umbrellas of the hot dog vendors that looked like tiki drink decorations from above, the pedestrian crossings so far below that several white stripes looked like one.

Evelyn found the angle where the original photo was taken, it must have been here, she placed her hands on the railing, looked out over Central Park, and felt the building breathe, she wondered which of the men on the beam was her great-grandfather, which of them was the reason she stood here now, the limestone spoke to her, for a few seconds she felt at home, then it began to rain, miniature people on the street pulled out their umbrellas, people argued over taxis, the beige color of the building turned brown, they went back inside, and when everyone on the observation deck gathered indoors, it became so warm that the windows fogged up.

Chapter One Hundred Eight

'm writing these words in January 2022, sitting in my assigned office at the New York Public Library, a new wave of Covid has led to new restrictions, and everyone is still wearing face masks, on the subway, indoors, at school. The library is closed to the public today, it's just me and a few security guards here.

It's been nine and a half years since Mohamed called me and told me that Emma was dead, and I still find it hard to believe, I want to say it's like in the beginning, the first years, that I still see Emma everywhere, her face in that of a barista, her hair on the subway, her gestures in a dog owner's, but it hasn't happened in years now. The truth is, she has faded away, I don't think about her very often, it happens now and then, maybe every three months, when a particular Gil Scott-Heron song plays randomly, when I come across an old photo on the computer, when the calendar shows that Midsummer is approaching, or when someone laughs at Target on Atlantic Avenue, and the laughter has the same hoarseness as Emma's voice.

But even though the memory of her is much less active now, even though it's almost been ten years, I still can't grasp that she is dead, I understand she's not here, but the fact that she's dead just doesn't sink in, sometimes I try to focus on the concrete details to make it graspable (the steel wire, the hallway door, Fijona getting worried on Midsummer Day and going over to peek in Emma's mailbox, the scream that made the neighbors call the police), sometimes I try writing it down to see if it changes anything (Emma is dead, Emma is dead, Emma is dead, Emma no longer exists, her body is not alive, she no longer exists, she's part of the past, she rests in peace, she rests in fireworks, her body has decayed into the earth, her nonexistent remains rest under a gravestone in the cemetery at Katarina Church on Södermalm in Stockholm), but whatever I do, some part of me insists on believing that she will come back someday, that now, when I finish this text and leave the library and head for the subway, she will be perched on a tree at Forty-second Street with a rotted, hollowed-out face, earthy clothes, overgrown decimeter-long nails, glowing green eyes, a smirk and a hoarse laugh as she hisses: That whole death thing? Come on. You didn't really buy that, did you?

Chapter One Hundred Nine

There was something bizarre about time in New York, it moved so much faster than any other time Evelyn had experienced. They had only been in the city for a few hours when Ina and Anastasia started reminding Evelyn that they would soon need to go home. The first day was Rockefeller Center and Columbus Circle, then down to Chelsea and the High Line. The second day was Battery Park, the Statue of Liberty, Freedom Tower and the Staten Island Ferry. In the evening, Evelyn searched for "Mikkola" in Ellis Island's archives, getting 299 matches. Mikki Mikkola arrived in 1890 on a ship named *Ems*, Konstantin Mikkola came in 1909, Samuli Mikkola in 1917, but none of the men felt right, and even if she had known her great-grandfather's name, she had no idea how to find him.

The third day, Central Park and the lake and the John Lennon memorial and an unassuming yet fantastic salad bar on the Upper West Side. Anastasia kept reminding Evelyn to take notes, and she did as instructed, she took out her notebook and wrote a couple of words, but often she wrote sentences such as "writing this to make Anastasia think I know what I'm doing" or "writing another note that means nothing just to pretend I have a fucking clue about what I'm doing." Each time she finished a note, she saw Anastasia proudly flash a thumbs-up.

In the afternoon, the sisters returned to the library at Bryant Park. They took the subway to Forty-second Street, passed the lion statues and climbed the marble steps to the entrance that looked like a castle, complete with metal nonautomatic revolving doors. Ina talked to a librarian and explained what they needed. They couldn't borrow any books but were allowed to sit in the Reading Room and go through the books recommended by the librarian. Ina read a book called *Building a Skyscraper*, Anastasia read *Steel Beams & Iron Men*, while Evelyn just sat there, surrounded by dark brown wood panels and symbolic paintings, with a book called *Skywalkers* in front of her. Sometimes she pretended to read, and other times she wrote something in her notebook, but mostly, they were mock words. She tried to look like a person collecting material for a monologue she knew she'd never deliver. She convinced herself that she was here to tell the story of how her great-grandfather arrived from a small village near Falkenberg eighty years ago. She would describe how he came to Ellis Island, found a friend in the passport queue, got a shared room in Brooklyn, ventured into Manhattan in search of work. "There's always work in Manhattan," people told him, but oddly, there was never work for him, he would soon run out of money, be hungry, miss his wife and children, wonder if coming here was the right decision, he had promised his wife not to take any hazardous jobs, especially not construction work, as people died like flies in such jobs, it was too dangerous, however, a week later, he stood in the queue at a construction site, and as soon as someone got injured or died, the next person in line was called forward, they told him he was too weak to get a job, too thin, too young, but he kept showing up, and eventually, they gave him a job as a runner, then he advanced to be part of a raising gang, six men and a pusher, he worked as a hooker-on, then a tagline man, and soon he became a roughneck, calling other newcomers snakes and . . .

No, Evelyn had no idea what he did or how he did it, he was here, he was part of the group that built a skyscraper that still stood to this day, he was photographed, and now he was dead, if she had been from a different family, she would know his story, know where he was buried, be able to contact him before he died to ask if it was scary up there, if he ever saw anyone fall to the ground, what happens to a body that falls from two hundred meters and collides with the

ground, what remains afterwards, what does it sound like, is it true
that Native Americans weren't afraid of heights, and was the photo
arranged for the marketing campaign, or did they really have lunch
up there on the steel beam, and which one was he, was he the one with
the empty bottle or the one with the newspaper and what was in the
bottle and did he ever stand up there, with the wind in his hair and the
steadily growing city beneath him, thinking he was exactly where he
was supposed to be, did he ever regret leaving his family and finding a
new wife here, did he ever return to the building after his retirement,
or as a ghost after his death, and place his hand on the limestone facade, thinking to himself: We built this, it was me and McDougal and
Eckner and Curtis and Smith and Johnson and Williams and Jones
and Brown and Davis and Jackson and Miller and Thomas and
Wilson and Lee and Taylor and Harris and Moore and Anderson
and Thompson and White and Robinson and Martin and Lewis and
Walker and Young and Clark and Allen and Scott and Wright and
Hill and King and Green and Carter and Mitchell and Adams and Hall
and Nelson and Baker and Turner and Campbell and Edwards and
Evans and Roberts and Nguyên and Parker and Phillips and Collins
and Stewart and Morris and Washington and James and Howard and
Cooper and Brooks and Reed and Rogers and Richardson and Cole-
man and Morgan and Bailey and Cook and Watson and Wong and
Gray and Singh and Sanders and Henderson and Bell and Alexan-
der and Murphy and Ward and Jenkins and Perry and Butler and
Ross and Foster and Simmons and Powell and Kim and Barnes
and Jordan and Price and Bennett and Woods and Kelly and Rus-
sell and Patterson and Peterson and Bryant and Cox and Ford and
Hughes and Hamilton and Wallace and Hayes and Griffin and Long
and Owens and Wood and Gibson and West and Marshall and Gra-
ham and Hunter and Ellis and Dixon and Myers and Harrison and
Cole and Fisher and Reynolds and Freeman and Khan and Henry
and Daniels and Wells and Mason and Patel and Stevens and Craw-
ford and Tucker and Porter and Simpson and Murray and Hunt and
Holmes and Gordon and McDonald and Boyd and Hicks and Sul-
livan and Hawkins and Spencer and Shaw and Warren and Chang

and Ali and Payne and Webb and Franklin and Grant and Willis and
Kennedy and Palmer and Ferguson and Watkins and Robertson
and Black and Tran and Banks and Mills and Armstrong and Berry and
Matthews and Stephens and Perkins and Rose and Burns and Garcia
and Bradley and Duncan and Lawrence and Rice and Sims and Hud-
son and Knight and Stone and Greene and Andrews and Harper and
Gardner and Pierce and Nichols and Fields and Kelley and Lane and
Oliver and Cunningham and Fox and Austin and Riley and Chen
and Hart and Montgomery and Dunn and Ray and Douglas and
Elliott and McCoy and Weaver and George and Silva and Harvey
and Arnold and Chapman and Garrett and Carroll and Jacobs and
Lawson and Peters and Richards and Santos and Reid and Joseph
and Dean and Burton and Carr and Wheeler and Byrd and Carpen-
ter and Johnston and Morrison and Love and Neal and Fuller and
Wade and Lucas and Olson and Gilbert and Cruz and Martinez and
Snyder and Frazier and Shelton and Chin and Williamson and Lowe
and Miles and Holland and Fowler and Lopez and Wagner and Cald-
well and Pearson and Hopkins and Chambers and Bishop and Brewer
and Bowman and Le and Terry and Parks and Watts and Barnett and
Lynch and Ryan and Welch and Day and Meyer and Burke and
Vaughn and Little and Sutton and Hansen and Newman and Mc-
Gee and Jennings and Howell and Fleming and Graves and McKin-
ney and Rodriguez and Thornton and Logan and Barrett and Holt
and Davidson and Jefferson and May and Chan and Bates and
Reyes and Haynes and Horton and Hale and Ahmed and Fletcher
and Craig and Dawson and Stanley and Stevenson and Park and
Francis and Hampton and Cummings and Mack and Norris and
Hardy and Gregory and McDaniel and Bimont and Curry and Hail
and Saunders and Dennis and Tyler and Steele and Tate and Ly-
ons and Perez and Mann and Walton and Hoffman and Schmidt
and Cross and Chandler and Rhodes and Lindsey and Reeves and
Chung and Daniel and Larson and Hanson and Ramos and Blair
and Rodgers and Fernandez and Benson and Page and Barker and
Hernandez and Carlson and Lambert and Hines and Wang and Bar-
ber and Glover and Burgess and Webster and Moss and Jensen and

Leonard and Hubbard and Flowers and Baldwin and Cannon and Houston and Ho and Yang and Bowen and Harmon and Clarke and Ramsey and Blake and Shah and Garner and Warner and Flores and Malone and Townsend and Ingram and Beck and Simon and Gill and Roberson and Sharp and Burnett and Reese and Floyd and Pham and Norman and Manning. But no one remembers us, not the tourists, not the office workers, not the city planners, not the architects, not the politicians, not even our great-grandchildren remember who we were.*

Evelyn closed her notebook, turned it upside down, and on the last page, she wrote a sentence. Then another. And another. She wrote a page, two, three. Ina and Anastasia glanced at each other, but Evelyn didn't care, she kept writing, she wrote while Ina went to get more books, while Anastasia went out for a cigarette break, while Ina got even more books, while Anastasia sighed and whispered that it wasn't possible for Ina to read that quickly, she wrote as if she had never written before, but she didn't write a word about her ancestor or the construction of a skyscraper, but at least she wrote, words came out of her, and she was so thankful that she didn't stop to question what the words were saying until the tired security guards told them the library would soon close.

They returned to Fabricia's studio, and when Evelyn was sure her sisters had fallen asleep, she took out her notebook again and kept writing, she had no idea where the words were coming from, but they seemed to have been waiting for her, and when she finally fell asleep, it was four in the morning, and she knew that this was something, maybe it wasn't a monologue, maybe it was more of a letter, and it might be more about her than about a historical person who built a skyscraper, but it didn't matter, what was important was that something was coming out of her, and for the first time in her life, she felt close to something that resembled meaning.

---

* There is no documentation of the approximately forty thousand workers who built Rockefeller Center in its archives.

Chapter One Hundred Ten

On a sunny Saturday in 2013, all of Emma's friends gathered to commemorate one year since her passing. Emma's parents were bringing sparkling wine, since Emma loved bubbles, and I also brought wine, I spent twenty minutes at the liquor store contemplating whether to bring champagne or sparkling wine or maybe one of each, or some beer, or a Riesling and a Pinot Noir, in the end, I chose a bottle of sparkling wine with a nice label, paid for it, five minutes later I was back in the store, to exchange it for another bottle or perhaps two, I did this while holding my phone in hand, to show the cashier that I wasn't crazy, that I was just trying to fulfill some picky girlfriend's or absent-minded aunt's requests, I bought two other bottles, used the same bag, and headed to Emma's friend's apartment. I was a bit early so I circled the block a few times, to arrive ten minutes late.

The apartment was located in a beautiful old building on Ringvägen, the woman who lived there was a theater director who had adapted my first book for the stage ten years ago, in an interview she had said that I was "Sweden's Bill Cosby" because I had the ability to make immigrants beloved by a broad white audience, she tried to convince me that she had meant it as a compliment, I never forgave her. She opened the door with a forced smile.

You haven't been here before? she said.

No, I said, but I wondered if I hadn't been here years ago, at a housewarming party, with Emma and Shang . . .

The hallway floor was filled with shoes of various sizes, indicating that other guests had arrived, but the apartment was oddly quiet.

Come in, she said.

I handed her the bag with my bottles.

Thanks, she said. It really wasn't necessary. She looked at the labels and placed the bottles in a cupboard.

I took off my shoes and entered the apartment. To the right, I saw a minimalist kitchen with gray cabinet doors, looking newly renovated, she had expensive scented candles, grapes, crackers and cheese on a large metal tray with a handle, on the other side of the kitchen was a small balcony. Emma's parents were in the kitchen, setting out glasses and opening bottles, I hugged them both, her father had aged, her mother was her usual energetic self, remarking that I had grown, which was an ongoing joke between us because I had always been about twice as tall as her. I continued towards the living room on the left, passing a closed door that I assumed led to the bedroom. I couldn't help but think that this apartment had the exact same layout as Emma's last apartment on Åsögatan, the kitchen to the right, the living room to the left, and the bedroom in the corner, even the balcony was on the same side.

Everyone was already there, even though I was only ten minutes late. Emma's older sister, her old friends from high school, her new friends from work in theaters and burlesque clubs, I hugged the people I knew and nodded to those I vaguely recognized, the sofa was full, so I sat on the floor beside it, everything was eerily silent, no one seemed to know how to behave, should we talk as usual, or should we talk only about Emma, or should we avoid talking about her altogether, nobody knew, and everyone remained quiet.

Sitting next to me, but on the sofa, was a girl with short hair, I knew she worked at the National Library, we had seen each other over the years but had never really spoken, now we had the chance, I could ask her if it was true that she had been eating the same thing for lunch for more than a year, trying to simplify her life, we could have talked about books, libraries or how I too had gone through periods of eating the exact same thing for months, but instead I just sat there, blinking.

Chapter One Hundred Eleven

When they woke up on the fourth day, it was sunny, and Ina suggested they go to Coney Island. They took the subway and arrived just before lunchtime. The amusement park was closed, the boardwalk deserted and the beach empty except for a few enthusiastic dog owners. It was their last full day, and Ina asked Evelyn if she wanted to show them what she had written so far.

I have absolutely nothing, Evelyn said.

Of course you do, Anastasia said. You have the flight here, the pirate on the subway, the fruit in Chinatown, the woman on the Staten Island Ferry, the mating dogs in Battery Park, our visit to Rockefeller Center. You have everything you wrote yesterday at the library and last night when you thought I was asleep. Tell us what you have, and we can help you move forward.

Evelyn reluctantly stood in front of them on the beach, the wind blew through her hair, her feet sank into the sand, which was warm on top and cool below. She cleared her throat and began speaking, but it was not a monologue about the construction of Rockefeller Center or their great-grandfather's story. Instead, it was a letter addressed to her sisters.

My dear sisters, she said without looking down at her notebook.

My dear sisters, she repeated, the notebook lying open in the sand, but she didn't pay attention to the words, the pages fluttered in the wind, Evelyn gathered strength, she bent forward as if she would vomit, she made strange sounds, then she looked up and said:

I hate you, I hate everything about you, absolutely everything, I hate how your appearance reminds me of my own aging body, how your voices sound like Mom's, how your career ambitions make me feel like a failure, how every good thing that happens to you makes me jealous, I hate your children (Ina gasped), I hate that you work in advertising (Anastasia smiled), I hate that you're always there for me, I hate that we always have each other, I hate our shared history, I hate our dead parents, I hate that you're all I have, making it impossible for me to let you go and disappear, I hate Simon and Hector and Åhdal, I hate Stockholm, New York, and Borås. I, I, I . . . Evelyn searched for words, glancing down at her notebook, the wind intensified, making it harder to hear her words (Borås, Ina thought, have you even been to Borås? What's wrong with Borås now? It's a nice little town, they have their textile high school and their city park and that debut prize for new authors, why out of all the small towns must you . . . but she didn't get to think further because Evelyn was on a roll again), now she didn't just hate Borås, she hated the whole world, she hated this beach, she hated her classmates, she hated zucchini, she hated her teachers, her friends, she hated that stupid curse, she hated the false hope that she was something other than her past, she hated that this text became nothing but a long list of things she hated, and she desperately wanted it to be something else, something with a beginning, a middle and an end, she hated phone plans and cats, fashion and theater, herself, her body, her hate, her rage, her impatience, her inability to finish things, her fear of connecting with the world, her feeling of constant emptiness, her fake self, her inability to live close to other people, she hated her voice, her knees, her shoulders, but most of all, she hated her smile, that fake ingratiating grin that had given her so many advantages in life, the impulse to face the world with a polished exterior, her fucking face that she had dragged around for so many years and that never seemed to want to . . .

Evelyn fell silent, she leaned forward and scooped up a handful of sand, rubbing it on her face, when she looked up again, she had red streaks on her cheeks, Ina wondered if this was part of the monologue, Anastasia listened and nodded, Ina wondered if Evelyn had lost it,

Anastasia thought it was fantastic, even though the wind stole more and more of Evelyn's lines, tossing them out over the sea, Anastasia was convinced that this was the monologue that Evelyn had to perform at school, it was the truest, most unsettling version of Evelyn she had ever presented to the world, she had never allowed herself to appear uglier than this, and there were muscles in her sandy face that had never relaxed before, but now she let go, she just stood there muttering and screaming alternately and when a passing jogger approached to check if everything was okay, Evelyn started talking to him as if he were Simon, she spoke to him in Swedish, explaining why she had to leave him, it wasn't because he thought she was cheating on him, which she was, it wasn't because he tried to get her to sign up for a phone plan, which she refused to do, it wasn't because he insisted on getting a cat, which was just a precursor to having children, it wasn't because he insulted her friends, which he did by giving them strange compliments, it wasn't because he felt threatened by her sisters, which he did, it wasn't because he had replied, "Why do I have to choose?" that time when she asked if he loved her more than his career, no, she had to leave him because every time they argued and he called her a whore, a traitor, fake, disgusting, every time he promised to be a little more gentle, not to slap her during sex, not to grip so tightly, every time he apologized after they had had sex and he had hit her, choked her, pulled her hair, whispering insults in her ear, she realized there was something in his aggressiveness, something in his pent-up anger that drew her to him, and that was why she had to leave him, not because he treated her badly, but because she realized the only way she could accept staying was if he treated her worse, and . . .

The jogger had disappeared. Evelyn turned away from her sisters and addressed the sea as if it were their mother, the wind stole even more lines, Anastasia and Ina could only catch a word here and there, Evelyn seemed to be yelling curses and insults at their deceased mother, and when words weren't enough, she screamed straight out at the horizon, she screamed until her voice gave out, screamed until she couldn't scream anymore, and then she screamed a little more,

Ina was moving towards her but Anastasia held her back, Evelyn screamed and screamed and screamed, and then she took two steps sideways and collapsed at the edge of the sand, but she never truly fell because her sisters rushed up and caught her, embracing her, Ina from the front, Anastasia from behind, and for several minutes they just stood there, holding her while the waves came and went, came and went.

I'm so sorry, Ina said.

That was incredible, Anastasia said.

A few days later, when Ina had returned home, unpacked her suitcase and the children had revealed how much screen time they had had, when Hector had spent more time explaining how incredibly difficult it had been to be alone with the kids than Ina had spent recounting the trip, she told Hector that even then, as they left the beach and headed for the subway, past the closed amusement park, along the deserted streets, she had a feeling that Evelyn wouldn't be coming back home with them.

Chapter One Hundred Twelve

The director who lived in the apartment came from the kitchen with a tray full of sparkling wineglasses. Most of us declined a glass, perhaps because it was only two in the afternoon, maybe because it felt awkward to have a glass of sparkling wine when Emma's parents entered the room. But it was their idea that we should drink bubbles, and they came into the living room with their own glasses. If Emma saw us now, she probably wouldn't want us sitting here and drinking tea, right? Of course not. So, more and more people reached for a glass, and we refilled our glasses, and sometimes someone broke down and started sobbing, and the person next to them leaned forward to offer a hug, I held it together, on some level I suspected her friends thought everything was my fault, just like I thought everything was their fault, where the hell were they when Emma decided not to go on living, and why the hell hadn't they gone over to check on her (and more important: Why hadn't I?).

After half an hour of uncomfortable silence, someone rang the doorbell, the ringing was way too energetic, too many rings, it had to be, yes, of course, Achilles entered the room, wearing baggy shorts, an oversized turquoise basketball jersey and a brand-new Miami Dolphins cap. He dressed like a rapper but had the energy of a cheerleader.

Darlings! he shouted and started walking around the room, cheek-kissing even people he didn't know, his legs straight like a ballet dancer's, his back straight as he leaned forward.

Let's get this party started!

I assumed that Jesper and his boyfriend would dislike Achilles just because he wore too much perfume, spoke too much English and was too much of a walking cliché, apart from his clothes. But they smiled and kissed him back.

Are all these for me? Achilles said and downed one glass of sparkling wine, and took a second glass with his other hand.

Who wants the pleasure of giving me tonight's first cigarette? he said, even though it was still afternoon, and more than three people quickly got up from the sofa to go to the balcony and smoke.

I stayed in the living room, at least for the first hour. I talked to Emma's dad about the housing market in Stockholm, and I talked to Emma's sister about the similarities between her daughter and Emma, then I also took turns going out to the balcony.

In the kitchen, the director was opening more bottles. She asked if I had any new plays in the works, and she told me that she had directed four plays at the Royal Dramatic Theatre and had just been invited to do something "on the Main," which for those in the know meant her next play would be on the Royal Dramatic Theatre's main stage.

Who will be in it? I asked.

She listed some names from the Royal Dramatic Theatre's ensemble.

Sounds great, I said.

I know, she said. But I wonder if it's not a bit too . . . predictable. There's a new girl graduating from Nama this spring. Evelyn . . . something . . . Evelyn . . . Evelyn . . . It's not a . . .

She took out her phone and showed a photo of Evelyn.

Mikkola, I said.

Mikkola, she said. Exactly. Evelyn Mikkola. Look. She's incredible. Do you know her?

A long time ago, I said, leaning forward to see the photo. It was a typical black-and-white actor headshot, very serious, very intense, the kind of photo that makes you want to lean into the picture and tickle the person sitting on the stool, trying to look deep. The kind of photo that makes you want to crack a fart joke just to see a bit of life seep into the picture. Evelyn looked older than I had imagined.

I'll watch her monologue next week, the director said.

On the tiny, overcrowded balcony, Achilles talked about a guy he had met and had sex with in Jordan. He talked about the challenge of giving a blow job when you have a cold.

The secret is to take small breaths, he said. Otherwise, you'll suffocate.

This was particularly difficult for Achilles because he was allergic to birch, so his blow job capacity diminished every spring, but in the fall, my God, he sucked cock left and right, there should be awards, no, streets, no, parks named after him, considering how many cocks he had sucked.

I looked through the glass door of the balcony. Jesper and his boyfriend were about to go out to smoke on the balcony but turned back when they heard Achilles's voice.

An hour later, Emma's parents came to say goodbye, they thanked everyone for this opportunity to mourn Emma, we thanked them, thanks for the invitation, for the sparkling wine, let's meet up soon, maybe at the gravesite, maybe somewhere else, yes, let's do it. We waved from the balcony and Achilles sat down on the librarian's lap. He was silent for a few minutes. She held him. He continued wiping his cheeks while looking at the clouds.

She was so afraid of looking stupid, he said. And then she goes and does this, which is the stupidest thing a person can do.

No one answered. The librarian offered him a cigarette, and the director came out on the balcony with a bottle to refill our glasses. We had only eaten grapes and crackers, and now we were too drunk to keep track of our phones. Achilles held out his glass, asking her to fill it to the brim. Then he sighed and said that the biggest problem with fucking someone in the ass with a dildo was that fingers and dicks have completely different textures and . . .

Ten meters away, there was another balcony where an old man had just settled down with a cup of coffee and a newspaper. He looked

at Achilles and cleared his throat. He looked as if he hoped our balcony would detach and fall into hell. Achilles waved and smiled and
shouted:

Sorry, there's a ring on this finger, pointing to his middle finger
(where there was no ring).

A few weeks later, I passed by the drama school to see the graduating class's monologues. I convinced myself I was there for work
reasons, I had written some plays, and it was good for me to keep an
eye on the new generation of actors. But truthfully, I was only there
to see Evelyn. In the program, it said that Evelyn's monologue had
been "canceled due to illness."

Chapter One Hundred Thirteen

Thank you. I love you. See you at the airport.

It was Evelyn's handwriting. She had written it on the back of one of the receipts from the bookstore. Her suitcase was missing, including the toiletry bag that had been in the bathroom, in which Anastasia had accidentally left the wristwatch she had found in her mother's basement.

Anastasia turned the receipt over and upside down, trying to find new words, new clues about where Evelyn had gone. Maybe she just wanted to see Rockefeller Center one more time, maybe this was some sort of practical joke that Ina was in on? But if Ina was in on it, she played her part well because when Anastasia woke her up and told her that Evelyn was missing, she continued to smile as if she couldn't be fooled. It was only when Anastasia swore on their mother's gravestone that she didn't know where Evelyn was that Ina started to worry.

We have two hours before we need to go to the airport, Ina said. But Anastasia knew that if Evelyn had been here, Ina would have already ordered a taxi, and because this was New York time, two hours disappeared in an instant.

Anastasia and Ina took a silent taxi to the airport. Anastasia looked at her empty left wrist, she missed the watch more than expected. She had paid for all the taxi rides so far, and now it was Ina's turn. Ina paid and Anastasia noticed that for once, she didn't ask for a receipt. Instead, she walked straight to the check-in counter to ask if their sister had checked in or if she had changed her ticket. The lady behind the counter said that for privacy reasons, they couldn't answer questions about other passengers.

This is my sister we're talking about, Ina said, looking like she was seconds away from imploding. My sister!

The woman behind the counter apologized and returned to her computer screen. For a few seconds, Anastasia thought she would help them, but then she looked up at the line and waved the next group of passengers forward.

This is all your fault, Ina said as they went through security and continued towards the gate.

How can it be my fault? Anastasia asked.

If it weren't for you, Evelyn would be home now, getting ready to finish her monologue.

First of all. No. Second of all: How would that be better?

Anastasia still believed that Evelyn would make it in time, when everyone had taken their seats and the flight attendant announced that they were waiting for one last passenger, one last, with her well-manicured finger pointing at the airplane ceiling, then, right then, exactly when they were about to close the gate, she would come running, Evelyn, sweaty and smiling, ready to return to Stockholm.

She won't come, Ina said.

How do you know? Anastasia asked.

I just know, Ina said.

The flight attendants closed the door, turning the large white handle that looked like it belonged on a bank vault. The plane began to taxi, and Anastasia still believed that Evelyn would make it. She would find a way to stop the takeoff, she would charm someone in the airport staff to drive her out to the runway in one of those strange little stair cars. But the plane reached the runway, the flight attendants buckled up, the engines roared and the plane took off without Evelyn.

Chapter One Hundred Fourteen

Later that autumn, I heard that Evelyn had gone to New York with her sisters and never returned. She never finished her monologue, she never graduated from drama school. What was she doing in New York? No one seemed to know. A rumor said she had paid an American to marry her and get her a green card, which was absurd because Evelyn was far too beautiful to need to pay someone. Another rumor said Evelyn was in Hollywood, trying to get a film agent, which also felt strange because if she really wanted to be an actress, wouldn't it have been more logical to come home and finish her education in Stockholm? Someone claimed that Evelyn had come back to Stockholm but was here incognito, ashamed of the unfinished diploma, avoiding her sisters, living in Rågsved in a sublet and applying to some university programs. But before she received any replies, she moved to London of all places, as the person who made this claim knew someone who had seen her folding merino sweaters in a clothing store on Poland Street a few months ago.

It would be eight years before we saw each other again.

BOOK 5

2020 (One Week)

Chapter One Hundred Fifteen

The first time Ina understood that her friends were really her friends was during a long hike in the forests outside Ödeshög in autumn 2020. Ina was forty-five years old and had never been walking in the woods, at least not like this, with a large backpack and special waterproof shoes.

They had spent three weeks texting back and forth to find a suitable date, what about August, or early September, or mid-October, but there was always something that made it impossible. Saskia's daughter had a piano performance, Laura's husband's family came over from Spain, Saskia's husband had an "important work thing," and sometimes Ina wondered if her two best and oldest friends noticed that she was the one in the trio who was always available. She always said yes, of course, she had a life too, she had job deadlines, soccer tournaments and birthday parties, her husband also had "important work things" he needed to be present for, maybe not the same kind of work things as Saskia's and Laura's husbands, but still. While their husbands traveled abroad to conferences, located at hotels with spas, her husband spent his weekends at book fairs held at bars in Södermalm, while their husbands gave presentations livestreamed to conference rooms in Asia, her husband sat behind a rickety table with piles of unsold publications in front of him, while their husbands talked to CEOs and politicians, Hector talked to strange men in trench coats who sneaked up to his table to admit that they really liked the latest collection of feminist rape porn.

Ina had seen these men before, they always looked both ashamed and excited that they liked the books Hector published, and even though she had never been to any of their homes, she knew they lived alone, she knew they had a large collection of World War II memorabilia, she knew they talked to their moms every day, and sometimes Ina noticed doubt in Hector's gaze. For him, the publication of all these obscure books was part of something bigger, he wanted to challenge the publishing world's status quo, he wanted to publish books that no one else would publish, but sometimes she saw that he doubted what he had wasted his savings on, was it really worth it, to take all the money and invest it in publishing texts that only a certain part of the male population seemed to like? She wasn't sure, and neither was he, but he continued to throw his money into the bottomless pit that was the publishing house, and the strange thing was that sometimes, very rarely, but every fifth year or so, Hector published a book that became a commercial success, usually prompted by an angry piece in a culture magazine questioning why a contemporary publishing house even bothered to publish such provocative nonsense, and every time they made a profit, Hector immediately decided to spend the money on four books of Greek drama with leather covers, in a font so small that the plays were almost unreadable, and the price was so high that even libraries refused to buy them. Ina wasn't sure what was going on, why Hector reacted as if all the money he earned was contaminated and had to be spent quickly, and she felt that she needed her friends now more than ever.

Finally, they found a date, it was late autumn 2020, but hopefully, it wouldn't rain, and if it did, Saskia had "tarps" for everyone.

What's a tarp? Ina asked in their group chat.

A type of rain cover, Laura said. We can use them over the hammocks.

Saskia liked Laura's comment, and Ina hearted it, wondering within herself when they had learned all this, how old were they when their parents took them out into the woods and taught them that this is a tarp, and this is a tent, and this is a knife, and that's a gas-powered stove, and this is a compass, and those are eagles, and those are geese, and if we just go north and then east, we'll arrive at our base camp before the sun sets.

   As the weekend approached, Laura listed everything they should bring in the chat: lighters, sleeping bags, extra socks, food, wine, beer and liquor. Saskia added even more things, things Ina barely knew what they were, "sporks" and fire starters and water purification filters. In the chat, Ina asked if she could wear regular sneakers (better to have waterproof shoes), did she need a sleeping bag (no, but bring extra pants and a warm sweater because the hammocks can get quite cold in the early morning) and how the hell were they going to carry all this (no worries, Saskia replied, we can take turns, Laura said).

   While Ina was in the kitchen preparing her backpack, a regular backpack, not one of those hiking backpacks with special pockets for flashlights and double water bottles, Hector asked her if she was sure about this.

   What do you mean? Ina said.

   Don't you remember last time? Hector said.

   That was a long time ago, Ina said.

   And it was, it must have been five years since all three of them met, it was on Gotland, Saskia had driven up from Malmö and Laura had driven down from Stockholm, first a pleasant and not too quiet car ride down to Nynäshamn, Laura drove and Ina sat beside her, then the big ferry down to Visby, Saskia was waiting for them at the harbor, and they hugged one another and bought way too much alcohol, loading it into the already full trunk of the car before driving up to the plot of land Laura and her husband had bought a few years earlier.

   Wow, this is amazing, Ina said when they drove onto the uncut grass and she saw the square of forest. No sea view, far from the nearest town, no real house, just an old toolshed they had left there to have somewhere to sleep while they planned where to build their house. Saskia lit a fire outside, and Laura unlocked the door to the shed, and Ina just stood there in the twilight, wondering where or when she would find a place where she would feel as much at home as Laura seemed to be here. They drank, they ate chili Laura had prepared at home, they toasted to their fortieth birthdays. When night fell, they heard a scream, someone was drowning, someone was being attacked by a racist rapist.

No, Laura explained, that's just a bird. It sounds like that. It lives down by the water.

Are you really sure it's a bird? Ina said, but she heard her mouth say something more like: Are you completely freaking stupid? If that's a bird, then I'm a cat, because there's no chance in hell that sound could have been made by something with a beak.

Laura and Saskia looked at each other.

Just wait, Laura said, it will scream again.

It was silent, and Ina noticed Saskia wasn't the least bit worried, or was she? No, she wasn't, she just sat there by the fire, while Laura lit another cigarette and teased Ina for going to get the axe, just in case. Ten minutes later, the bird screamed again, and again, but Ina still wasn't convinced, not even when Laura brought out her phone and showed her a video of the bird, which did have a similar scream, did Ina let go of the axe. The person out there in the dark, the one who obviously liked to torture people so they sounded like birds, if he made his way all the way to their shed, she wouldn't give up without a fight, not her, never. Then she had five more glasses of wine and ate a bit more chili and forgot about the bird, or the rapist, until they were about to sleep, when she asked Laura to double-check the lock on the toolshed and then opened the door herself to sneak out and get the axe, just in case.

The next day, Saskia and Laura could have made fun of her, but they didn't, and she was grateful for that, they didn't pretend as if they got scared every time they saw a sparrow, instead they had breakfast and tried to cure their headache with coffee and painkillers, and then they went to an abandoned peninsula with an old limestone quarry.

It's the low season now, Laura said, looking out over the empty landscape. It doesn't get more beautiful than this.

Ina tried to look at the scenery with Laura's loving eyes, but she couldn't, all she saw was wind, limestone and gravel, and she longed to go back to the city. As they walked back to the car, Ina asked them about the future, what they hoped to achieve in the next five years.

Laura said she just wanted to be happy. And get better at karate. It would be fantastic to have a black belt before fifty, she said, looking out over the violent sea.

And you, Saskia? Ina said.

I'm still dreaming of releasing an album, Saskia said.

Laura laughed. Saskia looked at her, and Laura stopped laughing and focused on removing something from her left eye.

What?

Nothing.

What's so funny?

No, I just thought, sorry, I thought you were joking.

Why would I joke?

I don't know, Laura said, looking like she was about to start hyperventilating. Sorry, I don't know why I laughed, it's just that it's been so long since you talked about making music, so I thought you had said goodbye to that dream, I just, I don't know, sorry, are we okay, are you mad, or?

Saskia smiled.

Of course not.

Ina wondered how it was possible for Laura to spend her workdays negotiating contracts with subcontractors and arguing with labor unions when she seemed so terribly afraid of her closest friends' anger. Or maybe it was only Saskia's anger that Laura feared. When they got back in the warmth of the car, with Saskia in the front seat and Ina squeezed in the back, she asked them if they weren't curious about her five-year plan.

Of course, they both said but added that it wasn't hard to guess, and as the peninsula disappeared into a cloud of dust, Saskia said that Ina probably wanted Hector to close down his publishing house and get a real job (Ina nodded), and she probably wanted Primo to do well in his new school (Ina nodded), and she probably wanted Evelyn to come back from New York (Ina nodded), and . . . Ina smiled and nodded, astonished that her friends knew so much about her hopes for the future, even though she hardly talked about them, and it wasn't until later, lying awake in the toolshed and listening for the bird's screams, that she realized all their ideas about her future dreams were connected to other people, and none were about her.

Now, five years later, during a pandemic that had struck the world, they were meeting again to hike a trail, one night at a hotel and then one night in the woods, sleeping in those high-tech hammocks that Saskia had praised for years.

It's like sleeping in a tent, she said, but a thousand times more comfortable and completely insect-free.

Saskia had bought the hammocks on the company card when they were doing some kind of team-building exercise at work, and she had used the equipment when camping with her family and during a weekend in the woods with her friends from Malmö, and now the equipment was in the trunk of her jeep, heading north from Malmö, while Laura and Ina were driving south from Stockholm. Laura brought the stove she had received from Saskia as a birthday present, and Saskia brought the green pocketknife that was a gift from Laura, and in the car heading south, Ina wondered when they gave each other birthday presents and why they never gave her any. The night before, she had woken up Hector and told him she really didn't want to go, she didn't want to feel left out again, there was something about Saskia and Laura that always made her feel like she was almost included, almost part of them. Hector didn't sigh, he just held her and comforted her and convinced her everything would be fine.

If you don't go now, you'll regret it, he said, stroking her back with his fingertips. I'll hold down the fort. You really need a break. I'll take care of the kids. Go.

The next day, Laura picked her up in her station wagon, the back seat had clean squares where the child seats had been and the trunk was full of dog hair. After a few hours' drive, Laura and Ina arrived at the hotel in Ödeshög. Ina could hardly believe her eyes when they left the motorway and followed the small road towards the towering dark forest.

I've actually been here, she yelled. Once, like, twenty years ago, Hector and I had just started dating, we drove to his mom's summer place on the west coast, we tried to find something to eat, so we left the motorway and ended up here, at this hotel, we parked outside and knocked on the door, it was closed for renovations!

Laura looked at her and smiled.

What a strange coincidence, she said. Ina wasn't sure why the sight of the hotel made her so happy, and she wasn't sure why Laura's reaction made her feel guilty, as if there was something wrong with her happiness, or as if Laura thought she was spoiling their special moment with this story from the past, but there was nothing special to spoil, they were just two friends checking in to a hotel, in the middle of nowhere, to spend two nights in the woods.

Chapter One Hundred Sixteen

On February 10, 2020, I received an email from Salvatore Scibona, the head of the Cullman Center in New York. I saw the email just before going to bed, around midnight. My children were asleep in their bunk bed, Diane had just turned off her lamp. Scibona wrote that he had tried to call me, but the number seemed to be out of service. I immediately noticed that a digit was missing from the phone number. The previous autumn, I had applied for a fellowship to write a book at the New York Public Library. I didn't have high hopes of getting it, since I had applied twice before, the first time, I received a response encouraging me to reapply, the second time, I received a standard rejection. In my third application, I claimed that I wanted to write a book about three sisters whose great-grandfather was involved in building Rockefeller Center. I wrote that I needed to come to New York to research the book, and I asked my references to resend their recommendation letters. Now, half a year later, the head of the fellowship had sent an email. I assumed that he wanted me to provide some additional information or was going to explain why I didn't get it this time either. My first impulse was not to call back, it was more comfortable not knowing than knowing.

Diane turned on her lamp and looked at me as if I were crazy.

Call him now, she said. I sneaked into the kitchen and made the call. He told me that I had received the fellowship. In September 2020, we would move to New York. For the family to get visas and come along, Diane and I needed to get married. To find housing, we needed to use our own contacts. To accept the fellowship, I needed to respond within twenty-four hours. After hanging up, Diane and I spent three minutes jumping in the kitchen. Then we forced ourselves to drink rosé bubbles and eat chocolate, even though we had brushed our teeth. We made plans for the future, trying to grasp that what we had talked about and dreamed about since we met was about to happen. We would get to live in New York. Diane, who had no family in Sweden, would be closer to her brother. The children would learn English, and I would finally write that novel about three sisters and Rockefeller Center, the one I, according to my application, had dreamed of writing my whole life.

When I tried to sleep in the dawn of February 11, 2020, I thought about Evelyn and wondered if she was still in the USA. I wondered what she would think of me borrowing inspiration from their lives to get money for a book project. I convinced myself that the application was one thing, and the actual book was something else. Once I got to New York, I would be free to write whatever I wanted, and I wasn't obligated to write a single word about the sisters or Rockefeller Center if I didn't want to.

In the following weeks, we express-planned our wedding. We visited venues and compared menus, booked a bus service and made guest lists. We set up a wedding website and invited friends and family to save the date: May 25, 2020. We weren't worried about that strange virus in China. We joked about it with our guests who were flying in from Buenos Aires, New York, Toulon, Douzains, haha, make sure to wear your face masks. By the end of February, we started to worry, my doctor brother advised us to start storing supplies, buy toilet paper and medications, be ready for a lockdown, we didn't take it seriously, in early March, Diane's father said, As long as they don't close the borders, we'll come up in May, closed borders within the EU was an unthinkable idea, a few days later, the borders closed, we canceled the wedding, we got married at City Hall on March 21, 2020, during peak pandemic, the only attendees were Diane, me, and the children, an administrator acted as a wedding witness and wedding photographer, on our way there, we listened to Frank Ocean, on our way back, we picked up takeout, now we were married, and we still hoped that we would make it to New York, everything else was canceled, all plays, all lectures, all sources of income, but the New York Public Library was still there, and everything depended on us making it there in September 2020.

Soon we realized it was impossible. The embassy didn't issue visas, and the libraries in New York were closed to the public, though we still hoped we could postpone the fellowship for the following year. In the fall of 2020, the same autumn when Ina went camping with her friends near Ödeshög, I began trying to find Evelyn in the USA. In an attempt to cope with the grief and anger of not being able to go, I reached out to acquaintances in North America, fellow writers I had met at some festival, friends of friends, and asked them if they had come across a Swedish woman named Evelyn. If our email conversations had been phone calls, they might have gone something like this:

Them: Evelyn?

Me: Yes.

Them: Evelyn what?

Me: Evelyn Mikkola, but she might have gotten married and changed her last name.

Them: And she is . . . ?

Me: A childhood friend, sort of.

Them: Swedish?

Me: Yes. Or Swedish in the same way I'm Swedish. She has been in the USA since the spring of 2013, and I'm just curious if you might have come across her by any chance.

Them: You're aware that the USA has about 330 million inhabitants?

Me: I know.

Them: So the odds of me running into her here in [Seattle, Austin, Vancouver, Boston, Wyoming, New York, Queens, Greenpoint, Delaware, Venice Beach] are . . . quite small, to say the least.

Me: But if you happen to run into her, could you say hi from me? And ask her to get in touch?

Them: Uh, okay.

No one seemed to have heard of anyone named Evelyn. No one bumped into her in a conference room, no one saw her appear as an extra in a low-budget indie film and no one attended a wedding where they heard, "Oh, this is Evelyn, our wedding planner." If someone had asked why I was so focused on the sister who had disappeared and didn't care as much about Ina, who apparently lived with her children in Bagarmossen, or Anastasia, who apparently had "cashed out" and lived in an attic apartment in Södermalm, I don't know what I would have answered. Perhaps my nightly searches with terms like "Evelyn Mikkola New York actress" were just a sign of me trying to avoid the real pain of losing contact with my real half sister. Or maybe there was something about Evelyn that reminded me of Emma, and now both were missing, but one could possibly be saved. I didn't know then, and I don't know now, but during the fall, I continued searching for Evelyn, amazed that she had managed to disappear, how can a person erase themselves from the internet, it was a mystery to me, she must have changed her name, she must have moved to a place where they use a different alphabet, she must be dead.

Chapter One Hundred Seventeen

Saskia was late, really late, she had been called to an unexpectedly late Friday meeting, and Laura and Ina were having their pre-dinner drinks alone in their shared room, dark green wallpaper, golden lamps, and walls so thin that they could hear other guests passing by in the corridor. Ina had brought a bottle of champagne to celebrate her recent birthday, but it felt wrong to open it without Saskia there, so instead she and Laura sat on the balcony, looking out over the dark fog rolling in over the black lake while taking small sips of whiskey from the pocket flask that Laura had brought.

It was never quiet, of course not, they were friends, after all. Their mouths uttered vowels and consonants, their ears registered the sounds and their brains transformed the tonalities into words and sentences, but in the short pauses that occurred from time to time, Ina wondered if what they were engaged in could truly be called a conversation. Instead of getting to know each other better, they filled the potentially uncomfortable silence with factual information, and it wasn't Laura's fault, really not—it was Ina who asked about the cost of laying the foundation for Laura's house on Gotland, the materials they used, and how the gradings worked in different karate organizations, it was Ina who didn't come close to saying anything that could create a bad atmosphere, like, for example:

"Why do we meet so rarely in Stockholm, even though we live so close to each other? Why do we always have to have Saskia with us as a reason to meet? Why do you and Saskia plan family vacations without asking if we want to join? Yes, I know your kids are closer in age and play better together, and yes, you both grew up in similar suburbs, and your parents have similar backgrounds, but sometimes I wonder if the biggest difference between you and me is that you and Saskia are pink, and I am brown, and sometimes I wonder if you will ever understand what it was like to grow up in this fucking cunt country as a person with brown skin—you'll never grasp the struggle to fit in, the struggle to do the right thing, the struggle to stand out—the constant balancing act between being yourself and being someone else, between being authentic and being fake—and every time I accidentally say something that reminds you both that we're not the same, that there's something fundamentally different about our backgrounds, you look at each other as if I'm crazy, and who knows, maybe you're right, maybe I'm going crazy after forty-five years here, I don't even know what's racist anymore, was it racist when the lady at the pharmacy the other day asked me if I wanted something for my skin, or was it racist when Primo's teacher asked us what language we spoke at home, was it just routine when the police stopped Hector to check his driver's license? I don't even know anymore, last summer when Pikko and Saga were climbing a tree on the west coast, an old man with a cane passed by and said with a sly grin, 'I didn't know we had monkeys in these woods,' and I got furious, but Hector tried to make me understand, over and over again, that the old man didn't mean anything by it, that he would have said the exact same thing to blond kids climbing trees, but I don't know, would he have said that? I guess so, but I can't share stuff like this with you because whenever I try to tell you things that remind you we're different, that there's something different about our backgrounds, you look at each other as if I'm making shit up, as if I'm overly paranoid, and maybe I am, maybe I'm turning into Mom, maybe that's how it starts, but I still think we should be able to talk about it too, because we've been friends for over thirty years, and I love you both, and I want us to be friends until we die, and I'm not like Evelyn, I can't just move to a new city and start over, I am me, and I can't believe we're *still* sitting here on a balcony outside Ödeshög, and instead of talking about what we should be talking about now, we've spent thirty fucking minutes talking about the differences among various international karate organizations!"

Saskia texted that there was an accident near Ljungby, and she would be here soon, but she'd be late for dinner. Ina noticed Laura's nervousness, their table was booked for half past six, and they planned to have a three-course dinner, sleep well and then venture out into the wilderness early the next day, but now Saskia wasn't here, and someone needed to go down to the restaurant to let them know. Ina left the room and took the creaking stairs down to the reception, she spoke to the kind lady in charge, no problem at all, they could come half an hour later, and if their friend hadn't arrived by then, she could have larger portions of the later courses. Ina thanked her and went back to Laura to explain the situation.

They weren't angry? Laura said.

Of course not, Ina said. Why would they get angry?

I just had a feeling they might get angry, Laura said, taking another sip from the pocket flask.

At seven o'clock, they changed clothes and headed down to the restaurant. Saskia hadn't arrived yet, and Ina felt a growing irritation. The whole point of the weekend was to spend time together as a trio, and here she was having dinner with Laura, who was more Saskia's friend than hers. Ina hesitated when the waitress asked about the wine—separate glasses or the wine package? She chose separate glasses because she couldn't see the price of the wine package in the menu, Laura chose the wine package, and Ina couldn't stop thinking that she had made a mistake, she should have taken the wine package, why didn't she choose the wine package, she knew Saskia would take the wine package, and then Saskia and Laura would be the wine package gang, and she would be the lonely single glass person, just like last time. They had just finished the appetizer when the restaurant's ceiling was lit up by a car driving up the hill and parking outside. Saskia came into the lobby with her distinct perfume scent and a backpack big enough to fit a grand piano.

Sorry! she called out when she saw them. I'm terribly sorry, what have I missed?

Nothing, Laura said, pulling out the chair next to her. The waitress welcomed her and asked if she wanted separate glasses or the wine package.

What did you choose? Saskia said.

Wine package, Laura said.

Separate glasses, Ina said.

I'll have the wine package, please, Saskia said, taking the chair next to Laura.

Chapter One Hundred Eighteen

Evelyn was not dead, she was very much alive, for the first three months of her absence, Anastasia did her utmost to persuade her to come home, she threatened her, saying that if she stayed longer than three months, she would never be allowed back into the USA, and if Evelyn returned home, she could always go back later. She promised that if Evelyn came home, she, Anastasia, would write the monologue, and all Evelyn would need to do would be to go onstage and recite Anastasia's words, but Evelyn refused, she said she was happier in New York than back home, she lived cheaply in Queens and worked for tips and cash at a nearby café.

When Anastasia gave up, Ina took over, during the first year, she tried to entice Evelyn to come home by calling her in the spring (always from her work number), she told her that the lilacs would soon bloom, she opened the window of her office so that Evelyn could hear the chirping of willow warblers and chaffinches. As Midsummer approached, she called again, telling Evelyn they would dance around the Maypole on the west coast, Anastasia and Åhdal would come down, everyone would be together and Anastasia was pregnant (she didn't mention that Primo would probably have a tantrum and Hector would likely drink too much and get too affectionate with the neighbors' teenage sons). As Christmas approached, Ina sent pictures from her children's Lucia celebrations, saffron buns and gingerbread cookies, a blurry procession of children dressed in white nightshirts, girls with battery-powered light-up crowns in their hair, boys with cone-shaped paper hats (Evelyn replied: *Is that a KKK rally?* And Ina didn't respond for several months, she didn't mention that Anastasia had suffered yet another miscarriage).

When the emotional approach didn't work, Ina tried facts. After a few years, Evelyn started receiving links to articles and PDFs, all suggesting that the days of the USA as an empire were numbered, its impending downfall was inevitable, a society without social security would soon implode, the human cost was too great, all this wealth, yet life expectancy was declining, the American dream was a nightmare, the working class was dying from drugs and poverty, the middle class was a house of cards. There were many things Evelyn agreed with, but what Ina never understood and probably never would was that there was a difference between theory and practice, some things were not measurable, Evelyn stopped skimming the articles, she never downloaded the economic dissertations, she was preoccupied with survival, and perhaps it wasn't logical that she felt at home here, with all her friends and family far away, but she did, she knew she could breathe here, be herself, blend into the streets, think more freely, be happier, and not even Ina could change that.

After five years, Ina seemed to give up and accept that Evelyn wouldn't come back. When she stopped trying to persuade Evelyn to return, they managed to stay in touch despite their lives becoming increasingly different, Ina had two—soon three—teenage children, and a husband who seemed to be aging backward, Evelyn had two cats named Chloé and Morris, Ina lived in a yellow town house in Bagarmossen, Evelyn moved around, a minuscule studio in Flatbush, a shared two-bedroom in Flushing, fourteen months ago, she moved in here, a one-room apartment with a turquoise bathtub in Bed-Stuy, she was taking care of the apartment and the cats while their owner went back to Australia for three months, then six, and after fourteen months, he transferred the apartment to Evelyn, and the cats came along. Ina spent her weekends at home, watching family-friendly game shows on TV, hoping someone in the family would sit beside her on the couch, but everyone was preoccupied, the kids had their tablets, Hector had his books, there was always a short story collection of gay porn that needed editing or a new obscure poetry collection that needed a release party, he was still in contact with his old university students, Klara, Stephen and Arkan called regularly to talk to Hector, and every time, he locked himself in his home office. Especially long were the conversations with Klara, who had become a PhD student at Södertörn and then returned to Stockholm University for a position similar to the one Hector had left.

So Klara benefited from you quitting? said Ina.

Stop it, Hector said. It's good for everyone that she's there.

Good for everyone except us, Ina said.

Lagerhjelm has improved, Hector said.

Ina tried to FaceTime Evelyn without video, but she rarely got a response, the time difference made it tricky, when they did manage to talk, Evelyn told her that she spent her weekends at the Forty-second Street Library, for months she had tried to research the names of the men depicted on the steel beam, she had become close friends with a new librarian named Awa, she helped Evelyn with material and sent her links to documentaries about the iconic photograph, although it wasn't allowed, Awa opened the door to the archive and allowed Evelyn to accompany her into the hidden heart of the library, there were endless rows of movable metal bookshelves, the smell of projectors, broken office chairs sat in the corners, and when Ina heard about this, she couldn't stop her mouth from making a wincing sound of envy.

Evelyn sat in the large reading room with clouds painted on the ceiling, reading all the books about Rockefeller Center and making long lists of possible names for the workers, most seemed to be from Ireland, two might have been from Italy, one or two or possibly three might have been Native Americans, and it was not impossible for one or two to be Swedes. But the name Mikkola was nowhere to be found.

What would change if you found out that one of them was actually named Mikkola? Awa asked one Saturday in October 2015, when Evelyn had stayed in the USA for two years and four months too long.

I guess I would try to find his relatives, Evelyn said. I would go to them, introduce myself and tell them that we are related.

And then what?

I don't know, Evelyn said. Maybe it would prove that my father wasn't a liar. And that we come from a family that built things, rather than a family of lunatics. I mean, if my great-grandfather had the ability to build a skyscraper that still stands, then I should be able to finish a twenty-five-minute monologue, right?

Awa smiled and nodded, taking off her round metal glasses to clean them, which she often did when she wanted to avoid pointing out to Evelyn that her monologue should have been finished years ago and was it even possible to show up at school three years late and expect to graduate? Wasn't this project, this life, just a big waste of time?

But as the gifted librarian she was, Awa never said these things and in the spring of 2016, Evelyn stopped going to the library, but she continued making notes for her ever-growing monologue, she started considering turning her text into a full-length play, or a movie, or a nonfiction book, or a novel.

She held seventeen different jobs over five years, working as a waitress at a Mexican restaurant where she learned some Spanish, a receptionist at a local TV station where she discovered that meteorologists were the most self-absorbed people on TV, she was responsible for storing and washing furs at a luxurious dry cleaner in Midtown, she helped out at a family-owned pharmacy in Queens. The only time she used her acting training was when she was paid by the hour to record advertisements that were mass-produced and sent out to hundreds of thousands of random mobile numbers. The challenge was to try to make the recipient believe that the prerecorded message was genuine, if they thought it was a real person calling, it was harder for them to hang up, and if they didn't hang up, there was a better chance they'd buy the detergent, donate to the victim support line or support the nurses' union. Evelyn was fantastic at signaling that hesitant authenticity that made people listen to the message, sometimes she coughed just before introducing herself, apologizing, sometimes she hushed an imaginary child before addressing the person who answered, and sometimes she used sound effects, as if she were washing dishes or receiving a vibrating text message, but after a while, it turned out that the most effective technique was to remain silent for a few seconds before introducing herself. This silence made the recipient pause, and then, when they heard her voice, her fake name, her story, it was too late for them to resist.

During the first few years, Evelyn told herself that she would go back, soon, next year or the year after that. Maybe she could contact the drama school and explain what happened.

Perhaps she could get her degree, or maybe she could reach out to Simon and salvage what was broken. But the longer she stayed, the more unthinkable it became to return to Sweden.

Simon moved on a long time ago, Anastasia said when they spoke in the fall of 2019.

Good for him, Evelyn replied.

He has a wife and two children.

And probably three cats, Evelyn said.

You know her.

Who?

His wife.

Before Anastasia said her name, Evelyn knew who it was, and when she mentioned Cecilia's name, Evelyn chuckled.

Of course, Evelyn said. I hope they're happy together.

Both of them miss you.

Sure.

It was the grief and longing for you that brought them together.

Definitely.

So what are you afraid of?

I'm not the least bit afraid of coming home, Evelyn said. The only thing I'm afraid of is not being able to come back here.

But sure, there were moments during these years when Evelyn wished she could teleport back to Sweden. Like when Anastasia finally had her first child. Or when she heard that Ina's son Primo had been arrested for vandalism. But Evelyn convinced herself that time passed quickly, and soon Anastasia's daughter, Nina, could cross the Atlantic on her own. So Evelyn stayed and time went on.

Chapter One Hundred Nineteen

The next morning they woke up much later than planned, the dinner had lasted until the waitresses needed to go home, as soon as Saskia arrived, their conversation picked up speed, no more talk about wine varieties or karate belts, not with Saskia around, she sat down and had three conversation topics ready, she asked them about their relationship with their bodies and suggested that they spend at least half an hour going through their bodies, from head to toe, or vice versa, and share their thoughts about each body part, and as always, when Saskia had an idea, Laura and Ina gratefully complied, four hours later, they had finished their desserts and consumed all their wine, but they still hadn't reached their feet, Saskia said she had always hated her body for being too big and sweaty, but her calves were her pride and joy, which was why she loved shorts and hated rain boots and Laura, mindful of the waitress circulating nearby, suggested they continue the discussion up in their room.

They left the table and smoked a quick cigarette outside, even Ina smoked one, up in the room they were too tired to continue talking about their relationship with their feet and too tired to open Ina's bottle of champagne, instead all three of them fell asleep, except for Ina, who lay awake wondering why she felt like she was imitating herself with these old friends, why she felt left out, why she couldn't shake off her irritation at the fact that Saskia looked so much older than when they last saw each other, why she didn't dye her gray roots, how she could accept all those wrinkles, why Laura seemed so deeply content.

Just as Ina was about to fall asleep, she received a misspelled text from her oldest son. Primo didn't ask how she was doing or how it was in the woods. Instead, he asked if she could send him some money. A producer he had dreamed of working with for years "had an opening," and Primo had a lot of money coming in, but right now, his account was "low," and he needed the money "now."

Ina closed her eyes and lay there for a few seconds before asking him how much he needed. He wrote the amount. Ina shook her head, took a screenshot of their conversation, and sent it to Hector. One weekend. She would be away for two nights for the first time in five years. Yet they found a way to hijack her attention. And that sum of money. It was way too much for a normal teenager to be carrying around. Did he need it for drugs? Would he use it to film a video and return the money afterwards? She had seen some of the clips that Primo and his friends posted online, always showing off bundles of large bills and weapons that she knew were replicas, expensive watches they borrowed and gold chains that couldn't possibly be real because they looked too heavy to be held up by Primo's thin neck.

Ina couldn't understand how anyone could take these boys seriously, but lately, people had stopped Primo on the street and asked him for autographs, and at first Ina found it entertaining, but lately, she had grown more and more worried. He was only sixteen years old and heading into a world full of violence and weapons. Last spring, one of Primo's idols had been kidnapped and extorted for money. The culprits released humiliating pictures, showing him bruised and wearing panties, and Ina knew that Primo wouldn't end up in a similar situation, but there was something about the desperate tone in his message that made her wonder if she would manage to fall asleep. She put her phone in flight mode, lay on her side and fell asleep within seconds, completely exhausted from trying so hard to be herself.

Chapter One Hundred Twenty

E velyn had lived undocumented in New York for seven years when the world shut down due to a pandemic. Restaurants and schools closed, museums and libraries too, everyone stocked up on toilet paper, neighbors who wanted to survive took the stairs, while those feeling daring took the elevator, but they never entered without face masks, and they only touched the buttons with their elbows. Evelyn worked at yet another café (her third, which only offered takeout), and one of her regular customers told her that she lived near a hospital in Fort Greene and that she was moving away because she couldn't bear any more sirens and body bags. Those who could left for a house upstate or their parents' farm in Maine, and those who stayed behind saw their family members on screens and dreamed of having a place to escape to.

For the first time in seven years, Evelyn contemplated going back to Sweden. Not because she longed for home, whatever home was, but because she knew that Sweden hadn't shut down, and if she got really sick, she would need a hospital and here, they would ask for her social security number, and she would have to admit that she didn't have one and that she had "overstayed her tourist visa by about seven years," and then they would force her out of the building, or call the police, or make her pay a bill that would be higher than her annual income. She had heard several horror stories—a friend of a friend who broke their foot and received a $700,000 bill, an uncle of a colleague who fell from a roof, injured his back and had to sell the house he had been repairing the roof of to pay his medical bills. The bills just kept coming, month after month, in astronomical amounts.

On June 20, 2020, Evelyn received a strange email from a man she had known somewhat superficially as a child. He claimed they were old friends and told her he had devoted his entire existence to understanding his life through Evelyn and her sisters, they got to know each other in Drakenberg, where they biked around and "played *Top Gun*" and climbed up Tanto Mountain and bonded over the fact that he had two brothers, and she had two sisters, and their parents knew each other, "and a bunch of other similarities that I won't bore you with," he added, and it was only in the second paragraph of the email that Evelyn realized he was writing to her in English, although it was clear that Swedish was his native language, it showed in the structure of his sentences, his choice of words and the occasional strange Swedish-English expressions that popped up, the only thing that wasn't Swedish about his email was that the sentences never seemed to end, they flowed from one paragraph to the next as if he were terrified of using punctuation, as if every period meant an end, as if everything he wrote somehow had a vital connection to the next thing, he claimed he was a writer (but Evelyn had never heard of any of his books), he said he had received a grant to write a book at the New York Public Library (but was "stuck in Stockholm due to the current situation") and he shared that he had contacted the library and was referred to a librarian named Awa, who was apparently an expert in books about the Great Depression, towards the end of their first virtual meeting, Awa mentioned that she had actually met another Swede researching a similar topic, Awa had refused to give out Evelyn's email address, and the man writing the email admitted that this was a pure guess, he didn't know if Awa was talking about Evelyn, he didn't know if Evelyn's email address consisted of her first and last name @ the most popular mail server, and he assumed the email would bounce back, so these words would probably mean nothing, or they would mean everything. And now, before hitting send, he just wanted to ask a few questions, and then the questions came, one after another, they weren't numbered, they had no structure, there must have been fifty, no, seventy questions about Evelyn's monologue, Ina's education, Anastasia's career, their mother's curse, their father's cancer, and he wrote that he understood if it felt weird, and he added that, on some level, he knew Evelyn would never read this, but if it didn't bounce, he would at least assume it had reached the right Evelyn, and that she was out there somewhere reading this, so he wanted to thank her for reading all the way to the end.

Evelyn didn't respond, and a few days later, another email arrived, with the same long sentences, but now he was writing in Swedish. He wrote that he understood if Evelyn didn't want to reply, he asked if she remembered him, he wondered how Ina and Anastasia were doing, he told her that he lived at the top of a building in a suburb just south of Stockholm, with his wife and their two children, he shared that the building was designed by the same architect who designed the houses in Drakenberg, and the kitchen he was sitting in while writing these words looked exactly like the kitchens they grew up in, with the same elongated shape, the same cabinet doors, the same metallic plastic handles, he wondered what strange force led him to search for an apartment for years and finally buy an apartment that looked so similar to the one he grew up in, only this one was bigger and had an unobstructed view and was outside the city instead of within the city's borders,

and

and

several blank lines followed, and Evelyn thought the email might have ended, but the previous sentence had two loosely hanging "ands," then the email continued as if he needed a couple of pages of space to dare to write what he really wanted to write, but now he switched to English, writing that he felt like he was sinking in quicksand, that he was forty-one years old and had dedicated his life to fleeing the deep depression that hit his father when he was forty-two, there were six months left, it felt like a curse, he told her about his mental problems, his suicidal thoughts, he avoided bridges and took detours to avoid getting too close to train tracks, he wrote about his recurring depressions, which he only now realized were depressions, he wrote about his financial worries, apparently he had spent the spring investing all his money in various index funds and now his life savings had gone up in smoke, he wrote about a half sister with HIV and a friend who had taken their own life, he wrote that his biggest fear in life had always been to sink into a deep depression like his father and realize too late that he needed help, and now, this fall, when everything shut down and he, for the first time in his life, couldn't rely on "external stimuli" (Evelyn wondered if he meant writing projects or drugs or both) to escape, he was occupied by an evil voice, echoing within him, he called it the Hyena, it was new, but it wasn't new, it had been with him since childhood or at least since his parents' divorce, since his father left the family, the Hyena hissed that there was something seriously wrong with him, it monitored his thoughts, behaviors, breathing, relentlessly criticizing him, every three seconds, it whispered that this was a sign that he was broken, unlovable, incapable of love, overweight, weak, skinny, manipulative, cowardly, and every time he met someone who didn't see through how broken he was on the inside, the Hyena began attacking that person as fervently as it attacked him and sometimes he wondered how much longer he could live with this voice in his head, sometimes he wondered if it wouldn't be better to

The email ended mid-sentence, without any periods or commas. Evelyn shook her head as she read it. She had considered responding to the first email, wanting to give it some time, a week or two, to show him that he couldn't control her, but this email disgusted her. Who the hell did he think he was sending stuff like this to her in-box? She wasn't his therapist. He didn't even know if this was her email address. They had known each other superficially a hundred years ago. And why on earth should she care that some middle-aged man in a foreign country walked around with a hyena in his head?

Chapter One Hundred Twenty-One

When Ina woke up, Saskia was already up, she had brought all the equipment from the car and placed it on her bed.

One good thing about the hammocks is that we don't have to worry about insects, she said, looking down at the bed, which seemed to creak under the weight of all the equipment. Hammocks, extra clothes, water pump, specially bought firewood, freeze-dried food, candy, beer and a green knife. Laura picked up the knife and asked Saskia if she was satisfied with it.

I love it, Saskia said.

How does the camping stove work?

Incredibly well.

After a quick breakfast, they returned to the room and tried to fit all their belongings into their backpacks. It didn't matter that Laura and Saskia had backpacks as big as refrigerators with lots of smart compartments on the sides. They would never manage to carry everything up to the top of the mountain. While Saskia and Laura tried to stuff things into each other's backpacks, Ina sneaked down to the reception and asked if there was any parking closer to the mountaintop.

We can drive up to the top, Ina said when she returned to the room, thinking it was good news.

I liked the challenge of trying to carry everything, Saskia said.

Me too, Laura said.

But we will never get all this stuff up there, Ina said.

Saskia tried to put on her backpack but couldn't get up from the bed.

Okay, she said with a smile. Let's go with plan B.

They carried everything down to Saskia's car and drove up to the top of the mountain. A small mountain led higher and higher up. They passed dog owners in rain boots and families in matching rain gear, possibly with baskets filled with mushrooms. The higher they went, the greener and denser the forest became.

Is this it? Saskia said.

I've lost my map, Laura said.

No, there's another parking lot a little higher up, Ina said, proudly holding her map from the reception desk. They continued upwards, Saskia drove slower and slower as the road became narrower, at the most unexpected moments, five muddy middle-aged mountain bikers could flood out onto the road and disappear into the next trail as quickly as if they had been deer.

Finally, they reached the right parking lot. When Ina got out of the car, she received a fourth message from Primo. He wrote that Hector refused to send him money, and he really needed it today, otherwise he would miss this opportunity, which was the chance of a lifetime. She forwarded the conversation to Hector, hoping they could solve this without her.

Before Ina and her friends chose a hiking trail, they wanted to see the summit, so they took some water bottles and went up the small trail. On the map, it didn't look like more than ten minutes to the top, but it had rained overnight and the path became steeper. As they walked, Ina noticed that her mobile phone lost reception and didn't get it back until they were near the summit. Hector replied that he would "take care of it."

Are you sure this path leads to the top? Laura said, and Ina nodded. She wasn't sure, but there was no other trail nearby, and the color markings matched, and they were heading upwards, which was a good thing.

In the middle of the forest, there was a sign warning that they were approaching a precipice, and a few minutes later, they reached the top, the world ending in a deep ravine with a breathtaking view of the lake, countless treetops and an endless sky. They stood there for a few minutes and just breathed. Ina resisted the urge to scream to test the echo.

This is our place, Saskia said.

Definitely, Laura said.

Her friends went to find suitable trees where they could set up the hammocks. Ina stayed by the edge, looking down at the sharp cliffs, the pine trees, thinking of her mother, imagining herself taking one, two, three steps forward, tumbling into the ravine. It would take a few days for the helicopter to find her, stunned friends, Hector devastated, their children's lives ruined forever, no, everyone would say, there was no sign that she was sad or depressed, she was just her usual self, Evelyn would return from the USA, she would speak at the funeral, she would say that Ina always had sorrow in her eyes, that she took responsibility for her sisters early on, that she had a strong belief that the world would end if she relaxed and enjoyed life, she had very high expectations for herself, and sometimes it felt as if she was only truly happy when she read, because in the world of books she escaped the mundanity of life, she escaped herself, but in life, she had a hard time relaxing, she was something of a perfectionist, but a perfectionist without the ability to be perfect, so she was a constantly disappointed perfectionist (Amen, Anastasia would shout), and that's why it was a bit challenging to be with her, because she always felt left out, and always wanted conversations to be interesting, every thought to be new, and every moment to have meaning, the same way events had meaning in her favorite Russian novels, and if everything wasn't perfect, it felt like she was slowly dying, and to be completely honest, it was damn tough being her sister, I don't want to say that I'm glad she's dead because that would be a terrible thing to say, especially at her funeral, but it actually feels like a relief that she's gone, there was something about her expectation that life should always be more than life that made her very difficult to be with, to travel with, to live with, I see Hector nodding in agreement . . .

Are you okay? Laura said. She touched Ina's shoulder softly.

Absolutely, Ina said and took a few steps back from the edge.

Chapter One Hundred Twenty-Two

n the middle of July, a new email arrived from the man in Stockholm, Evelyn saw it and decided not to read it, she was busy, she needed a new job to afford rent, one of her cats had an eye infection that she was trying to cure with home remedies, in the evening, she ended up reading the email anyway, there was something in the man's words that reminded her of a feeling she sometimes had, even though she didn't have a hyena in her head, but perhaps a parrot or a ferret, or maybe it was a badger.

He wrote that it had been decided that the move to New York wouldn't happen, not in the autumn, maybe never. He apologized for the previous email; he had been in a dark place, and he still was, but now he had at least decided to seek help, he couldn't bear it anymore, for the first time in his life, he had confessed to his wife what was going on, she convinced him to go to the doctor, he didn't dare seek help for depression, so he sought help for a pain in his right thumb, he did have some pain in his thumb, he had jumped from a diving board and the thumb was slightly out of alignment, when he visited the doctor, he showed his thumb, and she gently pulled on it, moving it up and down, and the pain instantly disappeared, he broke down and told the doctor that the thumb felt fine, but there was something else that would never heal, for the past three weeks, he had gone to his work apartment, cried for hours and then returned home, he described each morning as a struggle just to get dressed, he recounted the other day when he was unpacking groceries and realized that the fruit basket was on the kitchen table instead of the sink, and he couldn't understand how he would have the strength to go over to the kitchen table to put the fruit in it, he'd need to lift his legs and stretch out his arm, and while all this was happening, he had a hyena tearing apart his insides.

Hyena? asked the doctor.

Hyena, he whispered and pointed to his temple, he tried to make the doctor understand, he told her about the insults and criticism from his father, about the divorce, he was ashamed that there was nothing more to tell, just a regular divorce, just a regular dad who criticized him and then disappeared, just a regular mom who did her best to keep the family together after a curse had been placed on them, but it didn't add up, he had friends who had fled from war, friends who crossed mountains as infants, friends who grew up in refugee camps, friends with alcoholic mothers and drug-addicted fathers, friends with relatives tortured in political prisons, and there he was, sitting on a chair in a local hospital, crying his eyes out because he had a hyena in his head.

It sounds like obsessive thoughts, the doctor said. It sounds like a deep depression and sometimes it's harder to grasp emotional abuse than physical abuse.

The doctor then gave him a choice: antidepressants, cognitive-behavioral therapy or both, he was terrified of medication and chose CBT, now he was waiting for someone to get back to him, the waiting lists were long, but hopefully, he would get to speak with someone soon because he didn't know how much longer he could handle this, he couldn't tell anyone else, not his brothers, not his mother, definitely not his father, not his friends, not his publisher, they wouldn't understand, they would laugh at his weakness and wonder how such small things from so long ago could have such big consequences so far into the future, they would understand that something must be seriously wrong with him, and the hyena would lift its ugly, scruffy, shrunken snout and nod in agreement. The only person he felt he could share this with was Evelyn, because . . . because . . . because he wasn't really sure why, maybe because he was writing this in English, maybe because she was his oldest friend, maybe because he knew she would understand, perhaps because he still wasn't sure if anyone would read these words.

Evelyn didn't respond immediately, but she thought of him now and then during the summer and autumn, wondering how he was doing, if he managed to tame his hyena, if he walked around with the hyena on a leash or if he had managed to transform the hyena into another animal, a panda, or a rabbit, or an owl.

Finally, on October 10, 2020, she replied. She did it quickly to avoid changing her mind, pressing the reply button, seeing his name in the address field, watching the cursor pulsate like a heart. Then she wrote:

Hi Jonas. How are you?

Chapter One Hundred Twenty-Three

They began their hike, first following the blue markings on the trees, then green and then yellow. They passed a small stream, Laura took out her water bottle, emptied it and filled it with water from the stream to test a high-tech water purification tablet.

That's so cool, Saskia said.

Saskia gave me this, said Laura. Was it last year or the year before?

They all tasted the water, which had an earthy tone, but Ina wasn't sure if it was real or if her tongue was tricking her into sensing something that wasn't there. They continued hiking. Ina wondered how their interest in nature had arisen, whether it came from being scouts as kids or if it was Saskia and Laura's determined way of reclaiming the forest from men, they had had such phases before, like when both suddenly started giving each other advice on grilling, or that winter when they began sending pictures from their long-distance ice-skating trips to each other.

The path narrowed, Saskia led the way, and both Laura and Ina tried to walk in the middle. They talked about their spouses, about sex, about a new TV series Laura and Saskia had watched but not Ina. After a few hours, Ina tried to walk in front, and when she did, she noticed that Laura and Saskia found a way to walk beside each other, behind her. When she slowed down a bit, Saskia took the lead, and they returned to walking in a line.

After five hours of hiking, they reached "Per's Sten," which had been marked as a highlight on the map, it turned out to be just a large stone, and the three friends pretended to be fascinated by it, taking photos next to it, pretending to roll it like a giant black snowball, pretending to be crushed by it. Then they continued along the trail and didn't stop until they reached a resting place with a magnificent view of the lake. Laura brought out the camping stove (I got this from Saskia, she said for the millionth time) and they made coffee and smoked, although none of them smoked regularly, only here, for old times' sake.

This is incredible, they said. This is so beautiful. This is fantastic. We should do this more often. Every year. As a tradition.

They said it, but they all knew that this was the first and last time. Now let's go back and set up our base camp, Saskia said.

And they began walking. They passed dog owners on their way back to their cars, they passed team-building men in T-shirts with the same company name, also heading back to their cars, they passed another or the same group of mountain bikers, in muddy clothes with shiny helmets, on their way back to their cars.

Have you noticed that we haven't seen anyone else with camping gear? Ina said. Maybe it's just us spending the night in the forest, said Laura, and Ina heard a faint sound of concern in her voice.

They chose the brown trail back up the mountain, the sun had started to set among the clouds, now they hadn't seen anyone for at least half an hour. Then they saw a couple standing where the trail divided, they had large backpacks with camping gear, sleeping bags and sleeping pads, a compass dangling on a string. The man was holding the same map that the friends had, he was turning and twisting it. The woman, who was younger and shorter, tried to help. They were probably tourists because they were the only ones in the forest wearing face masks, and not even a global pandemic had convinced Swedes that there were advantages to hiding their faces.

Ina walked first. She passed the couple. Hello, she said.

Hello, they said.

The unwritten rule in the forest: See each other on a sidewalk, don't say hello. See each other outside the forest, don't say hello. But see each other in the forest, on a trail, then we greet each other, to show that we can be trusted, that we're not just wild lunatics walking in the forest because we have nothing better to do. The couple waited for the three friends, and then they started following. The trail turned left and continued uphill, uphill, then widened into a gravel road. The tourist couple was still behind them, and they couldn't have been more than fifteen minutes from the trail to the mountaintop when Ina realized what they were trying to do. Ina increased her pace. She heard the speed of the tourist couple's steps increase. Laura understood, she too walked faster.

Where are you going? Saskia shouted.

But Ina didn't stop, and neither did Laura. They hiked faster and faster, and the tourist couple followed, catching up, how was that possible? Maybe they were professional racewalkers, they increased their speed, Ina just needed to reach the trail before the couple, if she reached the trail, they would be safe, they would establish the base camp at the mountaintop, the last trail was too narrow to pass anyone. With twenty meters to go, Ina started to run, running faster than she had in years, running as if her children's lives depended on her reaching the trail first and finally, she heard the tourist couple's steps give up and slow down. They understood that they had lost. Laura slowed down, but Ina kept running, rushing up to the top of the mountain, maybe the couple knew another way up, a secret shortcut, and she was responsible for the map, and if someone else reached the campfire before her, the whole weekend would be ruined, or at least not be as she had envisioned.

When Ina finally reached the top of the mountain and sank down by the empty campfire, her body ached, and gusts of wind cooled the sweat running down her forehead. She had done it. She had secured their base camp. Laura arrived a few minutes later.

Well done, she said, trying to catch her breath. Saskia, still down at the trailhead, called Ina, who put her on speaker. It had taken Saskia several minutes to figure out what was happening, but now she bombarded them with compliments on their great intuition because if that damn couple had arrived before them this whole . . .

Ina looked up, the couple was walking up the trail.

Hello, Laura said.

Hello, the girl said.

The man passed them. They stood and looked at the view for a few minutes, picked some leaves from a tree and put them in their backpacks, then they walked back down.

Sayonara, suckers, Laura said, handing Ina a beer.

Chapter One Hundred Twenty-Four

Evelyn had hardly left her apartment since the pandemic began. The café where she used to work had finally been forced to close, and she started looking for remote job opportunities. During the fall of 2020, she worked as a salesperson for a fitness website that aimed to get people to sign up for one-on-one personal coaching. The trainers and dietitians handled the actual customers, but when someone wanted a virtual introductory call, they met Evelyn on the screen. She talked about the personalized meal plan they would receive and the individually designed workout routine. She made sure to wear the right sporty outfit and always displayed the purple yoga mat sticking out of the basket, so it would be visible on camera. Sometimes, when she checked her email, she wondered why the author who had contacted her never got back, had he been scared that she actually existed, or had he been defeated by his hyena?

Instead, Fabricia reached out and asked if Evelyn was still in the city and if she wanted to have a Covid-safe, socially distanced outdoor coffee. Evelyn put on her face mask and walked from Bed-Stuy to Park Slope. She passed the deserted streets near Prospect Park, where people were so wealthy that they had the luxury to leave the city whenever they wanted. Town houses were closed up with wooden shutters. Brown nannies pushed strollers with white children. The coffee was twice as expensive here as at the café where Evelyn had worked. Yet, despite all this wealth, despite the art on the walls, despite the designer furniture residents put out on the sidewalk to give away, despite the parked shiny Teslas, Evelyn noticed that the sidewalk belonged in the third world, it was uneven and unbalanced, a large square of stone clumsily joined with the next stone square. She felt very Swedish as she walked and grumbled about how uneven the ground was, thinking that this kind of sidewalk would never be accepted in her home country. Mothers with strollers would have complained to the municipality, and the sidewalks would have been fixed immediately, because a country without smooth sidewalks doesn't deserve to call itself a real country. When she crossed the street towards the park, she wondered if this was the first time in seven years that she had thought of Sweden as her home.

Evelyn and Fabricia had kept in touch since the sisters borrowed her studio, which felt like a lifetime ago. They exchanged numbers and promised each other that they would have that coffee soon, but neither of them seemed to want it enough to reach out, or perhaps life just got in the way. Then the pandemic struck, and all Swedes in New York who could go home, went home, back to a safe world of smooth sidewalks and free healthcare. But Fabricia and Evelyn stayed, and when they met at the Garfield entrance to Prospect Park with their takeaway coffees in hand, they agreed that this was, in fact, a sort of test—the place you go when the world is hit by a pandemic is your real home and since they had stayed, it meant that they were certified New Yorkers. The big difference was that Fabricia had come on a J-1 visa, which had later converted to an O-1 exceptional talent visa, which could then be transformed into a green card, whereas Evelyn had come as a tourist and was here on no visa. Fabricia had a gallery, health insurance, a social security number and a credit score. Evelyn had her inherited cats.

They walked through the park, down to the Dog Beach, and farther into the woods, chatting about how they had coped during the times of lockdown and social distancing, the TV shows they had binged, the friends they had in their bubble, the sweatpants they had worn twenty-four seven. When they came out on the other side of the woods, Fabricia turned to Evelyn and said:

How is Anastasia really?

It was the "really" that signaled that something serious had happened.

Good, I guess, Evelyn said, using that vague tone that expatriate siblings use to hide that they probably missed something life-changing.

Have you seen what she's been posting? Fabricia said.

I don't do social media, Evelyn said.

Don't freak out, but . . . it seems like your sister has become . . . *religious*, Fabricia said, sounding as if Anastasia had caught a venereal disease.

Religious? Seriously? Evelyn said.

Not just religious, but like . . . *Christian*? Fabricia said, making it sound like Anastasia's venereal disease was the worst, most deadly kind.

She took out her phone and showed the pictures Anastasia had posted in the past year.

Evelyn expected Christian memes and Jesus quotes, but the first photo showed a sparkling glass wall with light seeping through blue and yellow stained glass, it took a few seconds before Evelyn understood the scale of the photo, because at the front, at the bottom of the picture, was a small altar and a few barely visible rows of benches, and there stood a little girl with a hooded sweatshirt, her head tilted.

Is that . . . ? Evelyn said.

Revelation Church in Hägersten, Fabricia said, shaking her head. Don't ask me why she started going there.

Evelyn reached for Fabricia's phone and zoomed in on the girl. Is that Nina?

Fabricia nodded. Evelyn couldn't believe her eyes. How could Nina have grown so big? How could she look so incredibly similar to Evelyn? She scrolled farther, hoping to see another picture of Nina, her lips, her posture, her gaze, it was like looking at an unspoiled version of herself. But instead of Nina, Anastasia had posted about thirty photos from something she called "restoration of wall paintings in Finja church." One of the photos showed a woman with short bleached hair, wearing a face mask, in front of a stone wall with a brush as thin as a pencil, filling in a red field in a mosaic. On another picture, a man with a face mask and work gloves carefully chiseled out a tiny piece of the wall. The caption read: "Color sample."

Who are these people? Fabricia said.

No idea, Evelyn said.

What is she doing?

Evelyn shrugged.

Aren't you worried?

No, Evelyn said. Not at all.

But what about Nina? Fabricia said.

Nina will be fine, Evelyn said, knowing it was true. She glanced at Fabricia, trying to understand why she was so upset. Was it because she thought religion was less scientific than finding her future in tea leaves and tarot cards? Or was it an irritation that Anastasia seemed more fascinated by thousand-year-old church murals than Fabricia's contemporary career? They continued to walk in silence.

Should we turn back? Evelyn said.

They turned around, passing dog owners and dogs, children and mothers, pensioners and healthcare workers, frisbee throwers and kite flyers, everyone wearing face masks except for the dogs. Fabricia checked her phone and cursed.

What's wrong? Evelyn said.

My girlfriend. She was supposed to join me for a thing.

What kind of thing?

A dinner thing.

Who dares to organize dinners now? Evelyn said.

One of them is a doctor, Fabricia said to signal that it was a safe event. Do you want to come?

Evelyn accepted, she hadn't been invited to anyone's home for several months, and at her place in Bed-Stuy, there were only two cats waiting.

Chapter One Hundred Twenty-Five

The forest was pitch-black, the fire still burning, their shadows dancing over the trees even though their bodies remained motionless. They hadn't spoken a word for ten minutes. Ina reminded herself that it was okay, it was a sign of true friendship that they could share moments of silence without panicking. Ina checked her phone. Still no update from Hector. She had tried calling him, but his phone was turned off. Primo's phone was on, but no one answered. The curse whispered that it was over, he's dead, I warned you not to get too attached to him, told you not to . . .

Are you okay? Saskia said.

I'm feeling fantastic, Ina said. I feel so happy to be here with you, in this forest, by this fire. I . . . Her phone lit up. A furniture company informed her about an upcoming sale.

What's going on? Laura asked.

Nothing.

You've been glued to your phone all day, Saskia said.

I just . . . Ina said.

What?

I'm a bit worried about Primo, Ina said, and the curse sneered, and Ina tried to hold it together because she knew that if she fell apart now, she would never be able to put the pieces back together.

What's he done this time? Saskia said, with a smile. She looked relieved that it wasn't anything more serious, since both Ina's friends knew that Primo was different, he had always had a different energy than the rest of Ina's family. In a home where everyone loved books, libraries and footnotes, Primo had preferred bounce houses, ball pits and wrestling matches, first, he had been an incredibly sleepless baby, then he became an extremely energetic toddler, then he was one of those children at preschool whom other parents loved because of his incredible energy and charm, but secretly, they were quite grateful he wasn't their child, he always stood a little too close to the person he was talking to, always climbing on an adult, a mailbox, or a (sometimes freshly painted) fence. When he was five, Ina had brought out a gingerbread cookie to do the marshmallow test on him, but before she could explain the rules ("I'll give you a cookie now, and if you wait two minutes before eating it, I'll give you another cookie"), he had eaten it. She sighed and brought out another cookie, this time trying to explain the rules before giving it to him, I'll give you this cookie, and if you wait, two, no, let's say one minute, then you'll get another one.

Why? Primo yelled.

Because this is an important step in becoming human, Ina said. You must be able to delay your rewards to grow up and become a fully functional member of society. If you can't pass this simple test, you will *never* make it out there.

No. Of course she didn't say that. Instead she told him it was just a fun game and that he would do his best not to eat the first cookie immediately when he got it. Ina handed him the cookie. Primo looked at the cookie. He sniffed it. He smiled. He ate the cookie. Ina looked at the clock. It had taken him seven seconds.

Why couldn't you wait for the second cookie? Ina said, trying to stay calm.

I wanted this cookie now, he said, laughing. Ina saw a little Anastasia in his defiant eyes.

When Primo was twelve, Saskia visited Stockholm for a conference and stayed one extra night in Ina's guest room. After Primo had gone to school, Ina told Saskia that she was worried about him.

You've always been worried about Primo, Saskia said. Since he was born. Since he couldn't wait for his second cookie.

This is different, Ina said. He has started stealing. From school.

What did he take? Saskia wondered, thinking it must be about money or computers.

Rubber bands, Ina said.

That's nothing, Saskia said with a relieved smile. Ina opened a desk drawer in Primo's room, it was filled to the brim with rubber bands, thousands of them, they shot out on their own and landed on the floor when Ina opened the drawer—blue, green, red rubber bands of different thicknesses and lengths.

How did he even fit them into the drawer? Saskia asked.

No idea, Ina said.

What does he do with them?

He makes balls out of them, Ina said with a sigh.

Balls? Saskia said.

He twists them together into these big bouncing balls, Ina said, shaking her head. Don't ask me why.

She leaned forward and pulled out a drawer from under his bed. It was full of hundreds of homemade bouncing balls in various colors and sizes.

But why? Saskia said. Is he selling them?

Ina shrugged and shook her head—the same gesture that mothers have made since the beginning of time to signal their best friend that they have no idea how the person they created in their womb could turn into such a mystery.

I love him, but I will never understand him, she added, and Saskia hugged her friend, saying it was entirely normal, and she felt the same way about her children. However, on her way home to Malmö, she wondered if that was really true because Saskia still felt that she understood her children, even when they drove her insane, she saw their endless stubbornness, how important it was for them that everything was fair, and how they forced her to fetch a ruler to check if all the siblings had gotten exactly the same amount of soda, they were still small versions of herself, she saw herself in them, and she hardly saw any of Ina in Primo.

Ina stared into the fire. She sighed.

It's probably nothing, she said and put away her phone.

Laura and Saskia looked at each other.

Ina, what's happening?

Tell us.

We're here for you.

Maybe we can do something?

You never tell us when you have problems. We only hear about it afterwards.

When you've managed the situation yourself. When it's too late for us to help.

Please. Tell us.

Chapter One Hundred Twenty-Six

The couple who hosted the dinner lived just ten minutes away from the park, and when Fabricia and Evelyn left the liquor store with a bottle of wine each (Fabricia's twice as expensive as Evelyn's) and continued down Garfield, Fabricia mentioned that they were "collectors," and Evelyn wondered what she would have in common with an old art-collecting couple.

The apartment smelled of garlic and tomato sauce, and it took Evelyn a few minutes to accept that the couple she had imagined as retirees (who else has the means and time to collect art?) were, in fact, younger than both Fabricia and Evelyn. The gathering was an intimate dinner for four people, and Fabricia made it clear that Evelyn was not her girlfriend, just a friend.

Welcome, said the hostess, placing her hands over her heart instead of greeting with her right hand. I'm Katia.

Evelyn, Evelyn said, mirroring the greeting gesture.

So nice of you to come.

So glad to be here.

Manas is in the kitchen preparing dinner, Katia said. I can show you around in the meantime.

Katia took them from the ground floor to the third floor, showing Fabricia some artworks she had purchased recently. She mentioned the artists' first names as if they were personal friends, and maybe they were. Evelyn had not heard of any of the artists and instantly forgot their names. However, Fabricia was increasingly impressed with the collection they had built, saying "that's beautiful" or "that's intense" about every other piece. Evelyn couldn't believe that the young couple had all this—all this art, all these sofas, all these rooms, all this wealth, all this happiness. They had bought their brownstone a few years ago and renovated it entirely, but Evelyn never quite understood what Katia did for a living or why they had so many rooms and no children. At least Manas was a doctor. He greeted her by extending his elbow, asked if she wanted wine and said the food would be ready shortly.

They sat down at a set table with heavy cutlery and designer plates, starting with salad.

Evelyn noticed that Manas looked at her a little too long, and she continued to be charming, telling funny stories about what happened at her local café during the lockdown. She didn't mention that she worked at the café, and, only once, inadvertently touched Manas's shoulder. Evelyn had no intention of making Manas fall in love with her and just before it happened, she asked Katia four or five questions about her job, her upbringing in a small American town.

Evelyn had no real interest in Katia's answers, she just wanted the room to see she wasn't as self-centered as some other extroverted people out there. She was a special kind, an extrovert who could also listen—at least appear like someone who could listen—while Katia talked, and Manas stared at Evelyn's neck.

Is the food almost ready? Katia said.

Yes, Manas said, rising and sitting again. Sorry, but . . . Evelyn, may I ask you to turn your head to the side, all the way to the right?

An embarrassing silence fell over the table.

Excuse me?

Please, stay seated and look towards the window, he said.

Please, Manas, Katia said in a tired voice as if this was something he did to all dinner guests.

Evelyn did as she was told, for a few seconds, it felt like she was back onstage, posing for a portrait painter.

How long have you had that? he said, pointing to Evelyn's neck.

What?

You have a lump on your neck, he said. How long have you had it?

Evelyn felt her neck with her fingers, and yes, just under her left jawbone, there was something hard, the size of a marble, with the texture of a testicle.

Is it okay if I . . . ?

Manas didn't wait for an answer, he was already standing, putting on a face mask, spraying his hands with sanitizer, and approaching her with his arms out, as if preparing to strangle her.

Does this hurt? Or this?

He pressed on her neck with practiced fingers.

Do you feel dizzy when you lift one arm over your head? Have you had a fever recently or any unexplained weight loss?

Evelyn shook her head. The warmth of his hands surprised her and made her strangely calm. She liked this, having a man she had never met before standing over her, with a tomato-stained light blue shirt, deeply focused on examining her neck.

It's probably just a swollen gland, he said when he sat back down. But I would definitely get it checked out if I were you. As soon as possible.

I will, Evelyn said.

No, she won't, Fabricia said. She hasn't been to a doctor in seven years. She's here without papers.

Really? Katia said, looking more impressed than concerned, as if her street cred increased by several percent thanks to this illegal immigrant from the poor Stockholm slums sitting in her kitchen.

I came here in the spring of 2013, Evelyn said. And then I just stayed.

What happened? Manas said. Did you fall in love and get stuck?

No, said Evelyn. I just came here and stayed.

You just stayed? Katia said. For political reasons? Was it right-wing extremism over there that made you . . .

No, Evelyn said. I just didn't feel like going back. So I clung on here.

Chapter One Hundred Twenty-Seven

The fire crackled, shadows danced, and after another five minutes of evasions, Ina started telling. She said that Primo had started making music, he had found Hector's old vinyl collection and begun listening to crackling '90s hip-hop. Hector had told him about his dreams of becoming a rapper when he was young, long before he started teaching at the university, long before he started his publishing company, he told Primo about the first Swedish hip-hop concert at the Communist-run Kafé 44, where no one had thought it was possible to rap in Swedish, but suddenly a group of people who all believed it was possible gathered in front of an audience of maybe forty people, in a venue with anarchist posters on the walls, and rapped over other people's beats, and everyone who was there became known a few years later, Petter was there and Dogge and Ayo and Blues and Feven, and even though the scene had just started and everyone knew each other, there was beef, the rappers from the red line were in conflict with the green line, and the blue line rappers beefed with both the green and the red lines, and when some random hype man got a hold of a microphone and shouted FUCK BLUEHILL, a big fight broke out onstage, and Ina said that it was the first time in Primo's entire life that he had sat completely quiet and listened to a story until it ended, he played his dad's records to pieces, Primo was from another generation, he had access to endless amounts of music, everything was available, yet he returned to his dad's old collection that he had bought when he realized he didn't have the talent to become a rapper and instead began dreaming of becoming a DJ, soon Primo started writing his own lines, the guys at his school saw him as a joke, he was seen as a villa kid, even though Ina and Hector technically lived in a row house, but his mom was a regular at the library, his dad had tweed jackets with leather patches, sure, his publishing company published violent pornography, but that wasn't enough to raise Primo's street cred, yet he stuck with it, it was the first time Ina saw him do something that he didn't abandon after half a semester, and after a while, he actually got better, he started developing his own style, that lisp he had always been ashamed of, he started emphasizing it when he rapped, in a phase when all rappers tried to sing, he insisted on rapping, when everyone used soul samples, he stuck to minimalist beats, and when everyone suddenly got tired of melodic hip-hop, they found him, a villa kid from the green line with a surprisingly sharp wit in his disses, he said he wanted a threesome with your mom, and it sounded charming, he killed a competitor with a spear in a Gucci apron to avoid getting blood on his Balenciaga slippers, and it sounded funny, just because it was so obvious that he was a teenager, just because he pronounced the "c" in Balenciaga like a "k," and lately, Ina noticed that his music was getting attention, kids came up and wanted to take selfies with Primo, teenagers looked at him and looked away, and she was proud of him, she was, even though she had spent most of his teenage years trying to convince him to stop making music. But that's enough for now, it's getting late, shall we go to bed?

Laura and Saskia stayed seated, the fire was about to die.

So what are you afraid of, then? Saskia said.

What do you mean?

Why don't you tell us what's going on?

Well, what's going on is that I'm worried about Primo, Ina said, and at the same moment, she regretted it because putting words to her worries only made them worse.

Worried about what?

That he's getting involved with a crowd where there are a lot of drugs and weapons. Do you remember what happened to . . .

Ina mentioned the name of the famous rapper who had been kidnapped and extorted for money.

But Primo is not really on his level, is he? Saskia said, and Ina wondered why she felt offended rather than relieved.

Primo's biggest dream is to be like him, Ina said. Last night he texted me about needing money, and this morning he needed more money, and now Hector's phone is off, and Primo's not answering when I call, and I panic because I'm here, in the middle of a damn forest with bad reception when he needs me, and I know something has happened, and if that damn curse didn't exist, maybe I wouldn't think like this, but now it does exist even if it doesn't, and I'm afraid that I never will be able to . . .

She stopped mid-sentence. Her phone vibrated. A message. From Hector. She picked up the phone with trembling fingers, expecting comforting words, knowing that she was heading for a strange place. He would bring her back to reality, back to life, back to her routine, just like he had done ever since they met at that New Year's party more than twenty years ago. "He's home," he would write. "I've got him." "He's okay." "We love you, try to enjoy the forest, see you tomorrow." But Hector wrote something else. She read the message. She stood up.

I have to go back, she said. Now. They have him.

Who has him? Laura said.

They have kidnapped my son, Ina said and started walking down the mountaintop, with the open empty backpack over one shoulder and using her phone as a flashlight to find her way back to the car.

Chapter One Hundred Twenty-Eight

During the summer, Mathias, Anastasia and Nina took the train south towards Germany. Nina was only four and a half years old, but it was actually her idea to travel by train. She had heard that cars emit exhaust fumes, and Anastasia, who had spent the past years in airports, lounges, security queues, rushing from commercial shoots to conference meetings, was the one who enjoyed the train journey the most, especially the slow local trains that tourists avoided because they were in a hurry to get to the next place. There were empty compartments on those trains and no Wi-Fi. Anastasia couldn't check work emails, and she didn't have to think about the latest campaign, which ended in complete disaster. She could just read the same story aloud to Nina over and over, play solitaire, nudge Mathias when he snored too loudly and watch the world pass slowly outside the train window.

As they arrived in each country, they learned a few sentences in the local language to explain their unusual setup, nein, vi är nicht together, nee, he's not her father, non, we are just old friends, des anciens amis.

I work in advertising and he is a conservator of mural paintings, Anastasia explained to a young couple with whom they shared a compartment as their train left Belgium and headed towards Germany.

Advertising sounds fun, the guy in the couple said, appearing very proud of his newly bought automatic watch.

It's not the least bit exciting, Anastasia said. Not compared to his job.

She gestured towards a sleeping Mathias and told them that he spent his workdays climbing up into dusty church attics, above the bell towers, hoping to find hidden paintings.

Sometimes they had been forgotten, sometimes they had been painted over. His job was to bring them back to life, the artworks that once existed there. He used fish glue and brushes, microscopy and analysis, to connect lines and find patterns that no one had seen in hundreds of years.

So why did you choose to focus on advertising? the girl in the couple, wearing clothes, backpack, shoes and even a hairband from the same brand, asked.

I didn't choose it, Anastasia said. It just happened.

Then she went back to talking about Mathias's work, how they had helped a legendary mural conservator restore a forgotten painting in Glanshammars Church last spring, how they had eventually realized that the blue color on the wall was lapis lazuli, yes, exactly, that gemstone from Afghanistan that has a bright blue color and has been used for thousands of years to ward off evil spirits.

My mom used to tell me that the Greeks and Romans offered lapis lazuli as a prize when someone was extra brave, Anastasia said. And the Egyptians and Babylonians believed it cured melancholy.

The well-dressed, polite couple nodded and said they would be getting off soon.

Cleopatra used lapis lazuli as eye shadow, Anastasia told the now-silent compartment. She spoke about Mathias's work not only because it fascinated her but also because it still hurt to think about her disastrous spring campaign. The client was a university in a smaller town in desperate need of students, and had contacted Anastasia's company because it had heard she was the best. It took her just a few days to come up with the idea, the clients' eyes sparkled when they heard her pitch, she suggested sending something to potential students that would give them the feeling that their future was at their doorstep, that a change was near, seeds they could plant? Not visual enough. Tarot cards? Too esoteric.

Cocoons, Anastasia said. We buy butterfly pupae and send them to the students with a letter that says: Here is your future. And a few weeks later, the brown, knobbly pupae turn into a colorful, fluttering butterfly that the students can release into freedom.

It was a fantastic idea. Thousands of pupae were purchased, the dates were checked and double-checked, it was crucial that the package was small enough to be delivered in mailboxes, everyone involved worked with that special frenzy that comes when a project has a greater purpose. The pupae were kept chilled just right, they were sent out on precisely the right day, all the calculations were correct.

Two days later, angry calls from upset parents flooded in. They called the university, the postal service, Anastasia's advertising agency, the press, local politicians, they shouted that this was a scandal, that it was the worst thing their children had experienced, their beloved children were getting ready to graduate, to enter adulthood, to say goodbye to childhood, and they became happy and flattered when they received a bright red envelope from a real university in the mail, and then they opened the envelope and found a decomposed butterfly corpse, with that headline that Anastasia had been so proud of: "Change is near. Are YOU ready?"

And every time Anastasia lifted the receiver and heard another parent scream that this was the worst thing their poor Lisa had been through, that she was traumatized, that she had lost all motivation to graduate, Anastasia had to bite her tongue to refrain from saying: If this is the worst poor Lisa has been through, then it's probably a sign that you've protected her a bit too long.

But sometimes, when the well-dressed young couple had disembarked or changed compartments, when Mathias was still sleeping, when Nina was watching another episode of *Paw Patrol*, when the train stood still waiting for an available track, somewhere on the way from the Belgian countryside to the German countryside, she wondered if she didn't know what she was doing when she planned the campaign, if she did it because she wanted to sabotage herself, because she knew she could never say goodbye to her job voluntarily, but if she made herself a liability, they would have to fire her.

Before their departure, Nina had made them promise: only one church a day, and if they visited churches, Nina would get to "watch something" in return. It seemed fair. Every time they entered a cool, dark church, in Denmark, the Netherlands, Belgium, Nina would sit with a tablet and headphones until they were done, and that's how they spent their first six days of the train journey.

The seventh day was a Wednesday. They woke up in a small German town. It was Anastasia who had suggested they stop there, not because there was a particular church, but because she had a friend who lived there, a friend she hadn't seen in . . . she had to count, ten, fifteen, seventeen years; they had studied Arabic together in Tunisia.

What's her name? Nina said.

Daniela, Anastasia said.

Is everything okay? Mathias said when he noticed Anastasia opening a square sugar packet and pouring the contents into her water glass instead of her cappuccino.

I'm fine, Anastasia said, looking nauseous. Just a little nervous.

Didn't you tell her we were coming? Mathias said.

Anastasia nodded and shook her head simultaneously.

Yes, surprise! Nina said, clapping her hands.

There was no luggage storage at the train station, but a kind hotel receptionist allowed them to leave their bags with him. Without asking, he started describing the way to the castle and recommended restaurants.

Danke, Anastasia said, but do you know how we get here? She showed him the address.

Why do you want to go there? he asked.

A friend works there.

Are you sure? he said. There's nothing there. Just a . . . hole.

They got into a taxi that automatically started driving towards the castle, and they had to explain to the driver that, no, they would like to see the castle a bit later, but now they wanted to go to this place, a little outside the town. The taxi driver shrugged as if to say it was their money, and he could drive them all the way to Hamburg as long as they paid.

When they arrived, it turned out that the hotel owner was right.

There was nothing there, just a construction site surrounded by fences and yellow excavators and square little caravans and men in round helmets and neon-yellow vests.

Wait here, Anastasia said and went up to a person whose age and binder made him look like a foreman.

Nina watched her mom gesturing with her arms to be heard over all the big machines passing by. She nodded and seemed to be apologizing. She took a few steps back and slumped down.

She wasn't allowed to go in, Nina said.

Guess you probably need to work here to get in, Mathias said. What do you think they're building?

A house, Nina said.

Could be, Mathias said. Or a tunnel. Look at the hole over there.

Yeah, it might be a house inside a tunnel, Nina said.

Very possible.

The foreman turned away and consulted his notepad. Anastasia tapped him on the shoulder. This time, he only took one side of his earmuffs off. Anastasia spoke for a longer time now, whenever he tried to interrupt her, she continued talking, she pointed towards Nina and Mathias, she may have said that they had traveled all the way here by train, she may have said that she hadn't seen her friend in seventeen years, and it didn't end well the last time they met at that language course in Tunisia, she may have said that she deserved a polished lapis lazuli medal as a reward for her courage in standing here, and she was ready to do anything not to end up like her mother, so please, could he be so kind as to make an exception to the very strict rules and please get Daniela now. Now. Jetzt. Bitte.

The man nodded and said something into a walkie-talkie. Then he went to a shed and brought out a neon-colored vest and a helmet.

Look, now Mommy also got a helmet! Nina said.

Mmm.

Are we going to be here for long? Nina asked.

I'm not sure.

Can I watch something?

Don't you want to see if your mom gets to meet her friend? Mathias said.

I'd rather watch something.

While Anastasia put on a neon-yellow vest and a red helmet, with movements that felt surprisingly natural, Mathias took out a tablet and headphones for Nina. For the thirtieth time that vacation, the signature melody of *Paw Patrol* was heard through the headphones.

How many times have you watched this episode? Mathias asked.

Many.

But it's still good?

Mmm.

But you know exactly what's going to happen?

Mmm. That's what makes it good.

Nina looked up and saw her mom standing there on a German construction site.

How long will she stand there? Nina asked.

I don't know. Maybe as long as is needed.

How long is that?

No one knows.

A woman came out of the tunnel, she walked slowly, as if afraid of what she might encounter out in the light.

Who's that? Nina said.

That's probably your mom's friend, Mathias said.

Anastasia extended her arms. Daniela began to run towards her.

She looks very happy, Nina said.

Mmm, Mathias said.

They hug for a long time, Nina said.

Yes, they really do.

Now she dropped her helmet, Nina said.

Mmm.

Now they're kissing, Nina said.

Mmm.

They're kissing for a very long time, Nina said.

They really are.

Are you sad?

Not at all.

Why are you crying, then?

I'm not crying. I'm just . . . I'm just happy for your mom.

She's not crying.

No, she really isn't. She's really not crying.

Nina and Mathias remained outside the construction site. Nina had paused *Paw Patrol*.

Now she's crying, Nina said.

Chapter One Hundred Twenty-Nine

Evelyn knew that there were things to do, and she needed to do them now, tomorrow, before the weekend, before the next Halloween, before Christmas, before Easter, sure she had limited resources and no insurance, but there were ways, people had dealt with such things before. The first step was to contact the doctor that Manas recommended. She was obviously very busy, but apparently, she had helped people without insurance before. Maybe she could squeeze Evelyn in. Perhaps Evelyn could go there with a lot of cash and charm her, and if that didn't work, she could contact that woman who put up flyers in the subway—Lady Almora. It was only twenty dollars for a basic package (curse removal + bad luck removal), thirty for a standard package (luck and positivity), and sixty for a premium session (luck and success in everything). While Evelyn pondered her options, time passed, autumn turned into winter, then into spring, the pandemic came and went, and came again. Evelyn returned to her job at the café, they had reopened but mostly operated as a takeaway. She noticed customers looking at her neck, they could see something was wrong, her boss told her to check it out, she said she had, her boss insisted she had to do something about it, she began wearing scarves around her neck, her boss said that customers had started asking him if Evelyn was okay, now the lump was clearly visible, it had grown from being the size of an almond to resembling a golf ball, Evelyn had grown accustomed to seeing the world slightly sideways because she had to tilt her head to reduce the pressure on the left side of her neck, she quit before getting fired, she went home and checked her savings, she had enough to live on, at least for a few months, but paying rent would be tough, she could look for a job where nobody saw her face, she could use her last money to go back home, or she could use the money to get her neck checked out, but instead, she just kept on living the way she had, she canceled her phone plan, asked her landlord for a rent deferral and continued to buy food for her cats.

After almost ten months of silence, she received a final email from the author in Stockholm, in May 2021, he apologized for his "radio silence," explaining that he had spent the past year in intensive CBT therapy, a young therapist had tried to understand why the Hyena was after him, why it criticized him, why it hated him, after a few weeks, the therapist began giving him assignments—every week, he had to do something that would create anxiety, something that would trigger the Hyena, most of the exercises involved doing something that felt luxurious and unnecessary, one week, he went into town to buy a bath bomb, and he was instructed to tell the cashier it was for himself, he wasn't allowed to buy something for his wife, he wasn't allowed to buy bath bombs in bulk to get a bulk deal, another time he went to a spa, and all of this turned out to be severely anxiety-inducing, the Hyena went crazy, but he did it anyway and wrote down his anxiety and now he was feeling better, he had been helped by something called ACT—it was all about attacking obsessions with voices, repetition and humor, he tried it out, using his phone to make videos where he said what the Hyena said to him while filming one of his child's stuffed animals, in the clip it looked like the harsh criticism (you are broken, you smell bad, something is seriously wrong with you, you have no real feelings, you are worthless, you will die alone, and everything is your fault) came from a fluffy seal or a kindly smiling panda or a small brown monkey. After a while, he experimented with manipulating the sound of the criticism so that the Hyena's voice transformed. Instead of sounding as it did in his head (like his father), he used an app with a filter so that the criticism sounded like it was coming from a helium voice, a robot voice, or like it was sung by T-Pain. His mission was to watch the clips five times a day, then three times a day, then once a day. The strangest thing happened, the Hyena withdrew, it disappeared, and whenever it came back, he returned to the video and reminded himself that this wasn't a hyena; it was a little pathetic chipmunk, a hunched, washed-out, pilling fucking chipmunk attacking him on repeat. And when he heard the voice now, it wasn't a sign that he was broken, it was just a thought among other thoughts that came and went, and another reason he had a break from the Hyena was that he started writing fiction again, he had a new project, about three sisters growing up in the area where he grew up, he hoped to go to New York in the fall to finish the book, and instead of asking Evelyn how she felt about the subject of his novel, instead of inviting her to contribute to the book, instead of offering her a percentage of royalties, he continued writing about his father, apparently, he had moved back to Sweden during the summer, he was seriously ill, he couldn't stay in Tunisia anymore, his depression had worsened, he couldn't manage his diabetes, he had paranoid hallucinations, he lost his Tunisian passport in Frankfurt, someone had stolen his leather jacket with 30,000 kronor in cash in one pocket, they were Romanians or Bulgarians, they surrounded him, or maybe he had just forgotten the jacket at the gate, now he lived in his son's work apartment, but he kept leaving the apartment because a red-haired woman sat in one of the plants, she had her family with her and wanted to take the apartment from him, they were dead but still wanted his couch, he ran out into the hallway and called his son, who came over to the apartment and tried to persuade him to go back inside, the son showed him that the plant was empty of red-haired women, he tried to make his father understand that it was all a hallucination, they made an appointment with a doctor, but his father refused to go, refused to put on his shoes, just wanted to lie on the couch and watch TV, it took two hours to get him downstairs to the car, he traveled in slippers, they waited for three hours and forty minutes in the waiting room before they were called in, the doctor measured his blood sugar and called an ambulance, his blood sugar was sky-high, in the ER, they found signs of cerebral bleeding, maybe he had suffered small strokes without anyone noticing, after a week he was moved from the ER to a hospital in Dalen, where they conducted tests on him, they asked him to try to draw a clock face, the clock looked like a melted blob of butter, the son thought of Dalí when he saw his father's clock, the poster he had on the wall in his room at the temporary housing, they asked him to sort ten numbers from smallest to largest, but he didn't understand the instructions, they gave him a diagnosis and pills, and then he was discharged, the son picked him up from the hospital and his father came home, he was back in his son's work apartment, surrounded by his son's books, his son's boxes, his son's binders, his son's awards, the son woke up to at least ten missed calls every morning, his father's desperate voice on the answering machine, the red-haired woman was back, along with her family, they chased him out of the apartment, one afternoon the son went over with his son, thinking that seeing his oldest grandchild might bring his father back to reality, the grandchild that the father always, for some unfathomable reason, called Alain Delon after an old French actor, the grandchild had just had his karate graduation, going from a red-white belt to a red one, he sat happily in the front seat of the car but became less happy when he realized they weren't going straight home but stopping at the work apartment to visit his grandfather, they went up to the apartment together, the grandchild saw his father fumbling with the keys to the apartment, he saw him going into the darkness with his shoes on, and he saw him coming out, saying that the plans had changed, he would sit here in the stairwell and wait because Grandpa wasn't feeling well today, Grandpa needed to sleep, wait here, and I'll be back soon, so the grandchild sat in the stairwell and waited, he heard voices coming from inside the apartment, his grandfather's hoarse voice, his father's calming voice, but he couldn't understand what they were saying, but it took a long time, far too long, finally he stood up and sneaked into the apartment, he wanted to show his grandpa his new red belt, the apartment smelled strange, there were medicines on the floor, he saw his father leading Grandpa into the small bedroom, he heard his father say that Grandpa needed to sleep now, he couldn't stay up all night, he needed to regain his strength, but his grandpa's body refused to sleep, even though he lay down, his body shook, his hands vibrated, his lips trembled, he mumbled strange things, the father squatted next to the grandpa, he reached out and patted his cheek, he kept saying the same thing over and over, vi förlåter dig, he said, we forgive you, nous te pardonnons, and then he looked up and saw his son standing there in his bright white karate suit, holding his new red belt in his hand, he went up to his grandpa and put a hand on his shoulder, it's okay, he said, sleep now, sleep now and everything will be okay.

Three weeks later, he was back in the ER, the sons wrote letters and called the local social worker, and finally, they got him into a care facility, it was in the heart of the city, just a stone's throw from Central Station, a few hundred meters from Drottninggatan, where he used to sell his watches, and a few blocks from the corner of Åhléns, where he always wanted to meet, this was the end, here he would be happy, here they would take care of him, and as if the movie version couldn't end better, it turned out that one of the nurses was from Tunisia, she recognized their father, they had flown down to Tunis together thirty years ago, she had traveled alone with three children and had panicked because her youngest wouldn't stop crying, the father sat across the aisle, he didn't need to help her, but he did, he magically produced chocolate coins from the five-year-old's ears, he chatted with the three-year-old, and when she needed to use the restroom, he offered to hold her infant, when she returned from the bathroom, her youngest was asleep in his arms, her husband was waiting at the airport, she told him about the wonderful man who had helped her on the plane, her husband became jealous, now it was her turn to take care of their father, he had become bald, his belly rounder, his teeth brown, he was convinced that there were red-haired women living in flowerpots, but she reassured him, she accompanied him to his room, showed him the balcony overlooking the water, while his sons brought in the furniture, they drank coffee and admired the view, it would be fine, she thought, it would work, his sons thought, if this were a movie the end credits would be rolling now, everyone was happy, everything had been resolved, he would stay here, be well, not see his lost daughter's ghost, not lie awake at night tormented by choosing the wrong life, and yes, wrote the son in his never-ending email, this is how it ends, he becomes happy, he doesn't see any women in flowerpots, he doesn't call my brothers ten times a night, begging to go back to Tunisia, he doesn't miss his language or his heritage, he is doing fine in a dementia care facility in Stockholm with his TV, or maybe he isn't, or maybe he calls non-stop and asks them to come over, he says he just needs a little human closeness, he says they have forgotten him, even though they were there the day before, he claims that the nurses are trying to poison him, he claims that everyone here wants to steal his room and his TV, there are still people living in his potted plants, a shadow family appears every time he goes to the bathroom, he always sleeps on the couch because once he pulled back the sheets and discovered a stiff, smiling dead body in his bed.

The email concluded with a few obligatory questions, how are you, what are you doing, do you have contact with your mother's sister? According to our family in Tunisia, your aunt lives in the USA, and I can check her address if you want to get in touch with her?

Evelyn noticed herself shaking her head and sighing, as if she wanted to show everyone present (meaning her two cats) how incredibly tired she was of men trying to meddle in her life and control her. Reading his email was like being cornered at a party and bombarded with facts about World War II by someone with bad breath. It reminded her of fighting with Simon. She just wanted to get out of there, into the fresh air, away to the dance floor, up to the bar, and yet she read the whole email, all those confused letters without punctuation, before casually deleting it. She would never, never, never even consider seeking out her mother's sister; it wasn't an option. She refused, the curse didn't exist, and going to a stranger's house in America and intruding on them would not only be incredibly stupid but also dangerous. And Evelyn was many things, but dumb was not one of them.

Chapter One Hundred Thirty

They took Laura's car and drove north, Ina sat in the passenger seat, Saskia in the back, but not entirely because she leaned forward over the gear lever, so the three friends were sitting in an almost straight line, heading north at the speed of light. They had left everything at the mountaintop, the food, the bottles of alcohol, the extremely expensive hammocks.

No one will dare to take them, Saskia said. And if they do, we can always buy new ones.

Ina thought about the tourist couple who had hoped to camp at the mountaintop, if they came back now, everything would be ready for them, food, drinks, sleeping spots, they would just need to make a fire somewhere else, since the friends had been careful to pour water on the embers until they stopped hissing. Ina had never seen anyone drive as fast as Laura did that dark October night when the car spent all its time in the left lane, and the speedometer only dropped below 150 when Laura saw a police car near Norrköping. As soon as the police car turned off, she pressed down on the gas pedal again.

Where are they? she said with her mouth almost closed.

I'm trying to find out, Saskia said.

Ina saw her friends go from being hikers to becoming friends, then turning into a nighttime emergency response team in just half an hour. Ina could hardly think, she could hardly move, she just sat there in the passenger seat, naming the people Primo made music with, his friends, the ones he had beefed with, she said she didn't know where he was or what he had done, but Hector had texted that he hadn't come home and claimed that "everything would work out," he urged Ina to stay in the woods, but now his phone had been off for hours. Could they have kidnapped the whole family, or were they all dead, or . . .

How much money did he want when he contacted you yesterday? Saskia said.

Ina said the amount.

Oh damn, Saskia said.

Don't misinterpret this, Laura said. But is it possible that he's involved with drugs?

No, of course not, Ina said. He's sixteen years old.

There was silence for a moment.

The car rushed north as they continued searching for clues. Saskia called Primo's friends, his ex-girlfriend, the ex-girlfriend's parents. She called the police, who repeated that they couldn't do anything until the person in question had been missing for a much longer time. She called the producer who had lived with Primo in Ina's basement until a few months ago. Ina just sat there in the passenger seat, focusing on breathing. Her family was dead, Primo had borrowed money from the wrong people and they had come to the town house with automatic weapons and . . . Saskia didn't give up, when she was young, she had worked as a radio journalist, and Ina heard her activating her professional voice, she introduced herself quickly to signal that it was urgent, she asked the person she was talking to if they knew where Primo was, when they last saw him, if they might know someone who was with him right now. Soon they had a picture of what was going on. Primo had a meeting scheduled with a well-known American producer who was in town. He had rented a studio south of the city. Saskia waited for the exact address, they should be there within forty-five minutes or half an hour at Laura's speed.

Wait, is that Primo? Saskia said, showing Ina a still image from a video he had posted a few weeks ago. Is that his alias? Are you serious? It has hundreds of thousands of plays?

In less than a week, Ina said, without knowing why she made the time even shorter than it actually was.

Can I play it?

Soon Primo's teenage voice echoed from the speakers as he rapped about being more genuine than most, holding stainless-steel Kalashnikovs, spraying enemies with bullets, selling snow and having threesomes at clubs with glass tables (a line that always made Ina wonder if glass tables could withstand threesomes or if it signaled that the club was luxurious because it had glass tables). He never mentioned that he lived in his parents' basement in a town house in Bagarmossen, nor did he reveal to the listener that what he referred to as his "hood" included both low-income housing and upper-class villas.

Laura nodded along with the rhythm as she flashed the high beams so that a sluggish taxi would understand it was time to leave the left lane.

He's really good, Saskia said. I get it if people are jealous.

Ina looked back at her friend and quickly wondered if Saskia was talking about Primo's competitors or herself.

Are we already in Södertälje? Saskia said.

Laura nodded and checked the time.

This must be some kind of record, she said. Where are we going?

I'm still waiting for the address, Saskia said from the back seat. I'll try again.

Ina looked at Laura as they passed another long-distance bus. She looked at Saskia, who held the phone to her ear with her left hand and scribbled things in her notepad with her right hand.

Whatever happened from now on, Ina knew this was real. They were her friends. When things happened that were beyond her control, they were there for her, and with them, nothing was impossible. They would find her son and bring him home. They would do it together. They had Laura's ten years of karate, Saskia's knife and Ina's height. They would do it together, and then they would celebrate. And then they would go back to the woods and retrieve everything they had left there.

I have the address, Saskia said, hanging up without saying thank you.

It was after midnight when Laura turned off the highway and parked outside a high-rise building in a suburb south of the city. As they stepped out into the cold, Ina recognized the soccer field and the path that led to the subway and an abandoned kebab place. It was closed for the night, closed for the year or permanently closed, it was hard to tell.

What do you want?

The hoarse voice came from a car, a dark Audi with tinted windows. Ina approached the car, and her first feeling was relief because they must be plainclothes policemen, no one else could look so typically suspicious. They were, of course, keeping the area under surveillance, knowing there were shootings and drug deals here daily. And now they had stationed a bunch of new police officers in this empty parking lot to ensure that no one else would get hurt.

I'm here to pick up my son, Ina said.

A short silence, the face disappeared, he seemed to be talking to someone in the back seat. He might be conferring with the police chief through a walkie-talkie. Ina thought she heard laughter from the back seat, but she wasn't sure.

Let's go, Laura said, pulling Ina's arm.

This doesn't feel right, Saskia said.

Have you seen my son? Ina said.

Who's your son? the guy in the car said, still speaking through the barely visible gap in the window.

Primo, Ina said. My son's name is Primo.

A burst of laughter erupted from the car, and the people in the back seat laughed so intensely that the car seemed to sway sideways. The guy in the hoodie didn't laugh, he took out his phone and made a call.

We have a situation, he said. He listened and nodded. His mom, he said. Another pause, and then he hung up.

You can go in and talk to him, the man said, closing the car window before she could reply.

What the hell was that? Saskia said as they left the parking lot and started walking towards the high-rise. Did he just give us permission to go inside the building? Does that mean Primo is actually here? This really doesn't feel good.

Please stop saying that, Laura said. We'll just go in, get him and go home.

They entered the elevator, three middle-aged middle-class women, with careers, retirement savings and summerhouses but no guns, no reinforcements, no one knowing they were here. It wasn't until the elevator stopped on the lower basement floor that Ina realized the guy in the parking lot had been their lookout, and if they wanted to kill Primo and get away with it, they would probably have done it and left by now.

Chapter One Hundred Thirty-One

I n the fall of 2021, during the third or fourth or fifth wave of lockdowns and face masks and pandemic panic, Evelyn was at home when someone buzzed. It couldn't be her landlord because he had keys, and it couldn't be a food delivery because Evelyn had no money for takeout. She pressed the listen button and heard a man's voice.

Hallå?

It was a Swedish "hallå," she was sure, no American could produce that drawn-out "å" sound.

Evelyn? Är du där?

She looked out and saw a tall man dressed in black leaning forward to speak into her intercom, as if trying to convince a child to put on their shoes.

Evelyn, it's me, he said, switching to English. It's Jonas.

Evelyn waited for ten seconds before letting him in. He came up the stairs, and she recognized him despite the face mask. His face had aged, his forehead had wrinkles, his eyes looked sad and his hair had turned gray at the temples.

Thank you, he said.

They didn't hug, they didn't even shake hands, because no one does that during a raging pandemic. She didn't need to ask him if he had sent her all those emails. He didn't need to ask her if she had received them. But why was he here? How did he get her address? He entered her apartment, looked around for a place to sit, and when he realized there was only one chair in the entryway-slash-kitchen, and that chair was occupied by not one but two cats, he continued standing.

I happened to be in the area, he said.

Chapter One Hundred Thirty-Two

Primo had imagined that this recording session would be different, the notorious producer visiting from Atlanta would have rented a flashy house in Djursholm, with a pool and catered food, multiple assistants and A&R people. But instead, Primo found himself in a studio that resembled all the other studios he had been in, two flights down in a basement to avoid disturbing the neighbors, vinyl records in blue milk crates, egg cartons for soundproofing, worn-out cables, headphones that smelled like other rappers' sweat. However, what made the experience different was the producer's beats. They managed to be both soft and hard at the same time. There was something about the soul samples he flipped inside out, something about the strings, it would be expensive, but now he was here, and soon it would be his turn to step into the booth and spit as if there were no tomorrow.

He sat on a black leather sofa, writing verses on his phone when someone knocked on the door. The producer himself had only said maybe three syllables to him so far. He mostly communicated through his beats, sitting and smoking behind the mixing desk while his assistant handled everything practical. They had brought in the speakers, they had turned off the doorbell so as not to be disturbed, they emptied the ashtray when it got full.

It was twenty to one when there was a knock on the door. Primo assumed it was the next rapper, he couldn't believe his eyes when he looked up from his phone and saw his mom. It was really her,

Ina, with a wild look, forest pants with pockets on the outside of the knees and an empty-looking backpack.

The room was full of smoke and shadows, the volume was so high that Ina couldn't understand how they could willingly sit in there. A guy opened the door for them, and another showed them into the room with the sofa. And there he sat, her sixteen-year-old son, who was not dead at all. In the square light from his cell phone, his pimply and confused face was visible.

Mom? his lips mouthed, or maybe he said it out loud, but the volume in the studio was so loud that no sound survived all the way to Ina's ears. Ina signaled to Primo that it was okay, they would bring him home alive. Primo got up.

Has something happened? he said.

Ina looked around. Was this her son's kidnapper? Was the chubby guy behind the mixing desk the famous American producer? He looked like he was sleeping. There were five other guys in the room, and the smell of weed was so strong that Ina had to squint. Who were these confused guys with brand-name shirts and wristbands and expensive watches who desperately tried and utterly failed to look like men? They seemed ashamed of what they had done to her son, so ashamed that they didn't seem to care that they had been caught. How old were they, twenty, twenty-five? Were they the same age as Ina had been when she met Hector at the New Year's party? Impossible. She was much older than them then, and she was much older than them now. These men were lost, they kidnapped her son today and would be locked up for life tomorrow, they dreamed of becoming music stars today and would be dealing heroin tomorrow, they hoped not to be criminals like their fathers in the morning and robbed a Forex in the afternoon, Ina stood there in the smoke and hated these men, living stereotypes, men who blamed society for their problems, men who would always choose violence over discussion.

Let's go, Ina said.

The producer seemed to wake up, he abruptly turned off the

music, the rapper in the booth continued screaming himself hoarse for a few seconds before realizing he was rapping a cappella. He took off his headphones and looked towards the mixing desk. The producer had stood up.

What's going on? he said, looking at Ina.

This is my son, Ina said. I'm here to bring him home.

She suspected that the producer and his henchmen would laugh at a famous Swedish rapper being picked up by his middle-aged mom and her friends. But the American producer looked oddly unsurprised that she was there.

Trevor? the producer said.

A man stood up behind the mixing desk, he was as big as a door and as wide as a car, he was so heavy that it took a few attempts before he got to his feet.

He hasn't paid yet, he said.

I'm his mother, Ina said again, since this was the phrase that had gotten them this far.

He's not leaving without paying, Trevor said.

No, he's coming with us, Saskia said. And you better get out of here fast because we've called the cops.

The men in the apartment started laughing. One of them looked at his watch and said, in a squeaky voice, Okay, guys, let's hurry, and everyone laughed louder.

Is that your watch? Ina whispered to Primo.

He has the same one, Primo said.

Our cops aren't like your cops, Trevor said, in Swedish this time. And he's staying until we've been paid.

I'm his mom, Ina said for what felt like the tenth time tonight.

And I'm his manager, Trevor said, nodding towards the producer. He took a few steps towards them.

We had a deal, Trevor said.

He had a name tattooed on his neck, an RIP tattoo on his forearm.

Out of the corner of her eye, Ina saw Laura getting ready. She took a deep breath, ten years of karate training would culminate in this moment, now was the time, after all the hours in sweaty training rooms, after all the exercises on advanced kick-punch combinations, Laura prepared, she raised her arms and slid back her leg to land in a fighting pose. She screamed from her gut as she attacked Trevor with a furious flying kick, which she would have followed up with a deadly right-left elbow combination if Trevor hadn't noticed her coming flying with her left leg stretched out like a heat-seeking missile. He stepped aside and gave Laura a slap so powerful it would have echoed in any room that wasn't a music studio.

Laura fell to the floor, and for some reason, Trevor leaned forward and caught her before she landed.

Thanks, Primo said, leading a bewildered Laura out to the stairwell. Ina and Saskia followed.

Give me one minute, he said to Trevor, with his index finger raised.

Trevor nodded but didn't close the door to the studio, he stood on the threshold, looking at Ina, Saskia and Laura. He rubbed the hand that had slapped Laura, he looked like he wanted to apologize, but his mouth muttered something about "crazy white bitch."

Primo went up to Ina. He took a deep breath.

Mom. Listen carefully now. I don't need to be rescued. Not now. Never again. Okay?

Before Primo went back into the music studio and closed the door behind him, he reached out and patted Ina on the cheek as if she were a child who needed comfort.

The three friends went out into the October night. Ina tried to call Hector, but his phone was still turned off, he must have put the kids to bed and forgotten to charge his phone. The car with tinted windows was still parked in the parking lot, but no one opened the window and laughed at them this time.

Laura drove Ina home, they hardly said a word the whole way. Laura's cheek glowed red when they hugged each other in the streetlight outside Ina and Hector's town house. Saskia and Laura were going back down to the woods, they were going to sleep in the hammocks and clean up the base camp. Ina felt grateful not to go with them, this whole trip had been a mistake, or maybe it had given her exactly what she needed, though she hadn't realized it.

Thank you, she said and hugged her friends. Thank you.

Chapter One Hundred Thirty-Three

They spend three hours together, drinking quickly cooling tea and sitting a bit too close to each other on a red sofa whose edges have been scratched by cats. These two people who were friends in another time, now they are in their mid-forties, every cell in their bodies has been replaced since they last met, yet they talk as if no time has passed, mostly, she talks and he asks questions, she tells him about all the times they moved when she was little, the small towns, the schools, the dining halls that always smelled the same, no matter where they were. At first, it feels a bit strange to speak Swedish, but after just ten minutes, her tongue warms up, and soon she feels that she has missed these syllables. The more she talks, the more she remembers. She tells him about their father's death and their mother's funeral, about Ina's children and Anastasia's career, and everything she says seems to interest him, though she doesn't quite understand why. She tells him about the pain of constantly having to start over and how much it hurt never to dare to commit to anything or anyone because she knew that as soon as she made any kind of connection, her mother would decide it was time to move to a new place with better energy, where the curse wouldn't reach them. Finally, she asks him, why are you here? Why do you want to know all this? He sits silently for a moment and then says:

I've always been fascinated by you. Maybe because we were such good friends. Or because you were the only other half Tunisians I knew.

She looks at him. How close friends had they really been? She has some memories of him from the park, she remembers being at his place once. But close friends? She's not sure. And there were plenty of other half-Tunisian families in Stockholm. But he persists. He says he has always tried to understand his life by looking at "their lives" and claims that there are "so many links" between them.

Like what?

I remember when I started studying economics, and then I heard that Ina had also studied economics! he says triumphantly, as if that proves something. And my one brother is an actor and went to drama school just like you. And my other brother lives in Söder, just like Anastasia. And I used to play on the same basketball team as Anastasia!

Wait, you played on a girls' team? Evelyn says. And Anastasia is younger than you?

No, it was a mixed team, he says.

Anastasia played with girls, Evelyn says.

But she also played in KFUM Söder. When you lived in Kista, and they called her the Crow.

Evelyn looks puzzled. She knows that Anastasia played in KFUM Söder, but she was pretty sure it was a girls' team, and Anastasia had a crush on someone on the team, and they had a tall American coach who had played in the NBA.

Are you a hundred percent sure you played on her team? she says.

Yes, he says. We had Terrance Branford as a coach. Who had played in the NBA.

Or maybe you just watched her from the sidelines and imagined that you were on her team? Evelyn says.

Haha, yeah, really.

He takes it as a joke, but she hadn't meant it as a joke. Instead, he starts talking about the time they saw a JAS plane crash on Långholmen. She shakes her head.

No chance, she says.

I remember this clearly.

I was on Långholmen myself. And then Ina yelled at me for promising to stand on the other side of Västerbron.

I was there too, he says.

Maybe you were, but we weren't there together. And if you were there, you saw me from a distance and imagined that you were there with me. Maybe that's what you've been doing your whole life, looking at us from the outside and hoping that you were with us so much that it became true.

He falls silent.

And maybe that's why you've continued to be interested in us all these years, because we've been just far enough away from you for you to turn us into imaginary figures, because if there's one thing I remember about you, it's that you had extreme difficulty living in reality, that it was impossible for you to care about real people and that you liked fictional characters much more, maybe because real people couldn't be controlled, perhaps because real people have a tendency to die, and you always had to add things to make reality less painful, and maybe that's your biggest problem in life, that you're incapable of connecting with anyone who is present and can only feel interest and empathy for someone who is far enough away for you to turn them into something unreal?

No.

Of course, she never says all that.

But he imagines that she does and he even shakes his head, even though he suspects that she's right about everything she doesn't say.

I searched like crazy for you, he says.

I was here all along, she says.

But you were trying to disappear, he says.

Not at all, she says. I was just trying to find myself.

Finally, Evelyn stands up and removes their cups of cooled tea. He remains seated. He had asked her about everything except the lump on her neck, and she is grateful that he doesn't mention it.

Sorry I didn't bring anything, he says.

Sorry I only had tea and cat food to offer, she says.

I thought you were dead, he says. I pictured you climbing up Rockefeller Center and jumping off.

She smiles.

Of course not, she says. I haven't been there since Ina and Anastasia were here.

Should we go? he says.

She doesn't reply.

What have you been doing all these years? he says.

Reluctantly, she sits back on the sofa.

Living, she says. Just living. And what have you been doing all these years?

The same thing, he says. Living, just living. And writing. How's the monologue going?

It's a work in progress, Evelyn says. It keeps growing and growing. At first, I thought it would be a twenty-five-minute thing, but now I'm thinking it could be much longer.

How much longer?

Eight, nine hours, she says.

He smiles, she smiles.

First I wanted to tell my story, she says. Then my story became intertwined with my sisters' stories, and our parents' stories, and then I thought it would be about the curse, and then the skyscrapers, and then I realized that the whole monologue has to revolve around time. So now I'm reorganizing all the material into seven parts, and each part covers a shorter and shorter period of time, from a year down to a minute. The goal is for the monologue to reflect the feeling of time passing faster and faster as we age. Like a countdown. Cheesy, huh?

Not at all, he says. It sounds fantastic. What's the title?

I don't have one, she says.

Of course you do.

No, she says.

But you've been working on it for eight years, it must have a working title.

Anastasia wanted it to be called *Sisters Raised to the Power of Three*, she says. But I call it *The Sisters*.

He falls silent.

What? she says.

Nothing, he says.

Do you like Anastasia's title better than mine?

I'd do anything to read it, he says.

Be my guest, Evelyn says. Both you and I know that I'll never finish this monologue. Ina says I'm terrified of completing things, but I don't know. Maybe I'm just lazy. Or maybe it's the curse's fault.

They are silent. He doesn't mention that he's in New York with his family to write a novel about her and her sisters. He doesn't mention that he's spent his entire life trying to understand why he can't connect with people who exist in reality. He doesn't mention that a part of him wants to turn time inside out so Ina stays in the woods and Anastasia continues to make art, and Evelyn goes home before it's too late, and his half sister is saved. Instead, he says:

My dad seems to believe we're related.

How so?

Because, according to him, your dad, rest in peace, couldn't have children.

That's nonsense, she says.

I know, he says. I agree.

If he couldn't have children, how could he have had me and my sisters? she says.

Well, my dad seems to think he might have been your dad, or at least one of you. He says your mom got in touch with her ex-boyfriends and asked them for a . . . contribution before you were born.

A contribution? she says. You mean sperm?

He nods. She starts laughing, throwing her head back and laughing so loudly that he worries the lump on her neck will explode and drown them both in white or possibly green pus.

Your dad is crazy, she says.

I know, he says.

So he thinks we're siblings, she says.

Half siblings, he says.

Which would mean we have no connection to the Swedish guy on the steel beam, she says.

Both fall silent.

Do you know what? she says.

What?

I'm not even sure if any of those guys are Swedish, she says.

Who?

The guys on the steel beam. And to be honest, I don't even care. I'm so tired of lies, so tired of the curse, even though I know in my heart that it's not real, I think about it at least ten times a day. I drop an egg on the floor and think about the curse. I miss a subway and think about the curse. I get a damn lump on my neck and think about the curse. I just wish I could stop thinking about it.

I understand the feeling, he says. What happens if we try to lift the curse?

We'll abandon our parents, she says.

And maybe it's time to do that, he says.

They were so much more than their curses.

Maybe we have to cut that tie to survive. Even if it feels scary.

But *how*? she says. How?

There's a way to set yourself free, he says, fumbling in his pocket. At first, she thinks he's going to take out drugs or medicine, but instead, he pulls out his phone.

I made this for you, he says, pressing play on a video clip. She quickly wonders if this guy is as mentally unstable as his dad. The video consists of three stuffed animals, a tortoise, a yellow elephant and a squirrel, taking turns staring straight into the camera, and with a manipulated voice, they say:

You're under a curse. Someone has placed a curse on you and your sisters. You will lose everything you care about due to this curse.

The animals repeat the same thing, again and again. The clip ends.

Do you want to see it again? I'll send it to you. This is the chipmunk filter, but I can also change the voice to make it sound like a robot.

She gets up and backs away.

You only need to watch it, like, three times per day, he says.

She shakes her head.

I'm serious, he says. This helped me defeat the Hyena. I know it seems weird, but it really works.

You need to leave now, she says.

It's scientific, he says. It's called ACT. It's about manipulating voices and using humor to change the brain's neurological connections.

Evelyn bends down and picks up one of her cats.

Did you know that the hyena is a catlike animal? he says.

She holds the cat in her lap as she opens the door, signaling for him to leave.

Well, it's either this or go upstate to meet your aunt, he says.

Evelyn holds the cat in her arms as if the animal will protect her if he suddenly does something unexpected.

I can go with you if you want, he says. You must do it, not just for yourself, but for all of us.

Who is "us"? she says.

All of us, he says. All who fight against curses.

She begins to close the door.

For your sake, he says. For Anastasia's. For Ina's.

Evelyn snorts.

Ina has never needed anyone's help, she says. Especially not mine.

Ina has moved in with Anastasia, he says.

Evelyn is so surprised that she drops her cat, it twists in the air and lands softly on its paws.

Chapter One Hundred Thirty-Four

na turned the key and stepped into her hallway. She peeled off the empty backpack that, for some unfathomable reason, she had been wearing since they left the base camp to rescue Primo.

On a hanger hung a coat she didn't recognize. Two shoes that weren't hers were on the shoe rack. Two half-empty wineglasses and three bowls of snacks were on the living room table. Olives. Nuts. Chips. Three different kinds, and none of them had been finished. Ina heard footsteps from upstairs.

It was nearly half past two in the morning when Hector came downstairs in his bathrobe.

I can explain, was the first thing he said. I can explain.

Before he could explain, Klara came down the stairs. She walked with her head down, not saying a word. She put on her shoes, took the coat under her arm and left what until just now had been Ina's home.

BOOK 6

2022 (One Day)

Chapter One Hundred Thirty-Five

n January 2022, they arranged to meet at Grand Central to take the train upstate together. The man who claimed to possibly be her half brother offered to join her, which was perfect, since Evelyn didn't have money to buy train tickets.

Is this considered a normal day or a holiday? he says when he has downloaded the ticket app.

Not sure, Evelyn says. Why?

Because if it's a holiday, we can buy off-peak tickets.

What's the price difference?

Five dollars, he says. Five fifty. Per person.

We're on a mission to break a curse, she says. Just buy the tickets. He purchases two round-trip tickets.

You're the oldest, right? she says.

Yes, why?

Oh, I don't know. You remind me a bit of Ina.

And you're not the oldest, right?

You know I'm not.

No, you really aren't, he says, and as they board the train and find two seats next to each other, she wonders what he meant by that. Passengers pass them, searching for available seats, children look at Evelyn and then look again, touching their parents' sleeves, pointing and whispering. Adults glance at Evelyn and try not to look again. Evelyn uses a scarf to hide her neck, she leans forward to see herself in the reflection of the window, she honestly can't understand how people can be so fascinated by a lump on an otherwise perfectly normal neck, sure it has grown, now resembling a mandarin rather than a golf ball, but she still can't fathom how a red lump can steal attention from her eyes, her hair, her mouth.

The train starts moving, her reflection vanishes as soon as they leave the tunnel, they pass through a never-ending city, and when it finally ends, it happens abruptly, suddenly they are in the country-side, passing ponds, forests and villages. At one point, the glisten-ing water from the river is so close that it feels like it could flow in through the train window.

Is this your first time going upstate? he says.

She nods.

Do you want something to read?

He takes out a stack of papers with printed text from his backpack.

Is this . . . ?

He nods.

The book I'm working on.

She reads the first paragraph. It's about three sisters in an elevator on their way to a New Year's Eve party. The text is written in English but clearly authored by someone whose native language isn't En-glish. Some sentences feel cut and pasted from Evelyn's monologue.

When Evelyn finishes reading, she looks up from the text.

Do you recognize yourself? he says with a proud smile.

Why did you give me a made-up name? she asks. And why do you try to make the reader believe you approached me at that New Year's Eve party?

It is a novel, he says. And in a novel, you can make things up.

The part where you describe my blow job talent is clearly written by a man, she says.

He tries to hide his disappointment.

I was just trying to create the most truthful portrait possible, he says.

Start by giving me my real name, she says. I'm tired of hiding.

From Beacon, they take a taxi to her aunt's address.

How do you even know if she's home? Evelyn whispers after they get out of the taxi and stand on the sidewalk, looking up at the big, light blue house with a garden, a garage and a separate little house that looks like a barn turned into an artist's studio.

Well, the lights are on, he says. And that's probably her car. He points to a red car in the driveway.

What if she doesn't want visitors? Evelyn says.

She'll be so happy to see you, he assures her.

How do you know that?

Wouldn't you be happy if your sister's daughter, whom you lost contact with, showed up at your home? What if Nina . . .

They stand in silence. Evelyn nods, wiping her palms on her pants.

I'm really nervous.

Of course you are. I'd be happy to come with you.

No, she says. I have to do this by myself. Stay here. I'm going now. I will just walk up there and ring the bell.

Good luck.

She doesn't move.

Okay, I'm going. I'm going in. Now I'm doing it.

Do you want a push?

I'm going in now. Now I'm doing it.

She reaches out her hand and opens the white gate. She crosses the garden with steps that look like she's heard the lawn is mined. She goes up the stairs with the confidence of a first-time burglar. She extends her hand and rings the doorbell, only to realize there's no bell, so she knocks instead. No response, just a wind chime gently swaying in the breeze. She knocks again, harder this time. She turns around and stretches her hands in the air to signal to him that she's done all she can, it's time to go back.

Knock again!

She knocks again.

Harder!

She knocks as hard as she dares. A hoarse, irritated voice comes from the second floor down to the veranda.

It's open!

It's her mother's voice, the same irritation, the same accent. She opens the door and goes in without looking back. He stays outside, waiting for a sign, certain that Evelyn will come back any minute now, she'll wave to him.

Sorry, she would say, I completely forgot about you. Come in, let me introduce you. This is my aunt, and these are my cousins, and everything would be like in that Denzel Washington movie. But instead, Evelyn disappears, it gets gradually colder, the January darkness settles over the house, after half an hour, he starts getting worried, after forty-five minutes, he starts walking around the block, he realizes that the door they thought was the front door actually seems to be the back door, from a different angle, he sees straight into the living room, and when he turns right, he sees the dining area and the kitchen, but it looks empty, and Evelyn is nowhere to be seen, after an hour, he tries calling her, and after ninety minutes, he gathers enough courage to go up and ring the doorbell, he's just about to do it when he sees Evelyn coming down the stairs, she smiles at him and gives him a thumbs-up before disappearing again, she goes back upstairs with a candelabra.

When she finally comes out, it's dark, he has gone downhill to find a café, hoping she'd come out and start worrying about him while he was gone, but when he returns with his takeaway coffee, she's still in the house, ten minutes later, she comes down the stairs, puts on her coat, leans forward to hug someone who's either much shorter than her or a child, then steps out onto the veranda, wraps her scarf around her neck, looks him in the eyes and says:

Now, let's go, with sharpness in her voice, as if she had been waiting for him the whole time.

Aren't you going to tell me what happened? he says when they decide to walk back to the train station instead of taking a taxi.

Soon, she says. When we're on the train.

Just tell me if she lifted the curse, he says.

She keeps walking. When they're on the train, she leans her head against the window and falls asleep as soon as the train starts moving. He sits beside her and takes the opportunity to observe her face, neck and forearms. She has a brown wristwatch on her left wrist with the same logo as the watches he and his father sold on Drottning-gatan. When she wakes up, he plans to ask her about the watch. He wants to ask her about everything that was said in the house. He has to write it down to remember it. But Evelyn sleeps all the way back to Grand Central, and from there, they have to take different subway lines back to different parts of Brooklyn. She promises to tell him everything soon, but not right now, she needs to talk to her sisters first.

The next time he visits Evelyn's apartment, a property caretaker opens the door. He complains that Evelyn left the apartment without removing her furniture, without cleaning, without emptying the freezer. There were two starving cats here that he needs to put down if he doesn't find someone to take care of them.

I can take them, the writer says. It takes him forty-five minutes to coax the cats into the red cat carrier. He takes them home to his children, who are overjoyed, they rename the cats Graypaw and Nightshade, even though he still thinks of them as Evelyn's cats.

Chapter One Hundred Thirty-Six

S o here they are now, together again, after nine years apart, three sisters in a hospital room. One of them mourns her wrecked marriage, one of them misses her American cats, one of them is madly in love with a German engineer who plans to move to Sweden as soon as her tunnel is finished.

One sister stands by the window, looking at the view—the dark blue water, the bright clouds, the gray rocks and the green forest on the other side. Time moves slowly since her marriage collapsed, time feels like sinking in quicksand, one day begins and never ends, all her life she has tried to optimize her time, move faster, take shorter showers, jog and buy vegetables on her way home, now her life has stopped moving and she no longer has time to rush, she just stands there and looks at the view. The unforgiving January sun moves slowly sideways, the weather is too beautiful for bad news, one second at a time, and then the next second, she remembers what their mother said about the long, dark winters in this country when the sun shone in January: "Spring makes it worth it," even though the daughter is unsure if that's true.

Another sister sits in a hospital bed, she's been back for three days, her body is still confused by the six-hour time difference, to get an appointment at the local hospital, she had to wake up at half past seven in the morning and call exactly at seven forty-five, if she called one minute later (which happened two days in a row), she got a voice-mail saying that the available time slots for the day were gone, "but try again tomorrow at seven forty-five." On the third attempt, she managed to get an appointment. When she arrived at the hospital, the woman behind the counter called a nurse, and the nurse looked at her and said she needed to see a doctor immediately. While waiting for the doctor, the nurse conducted some tests, and before the doctor could arrive, she told the sister that she had to go to the emergency room.

They admitted her right away, telling her to stay calm and reassuring her that everything would be fine. A male nurse said that in more than 50 percent of cases, such a lump is entirely normal, while a female nurse said that statistic probably applies only to people under a certain age. A third nurse asked the sister why she had waited so long to seek help.

I lived abroad, the sister said.

And there aren't hospitals abroad? the nurse said.

I lived in New York, the sister said, and then it was as if all three nurses understood, oh, New York, that makes risking your life a bit more logical.

Now she sits in her hospital bed, dressed in a white hospital gown, waiting for someone to bring the test results, the longer she waits, the more certain she becomes that the news will be bad.

The third sister paces in circles, she got her wristwatch back from the sister who returned from the USA, she left the advertising world and now helps Mathias with his restoration projects, she contemplates becoming a conservator too. Soon, Nina will start first grade, and soon, Daniela will come up from Germany. The eldest sister recently moved into the guest room, and the middle sister has been sleeping on the living room couch for the past three days. It's a bit cramped, but it will do, it's only temporary, soon everything will be different.

Didn't they say ten minutes? says one sister.

Take it easy, says another sister.

Throughout their lives, they've spoken English with each other, but now, for some unfathomable reason, they speak Swedish.

Thirteen minutes have passed, says the first sister. Soon, fourteen. I don't understand; if they say ten minutes, they must . . .

Strangely, it's not Ina who says this but Anastasia.

A sound from the corridor, footsteps stopping outside the door. Three sisters look towards the door as the doctor enters. Three sisters think about the curse. Three sisters watch the doctor and try to interpret his slightest movement. He looks calm and composed as if he prepared himself for this difficult meeting in advance. He closes the door so that no one in the corridor can hear the bad news. He sits down on the bed next to the middle sister, on her right side (which is on the opposite side from the lump, indicating it's deadly and although he knows theoretically that the lump is not contagious, it's still best to avoid death as much as possible).

He reaches for the middle sister's hand (this is bad, this is so bad, it can't get any worse).

It takes him exactly one second to say: You're going to be okay.

The eldest sister screams and jumps up and down, punching multiple holes in the air. She takes a selfie with the handsome doctor and thanks him again and again, as if the diagnosis were all thanks to him. The youngest sister falls to her knees beside the middle sister, clasping her hands, praising God, Yahweh, the Lord, the Almighty, Elohim. When she finally looks up, the white paper sheet is transparent with tears. The doctor tries to convey the details of the MRI and biopsy results, he talks about a benign lateral neck cyst, fluid collected in a gill duct remnant from the fetal period, and a straightforward surgical procedure to fix it, but no one listens.

When he finishes, he leans forward and places a warm hand on Evelyn's shoulder.

You're a real trouper, he says and stands up, leaving the room.

The middle sister just sits there, tilting her head slightly to allow air into her lungs, she nods and smiles, saying she's glad to be back, feeling at home, she says she's eternally grateful for the help, but deep down, she wonders if she made a mistake.

BOOK 7

2035 (One Minute)

Chapter One Hundred Thirty-Seven

She was dying, it was clear to everyone that she was dying, the strange thing was that she had been dying for months, the first time it happened the nurses noticed all the typical signs of death approaching, first a sudden burst of energy, she called the nurses to tell them about that time when her family took her to see Niagara Falls, then a steady decrease in blood pressure, reduced urine, difficulty breathing, loss of appetite, her lungs became congested, her feet and ankles started swelling up, and the nurses immediately sent out an alert, all over the city, her now-adult kids and her soon-to-be-adult grandchildren reached for their phones, they rushed out of board meetings, they closed their books and ran towards the exit of the library, they told a pregnant woman with her legs already raised in the air that this was an emergency and unfortunately they had to reschedule, they drove down from the mountain in their jeeps, they canceled a third date and a dentist appointment, they left a basketball game at halftime, they tore off their scrubs, they put on their coats, they didn't change out of their basketball uniform, they ran out to catch a taxi, they bent over to unlock their bikes, they ran all the way to the hospital in order to get there before it was too late, when they arrived the nurses talked to them in hushed voices, they had turned down the lights in the room, there were flickering lights in the windows, normally they only allowed candles with batteries for safety reasons, but this time they had actually used real candles, because their dying relative had explicitly said that there was nothing she hated more than "battery-operated damn fake candles," the family smiled at the nurses, yes, it was her, it sounded just like her, and all the way until her death, she would remain herself, the family slowly realized that now it was happening, the woman who had been the family's rock, the foundation, everything's center was about to leave them, and they gathered around her, they squeezed her hands, they cried and mourned her even before she died, a few hours passed, she didn't die, the nurses came in and looked surprised, after a few hours they came back to remove the normal candles and replace them with battery-operated candles, somehow she wasn't dying, and one by one the family members left the hospital, they returned to work, they played another basketball game, they went on a fourth and a fifth date, they gave presentations at trade fairs, they showed their dentist which tooth was aching, they shopped at discounted prices and paid insurance premiums and three weeks later, another alarm came, now it's happening, they gathered at the hospital once more, but this time it took longer for family members to arrive, her daughter concluded an appointment with a patient, her son stayed until the end of the board meeting, her other son finished a talk for schoolchildren about the importance of taking care of the forest before he rushed to his jeep, her grandchildren stayed a little longer at the library before heading towards the hospital, they told their friends that their grandmother is in the hospital, but she's old and she's been there for a while now and this is the second time the nurses have called us, but somehow she never died, and this went on for months, she was brought to the hospice in February and in May she was still there, nobody in the history of the hospice had lived this long, in June she had new energy, her children had stopped taking taxis to the hospital, now they took the subway, or if they drove, they passed a drive-thru on the way to the hospital, knowing very well that they would be there for a while, and the food at the hospice was only for the soon to be dying.

In late June one of the nurses said that a doctor had suggested that she could be moved to another unit, medically she should have died long ago, but her body refused to give up, a few days later she took a turn for the worse again, the death signs appeared, one after another, this time it seemed like it was actually happening, everyone was gathered, and the woman who was the beginning of everything woke up from a slumber and looked at them, she saw them standing there, everything she had created, a forest ranger, a basketball player, a gynecologist, a bank employee, a psychology student, a person who wore a lot of perfume, whom she barely recognized, it was someone's girlfriend, all this existed because she had been ready to leave and start anew, and she opened her mouth and began speaking with a clarity she hadn't had in months, she looked at her youngest grandchild, Mona, and told her about her life, she said she was from a poor village in the Tunisian countryside and everyone nodded and listened, even though they had heard this story before, they knew exactly what was coming, she would tell them about her sister, the sister who had stolen her passport and gone to Europe, that's why she always had a hard time trusting people, but no, this time she told another story, she said that her whole life changed when her sister was born, she realized that she would never be alone, she would always have someone, someone to fight with, yes, but also someone to run to when things got tricky, she didn't tell Mona that her sister had stolen her passport, she didn't tell Mona that her sister's boyfriend, a charming man who later would move to Sweden, had helped with the theft, she didn't tell them that in revenge she had put a curse on them both, instead she talked about that day when her sister's beautiful daughter had come to visit her, she just knocked on my door, she looked like an angel, sure she had a strange thing on her neck, it looked like a blood-filled melon, but the boil only made her more beautiful, she looked just like my sister, she had traveled all the way here to ask me to remove the curse I had placed on her mother, I explained that the only way to lift a curse was to say a countercurse and burn three strands of hair from the person who uttered the initial curse, we lit a candle, we took three strands of hair and burned them, I said a countercurse and asked her for forgiveness, I explained that I had placed the curse because I was so jealous of her mother, I also wanted a life in Europe, three beautiful daughters, a life full of freedom, and my sister, she felt so guilty for what she had done that

she believed in the curse, I didn't reveal to her daughter that I had
never put a curse on her mother, after the ceremony, we blew out the
candles, my niece said she had to go, she had a friend waiting outside, invite him in, no thanks, she said, and she left, I accompanied
her to the door, she thanked me, I thanked her, we hugged and said
goodbye. She fell silent, her family had gathered around the hospital
bed, listening, some valued every second, others felt a little jealous,
we are the ones who had to deal with your aggressive tantrums for
decades and now, on your deathbed, you choose to remember this
one person who happened to make a surprise visit thirteen years
ago, it doesn't seem fair, it doesn't seem logical, it feels made-up, but
of course they didn't say it, and maybe they didn't even feel it, because somehow they must have sensed that this was the last minute
they had with their mother and grandmother, her skin was going
yellow, her mouth stopped speaking mid-sentence, her eyes closed,
soon she would be gone, she still held on to the hand of Mona, her
family looked at one another with tears in their eyes, this was the
perfect ending, they smiled, they nodded, they waited, they turned
off the electric candles, they waited some more, her heart kept beating, one hour passed, two hours, three, the family started getting
hungry, they needed to use the bathroom, they looked at the steadily
beeping monitor that measured her heart rate, it just kept beeping,
she was still breathing, long slow breaths, finally the family gave up,
one went to the bathroom, one went to order food, one went out to
make some work calls, one took the opportunity to talk to the cute
nurse, only one of them remained by her bedside, it was Mona, the
youngest grandchild, she was almost too young to be here, she held
her grandmother's hand, she whispered: It's okay, Grandma, you can
let go now, we're here, you've built all this and nothing will disappear even if you let go, and when the rest of the family was outside
peeing and ordering food and stretching their legs and calling their
secretaries and asking a nurse if she'd like to meet up for a drink after
her shift, the woman who was the beginning of everything drew one
last breath and died.

Acknowledgments

The writer would like to thank:

Diane Bimont, Daniel Sandström, Ian Van Wye, Sarah Chalfant, Sarah Watling, Kristi Murray, Jacqueline Ko, Charles Buchan, Salvatore Scibona, the Dorothy and Lewis B. Cullman Center for Scholars and Writers, the Center for Research in the Humanities, the New York Public Library, Xavier Bimont, Johan Renck, Hari Kunzru, Katie Kitamura, Deborah Landau, Paul Malmström, Lawen Mohtadi, Every Ocean Hughes, Dinaw Mengestu, Rattawut Lapcharoensap, Masha Gessen, Esther Perel, Madeleine Thien, Kibo and Tilas.

This novel is dedicated to Diane.

A Note About the Author

Jonas Hassen Khemiri is the author of six novels, seven plays, and a collection of short stories and essays. His work has been translated into more than thirty-five languages. *The Family Clause* was a finalist for the National Book Award for Translated Literature. *Invasion!* won an Obie Award for best script. Khemiri is the recipient of a Cullman Fellowship at the New York Public Library, and his work has appeared in *The New York Times*, *The New Yorker*, and numerous other publications. *The Sisters* is his first book to be written in English. He lives in Brooklyn with his family and teaches creative writing at New York University.